One
Minute
to
Midnight

Amy Silver is a writer and freelance journalist, and has written on everything from the diamond trade to DIY dog grooming. She lives in London and has a penchant for vintage clothes and champagne cocktails. This is her third novel.

Also by Amy Silver

Confessions of a Reluctant Recessionista
All I Want For Christmas

One Minute to Midnight

AMY SILVER

arrow books

Published by Arrow Books 2011

4 6 8 10 9 7 5 3

First published in Great Britain in 2011 by Arrow Books
Random House, 20 Vauxhall Bridge Road, London SW1V 2SA

www.randomhouse.co.uk

Addresses for companies within The Random House Group Limited can
be found at: www.randomhouse.co.uk/offices.htm

The Random House Group Limited Reg. No. 954009

A CIP catalogue record for this book
is available from the British Library

ISBN 9780099564638

The Random House Group Limited supports The Forest Stewardship
Council (FSC®), the leading international forest certification organisation.
Our books carrying the FSC label are printed on FSC® certified paper. FSC is
the only forest certification scheme endorsed by the leading environmental
organisations, including Greenpeace. Our paper procurement policy can be
found at www.randomhouse.co.uk/environment

Typeset in Palatino by Palimpsest Book Production Limited,
Falkirk, Stirlingshire
Printed and bound by CPI Group (UK) Ltd, Croydon CR0 4YY

For Ben, my favourite New Yorker

Acknowledgements

Thanks to Lizzy Kremer and Gillian Holmes

Chapter One

Boxing Day 2011

I get up in darkness, while the house sleeps, slipping from the warmth of our bed unnoticed. I dress in the bathroom so as not to wake Dom, then pad down the stairs, taking care to walk on the left side of the staircase (less creaky for some reason). The dogs are curled up in their enormous basket in the corner of the utility room; Mick, the hulking great mongrel, an unholy mix of Alsatian, Rottweiler, some Pyrenean mountain dog and a host of unknowns, completely enveloping Marianne, our tiny, delicate golden lurcher. They look up at me sleepily as I open the door.

'Come on, then,' I whisper, jamming my feet into my wellies, the sight of which already has them scrambling out of the basket, Mick barking enthusiastically.

'Shhhhh,' I hiss at him uselessly, lunging for the back door so that I can let him out before he rouses the entire household. Wake everyone up and they'll all want to come.

1

The dogs bound out onto a lawn turned crunchy and white by a thin layer of snow just freezing to ice. I zip up my parka to the very top, tucking my nose under the material, hunkering down against a bitter whip of wind. Fingers of pale winter sunlight are just beginning to creep across the lawn, warming nothing whatsoever.

Tails wagging furiously, the dogs are waiting for me at the back gate, Mick's nose pushing against the latch. One day he'll figure out that all he needs to do is flick his head upwards and he'll be able to open it. Fortunately, he's not too bright, so that day is probably a long time away. If Marianne could reach the latch she'd have figured it out ages ago.

I glance up at the window of the spare room. Blinds still drawn, in-laws still slumbering. Probably not for long. The three of us slip away, out of the gate and into the lane behind the house, making for Wimbledon Common.

We head north-west-ish, the dogs running ahead, Mick at a gentle canter, Marianne racing out of sight then returning a moment or so later, anxiously bobbing her head up and down like a meerkat, wondering what's taking us so long. There's not another soul in sight. Usually by seven-thirty on a weekday there are plenty of runners and dog-walkers around, even in the dead of winter. Not today. Everyone's still sleeping off the turkey and mince pies. It's eerily quiet, there's no traffic noise, no birdsong, not even the faint drone of aeroplanes overhead. I quicken my pace, partly to warm up, but also because, despite myself, this silence is creeping me out a bit.

Dom hates me going out alone at this hour, with the sun barely up.

'No one's going to attack me when I'm with Mick,' I tell him, although we both know that while our beloved dog might look fierce he'd run a mile if there were any real danger. I've seen him back down in an argument with next door's kitten. Marianne would probably provide better protection; she's got a fierce temper when roused.

('Just like you,' Dom tells me with a wink, although he isn't really joking.)

We get as far as the windmill and I know I ought to turn back. They'll all be up by now, early risers my extended family. They'll be wanting their breakfast. Failure to have it on the table will be regarded by my mother-in-law as a dereliction of my wifely duties. Yet another dereliction: does one more really matter? The dogs have barely been out of the house in two days, they need a proper walk. And I have things to think about, mental lists to write.

On 29 December, in just three days' time, we're flying to New York. New York for New Year! Just the thought of it is thrilling: carriage rides through the park, ice skating at the Rockefeller Center, cocktails at the Met. But it's nerve-racking too. Of the many, many skeletons in my closet, a surprising number of them have, for one reason or another, decamped to Manhattan. They're waiting for me there. That aside, I've just got too much to do before we go: I need to take down all the Christmas decorations (too early, I know, but it'll depress me to come back to them after our holiday's finished and Christmas is well and truly over), I need to clean the house (our lovely Albanian cleaner is away until the end of January for some reason); I have to drive to Oxford to do an interview for the *Betrayal* TV programme I'm producing, email my assistant with our New York contact numbers, read through (and decline?) the *Girls Gone Mild* proposal from i! TV, shop for a dress to wear to Karl's party, get my hair cut, my eyebrows threaded and my nails done *and* take the dogs to Matt and Liz's place in Sussex. Oh, and at some point I probably ought to reply to that email from my father.

The first communication of any sort I'd had from him in more than two years, it had arrived on Christmas Eve.

Dear Nicole,

I hope this message finds you well. I imagine you'll be spending Christmas with your mother. Do give her my regards.

I'm afraid I write bearing bad news. I have been feeling rather unwell lately and after many doctors' visits have finally been diagnosed with prostate cancer.

The doctors assure me that my prognosis is good, the cancer is not too advanced. However, I am due to go into hospital for surgery on 2 January.

I was wondering whether you might be able to come and see me before I go under the knife? It is relatively minor surgery of course, but one never knows, does one? It's been so long since we talked, there are things I feel I ought to say to you.

I know that for one reason or another our relationship is almost non-existent these days. You might not believe me, but this is a matter of great regret for me.

I look forward to hearing from you.

Happy Christmas,

Dad.

I still haven't told anyone about it, not even Dominic. It's not just that it would have put a dampener on our Christmas celebrations, it's more that Dom can be a bit . . . *prescriptive* when it comes to my dealings with my father. It's only because he wants to protect me, I know, but I need to figure out what I want to do about it by myself.

The dogs and I get to the northern end of the Common, the point at which it meets the A3. Usually, we would cross over the road and carry on through the Robin Hood Gate across Richmond Park, right up to the brow of the hill. Not today. It's almost quarter past eight already. By the time we get back home it'll be after nine o'clock. I might just make it in time to start breakfast before Maureen, Dom's mum, is bathed and coiffed and downstairs ready to make me feel bad.

No such luck.

'There you are,' Dom's dad says, looking up from his fry-up as I come into the kitchen. 'We were wondering where you'd got to.'

Maureen is standing at the cooker, her back to me. 'You are going to eat this morning, aren't you?' she asks, without turning round. 'I've done you a couple of fried eggs and some sausages.' I turn to close the door between the kitchen and utility room, but I'm too slow. Mick pushes past me, padding mud across the white kitchen tile.

'Oh, do keep the dogs out of here, Nicole,' Maureen says, wrinkling her nose in distaste at Mick, who's now standing next to Dom, having a sniff at his breakfast. 'You should never have animals in the kitchen. It's so unsanitary. Just look at the mess he's making.'

I grab Mick's collar and drag him out, slamming the door before he has time to barge back in again. 'Sorry, Maureen,' I say guiltily, slinking back to the kitchen table like a scolded child. Dom squeezes my knee and gives me a wink.

6

We eat in silence, the minutes ticking by. Dom and his father wolf down the remains of their meal while I push the lukewarm bits of greasy egg white around my plate. I can't bear fried eggs but I'm not about to tell Maureen that.

Eventually, Peter, Dom's dad, interrupts the quiet.

'So, when are you two off to the States?'

'Thursday,' Dom says. 'Midday flight. Gets us there late afternoon.'

Maureen sniffs. New York is not a place she's ever had any desire to visit, and therefore doesn't see any reason why anyone else should want to.

'We're going to the golf club for New Year's Eve,' Peter says.

'That sounds lovely,' I lie.

'Oh yes, it's always quite a good night,' Peter says, 'isn't it love?'

'It is,' Maureen agrees enthusiastically, 'it's wonderful. The O'Neills will be there, Dom, and the Harris clan, of course. You remember Simon, don't you? He married such a lovely girl. They're expecting their third in April.'

'Always a good night,' Peter says again, 'perhaps you two could come along next year?'

'Definitely,' Dom agrees, without looking at me. 'We should definitely do that.'

More silence.

'Are you not enjoying your eggs, Nicole?' Maureen asks.

* * *

They're gone by eleven, heading back up the M1, back to civilisation. Yorkshire. The second the car pulls away from the pavement outside our house, Dom grabs me around the waist, kissing me passionately on the mouth.

'Three days and not a single stand-up row!' he says with a grin. 'That must be a record.'

I smile ruefully, instantly feeling guilty for spending the two weeks before they came openly dreading their arrival.

'It was good. It was nice to see them. It's always good to see them.' He laughs. 'I mean it, Dom.' And I do mean it, sort of. Peter's a lovely man. And I don't think Maureen means to criticise my every move. She just can't help herself.

'I know. I thought you did very well.' We're walking back to the front door, arm in arm.

'I should try harder with her. Next time we should go to a show or something.'

Dom laughs again. 'A show? Good god, woman, that's above and beyond the call of duty.'

As I open the front door Dom puts his arm around my waist, pulling my body back against his.

'Let's go upstairs,' he whispers into my ear.

'I had a bet with myself that it wouldn't take you long to suggest sex,' I say, laughing. 'But less than thirty seconds after they leave! Impressive.' Dom has a weird thing about not having sex when his mother's in the house (just his mother, for some reason, sex with his dad around is fine).

'Oh shut up and get your knickers off,' he replies, slipping his hand into the waistband of my jeans.

We only make it halfway up the stairs. Afterwards, while we lie there comparing carpet burns, Dom asks about New Year's Eve.

'Where is this party exactly? At a bar, I take it?'

'No, no no, darling. It's at Karl's new gallery. Much more glamorous.'

'Ri-i-i-ght.' Dom sounds dubious.

'It'll be fun,' I say, kissing the point on his temple from which his sandy hair is fast receding.

'It'll be full of terrifyingly cool arty types,' he grumbles. 'We won't fit in.'

'What do you mean we?' I ask, struggling to my feet. '*I*'ll fit in just fine.'

Dom grabs me again, pulls me back down beside him. 'Oh is that right?'

'It is. In any case, I'm sure Karl will have invited some other geeky and uncool people to keep you company.'

'Right, bitch, you asked for it,' he says, running his fingers lightly down my side, sending me into paroxysms of tickle-induced laughter. He doesn't stop until I beg for mercy.

'Let that be a lesson to you,' he says, eventually, wriggling back into his boxer shorts.

'Lesson learned,' I assure him breathlessly. 'But there's just one thing I ought to say . . .'

'What's that?'

'I just wanted to tell you that no matter how much I love you, no matter how good you are to me or how well you treat me I will never, *ever* go to the fucking golf club for New Year's Eve.'

Chapter Two

New Year's Eve, 1990
High Wycombe

Resolutions:
1. Start keeping a journal: write every day!
2. Read more! *A Clockwork Orange*, *The Grapes of Wrath*, *On the Road*, also some classics
3. Lose half a stone
4. Volunteer for a charity, do forty-eight-hour famine
5. Kiss Julian Symonds

I was going to my first-ever proper New Year's Eve party. Okay, it was at my house – for the first time ever I was being allowed to join in my parents' annual New Year bash – and okay, most thirteen-year-olds would sooner die than attend a party with their parents and their parents' friends, I'm well aware, but I had an incentive, and his name was Julian Symonds.

Julian was a couple of years ahead of me at school;

he was the son of one of Mum's nursing friends, he was fifteen years old and he was bloody gorgeous. Tall and skinny with dark hair which was always falling into his huge, brown eyes, he had high cheekbones and long lashes, he wore lots of black and listened to the Velvet Underground, he was into art, he read Rimbaud and the Marquis de Sade, he was languorous, sulky, androgynous, rebellious, dangerous, a smoker. He was *divine*.

Under normal circumstances, I'm sure Julian would have had far better things to do with his New Year's Eve than come to a party at my parents' house, but he was being punished. The story, told to me by my mum, who had got it from his mum, was that Julian had snuck out to a rave, stayed out all night and came home in the morning 'high on drugs'. He was grounded for three months, but since his parents couldn't trust him to stay home all by himself, and since they wanted to come to the party, he was being forced, very much against his will, to come along.

'Little bastard better not bring any drugs into this house,' my father said when he was informed. 'I'll break his bloody neck. And you,' he turned to me with a snarl, 'don't get any ideas. I don't want you anywhere near him. You hear?'

Oh, I had ideas. I had fantasies, daydreams, scenarios, imaginings, entire scripts written in my head. I'd greet him (and his parents) wearing acid wash jeans and my new pink halter neck top from

Jigsaw (which was the first overtly sexy piece of clothing I'd ever owned) and he'd be struck dumb, speechless with admiration. I, of course, would play everything really cool, but eventually he'd get up the courage to ask me to dance, and we would, a slow shuffle in the corner of my parents' living room, the two of us, alone in a crowd. 'Nothing Compares 2U' by Sinead O'Connor. I put it on the end of the mixtape I'd made for the occasion (after 'There She Goes' by The La's, The Stone Roses' 'I Wanna Be Adored', 'Suicide Blonde' by INXS). Just in case.

This was of course all total bullshit. For one thing, Julian Symonds – gorgeous, smouldering, achingly cool fifteen-year-old Julian Symonds – wouldn't look twice at me. He wouldn't even notice me. Why would he? I was average. Undeniably, boringly average. Average height, average weight (in other words, *not* thin), boring brown eyes – the only thing different about me was my hair. Mum (and Mum's friends) were always banging on about how lucky I was to have such lovely hair. 'Titian blond,' Mum called it, but to be honest in some lights it looked worryingly close to ginger.

Julian Symonds would never notice me. He never had before, in any case, we'd passed each other in the corridors at school a hundred times and he had never once glanced in my direction. I was a total nobody. And second, the chances of me slow dancing with anyone while my father was in the same room were remote. Dad wouldn't like it. And wherever possible, I tried to avoid annoying my father.

Dad worked in middle management at Swan (tobacco papers, filter, matches) and he was always pissed off about something. Interest rates, football results, the travesty that was *Rocky V*, you name it, Dad was angry about it. But mostly he was angry with Mum.

Mum could never do anything right. That's what she always used to say, anyway. 'No matter what I do, it's never right, is it? I never do anything right.' When I was younger this struck me as odd, because Mum *did* do everything right. She was a brilliant story-teller. When she was reading to me at night she'd have me in stitches, giving Peter Rabbit a broad Glaswegian accent or reading the whole of *The Cat in The Hat* in a Jamaican patois. She was incredibly patient: she was the one who taught me to ride a bike, to swim, to bake brownies, to play pool – Dad didn't teach me anything, except perhaps how to fish. And how to swear. So why, I wondered, did she think she never did anything right?

There may have been a time when my parents were happily married, but if there was, I don't remember it. I do remember, when I was much younger, that things were better. Dad and I used to be friends. That was a long time ago, though. For years now, there had been tension in the air whenever Dad was around. Mum and I were quieter when he was in the house;

we made ourselves small. We walked on eggshells; we tried not to get in the way. Things had been bad for a while now, and they were getting steadily worse. The screaming matches that had made me cry when I was little were now much more regular. And they weren't just screaming matches any more either; these days they always seemed to end with something – a chair, a plate, a window, my first, greatly treasured, Sony Discman – getting broken.

The Discman incident had taken place a couple of weeks before Christmas. The Discman itself had no bearing on the row; it had nothing to do with the row. It was an innocent bystander. The row concerned a shirt. An unironed shirt. The thing was, Mum, who was a nurse in A&E, had worked a double shift because one of the other nurses had phoned in reporting 'a family emergency' (read: hangover) and they hadn't been able to find any other cover at the last minute. So my mother, who was the senior nurse on the ward and a highly conscientious person, agreed to work an extra eight hours. Instead of coming home at six-thirty in the evening, she'd arrived back just after two in the morning and had gone straight to bed, without ironing the shirt my father had intended to wear to work the following day. This, it turned out, was a disaster.

In the morning, getting ready for school, I heard him shouting. 'I have a meeting today, Elizabeth! Jesus Christ! Can you never do anything I ask? Blue shirt, grey suit, I told you this. Why is it so bloody difficult to listen? You just never listen, do you?' Standing in the hallway, their bedroom door slightly ajar, I watched him shake her awake.

'Okay, okay,' I heard her say as she was groping on the bedside table for her glasses, 'I'll do it now.'

'It's too late, it's too bloody late now, isn't it? Or do you want to make me late? Is that it? Do you want me to look a fool at work?' He pushed past me and crashed down the stairs, taking two at a time, Mum followed at a run, shooting me an apologetic glance as she hurried by. Like she was the one who had to apologise.

I hovered on the landing at the top of the stairs, not wanting to listen to the row continuing downstairs, but unable to walk away.

'It's important for me, Elizabeth!' he was shouting again. 'This meeting is important. Jesus Christ, if you paid half as much mind to me, to this household, as you did to your patients, everything would be fine.' I could hear the sound of the ironing board being dragged from its resting place next to the washing machine, the clank of metal as it was brought to stand.

'I told you! I have to leave now, you're too late!' Miscellaneous banging and crashing. 'But could you please do me one favour? Just one thing?'

'What is it, Jack?' her voice was clear and even, the voice she used when she didn't want to provoke him,

16

but she was prepared to show that she wasn't afraid, either. She used that voice a lot.

'Will you tidy this bloody place up?' Crash. Something smashed. As I discovered later, it was my Discman hitting the kitchen wall. 'It looks like it hasn't been cleaned in weeks.'

That had been the last big confrontation. Since then, over Christmas and in the run-up to New Year's Eve, peace had descended on the Blake household. Dad had been off work, which always put him in a good mood, and – better yet – we'd had my uncle Chris staying with us. Chris, Dad's older brother, seemed to have a calming effect on Dad, who was an altogether more reasonable person when Chris was around. In the face of considerable provocation – Mum working long hours, the interminable pissing rain, even England's 'total bloody capitulation' in the second Ashes test – Dad didn't throw a single tantrum.

I spent most of that week preparing for the party. In addition to my outfit, my hair and make-up and the music, I was in charge of preparing snacks – this was the price I had to pay for my admission. I was also required to help clean the house on the day of the party, and to lug tins of beer and bottles of soda water from the back of Dad's car to the ice-filled bathtub.

Mum and Dad were always entertaining. Maybe it was because we weren't the happiest of households, they liked having other people around, it eased the tension. They were always having barbecues, fancy dress parties and loud birthday bashes with karaoke machines. The planning of these events followed a regular course: Dad would suggest the party, but as the date drew near he'd decide it was a terrible idea and that they didn't have time to organise it, he'd work himself into a furious rage about it and eventually wash his hands of the whole thing, Mum would do all the actual preparation, she would organise the drinks and make the food and invite the guests. At the party itself, Dad would inevitably get blind drunk and the following morning he'd say to her the next day, 'That was good, wasn't it? Good idea of mine, to have a party, wasn't it?' He'd say it with a half smile; I never knew whether it was his way of apologising.

They did throw good parties, though. They had lots of friends, mostly Mum's, most of whom were quite rowdy and enjoyed a drink. There would be lots of nurses and hospital admin staff, the occasional hospital porter and, even rarer, the odd doctor. A few of Dad's mates from work (who weren't so much fun) would also come, plus Uncle Chris, the next-to-next-door neighbours (Dad didn't get on with the people immediately next door) and a few other old family friends. This New Year's Eve we were expecting no fewer than thirty-five guests to cram themselves into our two-up, two-down semi in suburban High Wycombe. It was going to be a packed house.

The party was due to start around seven, although Dad and Uncle Chris had opened their first beers a couple of hours earlier. Mum was on duty until six, so she barely had time to get home and shower and change before the first guests started arriving. She looked great, in fitted black trousers, a gauzy, floral print top and pink kitten heels. She'd had her hair done specially, her blond hair cropped short, it gave her this cool, elfin, impish look, a bit like Annie Lennox.

I was in a state of feverish anticipation, my stomach was churning with nerves and too much Diet Coke. I wanted to play it cool, but somehow I just couldn't seem to manage it. I hung around the front door, greeting my parents' guests, taking coats, constantly watching the road outside for a glimpse of the Symonds' red Volvo.

When eight o'clock came and went and there was still no sign of Julian, I lost heart. None of my parents' other friends had brought their kids, so I was stuck making polite conversation with people in their thirties. It was really boring. After a while, I gave up and, heart heavy, installed myself next to the stereo where I could at least make sure none of the old people started putting on any of their music. The mixtape I'd lovingly put together wasn't due for a hearing until later in the evening – around ten-thirty, I thought – so I busied myself shuffling through our meagre CD and more extensive tape collections, putting things into order, a potential playlist.

I was lost in thought, deep in the sleeve notes for *Disintegration* when, as if from nowhere, he appeared at my side. Julian Symonds. He was dressed in jeans and a black biker jacket, a yellow smiley face peeping out from his T-shirt underneath. Its sunny demeanour contrasted perfectly with his.

'It's not nearly as good as *The Head on the Door*,' he said, pushing his hand through his perfect, floppy dark hair. 'Don't you think?'

I didn't know what he was talking about, so I just said, 'Oh yeah. Completely,' and I felt the colour rising to my face and looked down, scrutinising the CD cover as though it were the most interesting thing in the entire world.

It was a huge moment. It was the first time Julian had ever spoken to me. We'd never talked at school, obviously, because he was two years above me and we didn't exactly hang out with the same people. We'd encountered each other before, in town, both of us standing next to our respective mums, which was of course the most embarrassing bloody thing ever, so neither of us were likely to speak then. Everything I knew about Julian, his coolness, his edginess, his brilliance, was mostly stuff I'd heard from people at school, plus some things that his mum (Sheila) had told mine.

And now, he was here. In my house. I stole a glance at him, sitting on the sofa across the room, staring at the blank television screen, a study in boredom. He'd only been here a couple of minutes. The fantasy in which I opened the door and wowed him with my stunning looks, the one in which I'd play it so cool, in which he'd be unable to resist me, was well and truly forgotten. I got to my feet and crossed the room to stand awkwardly in front of him.

'Can I get you something to drink?' I asked him.

'Brandy and Coke,' he replied, not looking at me.

I laughed nervously. 'I'm not sure . . .' I started to say, but he silenced me with a withering gaze.

'Okay,' I said, and weaved my way through the guests towards the kitchen.

Mum was leaning on the counter next to the fridge, a glass of wine in her hand, laughing at something the man in front of her was saying. I'd seen him before, he worked at the hospital, but I couldn't remember his name. They were standing really close together, but the music was turned up quite loud so you had to be quite close to hear what the other person was saying.

'Excuse me, I just need to get some more Coke,' I said, squeezing past Mum's companion to get to the fridge.

'You remember Charles, don't you, love?' Mum said.

'Hello, Nicky!' Charles said.

I grabbed the two-litre bottle of Coke from the fridge, resisting the urge to correct him. I hate it when people call me Nicky. Dad came barrelling into the kitchen, bouncing off the door as he did.

'Everything all right in here?' he asked, a little too loud, beaming at us.

'Yes, fine, we're fine,' Mum said. I noticed that Charles took a step back, opening up the space between his body and my mother's.

Some more people came into the kitchen, Dad was offering them drinks, Mum returned to her conversation with Charles, no one was looking at me. This was my chance. I scuttled round the room to the opposite counter where several bottles of spirits were laid out for guests to help themselves. Gordon's, The Famous Grouse, Bacardi, Rémy Martin. That was brandy, wasn't it? I placed the Coke bottle on the counter in front of the Rémy Martin. Glancing over my shoulder to confirm no one was watching, I slipped my hand behind the Coke bottle and twisted the cap off the brandy bottle. I grabbed a plastic mug, sloshed a bit of brandy in, and then a bit more (he'd want a strong drink, wouldn't he?), topped the cup up with Coke and sauntered out of the kitchen, giving Dad a big smile as I went.

Julian, still wearing his leather jacket, was gazing sorrowfully out of the window; he had slumped even lower, he was disappearing among the sofa cushions. I presented him with the drink. He took it, wordlessly, took a sip and pulled a face as though he'd bitten into a lemon.

'Jesus,' he said, laughing (the sight of his smile almost stopping my heart), 'how much brandy did you put in that?'

'Home measures,' I said, smiling at him. I'd heard Mum use the expression.

'Thanks,' he said, raising his mug to me. He took another sip, a smaller one this time. 'You not having one yourself?'

'Not just yet,' I said. I planned on having a glass of wine later, but I didn't really like the taste and I didn't want to get sleepy too early. I sat down next to him on the sofa, a little too close. He shifted in his seat.

'Enjoying the holidays?' I asked him.

He shrugged. 'All right, I suppose.'

'I went to see *Presumed Innocent* yesterday,' I said. He looked at me blankly. 'You know, Greta Scacchi, Harrison Ford. Have you seen it?'

'Nah, not really into all that Hollywood shit,' he replied.

'No, right. It was all right,' I said. 'It was okay. It wasn't that good.'

He looked at me as though I were a complete idiot, and then he smiled. 'I'm more into French cinema at the moment. Have you seen *Betty Blue*?' I shook my head. 'It's amazing. It's about madness and love and obsession. And fucking. Lots of fucking.'

I flinched at the word, I wasn't used to it being used in the literal sense, not conversationally.

'It sounds cool,' I said. We lapsed back into silence.

The party was starting to heat up a bit, the music was turned up very loud, the laughter of some of the women turning shrill. I could hear my father, who was standing a few yards away from us, telling a dirty joke to one of his friends in a very loud voice. I'd heard it before. It wasn't funny. I could see that Julian was listening and felt embarrassed. I pointed to his mug.

'You want another one?'

'Yeah, go on then.'

The kitchen was heaving by this point, which was good news for me because it made it much easier for me to get to the brandy unnoticed. I stood on tiptoe and could see Mum on the other side of the kitchen, still leaning on the counter, still holding a glass of wine (though probably not the same one), still talking to Charles.

Back in the living room, I handed Julian his drink.

'Hey,' he said, beckoning for me to lean in closer to him, 'do you want to go somewhere for a smoke?'

'Umm. We could go to my room,' I said. I couldn't believe I was actually saying the words. I was inviting Julian Symonds to *my room*. 'But not together. I'll go up first, you follow in a minute. Otherwise my dad might . . . You know.'

'Bit overprotective?' Julian suggested. I nodded, not sure that overprotective was how I'd put it, but anyway.

I slipped out of the living room and up the stairs, unnoticed again. Or at the very least not remarked upon. I tore around my bedroom, getting rid of anything that could be construed as embarrassing: my

24

flesh-coloured 32AA bra, for example, and my well-thumbed copy of Jilly Cooper's *Riders*. Then I sat back on my bed, resting against the pillows, trying to look casual, as though I invited older boys to my bedroom all the time.

After a few minutes, there was a gentle tap on the door. Julian popped his head round and smiled at me.

'All right if I come in?'

It's a good thing I was sitting down, because by this point I was close to passing out from nerves. Julian wandered idly around the room, picking up things and putting them down again, his face betraying neither approval nor disapproval, until he spotted the poster on the back of the wardrobe door. *The Kiss*, by Gustav Klimt. Julian smirked.

'You don't like Klimt?' I asked, defensive and disappointed. He wasn't supposed to laugh at my Klimt poster; it was the last item in the room I expected to provoke derision.

He shrugged. 'Bit of a cliché, isn't it? Don't all fourteen-year-old girls have *The Kiss* on their walls?'

Fourteen? He thought I was fourteen! That almost made up for his not liking Klimt.

'I think it's beautiful,' I said. 'I could look at it for hours.'

'Fair enough,' he said, sitting down at the end of the bed and pulling a packet of ten Silk Cut from his jacket pocket. 'You want one?'

I didn't really. I had smoked before but hadn't much

enjoyed it. I took one anyway and got up to close the bedroom door.

'Just in case anyone comes up here.' He opened the window above my bed to let out the smoke, lit his cigarette and handed me the lighter. I lit up too, stifling a cough as the first drag hit my lungs.

'Klimt's okay, I suppose,' Julian said, 'just not really my thing. I like Rothko. Rothko, Hofmann, Newman – the Colour Field painters. Do you like Rothko?'

I didn't know who Rothko was, I'd never heard of him, or of Hofmann, or Newman or the Colour Field painters.

'I don't think I know his work,' I said, feeling like an idiot.

But Julian didn't treat me like one. 'Oh, you should have a look at his stuff,' he said, suddenly brighter, enthusiastic, the mask of impenetrable coolness slipping for a moment. 'Mark Rothko was a genius, a real radical. He used colour in the most amazing way. The Seagram Murals are incredible. He killed himself by cutting his arms with a razor blade, here, at the elbow,' he mimed the motion to underline the point. 'He cut all the way down to the bone.'

I wasn't really sure how I was supposed to respond to that, so I just nodded thoughtfully.

'Fucking cool paintings though. He studied at the Art Students League of New York. That's where I want to go. I'd give anything to live in New York, wouldn't you?'

I'd never given it much thought, although anywhere that wasn't High Wycombe sounded great to me. 'Anyway,' Julian went on, 'I've got a couple of books on Rothko at home. You can borrow them if you like.'

'Oh thanks, Julian, I'd love to,' I said, and I really meant it. I don't think I'd ever meant anything so wholeheartedly in my entire life.

Julian flicked his cigarette butt out of the window. 'Jules,' he said, 'my friends call me Jules.'

It was the greatest party ever. Jules and I spent the entire evening together. We couldn't stay upstairs in my room, but we managed to split our time between the living room and my bedroom fairly evenly, wandering up and down the stairs, always individually, never together, making sure we were spotted by enough people in the living room or the kitchen. I kept him in a steady supply of brandy and Cokes, and the more he drank, the more garrulous and friendly he became.

We talked about art, which I didn't really know anything about, and music, which I knew a bit more about, and books and films and the fact that Kathy Slattery had given James Tompkins a blow job in the boys' loos at school. Midnight drew nearer. I started to wonder, when twelve o'clock came, would it happen? Would I get a kiss? (I would never have admitted this, not even to my closest friends at school, but at the grand old age of thirteen, I had still never been kissed. Not with tongue, anyway.) I tried not to think about it. Thinking about it was making me sweat.

'Do you make New Year resolutions?' I asked Julian, a little timidly. I was worried he might think New Year resolutions were stupid, or pointless, or bourgeois, or something like that.

'Oh yeah, a list of five. Always five. Ten's a bit ambitious. You?'

'I have five, too.'

'Well, okay then, Miss Nicole,' he said, giving me that heart-stopping smile again, 'let's hear them.' He was leaning towards me, his face only a few inches from mine. I could feel the colour coming to my cheeks.

'You first,' I said, looking away. Oh god oh god oh god. Why did I start this conversation? Why did I tell him I had five resolutions? Why the hell didn't I tell him I only had four?

'All right,' Jules said, lighting yet another fag and settling back against the window sill, 'number one: get As for my art, English and French GSCEs. That's very important. I'm not all that bothered about the other subjects, but I want to do well in those ones. Two, cut down on the cigarettes. They're very bad for your health.' He grinned and took a drag. 'Three, get to London to see as many art exhibitions as possible. At least ten. Four . . .' He hesitated. 'No, hang about. This isn't fair. I've done three, now you do three. Then we'll do the other two.'

I was starting to panic.

28

'I should probably make an appearance downstairs,' I said to him. 'They might have noticed we're missing.'

'Bollocks!' Jules replied, laughing. 'They're all pissed by now.' As I got to my feet he grabbed my hand. 'You're not going to get away with it that easily.' He pulled me back onto the bed. For a second neither of us said anything. He was looking right into my eyes, he was still holding my hand. 'Come on then,' he said, softly, 'what are you going to do next year?'

And in that moment, I thought, I can tell him. I can tell him that I want to kiss him. This is the right time to tell him, it's the perfect time, and I opened my mouth to speak, but I never said anything because in that moment the bedroom door burst open and there stood my father, red-faced and angry-drunk. I snatched my hand from Julian's and got to my feet.

'What the fucking hell is going on?' He crossed the room and grabbed the mug of brandy and Coke from Julian's hand, took a sniff and threw it straight out of the window. An almost-empty pack of Silk Cut sat on the sill. 'You're drinking and smoking with my daughter? You little piece of shit. Get the fuck out of this room. Now!' As Julian got to his feet, my father grabbed his arm and yanked him towards the door.

'Dad!' I cried out, horrified, leaping to my feet. 'We were just talking. It's okay, we weren't doing anything . . .' He clipped me over the back of the head with his hand. I felt the tears spring to my eyes and through them I could see the look of shock on Julian's face, I'd never felt so humiliated.

'You sit back down, girlie. I'll deal with you later.'

I didn't sit back down, I followed him and a worried-looking Julian down the stairs into the living room where Dad started shouting again.

'Please, Dad,' I called out, but he wasn't listening.

'Sheila!' he was yelling, he was looking for Julian's mum. 'Where the bloody hell are you? Where the fuck is that woman?' Someone turned off the music, everyone was staring at him: a raving, foul-mouthed tyrant, he was a sobering sight. Sheila and Mum came rushing out of the kitchen.

'What on earth's going on, Jack?' my mother demanded.

'You!' Dad yelled at Sheila, ignoring Mum's question. 'You can just piss off out of my house and take this little shit with you.'

Sheila stared at him, open-mouthed.

'Jack,' Mum was shouting now, 'don't you dare speak to our guest like that. What is going on?'

'Yeah, you don't know what's going on, do you?' Dad yelled, rounding on her. 'You don't know what the fuck's going on in your own house. You don't know that your thirteen-year-old daughter is upstairs in bed with a boy, drinking and smoking, because you're too busy flirting with anything in trousers down here.'

That's when I lost my temper. 'That is not true!' I

screamed at him, descending the last few steps into the living room. 'We weren't doing anything and neither was Mum! Why do you have to do this? Why do you have to be like this?'

I felt a hand on my arm; it was Julian, standing at my side. 'I was drinking and smoking,' he announced, his voice loud and even. 'Nicole didn't do anything. And we weren't *in* bed, we were sitting on top of it. Fully clothed.'

'You shut your mouth, boy,' Dad sneered at him.

'I will not,' Julian said, his head held high, a look of contempt on his beautiful face. I don't think I've ever loved anyone as much as I loved him in that moment. 'And *you*, I really don't think you are in a position to criticise other people's parenting skills. A drunk who hits his own daughter? What kind of father is that?'

There was a collective sharp intake of breath around the room. Dad opened his mouth to reply but nothing came out; the shock of someone talking back in that manner struck him dumb. Mum, on the other hand, was roused to fury.

'You hit her?' she shrieked at him, pushing him in the chest. 'You hit Nicole?'

'It was nothing,' he retorted. 'I gave her a smack for being cheeky.'

Mum pushed him again, harder. She was starting to cry now. 'You bastard,' she was saying, 'you bastard.'

And then he smacked her, just once, very hard, in the mouth, with a fist, not an open hand. She toppled backwards and split her head open on the edge of the coffee table.

Mum and I spent the early hours of New Year's day in A&E. She had a mild concussion and needed seven stitches in the back of her head. Despite plenty of encouragement from her friends, the police were not called.

'You just make sure he is not in this house when I get back,' Mum had said to Uncle Chris as she was helped into the ambulance. He nodded gravely. He was white with shock – he knew his brother had a temper but I don't think he could possibly have imagined, as I couldn't have up to that point, that Dad would actually punch Mum.

A couple of Mum's nursing friends stayed with me in A&E until she was ready to go home at around four o'clock in the morning. As we passed through the main waiting room, I noticed that Charles was sitting in a corner, drinking a cup of coffee. He watched us go, but didn't say anything.

Chapter Three

Boxing Day, 2011

I'm supposed to be working. And if I'm not working I ought at least to be cleaning the house. I'm doing neither. I'm sitting at my desk in my tiny attic office, composing polite replies to my father's email, explaining that, while I'm terribly sorry to hear that he had been diagnosed with cancer, I'm not able to come and visit him before his operation. I just don't have the time.

How extraordinarily callous that sounds. It *is* extraordinarily callous. It's also true. I don't have time. I have three days in which to do a million things before we leave. And why should I change my plans for him anyway? What, to paraphrase Janet Jackson, has he done for me lately? It's just so bloody typical of him to come to me now he's vulnerable and feeling low. Where was he four years ago, when my whole life fell apart? And the language of his message! '. . . this is a matter of great regret for me . . .' – it sounds like he was resigning from a job, not writing to the daughter he's barely seen in twenty years.

Then again, I *am* going to be in Oxford tomorrow to carry out the interview that I ought to be preparing right now. And Ledbury *is* only about an hour and a half's drive from Oxford. I could always drop by after the interview. Show some generosity of spirit, a bit of kindness to an old man struck down by illness, even if he is a miserable old bastard who doesn't deserve it.

I should talk to Dom about it. Dom will know what to do. I wonder, briefly, whether I should contact my mother and let her know. We almost never speak about him; he's the elephant in all of our rooms. I can't tell her. Not now, she's in Costa Rica on holiday, having fun with friends. I'm not going to spoil that, not for him, not after everything he's put her through.

I pick up my phone and ring Dom's mobile.

'Nicole,' he says when he picks up. 'This is a ridiculous waste of money.'

'I've got five hundred free minutes,' I protest. 'I never use them.'

Dom is downstairs, in his study, a little annex off the living room on the ground floor of the house. Yes, it may sound like I'm being lazy and profligate but it's actually not that easy getting in and out of my office. Access is via a step ladder which has a tendency to slip and slide about, posing considerable risk to life and limb, not to mention fingers, which are liable to get jammed in the hinge as it moves. Despite its inaccessibility, I love my office. It's tiny, you can barely move in here, but from the Velux window there is the most amazing view across the common, a view that changes month to month, week to week, a view that never bores me. Also, even though Dom's not exactly towering in stature, he's still too tall to stand up in here, so it's the one place I retreat to and he can't follow me. And sometimes you just need that.

'What's up?' Dom asks.

I want to tell him about my dad, I want to ask his advice, but for some reason I just can't. I can't bring myself to say the words because I know that when I say them out loud I'm going to cry. And I don't want to cry over him. I've done more than enough of that over the years.

'I think we should make a start on the Christmas decorations,' I say instead.

'You phoned me to tell me that?' Dom asks, incredulous. 'You do realise that if you're going to help me take down the decorations you are going to have to leave your study and come all the way downstairs? Or are you just phoning me to issue instructions?'

'I'll be down in a sec,' I say, hanging up.

Some people find the taking down of the Christmas decorations to be a depressing ritual, but I can't say that I do. If I'm honest, I've always preferred New Year's Eve to Christmas. Christmas is cosy and familial; New Year's Eve is thrilling, filled with possibility, the scent of pastures new, the opportunity to start afresh, to push the boundaries. And to wipe the slate clean, of course. To put yesterday away, somewhere it can be forgotten.

Dom and I pack lights and decorations into boxes and ferry them upstairs to the wardrobe in the spare room, which was specially cleared for the arrival of Dom's parents. Its usual contents – books, papers, files full of old credit card and bank statements, notebooks from Dom's old cases and my old assignments – have been temporarily transferred to our room, where they were hidden under the bed so that his mother doesn't realise how disorganised we are. Dom stows the decorations on the top shelf, I start bringing the rest of the junk through.

'We really ought to sort through all this stuff,' Dom says, 'I'm sure a lot of it can be thrown away.'

'Not this week, Dom. We don't have time. When we get back.'

'Let's just do it now. May as well now we've got it all out. Won't take a minute.'

I sigh, plumping my lower lip out. 'It'll take forever.' He gives a little shrug, the way he does when he thinks I'm being difficult. 'Oh, all right then,' I say. 'You get started, I'll make the tea.'

By the time I get back upstairs, Dom's sitting cross-legged on the floor, two boxes at his side, their contents strewn around him. He's flicking through a notebook, shaking his head.

'What is it?' I ask, handing him the tea.

'No bloody idea, your handwriting's illegible.'

I glance at the notebook over his shoulder. 'Look at the front, it'll have a date on it.'

'November 2004. Madrid? Does that say Madrid?'

'Yeah, that one can go. Anything up to about 2008 can go.' I grab a third box and flip open the lid. It's full of papers. Letters, postcards. I close it again.

'What's in that one?' Dom asks.

'Just stuff. Nothing I want to throw away.'

Dom is looking at me quizzically but he doesn't say anything. I pick up the box and am about to place it at the back of the wardrobe when a slim slip of paper which has been caught in the folds of cardboard at the base of the box falls out. It drifts to the floor and Dom picks it up. He looks at it, gives a sad little smile and hands it to me. It's a photo strip, one of those ones you get from booths, four little pictures in a row. Me, Julian and Alex, a tangle of arms around necks, beaming at the camera, gurning, pulling stupid faces, hysterical with laughter. On the back is written 'London, 1999'. I put the strip back into the box.

'I think I'll put this one in the cupboard in the bedroom,' I say. I can feel Dom's eyes searching for mine.

'I'm going to Oxford tomorrow,' I tell him in an effort to direct the conversation away from dangerous ground as quickly as possible, 'I have to talk to Annie

Gardner, see if I can get her to do the interview for the *Betrayal* series.'

Dom sips his tea. 'Nic,' he started, tentatively. I know he wants to say something about the pictures, and I don't want to hear it.

'We also have to think about the dogs. Shall I take them to Matt's, or do you have time to do it?'

'Nicole . . .'

'I could do it on Wednesday.'

'Subject closed then?' he asks.

'Do you know what?' I say, ignoring his question. 'I actually think I feel like coffee. Do you want some?'

'I'm fine with tea,' he says softly, and goes back to sorting through the notebooks from my previous life.

I leave Dom to sort out the mess in the guest bedroom and decide to tackle cleaning the kitchen instead. There's nothing I hate quite so much as the thought of domestic drudgery, but actually once you get into it it's weirdly cathartic. And because it's so mindless, your thoughts can drift elsewhere. So while I'm scouring surfaces I sketch out a mental plan of the days ahead. Tuesday: interview in Oxford. Wednesday: to Selfridges to find dress for party; hair appointment and manicure in the afternoon; take dogs to Matt and Liz. Thursday: New York, New York . . .

The final traces of muddy paw prints have just been erased from the kitchen floor when Dom appears, a bulging orange recycling sack in each hand.

'Right, these are all the work notebooks and papers up to 2008,' he announces. 'Yours and mine. You sure you're happy for me to chuck it?'

'Absolutely.'

He takes the bags into the utility room, the dumping ground for recyclables awaiting collection. Mick and Marianne, spotting an opportunity, burst past him into the kitchen, bits of dried mud flying from the paws as they scamper happily into the warmth of the kitchen. I pretend not to notice.

'Do you want to go out to dinner tomorrow night?' Dom calls out to me. 'I was thinking we could invite Matt and Liz? They could stay the night and then take the dogs back with them on Wednesday. Save us having to make the trip.'

I hesitate. The email. I should tell him about the email. This is the perfect moment to discuss Dad's email.

'Ummm . . . Yeah. I'll be back by four-ish I expect,' I say. So that's that. I won't have time to get to Oxford and Ledbury and back to London by dinner. Dad will just have to wait. And in the meantime, his email can be added to the list of secrets, just one of many, that I am keeping from my husband.

'So I'll book something shall I? Local? How about that Lebanese place in the village?'

'That's fine, darling.'

I glower at the flecks of mud on the floor, now being trodden on and mashed up and smeared across the tiles. There's a reason I hate housework: it's so bloody futile. And I remember that I haven't cleaned the oven, which I probably should have. It's seen a lot of action over the past few days.

'Nicole?'

'Mmm?'

'Is everything all right?'

Oh, bollocks to the oven. 'Yeah, sorry. I was just thinking of Quentin Crisp.'

'I'm sorry?'

'You know: there's no need to do any housework, because after the first four years, the dirt doesn't get any worse.'

'Leave it then,' Dom says, giving the room the once over. 'Looks fine to me.' There could be rats taking residence in the sink and Dom would say the place looks fine. 'Come and listen to my speech instead.'

'What's it about?'

'The limitations of the 1995 Disability Discrimination Act.'

'Sounds *fascinating*,' I reply.

'Well, you can listen to me or you can clean the loo. It's your choice.'

'I'll just get the Harpic . . .' I say with a grin, but I'm already following him into the living room to listen to his speech.

And the extraordinary thing? It actually *is*

fascinating. Dom can make the dullest, driest, most tedious subjects interesting. He has a way of explaining complex concepts, of illustrating his points with everyday examples, which brings his subject to life. And his subject – labour law – does need livening up.

'It's great,' I say as he finishes, getting up off the sofa to give him a kiss. 'Really good.'

'You don't think that section in the middle on codes of practice goes on too long?'

'No, honestly, it's good. Who's this one for again?'

'It's for the Law Society dinner in January. I'm keynote speaker, remember? I did tell you about this Nic.'

'Yes, of course. I remember.'

He raises an eyebrow, sceptical. 'No you don't.'

'I do.' I didn't.

I'm incredibly proud of Dom. He's a very successful solicitor, made partner at thirty-two, he's forever getting asked to give speeches and appear on committees. But sometimes I do space out when he's talking about his job, and not just because employment law is not the most enthralling of subjects. It's because I'm jealous. It's pathetic, I know, but I can't help myself. Witnessing the steady, hard-won, well-deserved progression of his career from strength to strength only serves to highlight the painful decline of my own. And it's stupid, I know, because this isn't a zero-sum game: his doing well doesn't have anything to do with my doing badly. Still, it hurts.

Take, for example, my latest project, *Betrayal*. When I was first asked to produce the programme, the production company informed me that it was going to be a fairly sober three-part series 'examining the causes and consequences of domestic treachery'. Obviously I knew what the basic subject matter would be: divorces, affairs, Machiavellian goings-on in the workplace, that sort of thing. I also thought it might be quite interesting. The production company promised interviews with psychologists and psychiatrists, in-depth sessions with family counsellors, cultural references and historical comparisons – we'd look at the stories of Judas and Iago, Brutus and Delilah. I thought I might learn something. I thought it might help me deal with my own situation. Ha! I never learn. Turns out it's just another prurient, cruel trawl through the dirty laundry of people whose lives have just not turned out the way they thought they would.

Annie Gardner, the woman I have to visit in Oxford tomorrow, is a case in point. Annie is married to Jim. They have two daughters and, as far as Annie was concerned, they were perfectly happy. That was until Annie's sister, Suzanne, fell pregnant and announced to Annie that Jim was the father. Suzanne has decided to keep the baby and Jim, big-hearted chap that he is, has agreed to support it. Annie has forgiven them both. And into this domestic hell go I.

Annie is the ideal subject for the programme – and they're not all that easy to find, despite what a daily diet of Jeremy Kyle and Jerry Springer might suggest – but she's very nervous about airing her dirty laundry in public. Who wouldn't be? In any case, she's having second thoughts about participating and it's my job to convince her to go ahead. Now all I have to do is prepare a pitch which will not only convince Annie to take part in the programme, but which will also not be a cynical, manipulative lie, the telling of which will keep me awake at night. It is not going to be easy.

I wrestle with the subject all afternoon, eventually giving up around seven. I come downstairs and discover Dom in the kitchen, staring into an open fridge.

'What do you fancy for dinner?' he asks. 'We have turkey, ham, half a dozen mince pies . . .'

'Chinese,' I say. 'I feel like Chinese.'

We order crispy aromatic duck, black bean stir-fry, butterfly tiger prawns and spring rolls, seaweed and loads of prawn crackers. We eat this feast on the sofa in front of the TV, and afterwards lie there, sated and soporific, Dom's arms around me, the dogs snoring next to the fire, watching a marathon of *Blackadder Goes Forth* re-runs on Gold. Perfection. Solid, safe, domestic bliss.

'Nic?' Dom says sleepily, squeezing me a little harder. 'You fancy an early night?'

'What?' I ask, feigning shock 'Twice in one day?'

'No, I actually mean I want to go to bed. To sleep. I'm knackered.'

43

'All right, old man,' I say with a smile. 'I'll put the dogs to bed, you make the Horlicks.'

I wake with a start from a bad dream, the precise details of which I can't remember. I just know that it was horrible. Dom is sound asleep at my side, I slip my hand into his for comfort. He doesn't wake. I lie there, motionless, for a minute or two, just listening to his breathing. I feel suddenly and completely awake, my heart beating just a little too quickly.

I check the time on my phone. One-thirty. Five more hours of sleep. If only. I can't seem to shut my mind down; I can't stop thinking about New York. I've been looking forward to it for months, ever since Karl invited us over to attend his inaugural 'New York for New Year's Eve' party. I haven't been over there for years, not since 2005, and I love New York. It's one of my favourite places on earth. And I can't wait to see Karl again. But New York isn't just home to Karl; it was also home to Aidan and to Alex. How was it that some of the most important people in my life have ended up there, in glamorous Manhattan, while here I was stuck in boring old southwest London? This wasn't the way things were supposed to turn out.

I slip my hand from Dom's, flip my pillow over, lay my cheek on the cool cotton and close my eyes. Sleep. I must sleep. I can't sleep. Instead, I make a mental list.

* * *

44

New Year's Resolutions, 2011:
1. Get in touch with Aidan re job offer
2. Lose half a stone
3. Stop taking the pill
4. Repaint the kitchen
5. Sort out things with Dad

The sublime, the ridiculous and the incredibly vague: a perfect list of resolutions. I ought to write it down. Carefully, I swing my legs over the edge of the bed and creep out of the room. Padding around in the dark again. It was getting to be a habit. I can't go upstairs to my study – it's directly above our bedroom and the floor boards up there creak terribly – so I go downstairs instead. I tiptoe into the kitchen (don't want to wake the dogs up), and in the darkness search for the bottle of Scotch we'd opened on Christmas Day. I discover it next to the toaster, pour myself a large measure and, with the bottle still in hand, pad into Dom's study and switch on his computer. I log onto the Internet, open my email account and the message from my father. I click 'reply'.

Thanks for your message Dad. I'm very sorry to hear you're unwell.

That sounds lame, as though he'd written to me telling me he'd been a bit under the weather. I try again.

Dear Dad, I am terribly sorry to hear your news. Unfortunately, the timing is awful . . .

The timing is awful? What the hell am I talking about? Am I saying it's a bad time to tell me he has cancer, or simply that it's a bad time to get cancer? For god's sake. Just be direct:

Dad, I'm afraid that I cannot come and see you before your operation.

And that's just brutal. Nothing I write sounds in any way close to adequate. I sit and stare at the screen, reading and rereading his message, desperately trying to think of something to say to him, something I actually *feel*. Trouble is, I don't really know what I feel, other than horrible. I give up, delete what I'd written and close the message. Then I open another email account, the secret Hotmail one that Dom doesn't know about. I have three new messages. Two are spam, quickly deleted. The third, which arrived that afternoon, comes from arose@petersen.com. Alex. No subject line. I click on her name to open the message.

So, it's confirmed. Aaron's playing away. Checked his BlackBerry on Christmas morning while he was in the shower. Message from Jessica. And I quote:
   'Lying in bed, wearing new La Perla (thank you,

thank you!) and no one to play with. Can you get away Boxing Day? Happy Xmas my darling Jx'

I wasn't surprised, of course, but you were right, it **does** feel like someone's stuck a knife into one's chest and is twisting it, slowly, slowly, oh so bloody slowly. Haven't said anything to him yet. I've barely got out of bed since I saw the message. Feigning illness. So now he brings me chicken soup in bed and soothes my (allegedly) fevered brow and all I want to do is punch him in the face.

I guess you must think I got what was coming to me. God, I miss you Nic.

xA

I take a large gulp of whisky. Some of it drips down off my chin and onto my T-shirt. It's one of my sleeping shirts, I've got a few, all of them ancient relics from another life. This one is my *Different Class* T-shirt, Julian bought it for me when we went to see Pulp play at the Brixton Academy in the first term of my first year at university. It's soft, worn thin over my shoulders, holes appearing along the seams. It will disintegrate to rags before I throw it out. I take another swig of my drink, shut down the computer, wipe the tears from my eyes and go back to bed.

Chapter Four

New Year's Eve, 1991
High Wycombe

Resolutions:
1. Enter the *Seventeen* short story competition
2. Lose half a stone
3. Phone Dad at least once a week
4. Sign up for the photography course at the leisure centre
5. Forget about Julian Symonds

Charles was coming round for dinner, which really pissed me off. It wasn't that I didn't like him; he was actually really nice. It just seemed . . . insensitive. This, after all, was the anniversary of my parents' spectacular break-up and there was still part of me that blamed Charles for it. Charles, my mother, myself most of all. Somehow over the course of the past twelve months Dad's part in the whole thing seemed to have diminished in importance.

Mum suggested that I invite a couple of friends around to join us for dinner; grumpily, I declined.

'It's going to be *really boring*,' I pointed out. 'My friends do not want to come round here and watch TV with you and your *boyfriend*.'

'Okay then, darling, have it your way,' Mum replied breezily, which infuriated me further. This was not going my way. This is not how I wanted to spend New Year's Eve. I wanted to be going out to a party, or at least having a party at home. Actually, the thing I wanted most of all was to have last New Year's Eve back, a chance to do it over, minus the bloody ending. More than anything on earth, I wanted to be sitting in my bedroom with Julian Symonds.

Julian and I had not spoken since Valentine's Day. He'd called a couple of times in the summer, but I'd got Mum to say that I was out. I didn't want to talk to him, *ever again*. I didn't want to hear him say that he was sorry, or to tell me that it wasn't me, it was him. I didn't want to hear him say that he really hoped we could be friends. It was all just too humiliating, too painful.

The thing was, I should have been over him by now.

'You only went out for like, five minutes,' Emma Bradley, my *supposed* best friend at school pointed out to me the last time I flinched at the mention of Julian's name. 'Don't you think you're being a bit . . .

melodramatic? It's not like you were in love or anything. You didn't even shag him.'

True, I didn't shag him, but I *was* in love with him. And it wasn't five minutes. It was five weeks. Five torturous, blissful, rollercoaster weeks, the five most intense weeks of my entire existence, the weeks during which I was Julian Symonds' Girlfriend.

It was beyond my wildest dreams. After all, I'd returned to school a week after the New Year's Eve party in a state of panic. I was terrified of seeing Julian again, convinced that he would have told the entire school about the party; about my awful fucked-up family, what a total head case my dad was, and about how desperately uncool I was, with a Gustav Klimt print on the wall and everything. That first morning back, I made my way towards morning assembly with my head down. My entire body tense, I glanced up every now and again to check whether people were staring at me, whispering, pointing, laughing. They were not. No one said anything to me, apart from a couple of classmates saying hello and asking if I'd had a nice Christmas, until I reached the doorway of the assembly hall. Then, just as I was about to enter, I felt a gentle tug at my sleeve, and I turned around and there he was, towering over me, handsome even in the dull grey of his school uniform.

'Hello,' he said, not quite meeting my eye. 'How are you?' He looked nervous, he was shifting his weight from foot to foot, biting his lower lip.

51

'I'm fine, thanks,' I said, concentrating terribly hard on breathing and not falling over at the same time. 'How about you?'

'I wanted to ring you,' he said, 'to find out if you were okay. You and your mum. But I wasn't sure if I should . . . I was worried . . .'

'Dad moved out,' I said, 'so, you could have, you know, if you wanted to, you know, called me.' Jesus, I sounded retarded.

'God, Nicole, I'm so sorry. I'm so sorry about your parents. That's just awful. I feel really terrible about this.' He looked genuinely upset.

'It wasn't your fault,' I said.

'It kind of was . . .'

'Julian . . .'

The second bell went, the signal for everyone to get into the assembly hall immediately unless they wanted a week's detention.

'Can I come and see you?' he asked me. 'After school, some time this week?'

My heart was hammering so hard in my chest I thought I might pass out.

'Of course,' I squeaked. 'That would be . . . nice. I have piano today and gymnastics on Thursday, but any other day would be fine.' Christ, now I sounded like a nine-year-old.

But he didn't seem to think so, he just smiled and said, 'Great. I'll come over tomorrow.'

As I walked into assembly, I glanced around again,

holding my head high this time, no longer hiding. No longer was I hoping that no one had noticed me, now I was praying that someone had seen. Please, please say someone had just witnessed me, Nicole Blake of Year Eight, talking to Julian Symonds of Year Ten, not just an older boy, but the best-looking boy in school.

As promised, he visited the next day. The day after that, he sought me out during our lunch break at school, he actually *sat next to me*, at my table, *in full view* of other Year Tens. That Friday, he came round to the house again. I was upstairs in my room, sulking, because I'd come home from school to find Mum sitting in the kitchen with Charles, giggling like a teenager. *So* undignified. After Charles left, Mum and I had a row. She said I'd been rude to Charles.

'Just because I don't fawn all over him like you do doesn't mean I'm being rude,' I said to her.

'Don't be like that, Nic,' she said. 'He's my friend.'

'Oh, is that what they're calling it these days?'

'Nicole!'

'Well, maybe Dad was right . . .'

'Go to your room, Nicole,' she said, cutting me off. 'Now.'

And I went upstairs and lay on my bed, wondering why I felt the need to be such a bitch to her. I knew she hadn't done anything wrong.

I was still lying there when I heard the doorbell ring. A few moments later, there was a soft knock at my door.

'What?' I snapped.

Mum pushed the door open. 'There's someone downstairs to see you,' she said.

'Who?'

'It's Julian,' she said, and I leapt to my feet in a panic, tearing off my school uniform and rushing around the room looking for something to wear. Mum stood in the doorway watching me.

'I really ought to send him home,' she said.

'No!' I cried, horrified. 'Please don't.'

'You've been really unkind to me, Nic. I'm not sure you should be allowed to see friends tonight.'

'Please, Mum,' I begged her. 'I'm so sorry. I'm so, so sorry.'

She just looked at me, implacable. Then she smiled. 'The red top, that one we got on Oxford Street last summer. Put that on. You look lovely in that.' I flung my arms around her neck and squeezed. 'Yes, all right. You get dressed and I'll tell Julian you're on your way down. And Nic?'

'Yeah?'

'I would never be rude to your friends. Please do me the same courtesy.'

I pulled on some jeans, threw on the red top and drew a line of black kohl under my eyes. I glowered at myself in the mirror. I was hideous. But there was nothing to be done about it now. I took a deep breath, pushed open my bedroom door and made my way downstairs.

Julian was standing in the hallway. Dressed in black jeans, his biker jacket and Doc Martens, he looked perfect.

'Hey you,' he said with a smile, 'hope you don't mind me just coming by like this.'

'Course not,' I said. As I got to the bottom of the stairs, he reached for my hand. I thought I was going to die. He pulled me closer, glancing quickly over my shoulder to make sure that we were alone (we were – my wonderful mother had disappeared into the kitchen), then he leant over and kissed me on the lips.

'Even better,' he said softly.

'Even better than what?'

'Than I'd imagined. And I've been imagining that since New Year's Eve.'

So it began, and it was even better than I'd dreamt it would be, too. It was perfect. He was so easy to be around, and beneath that whole cool façade, he had a wicked sense of humour. For the five weeks we were together it seemed like we never stopped talking – about everything: my family, his family, our friends, films, music, art . . . And I was so proud to walk down the halls with him, holding his hand, or with his arm draped around my shoulders – and he was so cool about stuff like that – he wasn't like those idiots who refuse to show their girlfriends any affection in public, but once they're alone immediately begin ripping their clothes off. Julian was happy to be seen with me.

Except, of course, that it wasn't perfect. Because

although he was lovely and affectionate in public, he was nothing more than lovely and affectionate in private, too. Not that I actually *wanted* to do anything with him (not yet, anyway), but it seemed really weird to me that *he* didn't want to. I never ever said anything about it (of course), but privately, I tortured myself. Why didn't he want me? What was wrong with me? Well, aside from my thighs (flabby), breasts (small), hips (wide) and so on. I tried to reassure myself that he was just being respectful of me, but in my heart I knew this was total crap. I was fundamentally undesirable.

A fact which was confirmed in brutal fashion on Valentine's Day, a date that I had been anticipating with feverish excitement and not a little anxiety. For the first time ever I was going to get a Valentine's card. A real one, not one written in my mother's poorly disguised hand. I might even get flowers. The anticipation was killing me. The post hadn't arrived by the time I left for school that day, but that didn't matter. He'd probably give me the card when I saw him anyway, and that would be even better, because then I'd have an excuse to show everyone. It was the complete contrast to the first day of term: me desperately hoping to bump into him, searching him out all day, failing to find him. I hung around the school gates for half an hour after classes, convinced that he'd be along any minute, but no such luck. I went home, deflated.

Until I pushed open the front door, and saw there on the mat, peeking out from under a large, official-looking manila envelope, a corner of brilliant vermilion. My heart leapt. I threw my bag onto the floor and scooped up the mail, flinging the bills and junk mail back onto the carpet. I ripped open the envelope and was surprised to see an impressionist scene on the front of the card: Monet, the artist's garden at Giverny. Not very Julian. I flipped open the card and read: *Dearest Elizabeth, Happy Valentine's Day. With love, C.*

It was only then that I looked at the front of the envelope, which I hadn't even checked in my haste to get to the card. It was addressed to Mrs E. Blake. It wasn't for me, it was for Mum. And it wasn't even from Dad, it was from Charles. Were they lovers now?

Feeling sick to my stomach, I ripped the card to pieces and threw it in the bin, making sure to cover the evidence with banana skins and tea bags. I couldn't believe it. Nothing from Julian for me, something from Charles for Mum. It was the worst possible combination. I dragged myself upstairs, stuck *Nowhere* on the stereo, turned 'Dreams Burn Down' up to ten, and flung myself face down onto the bed.

I was still lying there, in my school uniform, face buried in the pillow, when I heard the doorbell go downstairs. For a moment, I didn't know what to do. What if it was Charles? What if it was Dad?

'Nicole?' I heard a voice call out. 'You there?'

Julian! I was so delighted to hear his voice, I didn't

even worry about the fact that I was still in uniform, that I looked like hell. I tore down the stairs and yanked open the door, grabbing him around the waist and kissing him until I noticed that he wasn't kissing me back.

Something was wrong. He didn't meet my eye as he pushed past me into the house. He seemed agitated, distracted. In the kitchen, I poured us both a glass of juice. He waved me away as I offered it to him.

'Stick something stronger in there for me, will you?' he said.

'Jules,' I laughed, 'it's five-thirty in the afternoon. Mum's going to be home soon. She'll kill me if—'

'Oh for fuck's sake, Nicole.'

'What? What's wrong?' I reached out my hand to take his. He pulled away.

'Nothing. I'm just . . . I felt like having a drink.'

'Well, you can't have one here.'

'Fine, I'll go elsewhere then.'

'Julian . . .' I reached out for him again, but he was already heading out into the hallway.

At the front door, he turned. He looked straight at me, unflinching, direct, and said: 'This is just not working, is it? You and me. You're a great girl, Nic, but this isn't right . . .'

'Jules, please don't . . .' I said, already starting to cry. 'Oh don't . . .'

'Julian, I love you.' It was the first time I'd ever told him that, and I meant it.

'No you don't, Nic,' he said sadly, and turned to go, leaving me sobbing on the stairs.

And that was the last time we spoke. And it was so awful, because although it sounds silly (as Emma Bradley never tired of pointing out), we'd become so close in those weeks together, it was like Jules and I were best friends, which is probably why Emma was always so down on me when I talked about him. So it wasn't like I'd just lost my boyfriend, I'd lost my friend, too, and that was so hard. He was the one person I wanted to talk to about how I was feeling, the only person who would understand, and of course he was the one person I couldn't talk to about it.

When he called me in the summer, I was tempted to speak to him, I really was. The thought of being able to chat to him again, to talk about the books I'd been reading and find out what he thought of *Kill Uncle* was almost irresistible. Plus, I wanted to know if he was okay. That sounds weird, I know, because after all *he* dumped *me*, but there had been all kinds of rumours about him at school, and I was actually a bit worried.

He'd been bunking off school a lot lately, more and more as the year went on. At first it was a relief: the fewer chance encounters in the halls at school the better as far as I was concerned, but after a while it just seemed strange and out of character. I knew he had a rebellious streak but I also knew that it meant a lot to him to do well in his exams because he wanted to get into a good art school. Mum, who was still close friends with Julian's mother, told me that skipping school was just the start of it. He'd been getting into loads of trouble, she said, he'd been coming home drunk or high or not at all, he'd been in fights, he barely spoke to his parents at all. 'Sheila's at the end of her tether,' Mum told me. 'She just doesn't know what to do about him.'

Rumours at school were rife: Julian Symonds had got into serious drugs; Julian Symonds was a Satanist; Julian Symonds had become a complete loner, a weirdo, a drop out. Deep down, I was anxious that this was somehow all my fault. Had he been shunned by the cool set as a result of his inexplicable decision to go out with a nobody from Year Eight? And there was a part of me – the uncharitable part, I suppose – that thought it served him right. He'd broken my heart; I'd ruined his life. No more than he deserved. Except I didn't really believe that, not at all. The part of me that had been his best friend for those five glorious weeks was terribly worried about him. Still, I resisted the temptation to seek him out and tried, as best I could, to put him out of my mind.

On New Year's Eve, however, that was never going to be possible. Particularly as I had nothing more exciting than dinner at home with Charles and Mum to distract me. They'd been seeing each other since the summer. Well, that was the official line, anyway. They'd been 'spending time together, just as friends' since about five minutes after Dad left. It was a bit unseemly. In the early days, particularly in the wake of my break-up with Julian, Mum and I had fought about it quite a bit. It only took a couple of drunken late-night visits from Dad to get me back on her side, though. Why wouldn't she want to be with someone like Charles – quiet, considerate, with a surprisingly dry sense of humour (and a doctor, too) – when the alternative was my permanently pissed-off, unreasonable father?

Plus it was hard not to like Charles. He'd been really nice to me, and not in an annoying, I'm-trying-to-replace-your-father or (even worse) an I'm-trying-to-be-your-best-friend way. He was just friendly. He included me. When he and Mum were going to the cinema, he always asked if I wanted to come along too, even if the film was an 18 and I wasn't really allowed, and even though he knew I'd say no (seriously, who goes to the cinema with their parents?), and whenever I did say no, which was always, he never pressed the point. He just said, 'All right then. Shall we bring you some wine gums?'

And he'd lent me a ton of books. He had a much better selection than had ever been available in our house, including loads of stuff I'd never heard of, like *The Rules of Attraction* by Bret Easton Ellis which was really shocking and explicit. I actually wasn't all that sure I liked it very much, but it was probably the sort of challenging thing I ought to be reading.

Best of all, though, he made Mum really happy. It wasn't until I saw her with him, completely relaxed, always laughing, that I realised just how unhappy she'd been before. I suppose I hadn't noticed it, because it crept up on us over the years, but we'd become quite fearful in our day-to-day lives. And now Dad was gone we both became louder, messier, more chaotic, more ourselves.

Even so, I was still annoyed that Charles was coming for dinner on New Year's Eve. I'd imagined it would just be Mum and me, and that would be something different. Maybe we could talk a bit, about Dad, maybe Mum could help me understand why whenever I called him he sounded disappointed. He'd pick up and go, 'Hello?' and I'd say, 'Hi Dad, it's Nicole' and then he'd go, 'Oh.' And he never asked how I was getting on at school, or anything like that. He always said, 'How's your mum? She doing all right is she?'

Charles arrived just before seven brandishing a copy of Marco Pierre White's *White Heat*.

'Makes a change from Delia Smith, don't you think?' he asked cheerily. 'You want to help out with the cooking?' In a low voice he added, 'I won't even bother asking your mother.'

'Not really,' I replied grumpily. For god's sake! Wasn't it bad enough that I had to stay in on New

Year's Eve with my mother and her boyfriend? Now I had to help in the kitchen?

'Oh, go on, Nic,' Charles said. 'We're having scallops and langoustines with cucumber and ginger, followed by noisettes of lamb with fettuccine of vegetables and tarragon *jus*.'

'All right then,' I said, trying my best not to roll my eyes at him (Mum hated that). I didn't like to admit that I had no idea what he'd just said.

And to my surprise, as I chopped shallots and thinly sliced a thumb of ginger (ingredients entirely alien to our kitchen), and as Charles poured me half a glass of champagne and talked to me about *The Handmaid's Tale*, which I was due to study in English next term, I found myself having quite a good time. Dinner turned out to be delicious, Mum was in a great mood, we had a Keanu Reeves double bill on video (*My Own Private Idaho* and *Point Break* – a special treat for me), so it really wasn't so bad after all.

And then, just before eleven, the doorbell rang and my stomach churned. Dad. It had to be. And he'd have been in the pub a good few hours by now. Charles paused the video and got up to go to the door, but Mum stopped him. I tried to follow her out, but Charles put his hand on my arm and said, 'Let's give it a minute, eh?' The pair of us stood in the living room, just behind the door, poised to spring out and save her.

She opened the door and then I heard her cry out,

'Oh my god!' and my whole body went cold. Something very bad was about to happen. Charles charged out into the hallway in front of me, I grabbed the phone, ready to dial 999. I heard her say again, 'Oh my god, what happened to you?'

Phone in hand, I ran into the hall. Mum and Charles were in the doorway, blocking my view.

'What is it?' I called out, trying desperately to quell the panic in my voice. 'Is Dad all right?'

'It's not Dad, love,' Mum said, and as she did she and Charles parted slightly, allowing the person at the door to step into the hall. I watched, dumbstruck, as she and Charles ushered Julian into the house. Julian, dirty and dishevelled, his shoulders heaving, his right eye swollen shut, blood all over his face. I burst into tears.

Mum took him upstairs to clean him up. I hopped around outside the bathroom, calling out. 'What happened? What's going on? Open this door! Mum! I need to see him. He's *my* friend!'

Eventually Charles came upstairs, handed me a cup of tea and persuaded me to go downstairs, and an agonising ten or fifteen minutes later, Mum and Julian joined us in the kitchen. The four of us sat around the kitchen table for a minute or two, nobody saying anything, everyone sipping their tea. Julian looked horrendous. The right side of his face was swelling up, his skin turning an angry purplish red. His lower lip was split; he dabbed at it occasionally with a tissue.

I couldn't take my eyes off him; he hadn't once looked over at me.

After what seemed like an age, Mum spoke. 'I think I should call your parents, Julian.'

'Please don't, Mrs Blake.' He looked stricken. 'I don't want to talk to them now.'

'They'll be worried about you,' Mum said.

'No they won't. Not yet. They won't be expecting me till after midnight.'

'Well, I'm going to have phone them some time.'

'Not yet, please.'

There was another moment or two of silence interrupted by tea slurping, and then Charles said, 'At any rate we ought to call the police.'

'No!' Julian jumped to his feet. 'You can't do that. It'll only make it worse.'

'Julian, you've been badly beaten, you can't just let this go . . .'

'I won't press charges,' he said. He looked as though he might start to cry.

'Julian . . .'

He grabbed his jacket from the back of the chair. 'Thanks for the tea, Mrs Blake. I'll get out of your hair now.'

I grabbed his arm as he turned to leave. 'Just hang on,' I said, and for the first time he looked straight at me. 'Maybe Jules and I could have a chat alone for a minute,' I said. He reached out his hand and brushed away the tear rolling down my cheek. 'Please, Mum?'

So there we were again. Julian and I, sitting on my bed at a few minutes from midnight. We sat in silence while he smoked a cigarette, then he threw it out of the window and took my hand.

'How are you, Nic?' he asked, staring down at the bedspread.

'Julian, what on earth is going on? Who did this?'

'I'm so sorry I hurt you,' he said, still not meeting my eye, 'I never wanted to. I just . . . I just didn't know what to do.'

'What to do about what?'

'Everything.' He let go of my hand and got to his feet.

'Don't go, Jules. Please tell me.'

He stood with his back to me, all attention apparently focused on the Klimt on the opposite wall.

'I went to a party at Craig's house,' he said at last.

'Tonight?'

'Yeah. And . . . I've been thinking about this for ages . . . I needed to talk to someone . . . It was totally the wrong time of course, it was fucking stupid, but I had a couple of beers and just thought, you know what? Fuck it. Craig's a friend, we've known each other for ages.'

'Okay,' I said, completely mystified as to what the hell he was talking about.

'So, we went outside for a spliff and I told him.'

'Told him?'

'That I'm gay.' He turned around and smiled at me,

the saddest smile I'd ever seen. I opened my mouth to say something, but nothing came out. 'But then, you knew that already.'

'No I didn't,' I said, finally finding my voice. 'I had no idea . . .'

'Nic. You must have known . . .'

'Is that why . . . that's why you broke up with me. That's why you didn't want me . . .'

He sat back down on the bed and put his arms around me. 'I wanted to want you,' he murmured into my hair. 'I really wanted to.'

For a while we stayed like that, our arms wrapped tightly around each other, both of us crying a little. Finally, we broke the embrace, blew our noses and giggled a bit, embarrassed. From downstairs I could hear the countdown to midnight on the television.

'Happy New Year, Nic,' Julian said as they reached zero, gingerly giving me a kiss.

'I can't believe Craig did this to you,' I said, gently touching his lip.

'Oh, he didn't. He was totally cool about it. He was actually really nice, told me he was quite relieved – they'd been worried that I'd become a Christian or something.'

'So who then?'

'Turns out Craig's brother, who is an absolute fucking tool, overheard the whole conversation. He was lurking in the bushes or something, the complete freak. Anyway, he was there with a bunch of his retarded mates who apparently don't like gay boys all that much. When Craig and Al went to the offie to get some more beers, his brother and the rest of the cowardly Cro-Magnons took me outside and gave me a good kicking.'

'Bastards! You have to tell the police, Jules.'

'It'll make it worse, Nic. It'll create all kinds of hassle between me and Craig – his brother might be a prat but he's still his brother. I'm going to need my friends, Nic. You know what it's going to be like at school. I really don't want to get the police involved. Okay?'

'All right,' I said, feeling that I was letting injustice prevail, 'but there's no way Mum's not going to ring your parents.'

'I can't face my dad yet,' he said in a small voice. 'That's why . . . that's why I came here. I knew I could count on you, I knew that even though I hurt you and even though we haven't spoken for ages, I knew you'd understand, because that's just the kind of person you are. I knew that if I was with you, I'd be okay.'

I left Julian in my room and went downstairs to persuade Mum to ring Julian's parents to ask if he could stay with us for the night.

'If you just say that he'd had a couple of beers and got into a bit of a fight, but that he's fine, he's just sleeping it off . . .'

'Nicole, I am not lying to Julian's parents.'

'But . . . it isn't even really a lie. He did have a

couple of beers, he did get into a fight. He doesn't want to talk to his dad yet.'

Mum chewed on her nails nervously. To his credit, Charles stayed out of it. I'd just about got her to agree when there was another knock on the door.

'Shit,' my mother and I said in unison.

'Don't answer it,' I whispered to her.

'He'll have seen the lights . . .'

'Hello?' a voice called out from the porch, and it wasn't my father's.

'Maybe it's Craig,' I said, edging in front of Mum to get to the door first.

It wasn't Craig. On the doorstep stood a tall, dark-haired man holding a motorcycle helmet in his hand. I'd never seen him before, but he was instantly familiar to me, with Julian's high cheekbones and long lashes, just situated on an older, more world-worn face. And while Julian's eyes were brown and soulful, this person's eyes were green. Bleary, a little bloodshot, but definitely green.

'Hello, young lady,' the man said, giving me a rakish smile. 'You're up past your bedtime, aren't you?'

Past my bedtime? 'Who the hell are you?' I demanded, annoyed.

He laughed. 'Is your mum in?'

'Seriously,' I said, really pissed off now, 'who are you?'

'Name's Aidan,' he said, holding out his hand for me to shake. He had the faintest trace of a Glaswegian accent, that and something else, Manchester maybe. 'I'm sorry to call so late, but I understand you're giving refuge to my young cousin.'

'You're Julian's cousin?'

'That's right. I was meant to pick him up from the party, but they told me he'd left. Said I might be able to find him here. I didn't realise he had a girlfriend.'

'I'm not his girlfriend,' I said. 'I'm his ex.' Aidan found this inexplicably funny. 'He's staying here tonight,' I told him.

'Oh, I don't think so,' Aidan said, stepping a little closer to me and peering over my shoulder into the house. He smelt of lemons and cigarettes. Weird combination. I stepped across him to stop him looking into the house, folding my arms across my chest.

'He's staying here tonight,' I repeated.

Aidan started to laugh again. 'Any chance I could speak to him then?'

'I'll go and see if he wants to talk to you,' I said, and turned on my heel, closing the door in Aidan's face. Annoying bastard, I thought, and yet I could feel my face colouring and my heart racing. It's just because he looks like Jules, I thought. He's patronising and smug. And really old.

Upstairs, I found Jules sitting at my dressing table, examining his facial injuries in the mirror.

'Can I stay?' he asked anxiously when I appeared.

'I think so, but you have to go downstairs and talk to your annoying cousin first.'

70

'Oh crap! Aidan. Shit, I forgot all about him. He said he'd pick me up after the party.' Then he grinned at me. 'Why did you say he was annoying? What did he do?'

'He's just . . . really patronising,' I said, but I could feel myself blushing again.

'Okay,' Julian said, still smiling at me, a little quizzically. 'I'd better go and talk to him.'

Julian and his cousin talked outside. I watched them from behind the curtain in the living-room window. Jules telling his story, shuffling from foot to foot, every now and again pausing, his head in his hands; Aidan, leaning against his motorbike, smoking, listening passively. Until, presumably at the key point in the story, he threw the cigarette down and started to yell.

'Why didn't you call me? I would have come straight away.' Then he put his motorcycle helmet on and swung one long leg over the bike

'Where are you going?' I could hear Julian ask him.

'To sort those fuckers out,' he replied, kick-starting the bike into life.

After that, I couldn't hear anything they were saying over the noise of the engines, I could just see Julian gesticulating, obviously pleading with him not to do anything stupid. Fat chance, I thought to myself. Aidan looked like the sort of guy for whom stupid – or at the very least reckless – came naturally.

I was just wondering whether I ought to go out and intervene when I heard the front door slam and, to my horror, Mum strode out into the driveway, and I *could* hear her yelling over the engine noise.

'Enough!' she shouted, holding up her hands. Aidan cut the engine. 'You,' she said, addressing Aidan, 'can get going now. And I don't want to hear about you turning up at Craig's parents' place in the middle of the night. Julian, go inside. I've spoken to your mum, it's all right for you to stay. But you can go to bed right now. I've made up the bed in the spare room.'

Despite my embarrassment, I couldn't help smiling. The two boys, instantly recognising they were no match for my mother, did exactly what they were told. Aidan started up his motorcycle once more, and rode off at a sensible speed, while Julian came back into the house and hurried straight upstairs to bed.

It was about just after one when I heard my mother's bedroom door close and realised it was safe to sneak out. I tiptoed down the hall, pushed open the door to the spare room and slipped inside.

'Are you awake?' I whispered.

'Yeah.'

'Are you okay?'

'I think so.'

'Do you want to talk?'

Julian flung back the bedspread in reply, and I crept into bed, nestling myself up against him.

'Shall we do resolutions?' he asked me.

'You first.'

'Okay, at number one I had "come out to my

friends", so I've jumped the gun a bit on that one. Number two, "come out to my parents".'

'Your parents are good people, Jules, they'll be fine.'

'Mum will. Dad's going to be disappointed. I know he won't want to be, but he won't be able to help himself.'

I slipped my arm underneath his body and squeezed him.

'Not too hard,' he mumbled. 'I might have a broken rib.'

'Sorry.'

'Number three: quit smoking.'

'You had that last year.'

'I'll probably have it next year, too.'

'Four: really concentrate on work. I really want to go to St Martin's next year, and I'm going to need As to get in.'

'You'll have no problem getting in, Jules. You're so talented.'

He kissed the side of my head in the dark, squeezed me a little tighter.

'And five: well . . . It was going to be to make things right with you. But maybe . . . I don't know . . . Do you forgive me, Nic?' There were tears in his voice, and I started to cry, too. 'I'm sorry I hurt you . . .'

'I'm sorry I wasn't around when you needed me.'

We lay in silence for a bit, arms wrapped around each other, my heart full, completely safe. I told him my resolutions, and then I got up to go back to my room.

'I'd better not fall asleep here,' I told him. 'Mum will kill me.'

'You did just tell her I'm gay, didn't you?'

'She'll still kill me.'

'Okay.'

'Will you be all right?'

'I'll be fine. Night, Nic.'

'Night.'

I tiptoed back to my room and crawled into bed, falling asleep almost instantly. I dreamed that Julian and I were on holiday, riding through a desert somewhere on a motorbike. The sun was setting and we stopped to take pictures, but when Julian took off his motorbike helmet I realised that his eyes were green, not brown. It wasn't Jules at all, it was Aidan.

Chapter Five

27 December 2011

I get up in darkness, again. This time there's no time to walk the dogs. Hop in the shower, get dressed, get my notes together, drink my coffee, out the door. I need to be in Jericho, in Oxford, by nine-fifteen. If I leave at half seven I'll make it.

At seven forty I dash back upstairs to say goodbye to Dom. He's just stirring.

'You off already?' he croaks sleepily.

I kiss him on the head.

'You'll be back for dinner, yeah?' he asks. I don't say anything, I just kiss him again. 'Have a good day, love,' he says. 'Good luck with the interview.' On my way out of the front door I catch sight of myself in the hallway mirror and recoil slightly. My hair, which was cropped quite short in the summer, is now in that awkward neither short nor long phase. I could definitely do with some styling. And I look pale, a little tired. Like someone who's been inside for too long.

* * *

I get stuck in traffic on the M40. Traffic. The day after Boxing Day? Where the hell is everyone going? Hopefully, I root around in the glove box. And there it is, contraband. A packet of Marlboro Lights, half full. Dom would kill me if he knew.

I light a cigarette and flick on the radio. Some mindless chatter for a minute or two, then The Pogues with Kirsty MacColl, 'The Fairytale of New York'. This, just as I'm passing the sign for the off ramp to High Wycombe. It feels like a sign, or a horrible cosmic joke. In reality, it isn't so remarkable – after all, they play this song to death every single Christmas now, now it's been voted Greatest Christmas Song in the World Ever.

Still, for a moment all I can see is Julian, twirling my reluctant mother around the kitchen, singing at the top of his lungs in a terrible fake Irish accent. That was what, twenty years ago? Me, Mum and Jules, drinking illicit sparkling wine and scoffing mince pies, the year Jules' parents went to visit his aunt in Australia, the first Christmas we ever spent together. I turn off the radio and put out my cigarette.

The car in front of me moves a few yards, brakes, trundles a little further on, brakes again. I force myself to keep my eyes on the bank of red brake lights ahead, refusing to look over to the right hand side of the road, to my old hometown. The sky above looks ominously grey. Somehow the weather always seems miserable at this point in the road. I light a second cigarette (bad, bad girl) – anything to distract me. But as soon as I get past the turnoff to High Wycombe I start to feel better. Not going back there always feels like a little victory.

I can hear my phone ringing from the depths of my handbag. As luck would have it, the traffic's just started to move again, so I can't answer. I've already got six points on my licence and I don't fancy any more. As soon as we grind to a halt, I grab the phone and dial into my voicemail.

'Hello? Ms Blake? It's Annie here. Annie Gardner. I'm really sorry to inconvenience you, but I can't do nine-fifteen. I've got a meeting here I can't get out of. I could meet you for lunch though. Really sorry to cancel at such late notice. Please give me a call when you get this message.'

My heart lifts a little. It's like hearing you have a snow day when you're supposed to have a test at school. A temporary reprieve. With the traffic still stationary, I ring Annie back to say that lunch will be fine. Browns at one o'clock.

By the time I actually get into Oxford and find some- where to park the car, it's after ten o'clock, so it's a good thing Annie had that meeting. I have a few hours to kill before lunch, but the good news is that the sky over Oxford is clear; it's a bright, crisp winter day, the perfect sort for wandering around one of England's loveliest cities. All the more so out of term time: with no students and not too much traffic, Oxford is a joy.

I park at the shopping centre near the station and wander along George Street into town. Past Balliol, past Trinity, the Sheldonian theatre and the Bodleian Library, I turn right at the King's Arms and walk through the heart of the university. On every street, around every corner, there are ghosts. Alex and I, reeling along Holywell Street, singing at the tops of our voices, arms linked, kebabs in hand, after a long, boozy afternoon in the Turf Tavern. Alex, stripped of her ball gown, right down to bra and knickers, jumping off Magdalen Bridge – in clear defiance of University rules – on a freezing May morning in our second year. Despite myself, I can't help but smile. I found myself wandering along, laughing out loud, occasional passing tourists shooting bemused glances in my direction.

I turn back, ending up, inevitably, walking down Parks Road towards our old college. There we were again, Alex and I, sunbathing in the gardens of Rhodes House or drinking wine in the university parks that sweltering summer that Julian came to visit, watching the boys play cricket. I reach the solid, dark oak doors of the college and, butterflies quivering in my belly, step inside.

'Can I help you?' A porter emerges from the lodge, a frown fixed upon his face.

'I just wanted to take a look . . .'

'College is closed to visitors,' he says abruptly, indicating the sign to that effect.

'I used to go here. This is my old college.'

'Closed to visitors,' he repeats. 'It's open in term time.'

'I just wanted . . .'

'We're closed,' he snaps, virtually pushing me out of the door. The porters always were miserable old bastards. As I walk slowly around the college, back towards St Giles, I have another flashback, of Alex and I getting a bollocking from the head porter for making a racket when we came back to college one night, and of her, hoiking up her skirt, bending over and showing him her arse in reply. I start to giggle again. With everything that's happened over the past couple of years, sometimes I forget how happy we were. Back then, it was impossible to be miserable when Alex was around.

There's a coffee cart on the corner of Keble Road and St Giles – a new innovation, that certainly hadn't been there in my day. I buy myself a large latte and find myself a quiet spot to drink it on a bench in the graveyard of St Giles Church. Protected from the wind by a line of firs, and with the sun on my face, it feels quite warm. I lean back on the bench, close my eyes and try not to think about the day ahead. After a while, I couldn't really say how long, a shadow looms over me. I open my eyes.

'Are you all right there?' It's the vicar.

'Sorry,' I say getting to my feet. 'I suppose you don't encourage loitering.'

He laughs. He has a broad, open face and dreadful teeth, yellow and gapped. 'Not at all. Loiter all you like.' He gestures for me to sit back down on the bench and takes a seat beside me. 'Bit warmer today, isn't it?'

'Mmm-hmm.'

'Are you visiting?'

'Just here for the day.'

'Have you seen the sights? It's quite a climb, but I'd recommend you try the top of St Mary's tower. There's a marvellous view.'

'Oh, I've been before. I actually studied here. A long, long time ago.'

He smiles at me. 'It can't have been that long ago. You have good memories of the place?'

'Wonderful,' I say, and I can feel tears pricking my eyes. Ridiculous. I must be pre-menstrual. I grab a tissue from my bag. 'Sorry,' I say, embarrassed, 'for some reason coming back to Oxford always makes me nostalgic – you know, lost youth, missed opportunities, all that.'

'Lost youth?' he laughs out loud. 'I'm sixty-three.'

'You know what I mean. It's just . . . when you come here, when you're that age – eighteen, nineteen, you know – you're so convinced that you can do *anything*, that you will do something amazing, that you're invincible. It's ridiculous, obviously, but I just miss the way that felt.'

'The way you feel before you learn to compromise,' the vicar says with a wry smile. 'Before real life gets you.'

'Exactly. And I miss the friends I made here.'

'You don't see them any more?'

'Some of them. Not all.'

'Well, you should do something about that. You should never be careless about friendship. You will find, the older you get, that new friendships do not come around quite as often as they once did. You should treasure those you have, protect them fiercely.' He nods sagely to himself. 'Plus, these days you have all those social networking sites, don't you? Spacebook, Myface, all that sort of thing. Makes it much easier to track people down.'

We sit in silence for a moment, and then he gets up to leave.

'My father has cancer,' I blurt out all of a sudden, and he sits back down right away.

'Oh my dear,' he says, placing his hand on my arm, 'I'm so very sorry. What's his prognosis?'

'I think it's okay,' I say. 'I'm not really sure. We don't talk. I haven't seen him for years.'

By the time I get to the restaurant, Annie Gardner is already there. A small, slight woman with a rather severe dark bob, she rises to her feet as I approach and holds out her hand for me to shake.

'I'm sorry about this morning,' she says, her voice so

soft I can barely hear it, 'it was unavoidable.' She looks nervous and uncomfortable; she doesn't quite meet my eye.

'Not at all,' I reply, beaming at her, 'gave me a chance to wander around a bit. I haven't been here for ages, so it was great to have the opportunity to see the sights again.' Already, I'm a little too jovial, a little too eager to make her like me.

We order lunch – a salad for her, fish and chips for me.

'Would you like a glass of wine?' I ask her.

'Oh no, I have to go back to work this afternoon, and I'm useless if I've had a drink at lunchtime.'

'Oh go on,' I say, cajoling, 'just one?' The more relaxed she is, the more likely I am to be able to talk her into this. Reluctantly, she agrees, and I launch into my pitch. I tell her how helpful the programme will be, how it will give her the opportunity to talk to qualified counsellors who can really help her to heal her family.

She shakes her head sadly. 'I just don't know,' she says, 'I don't know if it's the right thing. You don't understand . . .'

'The thing is Annie,' I jump in, interrupting her, 'I *do* understand. I know how you feel.'

She chuckles. She's very pretty when she smiles. 'I doubt that.'

'No, I mean, I haven't been in exactly your situation. But . . . my husband was unfaithful to me.'

She looks up at me, quizzically. I can tell she isn't quite sure whether to believe me or not. This was it, the critical point in my plan: the way to get Annie onside was to show her that she wasn't alone. *I* knew what she was going through. I'd been there myself, and I'd survived. *I* knew how she could come out of it the other side, her marriage and dignity intact.

'A couple of years ago. Okay, it wasn't quite your situation, but he had an affair. With a friend of mine. A close friend. My best friend, in fact.'

'I'm sorry,' she said. She looks stricken. 'I'm so sorry.'

'It was horrible. It was very painful.'

'You left him?' she asks.

'No,' I take a slug of my wine and set the glass back on the table, 'but I thought about it. I thought long and hard about it, in fact. We were separated for a while. But I love him very much, and I know he loves me, and I know that he made a bad mistake, a terrible mistake, and that he regrets it enormously. We had counselling, for several months, and we worked through everything. And, eventually, we were able to live together again, to be close again . . .'

I tail off. She's looking at me intently. 'And you forgave him? You really forgave him?'

'I did.'

'I'm afraid,' Annie says, gazing a little mournfully into her wine glass, 'that every time we argue, every time something goes wrong . . .'

'You'll throw this in his face? His affair, his betrayal?'

'Exactly. I'm afraid we'll never get past it. Or that I'll never get past it, anyway.'

This was the moment. The big sell. 'That's why I think you should do the programme, Annie.'

She shakes her head again

'No, I mean it. That's where the counselling will be invaluable. We won't be asking you sordid, tawdry questions, we'll be getting you – and your husband, and your sister – to really talk through your emotions, to deal with issues of guilt and recrimination. You can tell them how you feel, how they've *made* you feel. And I hope you'll find a way, just as my husband and I did, to move past this and get on with your life.' She's listening carefully, I can tell she's weakening, I have her on the ropes. I go for the jugular. 'I *know* betrayal, Annie. I know how it feels, and I feel sure that working with us on this programme can help you, and help others in similar situations, too.'

She looks down at the tablecloth and back up at me. There's hope in her eyes. In that moment I hate myself.

We finish our coffees, I pay the bill and we leave the restaurant.

'Thanks for meeting me, Annie,' I say, as we walk out into the watery afternoon sunshine. 'I really appreciate you taking the time.'

I want to ask her whether she'll reconsider doing the interview for the programme right there and then, but I feel it's best not to push. Instead, I shake her hand, give her my warmest, most reassuring smile, and head off along St Giles towards the city centre. I've only walked a few yards when she calls after me.

'Nicole,' she says, 'What about your friend?'

'I'm sorry?'

'Your friend? You said that your husband had an affair with your best friend?'

'Yes, that's right. Alex.'

'And did you forgive her, too?'

'Yes, I did. It took a while. For some reason, her betrayal seemed even worse than his. I mean, you expect men to play around, don't you? You don't expect it from your mates.'

'Or your sister.'

'No, quite.'

'But you're okay now, you and her?'

'We're fine,' I lie. 'We're good.'

She smiles at me warmly and, quite unexpectedly, gives me a hug. 'Thanks for talking to me, Nicole. I'll email your assistant with some times for an interview tomorrow.'

'You'll do it then?' I ask her, slightly incredulous.

'I'll do it.' As I watch her walking off down Little Clarendon Street, I feel a peculiar mix of emotions. There is the satisfaction of a task completed, of course, that mission-accomplished sense of jubilation, but there's certainly no pride. Quite the contrary. I feel ashamed of the lies I've told.

* * *

I check my watch. It's just after three: lunch went on longer than expected. What I should do, I know, is to go straight back to the car and drive back to London. Instead, I cross the road and enter the gloom of the Lamb and Flag, scene of many a good night back in my student days. I sit there, nursing a gin and tonic (for old time's sake), counting the lies I've just told a perfectly nice and obviously vulnerable woman.

One. Dominic did not have an affair. He had a one-night stand. Different thing entirely.

Two. We never went to counselling. Dom wanted to, he begged me to after we separated, but I refused. I didn't want to talk about it.

Three. And this follows from two: as a result, I haven't really forgiven him. And I haven't forgiven Alex, either.

I switch on my phone, which was turned off during lunch, and listen to my messages. One from the office, just checking how I'm getting on with Annie Gardner, one from my mum, who sounds like she's having a great time in Costa Rica, although to be honest the line's so bad she could be saying almost anything, and one from Dom.

'Hi love, we've got a table booked for eight. Matt and Liz are going to come round a bit earlier for drinks. Ummm . . . it's just after two now . . . give me a call when you get this. Hope all's well. Love you.'

On my phone, I Google B&Bs in Ledbury. I ring the

Ashton Guest House, 'a family friendly B&B standing on the hill slopes, overlooking the market town of Ledbury', and book a room before I can give myself the chance to back out. Then I ring Dom. Relief floods over me when the phone goes straight to voicemail. Cringing at my own cowardice, I leave a message.

'Dom, hi. You're not going to be very pleased with me. I can't make it back for dinner tonight. I've decided to go and see my dad. I know this is a bit out of the blue, but there is a reason, and I'll explain it all when I get back. Tomorrow. I'm going to stay in Ledbury. I'll ring you later, okay? Hope dinner's fun. Love to Matt and Liz.'

I end the call and turn off my phone straight away. I don't want to face his wrath just yet, and he's going to be furious. Not so much that I've cancelled dinner or that I'm not coming home right away, but that I've been secretive about something. He hates it when I sneak around.

Chapter Six

New Year's Eve, 1996
Cape Town

Resolutions:
1. Get a first in Prelims
2. Lose half a stone
3. Apply for internship with production house
4. Plan Julian's twenty-first. It has to be major!
5. Go rowing. Or hunt-sabbing.

Alex met me at the airport. Typically, effortlessly gorgeous in denim cut-offs and a white vest, Ray-Bans and flip-flops, her skin was already tanned a deep golden brown after ten days in South Africa *en famille*. I, on the other hand, looked like hell: dressed in black jeans and a grey polo neck, sweltering in thirty-degree heat, I was sweaty, smelly and bedraggled after a marathon, three-leg journey from London. Eight and a half hours to Nairobi, a three hour stop-over at Jomo Kenyatta International Airport, a four-hour flight to

Johannesburg, another two hour stop-over, and finally, two hours to Cape Town – for a girl whose previous longest flight was a couple of hours to Rome, it felt like I'd travelled halfway to the moon.

And as Alex drove me through the outskirts and then the heart of Cape Town towards her parents' home in Camps Bay, the moon might just as well have been where I'd landed, so alien did all this seem to me. I don't know what I'd been expecting, but it hadn't been this: the traffic-choked city, the high rises, the tangle of highways; and then, all of a sudden, a glimpse of the ocean, or a view of Table Mountain rising above us. I felt disoriented, almost panicky, my nerves not helped by Alex's erratic, high-speed driving. I clutched the door handle and ghost-braked all the way from the airport through the grimy, poverty-stricken district of Athlone, as we headed towards Camps Bay.

'Lock your door!' Alex yelled at me over the music as we screeched to a halt at a set of traffic lights.

'What?'

'Your door! Lock it!' I did as I was told. 'Car jackers!' Alex yelled cheerfully.

At the next set of lights I almost jumped out of my skin when a child appeared at my window, seemingly from nowhere, in the middle of four lanes of traffic. A little boy, no more than seven or eight, clad in shorts and a filthy T-shirt urging me to enjoy Coca-Cola. He grinned at me and held up a bucket.

'He wants to wash the windscreen,' Alex explained, giving a little shrug of exasperation. 'You get them at every bloody light.'

The child gazed soulfully at her through the window, his head cocked to one side. 'Oh, all right then!' she yelled at him, nodding her head. 'The water's so bloody filthy it makes things worse rather than better,' she said to me, but continued to smile sweetly at the child, who could barely reach the top of the windscreen with his cloth. The traffic lights changed to green, behind us, drivers lent on their horns. Alex rolled down the window and handed the child a ten Rand note. He thanked her, waving cheerfully at us as we pulled away, a tiny, raggedy figure standing in the middle of the road, apparently unconcerned by the cars and lorries trundling past just inches away.

I took a deep breath and leaned back in my seat.

'You okay?' Alex asked me. 'Glad you came?'

'Of course I am!' I replied, although I still couldn't quite believe I'd done it. Coming all this way for a one-week holiday – and spending half my student loan on the airfare – was probably the most daring, irresponsible thing I'd ever done. It was a ridiculous idea, one I'd be paying for all year – literally. But that was the effect Alex had on me. She made me reckless. And once Alex had decided that something was a good idea, she could convince just about anyone. I found her totally irresistible.

I hadn't been able to say no to her since the first

day I met her, during freshers' week. She turned up at my door at two o'clock in the morning, an obscenely short, red silk robe wrapped around her statuesque frame, asking if I had any vodka.

'I'm making cocktails,' she announced.

'I think I have some wine,' I said, pulling my own robe (floor-length terry cloth), a little tighter around me.

'That'll do!' she said happily, 'I'll get you a bottle tomorrow!'

She never did, of course, but she did show up a couple of days later armed with an enormous box of chocolates and a stack of books, suggesting we study together. We did no studying at all, but stayed up half the night comparing life stories. Since then, we'd become virtually inseparable.

'How's our favourite boy?' she asked me, turning down the radio so that we could have a conversation. Julian.

'He's very good. He's fine. He's incredibly jealous. But he sends his love.'

'He should have come.'

'He's flat broke, Alex, he just couldn't afford it.'

'I know. But it would have been so cool for all three of us to be here together.' (This was one of the many, many things I loved about Alex: she loved Julian, too.)

'So what's he up to tonight? Raging in London?' Alex, who had only lived in England for a few years, spoke accented English littered with South Africanisms.

Raging = partying, lekker = good, frot = rotten, that sort of thing. For some inexplicable reason she called traffic lights 'robots'. (Her directions to the Social Studies library had left me utterly mystified – turn right at the robots? What on earth was she talking about?)

'He's going to a party at Heaven, I think, as well as various others. You know what Julian's like. Likes to keep his options open. Much more importantly, what are we up to for New Year's Eve?'

'Well, we're starting off with the obligatory cocktail party at my parents' place.' She glanced over at me, caught my stricken expression and grinned. 'It'll be okay, not massively exciting, just some friends, some family – it's not a big deal. And we don't need to stay long. But we may as well have a few drinks on the olds before we have to start paying for our own.'

'Good plan.'

'After that, we're invited to a party at La Med, which is a cool bar down by the beachfront. Alternatively, there's a beach party at Clifton, which is likely to be *very* hectic, but also a lot of fun. We can always do both. We'll just have to get someone to give us a lift from the bar to Clifton Beach, because there's no way I'm driving tonight. I'm sure we'll be able to talk someone into giving us a ride.'

I had no doubt. Alex, tall, dark and beautiful with huge blue eyes, Brooke Shields' eyebrows and the widest smile you've ever seen, could talk anyone into anything. She was the kind of girl who on first sight I'd expected to be a total bitch (girls that beautiful usually are, aren't they?) but turned out to be utterly charming and unaffected. Which was all the more amazing given her exotic family background.

Alex's father came from Zambia where he'd been part-owner of a copper mine. She and her three older sisters had spent their childhood running wild in the grounds of some enormous rambling pile in the lush suburbs of Ndola, they rode horses, they spent their summers on safari in Kafue and Bangweulu, they went rafting on the Zambezi, they danced the night away in dodgy nightspots to which they were far too young to gain admittance. Alex's father, having made plenty of money, retired in the early nineties and moved the family to Cape Town. The Roses, Alex's family, had it seemed lived their lives in glorious Technicolor. I, on the other hand, felt distinctly black and white.

Arriving at the Roses' home hardly put me at my ease. We entered the property through high gates and wound our way up the driveway to the crest of a hill. Alex parked the car, hopped out, rushed around the car and opened the door for me with a flourish.

'Welcome!' she said, taking my hand and pulling me out of the car. 'Casa Rose!'

Once again, my expectations were shattered: this was not the grand old Cape Dutch house I'd secretly dreamed about, it was something else entirely. Large, sprawling, low, stark and modern, the villa was all glass and chrome, a magnificent contrast to the lush vegetation surrounding it. It clung precariously to the hillside, high up on the slope where Table Mountain rises out of the sea.

We grabbed my luggage (dirty and tatty-looking, I noticed all of a sudden) out of the boot of the car when the front door flung open. A woman dressed in a brightly printed kaftan swept through the door, her arms opened wide in greeting.

'There you are at last!' she called out. She had exactly the same wide smile that Alex did, 'I'm Karen, Alex's mum.' She kissed me on both cheeks. 'You look exhausted, you poor thing. Was your flight awful?' She took the suitcase from my hand and put it down on the ground. 'Here, leave that,' she said. 'Solomon will get it.'

'Oh that's okay—' I started to say, but she cut me off.

'No, leave it,' she insisted, and led me into the house.

If my first impression of the Roses' home amazed me, the second struck me dumb. From the entrance hall you could see all the way through the house, across a balcony to the ocean, shimmering under a low sun. It was jaw-dropping, awe-inspiring. High Wycombe, it was not.

Alex and Karen, standing a little to my left, were both smiling at me.

'Beautiful, isn't it?' Karen asked. 'I never get tired of that view.'

'I've never seen anything like it,' I breathed. 'You feel as though you could jump off the balcony and dive right in, right into the Indian Ocean!'

'Atlantic, actually,' a voice boomed out from somewhere deeper into the house.

'Hey, Dad!' Alex called out, and her father emerged from behind the bar to the left of the living room, a glass in hand. Scotch on the rocks, it looked like. Easily six foot three, Alex's father had white hair, a deep mahogany tan and thick, beetling eyebrows. He looked like a tall, scary Giorgio Armani. He held out an enormous hand for me to shake, his expression stern.

'If you want the Indian Ocean, you'll need to go about fifty kilometres east,' he told me. 'Our views are better, our restaurants are better and our beaches are better, but the water is a hell of a lot warmer over there, I can tell you.' He smiled. 'I'm Robert,' he said, his enormous hand engulfing mine and squeezing like a vice. 'We're very pleased to have you here with us, Nicole.' He took my arm and steered me towards a drinks cabinet in the corner of the room.

'What's your pleasure?' he asked. 'Gin and tonic? I understand you've been reading Marx? I used to be a communist. A long, long time ago. Only for about five minutes, though. Then I started making money and I realised it was all bullshit.' Realised, pronounced ree-lahzed. His accent was much heavier than Alex's. 'Gin and tonic, ja?'

Two gin and tonics and one frankly terrifying

discussion of the Communist Manifesto later, Alex escorted me down to the guest room, a palatial suite on the lower ground floor with French windows opening out onto the pool area. My grubby suitcase had been placed, presumably by the as-yet unseen Solomon, beside the bed.

'Is this all right?' Alex asked with a grin. Seeing the look on my face, she said, 'Don't look so worried,' and gave me a hug. 'Have a shower, get dressed and then you come up and meet my sisters. They're at the beach right now, but they'll be back any minute.'

The prospect of meeting the Rose girls, the *infamous* Rose girls, sent the butterflies in my stomach into overdrive. I had heard the stories, I'd seen the photographs: to say that these women were going to be intimidating was an understatement. First, there was Kate. The eldest at twenty-nine, Kate ran her own graphic design company and drove a Mercedes. Jo, twenty-five, was doing a masters in psychology. Lisa, twenty-two, was just back from Milan where she'd just got her first spread in *Vogue Italia*.

So, I muttered to myself, flinging open my suitcase and inspecting its contents with disdain, what does one wear to impress a supermodel? The ideal outfit, given the climate and the company, would be some sort of strappy sundress with high heels and just a smattering of jewellery. I, however, was not the sundress sort, strappy or otherwise. Never had been, and most likely never would be. Despairingly I rifled through my poorly packed and by now incredibly crumpled clothes. Oh god oh god oh god. I had imagined, before I'd arrived here, that New Year's Eve in South Africa would be a casual, jeans and T-shirt type of affair. Having seen the house, it was clear that jeans and a T-shirt were not going to cut it. With a mounting sense of panic, I scrabbled through the untidy pile of clothes, looking for something suitable.

I ended up settling on an elegant (I hoped) but rather dull combination of white trousers, dark green chiffon top and wedge heels. Not particularly practical, but I could always take off the shoes when we went to the beach. I showered, washed my hair and took a despondent look at myself in the mirror (I looked exactly like what I was: an English girl who hadn't slept for twenty-four hours). I slapped on as much make-up as my pale complexion could take, summoned up my courage, and tried not to fall over as I walked up the stairs.

At that moment, I felt a sudden pang of longing for Julian. With Jules at my side, I always felt invincible. He was almost always the best-looking man in any room he entered, so he was the perfect person to have on your arm. Perhaps I should just pop back down-stairs and give him a call? After all, I didn't want to miss him. I had to speak to him on New Year's Eve. It was tradition.

I turned and was just about to skulk back below stairs when I was accosted by yet another incredibly tall person: a woman with cropped dark hair, wearing the perfect strappy sundress for the occasion.

'And where do you think you're going?' she asked. 'You saw us all and decided to make a run for it, did you?' She laughed. 'Seriously, it's not going to be that terrible. Just get a couple of beers down you and you'll be fine. I'm Kate, by the way. You must be Nicole.'

'I must be,' I murmured, following the Amazonian girl out onto the terrace, where the beautiful people were gathering.

Alex was standing on the far side of the terrace, drinking champagne with two other girls, both of whom were slender and long-limbed and appeared to have wandered out of the pages of a fashion magazine. One of them, of course, had.

'This is Lisa,' Alex said, indicating the taller of the two, 'and Jo.'

They beamed at me and said hello, but they were sizing me up, too. I could feel their eyes run ever so quickly and almost, *almost* imperceptibly, from my head to my toes and back again. I felt like a midget. A rather pale, slightly overweight midget.

'You have the most beautiful hair I've ever seen,' Lisa said to me, immediately making me feel better. 'Is that colour real or out of a bottle?'

A man appeared at my elbow, a black man. He was serving drinks. 'This is Solomon,' Alex said.

'Hello!' I said, a little too brightly, holding out my hand for him to shake, but since he was carrying a tray of drinks he clearly couldn't shake my hand, so he just grinned toothsomely and nodded.

'Pleasure to meet you, madam,' he said. 'Would you like champagne or perhaps a beer?'

I took a glass of champagne and thanked him and thought about the child on the road, and looked around and noticed that the only black people at this party were the ones carrying trays, and I felt uncomfortable. Alex caught the look on my face and smiled.

'*Plus ça change,*' she said in a terrible French accent. 'It'll be better later, on the beach. It won't be so . . . monochromatic. Promise.'

We hung around for a couple of hours making polite conversation with Alex's parents and their guests, and were just inching towards the front, about to ditch the cocktail party and head for the real action, when we spotted Robert heading purposefully in our direction.

'Oh crap, he's going to try and make us stay . . .' Alex muttered, but in fact he wasn't.

'There's a telephone call for you, Nicole,' he boomed at me, brandishing a cordless phone in my direction. 'An English bloke. Charles, I think he said his name was.'

Alex grinned. 'Jules.'

I grabbed the phone with unseemly haste from Robert's hand.

'Julian!' I squealed excitedly, ignoring the sideways glances of the assembled guests. 'Just . . . say . . . new year . . .' he said. I could barely hear him over the crackle on the line.

'What?'

'. . . wanted . . . say . . . Happy New Year!'

I scuttled inside in search of better reception.

'How are you?' I shouted.

'I'm still pissed off with you for leaving me here, all alone in London. What's it like there?'

'Hot,' I said. 'Scary. Exotic. Did I say hot?'

'Yeah, you did, and you can shut the fuck up about it too, because it's minus two and raining here.'

'I wish you were here, Julian.'

'God, me too, but I've barely got enough cash to keep me in beer and poppers.'

'Behave yourself tonight.'

'Don't I always? Have an amazing time, take lots of pictures and give Alex a big kiss for me. I'll be thinking of you at midnight.'

'You too.'

'Happy anniversary, Nic.'

'Oh shit, Jules, we haven't done resolutions . . .'

'Quickly, I'll go first—'

But then the phone cut out, there was some beeping and some crackling and I just stood there saying, 'Hello? Hello?', and for just a second or two, I felt bereft, but then I looked up and saw Alex out on the terrace, grinning at me, gesturing for me to join her, and behind her the sun was just starting to dip into the ocean, lighting it on fire, and my heart leapt. I realised that for the first time ever I was doing something exciting and extraordinary, and I had to hang onto every moment, I had to remember what everything looked like and sounded like, I needed to remember the smells and the textures and tastes, because this – new, exotic, terrifying – this is what I wanted my life to be like.

A few minutes later I found myself squashed into the back seat of Kate's Mercedes, with Lisa on one side and Jo on the other, long legs folded up so that their knees almost reached their chins. Alex sat in front with Kate, because she had to have control of the stereo.

'Seriously,' she told me, 'if it were up to Lisa, we'd be listening to the Spice Girls. She has the worst taste.'

I wasn't overly concerned about the music. I found myself gripping my seatbelt in terror as the car careened along a windy coastal road cut into the side of the mountain. Out of the window to my left I could see sheer cliffs dropping away to the sea. My stomach lurched.

'Just don't look down,' Jo said with a grin.

'Don't worry,' Lisa reassured me. 'Kate's never had an accident in this car. She wrote off the last one, but she's never crashed the Merc.'

'Don't tell her that!' Kate protested from the front seat. 'Honestly, I'm a great driver. The other accidents were always the other guy's fault.'

'Let's talk about something else, shall we?' Alex suggested.

'Of course. What are you guys going to get up to for the next few days?' Jo asked.

'We haven't really made any firm plans . . .' I said.

'Typical Alex,' Lisa said. 'So disorganised.'

'Spontaneous,' Alex corrected her.

'Well, you *have* to climb the mountain,' Jo said. 'It's an amazing hike.'

'I'm not really much of a climber . . .'

'There's an easy route,' Lisa reassured me. 'Only takes a couple of hours. I've done it with my grand-parents. Anyone can do it.'

'Oh, and you *must* go and see the penguins at Boulders Beach . . .'

'And you should go to Robben Island . . .'

'Go shopping in Green Market Square . . .'

'Take a drive out to Stellenbosch to do some wine tasting . . .'

'Actually,' Alex interjected, 'We'd quite like to spend some time just lying on the beach doing bugger all.'

'Don't let her drag you into her pit of apathy Nicole,' Kate warned me. 'If it's left to Alex, you'll go back to England in a week's time having seen nothing but the abs on the lifeguards on Clifton Beach.'

Kate dropped us off in the packed car park at Clifton at around ten. As far as the eye could see, the beach was lit by bonfires, around which hundreds of (mostly

scantily clad) young things were dancing. Others
thronged at one of the makeshift bars that had been set
up at various intervals, emerging from heaving crowds
with cans of beer or plastic glasses. From an enormous
sound stage a little way down the beach, boomed the
unmistakeable hook to Faithless's 'Insomnia'.

Alex grabbed my arm and we made our way down
some rickety wooden steps to the beach. With each
barefoot, bikini-clad girl we passed, I regretted my
outfit choice more keenly.

'Right,' Alex said, surveying the scene as we got to
the bottom of the stairs, 'let's head for the sound stage.
Anton's DJing tonight and there's bound to be a good
crowd there.'

'Who's Anton?' I asked her, stumbling along at her
side, shouting to make myself heard over the noise of
the crowd and the music.

'Met him on Christmas Eve,' she yelled back. 'Very
nice guy,' she added with a wink.

Anton, it turned out, was not the only guy Alex
knew at the party. She also knew Steve and Michael,
Danny and Graham, Wayne and Tod . . . a seemingly
endless parade of good-looking young men. They
greeted her enthusiastically, shook my hand politely
and then ignored me. I clung to Alex's side, feeling
awkward and intimidated. Eventually, I volunteered
to go and get us drinks. Copious alcohol consumption,
I reasoned, might be the only way to get through this
party alive.

Abandoning my wedge heels, I trekked back across the dunes towards a bar. Walking barefoot was not a great deal easier, since I was now stumbling over the hems of my trousers. The crowd at the bar was ten deep. For a moment I considered giving up before I started. After all, Alex would almost certainly be able to suggest that one of the boys fetch drinks for us. Not wanting to seem defeatist, though, I pushed myself into the fray.

What seemed like hours, but was probably more like fifteen minutes, later, I emerged victorious with four gin and tonics balanced on a plastic tray. Two for Alex, two for me. There was no way I was going to go back to the bar again any time soon. Gripping the tray as though my life depended on it, I started to make my way back towards the sound stage. I had got about three yards when I managed to put my left foot on my right hem, stumbled, righted myself, and was breathing a sigh of heartfelt relief that I hadn't gone arse over tit when a teenage boy, chasing after a Frisbee, came flying out of nowhere and charged straight into me. The drinks, and I, went flying. The teenage boy didn't even break stride. A roar of laughter went up from the nearest gaggle of people, although one kind soul grabbed my arm and helped me to my feet. I dusted myself down and grinned ruefully at the laughing crowd. I may have been hoping fervently for the ground to swallow me up, but I wasn't going to show it. I picked up my tray and went back to the bar.

I was just steeling myself for another assault on the bar crowd when someone tapped me on the shoulder and said, 'That was unlucky.' I turned around and found myself looking into the sleepy green eyes of a lithe, dark-skinned man with a mop of unruly black hair. He was wearing baggy, boarding shorts and a dirty white T-shirt. A cigarette hung from his bottom lip. I inhaled sharply, my mouth opened, but I was actually speechless.

'Of all the beach parties in all the world . . .' he said with a lazy smile.

'Aidan?' I said, eventually finding my voice. 'Aidan? Is that really you? What are you doing here? I thought you were in India. Or Pakistan. Somewhere in Asia.'

'I was, for a while. Now I'm here.' He spread out his arms and gave me a hug. I was still struggling to get to grips with the fact that I had just bumped into someone I know roughly six thousand miles from home, but Aidan didn't seem in the slightest bit fazed by the coincidence.

'Shall we have another go at getting you a drink?' he asked.

Inwardly I cringed. You don't see someone for years and the first time you do, you're falling over and throwing drinks everywhere. Typical. That would never happen to Alex. It would never happen to Julian. Only to me.

'What can I get you?' Aidan asked me.

'Gin and tonic,' I replied, 'but I'm not just buying for me . . .'

'Oi, Joe!' Aidan yelled, incredibly loudly, over the heads of the crowd.

One of the barmen looked over at us. 'Yes, chief!' he yelled back.

'Gin and tonic and a Castle!'

'Yes, chief!'

'Make it two Castles!'

'Yes, chief!'

He turned to me and grinned. 'You *are* old enough to drink, aren't you?'

A second or two later, I had a gin and tonic in my hand.

'Easy when you know how,' I said to him.

'Yeah, Joe tends bar at the hotel I'm staying at. He's moonlighting tonight. Twenty-three with three kids and a fourth on the way. Needs the money. Come on, let's find somewhere to sit.' He placed his hand between my shoulder blades, guiding me towards a quieter section of beach.

'Alex – the friend I'm with – will be waiting,' I said, not quite resisting.

'But I've bought you a drink now! You have to talk to me. You're obliged to talk to me. For five minutes at least. It's the law.'

We found ourselves a spot next to one of the less crowded bonfires and sat down.

'So,' he said, looking me up and down, 'Nicole Blake. Look at you, all grown up.'

He was running his eyes all over me. I could feel the colour rising to my cheeks. He grinned, that annoying, I-know-what-you're-thinking kind of grin, and asked, 'Didn't you know you were coming to a beach party?'

'I was at a cocktail party before,' I said, a little stiffly, 'and I didn't have time to change.'

'Oh, a *cocktail* party,' he said, putting on a posh English accent. 'Rather.' He lit himself a cigarette and offered me one. I declined.

'Good girl,' he said, patting my arm.

Patronising git. What was it about this man? Why was I simultaneously seized by the impulse to slap him across the face and rip his clothes off? Well, it was clear why I wanted to slap him, but the attraction was less obvious. Yes, fine, he was good-looking, yes, okay, he looked exactly like Julian, but there was something else, something underneath all that which made me want to get to know him. He had an air of dissolution, a raggedness around the edges that was somehow irresistible to me. I had an overwhelming urge to kiss him.

'I should go,' I said, swigging down as much of my gin and tonic as I could in one gulp, because if I stayed there any longer I wasn't going to be able to resist that urge. 'Alex will be waiting.'

'Oh, come on!' he protested. 'I haven't seen you in . . . how long's it been? Five years?'

'It was much more recent than that,' I said, a little disappointed that he couldn't remember the exact moment he'd seen me last, because I could. 'It was Julian's eighteenth.'

'Oh, that's right,' he said, starting to laugh. 'You and Jules took a couple of Es and you just about chewed a hole through your lip. Remember?'

I looked away, embarrassed. 'I remember.'

'And you told me I was quite good-looking for an old guy.'

'I did not,' I protested, feeling the blush rise to my roots.

'Yes you did,' he replied, laughing at the memory. 'You were off your face, though.'

Why was it that he made me feel like an idiot whenever I saw him? And why was it that he seemed to enjoy it so much? And why in god's name did I let it get to me?

'So tell me about this Alex, then,' Aidan said, thankfully changing the subject. 'Who's he? Captain of the rowing crew?' Ever so casually, he draped an arm around my shoulders, leaning in to whisper, 'I hope he's not the jealous type.' My stomach flipped, a shiver ran through me. He pulled me closer.

'You're not cold are you? I've got a jacket somewhere . . .' he looked around. '. . . not sure where I left it though . . .'

'It's okay,' I said, 'I'm not cold.'

'Sure?' He turned to look at me, his face was just inches from mine, he reached across and pushed my hair away from my face. My heart was pounding.

'You look good, you know?' he said. 'You look really good . . .' He leaned in closer, slipping his arm all the way around my waist – this was happening, this was really happening . . .

'Aidan Symonds!' And then it wasn't happening. A loud, harsh voice rang out, tearing through my perfect moment.

'Hey, hello!' Aidan called out, letting go of me and getting to his feet. He was immediately enveloped in the arms of an incredibly tanned blond girl with beads in her hair and a bright orange kikoi tied around her slender waist. She knew how to dress for a beach party. She was whispering something in Aidan's ear, he was laughing. I turned away and got to my feet.

'I really ought to go, Aidan,' I called out to him. 'It was nice seeing you.'

'Yeah, yeah, we should meet up again, you can introduce me to Alex,' he replied, half-heartedly attempting to disentangle himself from the clutches of the blonde. I just smiled, and waved, and walked away, furious with myself for feeling so disappointed.

Back in the shadow of the sound stage, I found Alex dancing up a storm.

'Thank god!' she yelled when she saw me, flinging her arms around me. 'I thought I'd lost you. It's almost midnight! Where the hell are our drinks?'

'Long story!' I yelled back as she dragged me onto the decking which served as dance floor.

'Never mind! I'll have one of the guys get us some champagne!'

By midnight, I'd forgotten all about my sartorial failure, the embarrassing fall on the beach, even Aidan and his annoying blonde. Intoxicated with champagne, dance-induced adrenalin and the simple joy of being with my second-best friend in the whole world, the only thing that could have improved my night would have been if Julian had been there too. At the stroke of midnight itself, Alex and I were jumping up and down, hugging each other tightly, a huddle of boys behind her waiting patiently for their New Year's kiss. As I let her go, I found myself spun around and, before I could protest, Aidan had planted a kiss on my lips.

For a moment or two, everything slowed down. That's how it felt, as though the rest of the world went into slow motion, the music was turned down, the noise of the crowd abated and the colours faded to black and white. There was nothing except for me and him, standing together on the beach, his arms around my waist, his lips on my mouth. And then he pulled away and the world came back, bright and loud.

'Happy New Year, Nicole Blake,' Aidan said.

'Happy New Year,' I replied.

He brandished an unopened bottle of champagne at me. 'Come on,' he said, 'let's go and drink this somewhere quiet.'

'What about your friend?'

He shrugged and laughed. 'I don't see her anywhere around, do you? What about *your* friend?'

I looked over my shoulder at Alex who was standing there, grinning at us.

Aidan laughed again. 'So *that's* Alex, is it? Prettier than I'd expected. Less butch.'

Alex waved me away. 'I'll be fine!' she called out. 'Go and have fun. I'll be hanging out around the DJ booth, like a groupie.'

We walked along the beach, heading away from the party, into the darkness. I felt reckless, as through I were teetering on the brink of something, possibly something dangerous, I wasn't quite sure what. I felt dizzy, I felt high. It felt amazing. Here I was, on New Year's Eve, on a beach in South Africa, drinking champagne with a dangerously handsome older man! This was an adventure! This was what I wanted. Also, if he tried anything untoward I could always brain him with the champagne bottle.

We walked in silence for a while, eventually turning to climb halfway up a sand dune, where we sat down and he opened the champagne. We took turns to drink from the bottle. We had walked far enough from the party so that we could no longer hear the music or the shouts of the crowd. There was no one else on the beach. I felt as though we could be the last two people on earth.

The moon, a sliver away from a perfect circle, hung low in an endless sky filled with more stars than I'd ever seen in my entire life.

'Don't get skies like that back home, do you?' Aidan asked me.

'You certainly don't.'

'How are things at home, by the way? Your mum all right?'

'She's fine. She's good. She's getting married next year.'

'Nice bloke?'

'He's lovely.' I was a bit confused. What were we doing here? Why were we talking about nothing in particular? Surely he didn't bring me all the way down the beach with a bottle of champagne so that he could ask me about my mother? I was suddenly aware that he hadn't actually told me what he was doing here in Cape Town. Nor, come to think of it, had he asked me what I was doing here. The weirdness of the whole situation just didn't seem to bother him at all. It bothered me, though.

'What is it that you're doing here, Aidan?' I asked him. 'I can't believe that Julian didn't even tell me that you were in South Africa . . .'

'He probably doesn't trust me with you,' Aidan replied with a grin. 'His precious Nicole.' His arm was around my shoulders again. I closed my eyes and leaned into him inhaling his scent. Citrus and cigarettes. Intoxicating, although not quite intoxicating enough to make me forget that he still hadn't answered my question.

'You still haven't answered my question,' I said.

'I'm working,' he told me. 'I'm with the BBC now.'
'Reporting?'
'I'm a cameraman. We're doing a documentary on the Truth and Reconciliation Commission. You heard of that?'
'I do read the papers,' I said, stiffening up again, pulling away from him.
He smiled at me. 'You're so spiky,' he said. 'I love how spiky you are. You're the easiest person in the world to wind up.'
'And how would you know that?' I asked. 'You barely know me.'
'Ah, but I've heard the stories,' he said. 'Plus, I remember the first time I ever saw you. I came to your house to pick up Jules, after he was in that fight, you remember?'
'I remember.'
'And you got all pissed off and hot under the collar because I asked you if it was past your bedtime.' He started laughing again.
I ignored him. 'So, that sounds interesting. The Truth Commission thing I mean.'
He chuckled. '*The Truth Will Out!* That's what they're calling it. Fucking ridiculous.'
'What do you mean? You don't think it's a good thing? I think it's incredible, so optimistic, you know? To try, in a really constructive way, to deal with the problems of the past.'
He laughed more loudly this time. 'You think it's a

114

good thing to let murderers go free? To say sorry to the victims' families and simply walk away?'

'That's not the point, though . . .'

'I know it isn't. I know. I've just been to enough places with dark pasts to know that this country's problems aren't going to go away because someone's convened a *commission*.'

'That's a bit cynical,' I said, and he smiled at me, that knowing smile. 'I'm not naïve,' I started to say, but he shut me up with a kiss.

Later, I asked him what he meant when he said he'd been to enough places with dark pasts.

'You name it.'

'Well? Where?'

'I've travelled all over the place. Spent a long time trying to get into print journalism, but there were a couple of problems. One, I didn't have a university degree and two, I can't write for shit. Anyway, eventually I decided to get behind the camera instead. I did some work in South-East Asia – mostly just filming stupid hippies on holiday. That was fucking dull, and I wanted to do something real, so when I read the first reports about the civil war in Liberia, I decided to go there.'

'Jesus.'

'Yeah, charming place.' He stubbed out his cigarette and immediately lit another. 'You wouldn't believe what people were doing to each other.' He was looking out over the ocean, his eyes fixed on some point in the distance. I touched his arm, and he shook his head, as though shaking off some unbidden memory. 'I got some great footage there. Liberia. I went to a few places where there weren't many other hacks hanging around, so some of my stuff got picked up by the BBC, CNN, people like that, and since then I've not been short of work. I was in Rwanda in 1994, Croatia in 1995, Chechnya this year. Last year, I suppose it is now . . .'

I was in awe. 'My god, that must be so amazing. So incredible to see all this stuff up close, to be right there, telling the story . . .'

He laughed. 'It is, if your idea of excitement is getting a couple of teeth smashed out with a rifle butt wielded by a crazed Interahamwe militiaman.' He bared his teeth at me and tapped the front two. 'Replacements. Or if you like the idea of crawling out of a burning vehicle because some Serb has sprayed your car with bullets and shot off your driver's head. It's all very exciting.' He shrugged. 'It's not for everyone. But I can't really imagine myself doing anything else. I don't think there's anything else I'd be any good at.' And when he talked about it, I thought that it was exactly the sort of thing I wanted to be good at, too.

For a while, we sat there, watching as a hint of grey appeared at the horizon, a precursor of dawn. The champagne was finished.

Aidan turned to me at last and said, 'I think you

116

should come home with me. To my hotel.' My heart was thudding so loudly in my chest I felt sure he could hear it. 'Will you come?'

I wanted to, I wanted to be with him, but I couldn't. I couldn't just run off and leave Alex. I couldn't just go to a hotel room with some guy I hardly knew. Could I?

'Aidan, I can't . . . Alex is waiting for me . . .'

'That's okay,' he said, ruffling my hair. 'I guess I never thought of you as the type to put out on a first date anyway.' He got to his feet and pulled me to mine.

'Oh, but you did think about it?' I asked him with a smile.

'Of course I did.' He put his arm around my shoulders and we walked down the dune together. 'After that party, Julian's eighteenth, when I drove you home and dropped you off . . . the night you told me I was good-looking for an old guy. God, I thought you were so incredibly cute.'

'Cute?'

'Well, cute, sexy, beautiful in this completely unassuming way . . .'

'Yeah, yeah, keep going . . .'

'Well. I told Jules all this, and he flipped out.'

'He never told me this.'

'Oh yeah, he had a right go at me: you stay the fuck away from her, don't you go anywhere near her . . . blah blah.' I laughed at his fairly accurate Jules imitation. 'I didn't know you were only sixteen. I thought you were Julian's age.'

'Still too young for you.'

'What can I say, I'm a dirty old man.'

'How old are you, actually?' I asked him, as we walked hand in hand towards the ocean.

'Thirty-five,' he replied.

'You are not!' I said, dropping his hand as though it were scalding.

'Of course I'm not,' he said, laughing and grabbing me round the waist. 'Jesus, do I look thirty-five? I'm twenty-eight.'

'That's still pretty ancient.'

'I'll show you ancient,' he said, raising me up into the air and over his shoulder in a fireman's lift. Ignoring my helpless pleas and flailing limbs, he carried me to the water and dropped me into it, diving in after me, wrapping his arms around me, covering my face and neck in salty kisses.

We found Alex sitting at one of the bonfires with a large group of people, a haze of smoke surrounding them and – from the smell of it – not just from the bonfire. Alex erupted in fits of giggles when she saw us.

'Hey there, lovebirds,' she said. 'Or should I say drowned rats?' Embarrassed, I dropped Aidan's hand. He reached for it again. My heartbeat sped up a few dozen beats per minute. 'What on earth have you been up to?'

We lay back on the beach as the sun rose, getting gently stoned as we waited for our clothes to dry off. Someone had come prepared, they'd rustled up orange juice and were cooking boerewors, a kind of spicy sausage, for breakfast.

When the sun was fully up, Aidan propped himself up on one elbow, stretched and said, 'I guess I ought to get going.'

'Oh, don't go,' Alex protested. 'Come back to the house. We'll go for a swim, have a braai, something like that. Just chill out.'

'That's kind, Alex, but I really can't. I've been on the lash since Christmas and I have to work tomorrow. At some point I really ought to get some sleep.' He leaned forward and kissed me on the neck. 'You got a number I can ring you on while you're here?'

I gave him Alex's parents' number and walked with him up to the car park to say goodbye. We had one last, intoxicating kiss before I watched him climb, slightly unsteadily, onto a motorbike and roar off into the distance. Without a helmet.

When he was gone, I returned to the bonfire on the beach, aware that I was grinning like the Cheshire Cat and unable to stop myself.

'Nice going, Nic,' she said, as I approached. 'He is delicious. Lekker like a cracker. Although kind of old, no?'

'Twenty-eight!' I said.

'No way!'

'But so, so sexy.'

'Definitely' she agreed. 'He looks just like Julian.'

'I think,' I said, sitting down next to her and draping my arm around her shoulders, 'that this has been the best New Year ever.'

'Not better than the Julian one?'

'Well, that was great and awful. This one was just great. God, this is such an amazing place.'

'Isn't it?'

'I think we should come back here. When we've finished our degrees. We could travel, teach, do something important, you know?'

'Gets under your skin, doesn't it?' Alex asked me with a smile.

'What does?'

'Africa.'

We sat there until the rising sun became too hot, and it was time to head back. Alex managed somehow to find someone sober enough to drive us home, where we snuck quietly into the house and went to bed. I didn't fall asleep straight away, though. I just lay there, hugging myself, going over every detail of the previous night, thinking of Aidan's laugh and his green eyes.

Chapter Seven

27 December 2011

I'm on the A40 heading west, listening to the radio and wondering why the fuck I'm doing this. I am seriously annoying my husband, risking all manner of nasty confrontations just two days before our holiday, purely so that I can go and visit a man who has pretty much never done anything but let me down.

Because he's my dad. That's why.

The last time I spoke to him was when he rang to wish me a happy thirtieth birthday. This was two years ago, the day I turned thirty-one. The last time I actually saw him was the night before my wedding. That was more than three years ago. He turned up for dinner the night before, had a drunken temper tantrum and left that night, so he never actually made it to the event itself.

Given our history, a surprise visit probably isn't the greatest idea, but somehow I just can't face picking up the phone and talking to him. Plus, I've turned off my phone because I don't want to hear Dom's irate messages, or read his angry texts. By the time I get to Ledbury, I realise that I'm not even sure I'll be able to find his house, it's been so long since I visited. And I'm right, I don't remember the way, so I drive round and round for forty-five minutes, still not wanting to phone, until finally I spot The Castle, the horrible pub that he drinks in, which I know is just round the corner from his place.

It's just after six when I walk up the concrete pathway to his front door. My hands are shaking. My mouth feels like something died in it – I've smoked six cigarettes on the way here and I don't have any mints. I ring the doorbell. No one comes and relief washes over me. This is the best possible outcome! I've tried to see him and I've failed – but it's not my fault. I can go to New York free of guilt. I turn and start off down the path, a spring in my step this time, but just as I'm pushing open the garden gate I hear the door open behind me and my heart sinks into my boots.

'Nicole?'

I turn around and there he is, gaunt, grey and slightly stooped, a hundred years older than I remembered him.

'You are here,' I say. 'I thought no one was in.'

'You should have phoned,' he says, and turns to go back into the house, calling out to me to follow as he goes. No kiss then, no hug, no tearful reunion. For a moment or two I hesitate at the gate, tempted by the almost irresistible idea of just getting back into my car and driving as fast as my Honda Civic will take me all the way back to London, to have dinner with my husband and friends.

'I'm not bloody made of money you know,' I can hear him shouting. 'It's freezing out and I can't have the heating turned up high all day and night. Will you hurry up and close that door?'

As I step over the hearth onto the ugly orange carpet I can hear him muttering to himself. 'Christ's sake. With me poorly and everything she leaves the bloody door open for half an hour.'

He's standing in front of the electric fire in the living room, rubbing his hands together like a miser over his hoard, his dirty grey tracksuit bottoms hanging from his bony hips.

'You've lost weight, Dad,' I say.

'Yeah, well, cancer will do that to you.' He turns and looks at me. 'Didn't know whether you'd come. You could have replied to my email. I don't have anything in for dinner.'

'We can get a takeaway,' I say.

'Money to burn, have you?'

'Or I could take you out somewhere.'

Dad sits down in the chair nearest the fireplace. 'There's nowhere decent round here these days,' he says.

I take off my coat and sit down on the brown velour-covered sofa. The room is unspeakably hideous, it looks as though it were decorated in 1978 by someone with absolutely no taste. Everything is brown or a dirty shade of orange. There are no books, no pictures on the walls, just an enormous flat-screen TV in one corner.

'How are you feeling, Dad?'

'Pretty bloody awful.'

'I'm so sorry. When did you . . . when was it diagnosed?'

'About a month ago. But I've been feeling rotten for a while.'

'You should have told me.'

'What? That I've been feeling unwell? What would you have done about it?' He picks distractedly at some unseen lint on his tracksuit trousers.

'Shall I make us some tea?' I ask him, already desperate to put some distance between us, even if it's just a matter of a few feet.

'All right then.'

Standing in the kitchen, waiting for the kettle to boil, I feel like I want to cry, out of frustration more than anything else. Why is he like this? Why can't he just make an effort? There's a feeling like nausea rising up inside me, a feeling I remember from a long time ago, from childhood. Fear and disappointment. Pity, too. God, he must be lonely.

I take the tea back into the living room. He's turned on the TV and he's watching Sky Sports News, the sound up high. He accepts the tea wordlessly, takes a few sips, ignores me completely.

'The operation's on the second then, is it? Is that in Malvern?'

Nothing.

'Dad? Could we turn the TV down a bit?'

He turns it off. 'I just wanted to see the scores,' he says, exasperated.

'I didn't say off, I said down.'

'Done now.' His mouth is set in a grim line. I want to slap him.

'I was asking about your operation. Are you going to the hospital in Malvern?'

'Gloucester.'

'Do you need someone to take you there? How long will you be in for?'

'Your uncle Chris is driving me. Only supposed to be in a couple of days, but you don't know with the NHS, do you? I'll probably get MRSA.'

Always look on the bright side.

We sit in silence, sipping our tea. He turns the TV back on, muted this time, and swears softly when he sees the football results.

'Did you have money on it?' I ask.

'Just a tenner.' He stares down at his hands, clenches and unclenches his fists. It's a gesture I remember from childhood, and I'm hit by another wave of nausea.

'How about that takeaway then? Do you have any menus?'

He jerks his head backwards. 'Second drawer down in the kitchen.'

I suggest pizza, but he wants Chinese, so for the second night in a row it's crispy aromatic duck and black bean stir-fry, only this time the duck is oversalted and the black beans are dry. Dad doesn't seem to notice, he wolfs his food down.

'I'm glad to see you've got an appetite, despite not feeling well,' I say.

'Well, I don't get to eat stuff like this very often. Too expensive. This is a treat,' he says, and he almost smiles.

After dinner, we drink our Tsingtao beers (two free with any order over fifteen quid), and I finally pluck up the courage to ask him what I'm doing here.

'Dad, in your email, you said that there were some things you wanted to talk about . . .'

He mutters something unintelligible and looks away. 'Come on,' I say, ignoring his embarrassment, 'what was it? I'm here now.'

'I was feeling a bit low when I sent that,' he says. 'It wasn't really necessary for you to come.'

'Oh. Well. I'm glad I did, anyway. It's good to see you.' Liar, liar, pants on fire.

Dad drains the last of his beer and puts the bottle down on the table. 'So. How's Dominic?'

'He's well. Working hard as usual.'

'Good. Good to hear it. Still no kids then?'

I laugh nervously. 'No, not yet.'

'Best get on with that, hadn't you?'

'Plenty of time,' I say.

'Hah! Is that right? You shouldn't waste time, you know. It's always later than you think.'

'Would you like some more tea, Dad?' I ask, eager to end this conversation, which has suddenly veered from mundane to morbid.

'How's your mother doing?' he asks, ignoring my question.

'She's fine,' I say, getting to my feet and clearing away debris from the takeaway.

'Spend Christmas with you, did she?'

'No, not this year.'

'Where is she then?'

'She's on holiday. In Costa Rica.'

An ugly sneer crosses his face. 'All right for some, I suppose. She still with that tosser, then? What was his name?'

He knows very well what Charles's name is, he knows very well that they're still together. I'm not getting drawn into a conversation about it: I know what he wants to do, he wants to rail at me about how badly she treated him, he wants to insinuate that Charles and Mum were sleeping together before the split, he wants to go over and over what happened, rewriting history as he tries to absolve himself of blame. We've been here before, and I'm suddenly furious with myself for coming: why did I think this time was going to be any different?

I clench my fists now, digging my nails into the palms of my hands. I can't shout at him, I can't storm out. His illness holds me hostage. I take a deep breath, sit back down opposite him and give him the brightest smile I can muster. 'Is there anything I can get you, Dad? Anything I can do for you?'

He shakes his head, passes his hand over his eyes. He looks exhausted. I bite hard on my lower lip in an attempt to stop the tears coming. He looks up at me, surprised. 'What's wrong?' he asks. 'Is something wrong? You're not going to cry, are you?' He hauls himself to his feet, shuffles across the space between us and sits down next to me. He takes my hand in his. 'I'm not dead yet, love,' he says, and I burst into tears.

I promise to visit again in the morning, before I drive back to London. On the way to the B&B I pick up a bottle of wine and twenty Marlboro Lights from a corner shop. The rooms at the B&B will be non-smoking, of course, but I can always hang out the window. Like a thirteen-year-old.

The B&B is nicer than I'd expected: a pretty Victorian house with large rooms and a distinct lack of chintz. I lie down on the queen-sized bed with a glass of red, luxuriating in solitude, wishing I could stay here for days. No one, I realise, knows where I am. I have disappeared. I am off the grid. It's delicious, the best kind of escape, completely irresponsible and utterly selfish.

I can't enjoy it for long, though, because my mobile phone, still switched off, sits on the bedside table, a silent, accusing presence. I have to turn it on some time. And so I do, and then wish I hadn't.

Message received today at 16.24.

'Nic, I can't believe this. What are you doing? I've already invited Matt and Liz – they're probably already on their way down. I said we'd go for a drink first. I just don't understand . . . Am I honestly supposed to think this was a spur-of-the-moment decision? Christ, this pisses me off.'

Message received today at 16.32.

'Call me back, for fuck's sake. You do realise we're supposed to be getting on a plane to New York the day after tomorrow?'

Message received today at 17.15.

'You know what, Nicole? Don't come crying to me when this turns out to be a disaster.'

After the third one I can't stand to listen any more, and now I know that there's no hope of me drifting off to dreamless sleep. I lie awake, I'm anxious, guilt-ridden . . . I open my laptop and make a perfunctory attempt to get some work done. I type up the notes from the afternoon's meeting with Annie, but that just makes me feel worse. Finally, I open my secret Hotmail account and check my messages.

There's another message from Alex, sent just an hour ago.

Alex to Nicole

Are we not talking again? Or are you just busy?
Maybe you're at the in-laws.
   Well, you'll get this some time. I confronted Aaron

about Jessica this morning. I meant to be all cold and businesslike about it, but then I just fucking lost it, screamed and cried and threw stuff. So humiliated now. He was contrite, begged forgiveness, told me it was 'a stupid, meaningless sex thing' – as though that's supposed to make me feel better. Fucker. So what do I do, Nic? He promised me (before I threw the soapstone elephant that you bought me in Cape Town at his head – don't worry, it's not broken), that he would end it with her, that he would never see her again. I don't think I believe him.

Ax

Nicole to Alex

I'm sorry. I didn't read your message until late last night (we've had the in-laws to stay) and I've been working all day today. I'm really sorry about Aaron. And of course I don't think you got what was coming to you. Well, maybe a little bit.

I know you think I can give you advice on this, but I can't really. Our situations are completely different. There was no question, not really, of me leaving Dom back then. You're not in a marriage yet. You can just walk away, if you want to. Do you want to? Do you love him?

Why is your taste in men so crap?

Alex to Nicole

Oh, pots, kettles and people in glass houses . . .

No one knows about me and Alex. No one knows about our secret email exchanges. No one would understand it. Well, no one except Julian. I certainly can't talk to Dom about it – he freezes up at the very mention of her name. He would never understand why I can talk to her, joke with her about what happened, but cannot bear to speak about it with him. Why should he? I can't understand it myself. Maybe it's just because I've loved her for longer than I've loved him. Sometimes I think it's because I loved her more.

Nicole to Alex

Oh, come on. My record has nothing on yours. There was that wanker Howard at college, there was that awful DJ in Cape Town, there was Mike, and now there's this guy. You have worse taste in men than Cheryl Cole. But . . . since we're on the subject of dark pasts, I should probably mention that Aidan called, just before Christmas. He left a message on my voicemail – he offered me some work with his company. I haven't called him back but I'm so tempted: he's been doing really interesting stuff over there. It would be so great to have real work to do again, to get away from the execrable nonsense I've been working on here. But I don't think Dom would stand for it.

Alex to Nicole

One — you don't think Dom would stand for it? Come on Nic. That's not like you.

And two — are you really sure you want to open up that can of worms? We are talking about the same Aidan, aren't we? The one who's been breaking your heart since 1997? I should warn you, before you do anything, that if you did decide to work with him, you wouldn't be safe. He's not over you. I bumped into him a couple of months ago at some fundraiser thing at the Met and all he did was talk about you. How is she, what's she up to, is she happy . . .

Oh, why did she have to tell me that?

I snap my laptop shut, annoyed. It's annoying that she told me, but even more annoying than that is the fact that she's right, and I know she is. Seeing Aidan again would be a mistake. He *has* been breaking my heart, ever since that encounter on the beach in Cape Town fifteen years ago. Because, of course, despite saying he would, he didn't call me the next day. Or the day after that. It didn't spoil my holiday; I had a great time. Alex and I climbed the mountain, we whale-watched, we sunbathed and went dancing, made our pilgrimage to Robben Island, drank vast quantities of Constantia Sauvignon Blanc. But I can't pretend that I wasn't disappointed that he hadn't called. I'd thought that New Year's Eve had been the start of something; obviously he hadn't.

But then, of course, the day before I was due to fly back to London, just when I had accepted the fact that it hadn't been anything special, it had just been a snog on the beach, *then* he called. We were planning a quiet night in – Alex's parents insisted that she spend her last night in South Africa at home with them – but, on witnessing my excitement at finally hearing from Aidan, I was excused from the family dinner.

Alex didn't approve.

'He doesn't call all week and the second he does you go running? Not clever.'

She didn't understand. No one had ever made her wait a week for a call.

He turned up just before sunset, a motorcycle helmet in his hand.

'What about you?' I asked when he handed it to me.

'I've got a hard head,' he replied, rapping his knuckles against his skull.

'What about the police?' I asked, but he just laughed.

I hopped up behind him on the bike, trying to appear nonchalant, not wanting to admit to him that I had never been on a motorbike before. I gripped the strap on the seat in front of me.

'You can't hold onto that,' he said, turning to smile at me. 'Not if you want to stay on the bike.' He took my hands in his and locked them around his skinny torso. I hoped he couldn't feel how fast my heart was racing. 'Just hold on tight,' he said. 'Lean when I lean and we'll be fine.'

We drove south along Chapman Peak Drive, the magnificent, winding, terrifying stretch of road that runs along the Cape Peninsula from Noordhoek to Hout Bay, where the western side of Table Mountain plunges into the Atlantic. Clinging onto Aidan's body, the wind whipping against us, eyes watering, the roar of the bike competing with the sound of the waves below, sun dipping towards the ocean, turning the sea and the sky from blue to orange to pink, I felt I was in heaven. I never wanted that ride to end.

It had to, though, and when it did we drove across the peninsula to Fish Hoek. We bought lobster rolls and a bottle of white wine and picnicked on the beach. Afterwards, when the wine was finished, we walked to his hotel, which was right on the bay, and went to bed. I remember being incredibly nervous, my hands trembling, fumbling to undo my jeans, almost incapable of looking him in the eye. I'd only ever slept with two people before that – Ben Maxwell, two days after my seventeenth birthday (awful), and Stewart Sommers, my tutorial partner at college (slightly less awful). Aidan was a different proposition altogether.

Afterwards, my brain drenched in oxytocin, flooded

with the joy of having just had my first-ever satisfying sexual experience (with another person, anyway), I wanted to tell him that I was falling in love with him, but I couldn't. It was ridiculous; we hardly knew each other. But I had to say something, so I told him that I'd never felt that way about anyone before, not ever. He didn't say anything in reply. He drove me back to Alex's place just before dawn, we kissed goodbye at the gates, he told me that he'd give me a call the next time he was in England.

'I'll probably be back in a few weeks,' he said. 'We can get together then.'

It was almost two years before I heard from him again. Michaelmas term, 1998. I had been going out with Stewart Sommers for six months by this time. It was not a passionate relationship, but it was a happy one. Stewart was sensitive, funny and fiercely intelligent. We were constantly engaged in intellectual debates, about the economic outlook of the former Eastern Bloc countries in the wake of the Russian banking crisis, the long-term prospects for peace in Northern Ireland following the Good Friday agreement, about whether or not Chumbawamba's Danbert Nobacon was justified in pouring a jug of water over John Prescott at the Brits.

It was late November, and Stewart was away for the weekend, he'd gone hunt-sabbing somewhere in Sussex. I was no longer living in college at that time, instead I was sharing a poky hovel in Jericho with Alex and three other girls. It was Friday evening and Alex and I were in her room getting ready to go out to the pub when the doorbell rang downstairs. One of my other housemates called up to me, saying there was someone there to see me. I went downstairs and there he was, looking exactly the same as he had when I'd met him on the beach: skinny and tanned, his hair tousled, stubble on his chin, looking as though he hadn't slept in a week.

'Hey, Nicole,' Aidan said, smiling that infuriating, irresistible, sexy smile. 'I've been back in the UK for a couple of days, and I've got nothing to do, and I was just thinking, if I could do anything in the world, what would it be? And I decided that it would be to visit Nicole Blake. Julian gave up your address. Reluctantly. I threatened his Fred Perry collection.'

I just stood gawping at him, unable to believe he was really there, standing on my doorstep, the man I'd spent weeks and months dreaming about, fantasising about, agonising over, the one who said he'd call and never did. The one I'd finally given up on.

'Nicole? Aren't you going to say anything?'

Finally, my brain kicked into gear, I took a tentative step forward, and gave him a hug.

'It's good to see you, Aidan. Come in.'

By this time, Alex had come downstairs to see what was going on. She looked at Aidan, back at me, raised an eyebrow and turned to go back upstairs.

'Nice to see you too, Alex,' Aidan called out after her, but she ignored him. I got him a beer out of the fridge and we sat at the kitchen table.

'Where have you been?' I asked him. 'Julian never seems to know where you are.'

He shrugged. 'Around and about, you know. It's not always easy to contact people when I'm on the road.' He slid his hand across the table and touched the ends of his fingertips to mine. 'I'm sorry I didn't get in touch after Cape Town. I meant to, but then there were some problems at work, so I ended up staying a lot longer, then when I did come back things were a bit complicated . . . with someone . . . so . . .'

I pulled my hand away. I realised that I was sitting very straight, like a schoolteacher. I made a conscious effort to relax, to loosen up.

'It's fine, Aidan. It doesn't matter.'

'No, I felt bad. I did think about you.' He had the good grace to look sheepish. He took a long slug of beer. 'In any case, I've got the weekend in Oxford now. Can we hang out? Can I take you out for something to eat tonight? We'll go somewhere nice. I bet you're living on curry and kebabs.'

'I'm supposed to be going to the pub with Alex,' I said. He looked genuinely disappointed.

'She can spare you for one night can't she? Come on, Nic. It's been . . .'

'Nearly two years.'

'Exactly. I want to hear about what you've been up

137

to, I want to know what's going on with you.' His hand was touching mine again, our fingers interlocked. I had goose bumps all over.

Upstairs, I asked Alex if she'd mind going to the pub with the others, leaving me with Aidan tonight.

She glared at me. 'I can't believe this,' she said. 'After all this time, you go running to him, just like that? Do you remember how hurt you were last time? Do you remember all those bloody nights you sat up, going over and over things, wondering why he didn't want you?'

'I know, but—'

'Go. Have dinner with him. But please, Nic, don't shag him. Think about how you felt last time. And think about Stewart. You know, the guy who loves you and would never treat you like shit?'

The problem was that all through dinner, I thought about nothing but how I'd felt the last time. I could think of nothing but how he'd made me feel, in his bed, in his hotel room in Cape Town, on that hot, sluggish, late afternoon in January. As we ate our nam tok and Thai green curry at Chiang Mai on the Broad, I listened to Aidan telling me about covering the fall of Mobutu Sese Seko in Congo, and the overthrow of General Suharto in Indonesia, about his kidnap (for all of twelve hours) in Bogota and his car accident in Bolivia, and I realised that I'd been ridiculous back then, after Cape Town, expecting him to ring me every five minutes, to come back to England to visit me. He'd had better things to do, important things. He'd been out in the world, having adventures, making a difference, bringing the stories of people in conflict and tragedy back to England. I could have listened to him talk all night, but that wasn't what I really wanted.

'Where are you staying?' I asked him when dinner was finished, pushing thoughts of Stewart to the back of my mind.

'The Randolph,' he said.

'Ooh la la.'

'Yeah, well, I spend most of the year living in fleapits, so I thought I'd splash out. It's very nice actually. You want to come up and see my room?'

We spent the weekend holed up in Aidan's hotel room, talking incessantly, drinking champagne and having the best sex I'd ever had. Aidan left on Sunday night, and on Monday I broke up with Stewart. Alex was incredulous. So was Julian. He rang me on the Tuesday.

'Alex just called,' he said. 'I can't believe you dumped Stewart. He was a nice guy.'

'It's all your fault,' I told him. 'You should never have given Aidan my address. You know I can't resist him.'

'He threatened my Fred Perrys, Nic. What else could I do? In any case, what's going on with you two now? I hope you're not expecting anything from him. I love the man like a brother, but you know what he's like. He's never around, and even when he is, he isn't exactly reliable.' He sounded worried.

'Of course I'm not expecting anything,' I replied, although of course I was desperately hoping that this might develop into an actual, full-blown relationship. 'We're just taking it slowly.'

'Good.'

'And we're going to spend Christmas together. Me and my mum and Aidan and you – since your parents are off jet-setting again this year. And Charles, of course. And Alex, if she doesn't go home this year. It'll be brilliant.'

'Okay,' Julian said, still sounding less than convinced. 'I hope you're right.'

A few days before Christmas, Aidan rang to tell me he wasn't going to be able to spend it with us.

'Things are hotting up in Iraq,' he told me. 'The disarmament crisis. We're going out to Kuwait for a few days, going to cover things from there. I'll ring you when I get back.'

I didn't see or hear from him again until the following summer. He turned up in Oxford again a month before I wrote my finals. The prospect of having him back in my life spun my head yet again. I couldn't concentrate on anything, I spent hours in the library composing cool but sassy text messages to him, instead of reading *Beowulf*. Two nights before my exams started, Aidan rang to tell me he was going away again, to the Congo. He wasn't sure how long he'd be, or when he'd be able to get back in touch.

I did not get the first-class degree I'd spent three years working for.

I flick open my laptop to rewrite my resolutions.

New Year's Resolutions, 2011:
1. ~~Get in touch with Aidan re job offer~~ Talk to old BBC contacts about work
2. Lose half a stone
3. Stop taking the pill (or at least admit to Dom that I'm still taking it??)
4. Repaint the kitchen
5. ~~Sort out things with Dad~~ Make an effort to see Dad regularly – monthly dinners?

There's one new message in my secret Hotmail account.

Alex to Nicole
Nicole? Are you still there? I have to come to London for work at the end of January. I was hoping I could see you. Any chance?

Nicole to Alex
I don't think so, Alex.

Alex to Nicole
Please?

Nicole to Alex
I'm not trying to hurt you, Alex. I just don't think I
can see you.

Alex to Nicole
Okay. I love you, Nic. I'll be thinking of you on Friday.

I close my laptop and ring Dom from my mobile, but
it goes straight to voicemail. I leave him a message,
telling him I'm sorry that I missed dinner, that I bailed
on him at the last minute, but it's a lie. I'm not sorry,
I'm pleased that I came. It was the right thing to do.

I rewrite my resolutions one more time.

New Years Resolutions, 2011:
  1. ~~Get in touch with Aidan re job offer~~ Talk to
     old BBC contacts about work
  2. Lose half a stone.
  3. ~~Stop taking the pill – or at least admit to Dom
     that I'm still taking it~~ Be honest with Dom.
     About everything.
  4. Repaint the kitchen
  5. ~~Sort out things with Dad~~ Make an effort to see
     Dad regularly – monthly dinners?

Chapter Eight

New Year's Eve, 1999
London

Resolutions:
1. Get a job! Any job! Preferably one in TV though
2. Lose half a stone
3. Go to Marrakech, take a trip into the Sahara (or the Atlas mountains?)
4. Read *The Times* and *the Guardian* <u>every day</u>
5. Go bunjee jumping. Or sky-diving.

'I just don't see why we're all making so much fuss when it isn't actually the millennium tonight.'

'Oh will you shut up with that?' Julian lobbed a pillow at my head.

'Well, it's true. The actual start of the third millennium is 1 January 2001, not 1 January 2000. We're a year early.'

Alex groaned and laid back on the bed. 'Will you

stop trying to spoil our fun? I don't care if it's the real millennium tonight or next year, *tonight* is when everyone's celebrating it, so stop being such a downer.'

'Exactly,' Jules agreed. 'Tonight we are, quite literally, going to party like it's 1999.'

'It *is* 1999.'

'Oh, just drink some champagne and cheer up, will you?'

The three of us were sitting on Alex's bed, drinking cheap cava and helping Alex choose her outfit for the evening. At that moment she was wearing a red Gucci mini-dress (bought with her entire student loan in the summer sale) and high heels.

'You'll freeze to death,' I told her.

'Yes, but her corpse will look fucking fabulous,' Julian said. He took a photograph of her; she posed for the camera, model-esque.

'Well, I'm wearing jeans,' I said. 'And lots of layers. A woolly jumper. And Doc Martens.'

Alex wrinkled her nose at me in disgust. 'You can't wear a woolly jumper, Nicole. We're on the guest list at Fabric.'

'Well if we're on the guest list, we should we able to wear whatever the hell we like. In any case, before we get to Fabric we're going to be standing on the banks of the Thames for hours, freezing our arses off. You'll be miserable as sin by eleven, I'm warning you.'

Alex kicked off her heels, unzipped her dress and

let it fall to the ground. She was wearing bright pink underwear. Julian took some more photographs.

'You'd better not show anyone those, Jules,' she said, as she rifled despairingly though another rack of garments.

'Oh, I was thinking of blowing them up and hanging them in the living room. If you've got it, you know, may as well . . .'

The two of them started giggling, which got on my nerves. I swilled back more cava in an attempt to perk myself up a bit. To be perfectly honest, I was feeling grumpy. I didn't want to stand for ages on the banks of the Thames looking at fireworks and I didn't want to go to some uber-trendy club where Alex and Julian would fit in effortlessly and I'd stand around feeling incredibly uncool. If it had been up to me, we'd have just had a party at home, but my flatmates refused. Not entirely unreasonably, it had to be admitted, since you couldn't fit more than fifteen people into our place at the very most.

Julian, Alex and I had been living in a flat on Heneage Street, just off Brick Lane, since the summer. A tiny three-bed with a galley kitchen and a shower room (no bath), it was poky and cramped, with paint peeling off the walls in the hallway and rising damp in the bathroom. We loved it. A stone's throw from the Whitechapel Gallery, a short hop to Shoreditch and all the curry you could eat right on your doorstep.

I couldn't remember being happier: Jules and I had been dreaming about sharing a flat (in New York, or Paris, or Barcelona, or London) since he was seventeen and I was fifteen. Having Alex in the mix just added to the fun. I loved our lazy Sunday brunches at the Cantaloupe, I loved the evenings spent sitting on our tatty sofa drinking cheap Rioja and eating pizza while watching *EastEnders*; most of all I loved the fact that Jules could crawl into bed with me at three in the morning after a big night out and tell me all about his adventures.

And so what if the flat wasn't exactly the luxury apartment of our teenage dreams? It wasn't like we had a lot of choice: it was all we could afford. Julian was earning peanuts working as an assistant for a freelance photographer, Alex had landed her dream job in a publishing house, but she was starting at the very bottom of the ladder so she was earning peanuts too, and I wasn't earning anything at all. My three-month graduate trainee-ship at Optimum, a TV production company, had ended without my being taken on permanently. That was five weeks previously, and I was yet to find a new job. Frankly, I was starting to panic.

Which was another reason for my being unseasonably grumpy that New Year.

'If I don't find anything in the next month, I'm going to have to move home,' I moaned to Julian, while simultaneously trying to feign interest in Alex's sixth wardrobe change.

'Never going to happen. I won't let you.'

'I'm running out of money, Jules. By February I won't be able to pay the rent.'

'Then we'll sub you one month's rent. You're not going home.'

'You don't have any money either, Julian.'

'I'll quit smoking. It's on my list of resolutions.'

'It's *always* on your list of resolutions.'

Alex pirouetted around in front of us in gold hot pants and a sheer black top.

'No!' I protested. 'I am not going anywhere with you looking like that. Seriously. You look like a stripper.'

'Now there's a solution to our money problems,' Julian said with a grin. 'Let's send Alex out to work at Spearmint Rhino. Oh my god!' he said, his eyes wide. 'You even have the perfect stripper name. "Lexi Rose"!' he exclaimed, waving an arm from left to right as though presenting the billing.

Alex threw a feather boa at him and downed the rest of her sparkling wine.

'Well, I think I look good in these.'

'You look amazing, Lexi Rose, you really do,' I said. 'But I'm still not going anywhere with you dressed like that.'

An hour or so later, we were ready to go. Alex was back in the red Gucci dress, Julian was devastatingly gorgeous in jeans and a leather jacket. I was wearing jeans too, though Alex had managed to persuade me out of my woolly jumper and Doc Martens and into a daringly low-backed top and heels. The three of us walked arm in arm along Brick Lane, heading north towards Shoreditch where we were planning to hit a few bars before making for the river. A motorbike roared past on our right-hand side. Alex jumped, almost tripping over the pavement in her haste to get out the road.

'Wanker!' she called out after the bike, flicking a 'V' sign at his back. To my alarm, the motorcyclist slowed, turned the bike around and headed back towards us.

'He can't have heard me, he can't possibly have . . .' Alex said.

'Might have seen you though . . .' Julian replied.

The bike came to a halt just in front of us. 'Oh crap,' Alex muttered. My legs had turned to jelly, but not because I was afraid of being beaten up in a road rage incident. I knew who it was even before he took off the helmet.

I hung back while Aidan and Julian embraced. Aidan looked tired and gaunt, there were dark circles beneath those beautiful green eyes.

'Wanker!' Alex muttered again. Then she grabbed my arm and pulled me closer. 'Do not, under any circumstances, sleep with him tonight,' she hissed in my ear.

I rolled my eyes at her. 'Of course I'm not going to sleep with him,' I whispered. 'I haven't forgiven him for costing me my first. Or for breaking up me and Stewart. I'm *totally* over him in any case.'

And then Aidan put his arms around me and buried his face in my neck, murmuring, 'Hello, beautiful,' and I felt like I'd come home. We held on to each other for just a little too long, oblivious to the noise and the people around us. Alex broke the spell.

'Hello, wanker,' she said. 'You nearly killed me back there, you know.'

'Nah, I knew what I was doing. Just giving you a little buzz.' He looked her up and down. 'Going to a tarts and vicars party, are we?' She slapped him, not quite playfully, across the face, then gave him a kiss on the cheek.

'Wash your mouth out,' she said. 'This is Gucci. And we're going to a party at Fabric later. *We're* on the guest list; *you* are not.'

'But you're very welcome to join us for drinks and fireworks,' Julian said, stepping in between the two of them. 'Although I'd imagine that an international playboy like your good self would have plans for the biggest New Year's Eve of all time?'

Aidan shrugged. 'It's not even the proper millennium, you know,' he said, and I wanted to kiss him.

Aidan parked his bike outside our flat and the four of us set off once again: Alex's mood just a little less chirpy, Julian delighted to see his cousin again, me in the state of emotional turmoil typically associated with

149

Aidan's proximity. Aidan, as usual, seemed completely oblivious to the impact he was having on everyone else.

Alex, teetering a little in her heels, linked her arm through mine as we followed behind the boys.

'So,' she said, giving me a knowing little smile, 'it's you, me and the Symonds boys for New Year's Eve. Who'd have thought it?'

I smiled at her. 'Well, it's made Julian's night,' I said. Julian and Aidan were walking a few paces ahead of us, chatting animatedly about Aidan's recent travels in Africa.

'It's funny, isn't it?' Alex said, smiling at them, 'how much Julian adores him. They couldn't really be more different.'

'Oh, I don't know . . .'

'Oh, come on. Okay, same smouldering looks, I'll grant you, but Jules is so sensitive and sweet and completely selfless, whereas Aidan . . .'

'You don't know him, Alex. There's a whole history there that you don't know about.'

Alex rolled her eyes, her expression pained. She'd never admit it but she hated hearing about that history, she hated the fact that she was excluded from a whole chunk of Julian and my friendship. 'Seriously, when Julian first came out, Aidan was amazing to him. Jules didn't have the easiest time of it – with his dad, with people at school, but Aidan was always there for him.'

'So that's it, is it?' Alex asked.

150

'That's what?'

'The reason you like him so much. Because he loves Julian as much as you do.'

'Well, not the *only* reason . . .'

'Yeah, I refer you back to the smouldering good looks.'

'There's more to him than that, Alex.'

She cast a suspicious sideways glance at me. 'Oh god, you're totally going to sleep with him tonight, aren't you?

'Of course I'm not!' I huffed. 'I told you, I'm over him.' Perhaps if I said it often enough, I might convince myself.

We arrived at the Bricklayer's Arms, scene of our first pint. Alex and I grabbed a table in the corner while the boys got the drinks in.

'We could always ditch them,' Alex said to me. 'You and I can go off and do our own thing. Pick up some exciting new boys for the new millennium. And if you say it isn't the new millennium one more time, I'm going to smack you.'

'We're not abandoning Jules on New Year's Eve, Alex. Plus, you've been looking forward to this thing at Fabric for weeks. And you're risking hypothermia just so you'll look good on the podium when we get there.'

'Just so long as it's Julian you want to be around,' Alex whispered as Julian and Aidan approached with the drinks. Gin and tonics for Alex and me, a pint for Julian and something that looked suspiciously like orange juice for Aidan.

'You planning on driving somewhere later?' Alex asked.

Julian shook his head ever so slightly.

'Just pacing myself,' Aidan replied. I shot Julian a quizzical glance, he shook his head again, mouthing, 'later' at me.

We drank our drinks, laughing hysterically while Julian regaled us with tales from the photography studio: the woman who'd brought in her seven cats 'to sit for a portrait' ('I spent four hours literally herding cats. *Literally.*'); the blond teenagers who came in and promptly whipped their tops off ('practising for page three, innit?'); the lothario from Lahore who came in with a new bride-to-be every other week – the ladies were to be professionally photographed so that he could send the images to his mother back in Pakistan for approval.

It struck me that it was the first time the four of us had ever sat around a table together and had a drink, and it felt so good, it felt *perfect.* I wanted to bottle that moment, to keep it forever: me, sitting at a table in East London, young and happy and drink in hand, with my best friends and Aidan. The man I was over. Completely over.

As we left the pub and headed for the next bar,

Julian fell back in step with me, while Alex and Aidan walked ahead, trading teasing insults as they went.

'What was that about?' I asked Julian. 'The orange juice?'

'Oh, he's just taking it easy,' Julian replied, without meeting my eye.

'Julian,' I said, taking his arm and turning him to face me, 'come on. Aidan's taking it easy? Seriously?'

Julian sighed. 'He's on antidepressants. The past year's been a bit harrowing, apparently. Don't say anything, he doesn't want to make a big deal about it. Just . . . I don't know. Be nice. And tell Alex not to be too hard on him, okay?'

'I'm always nice,' I replied, and Julian put his arm around me and squeezed.

'I know you are, my darling. I know you are.'

We swapped around again, Julian catching up with Aidan while I hung back with Alex, who was struggling to keep pace in her heels.

'He was asking lots of questions about you . . .' Alex told me as she took my arm.

'Really?' I asked, much too eager.

'Oh yes,' she replied, raising her eyes to the heavens, 'you're *totally* over him.'

'Piss off,' I said, giving her a friendly shove. I tried not to take the bait, I really did, but I couldn't help myself. 'So, what was he asking?'

'Oh, you know. How is she, what's she up to, is she

seeing anyone . . . That kind of thing. I told him you were shagging an investment banker with a big dick.'

'You did not!' I shrieked, shoving her again.

'Well, you did have a one-night stand with that investment banker, and I seem to recall you saying . . .'

'All right!' I cut her off. 'That's quite enough of that.'

She giggled. 'Okay, I didn't say that, but I did say that you had no shortage of offers.'

I smiled at her. 'Thank you, Alex. That's well put.'

'I still think you should steer clear of him.'

'I know you do. And I know he hasn't exactly treated me fantastically in the past, but I can't help the way I feel . . .'

'I thought you said you were over him? I thought you just said you hadn't forgiven him for last time.'

'But it's not *really* his fault I didn't get a first, is it? And it's not *actually* his fault I broke up with Stewart. I blame him, because it's easier to do so, but I was the one who let myself be distracted, I was the one who didn't work hard enough and I was the one who chose to run off with him the moment he turned up. No one had a gun to my head.'

We'd arrived at the King's Head, the next pub on our crawl. Alex dropped my arm, turned to face me and gave a sad little smile. 'One day, you're going to have to start saying no to him, Nic. Otherwise he'll just keep turning up, turning your life upside down and then disappearing off into the distance in search of a new adventure. Men like him never stick around, you know.'

I went to the bar to get the drinks. Aidan disappeared off to put something on the jukebox. When I got back to the table, Julian grabbed my arm.

'Guess what, Nic,' he said excitedly, 'Aidan's here to stay. He's got a job in London. He's sticking around this time.'

I looked across at Alex, trying not to smile. She rolled her eyes at me, raised her drink and said: 'I give up.'

After a couple more drinks we left the pub and weaved our way slowly (painfully, in Alex's case), southwards towards the Tower of London, and then inched along the river pushing our way through the crowds, taking turns to swig from the bottle of cheap champagne Aidan had purchased from a newsagent on the way. He and I had still barely spoken a word to each other – every time I looked at him, I could sense disapproval radiating from Alex. As surreptitiously as I could, I slipped my hand into Julian's and pulled him back a little, so that we could walk and talk.

'Is he really staying?' I asked.

'Claims to be. He reckons he's sick of travelling all the time. Plus his mum, my aunt Sarah, is unwell, so I think he wants to be around.'

'Sorry.'

'Don't be, she's a miserable old bitch. Hates me.

Whenever she speaks to my mum she asks "whether Julian's still queer".' I giggled. 'Seriously. She sent Mum a pamphlet from some insane church group that claims it can holy ghost the gayness right out of you.'

'Christ.'

'Exactly. Also – he didn't say as much – but I think you might have something to do with it.'

'To do with what?' I asked, knowing exactly what he meant. I wanted to hear him say it.

'To do with Aidan staying here. I'm pretty sure he wants to be with you.'

'Doubt it. He's barely even looked at me since he arrived.'

'That's because he's nervous. And feeling guilty. And getting evils from Alex.'

It was true, actually. He did seem nervous. Which was weird – Aidan, nervous and not drinking? Perhaps the two went hand in hand. Whatever the cause, I seemed to be making it worse. Because apart from that hug when we first saw each other in the street, he'd kept his distance from me. He hadn't been rude, or anything, it wasn't like he was ignoring me, he just seemed to be addressing either Julian or Alex when he spoke, only really looking at me when I wasn't looking back. I'd caught him doing it a couple of times in the pub: watching me and then looking away the second I looked up at him. And now, down at the river, he stuck to Julian's side. It was almost as though he was afraid to be alone with me. I wasn't sure what to think.

Inevitably, at midnight, as the fireworks went off, something had to give. Aidan took my hand and pulled me towards him, he was saying something but I couldn't hear him, the noise of the crowd and the pyrotechnics was so loud. He slipped his hand under my chin and bent his head to kiss me; I turned my head and offered him my cheek, then turned away, freeing myself from his grasp, wrapping my arms around Julian instead. My refuge. When I looked over at Aidan again he was watching me, he smiled, but he looked hurt. I don't know what it was he expected.

Alex, who was, as I had predicted, freezing cold and in pain because her shoes were so uncomfortable, was complaining. 'That was crap, wasn't it? Where was the river of fire? I couldn't even see it. Come on, I'm freezing. I want to be in the VIP area sitting on someone's lap. Let's go clubbing.' She turned to Aidan and kissed him on the cheek. 'Catch you later, maybe,' she said, grabbing my hand and starting off towards the tube.

'Alex, we can't just leave him here,' I protested.

'Yes we can. He'll be fine. I'm sure he'll find some way to amuse himself.'

'Alex . . .' I glanced over my shoulder. Julian was saying something to Aidan, Aidan was shaking his head in reply.

'No, no, you go on,' I heard him say.

'Nic,' Jules called out to me. 'You girls go to the club. I'm going to hang on with Aidan for a bit longer.'

'No!' Alex and I both replied in chorus.

'This is ridiculous,' Alex muttered. 'We had plans. He can't just turn up and—'

'Alex, be nice. Listen – you two go to Fabric. You and Julian. You're the ones who wanted to go clubbing. I don't even like clubbing.' Julian looked doubtful, Alex pouted. 'You know I don't like clubbing, Alex.'

'I'm think I should just get going . . .' Aidan said.

'Yes, go on. Fuck off,' Alex said, and we all started to laugh.

In the end we decided that Julian and Alex would go clubbing, while Aidan and I would 'hang out and catch up'. Aidan promised he'd make sure I got home safely. The four of us walked together as far as Tower Hill tube, then Julian and Alex descended into the station, while Aidan and I stood outside, just looking at each other, not sure what to say, buffeted by the crowds. After a moment or two of awkward silence, Aidan slipped his hand into mine and led me back down to the river.

'Let's just walk,' he said. 'Shall we walk?

For a while we walked in silence, hand in hand, against the mercifully thinning crowds. By the time we were level with London Bridge, a fog had descended, obscuring the remaining people. I was transported back to the beach three years ago, I had the same feeling of isolation, as though Aidan and I were all alone in the world.

'So, which do you prefer?' I asked him. 'The banks of the river Thames in freezing, foggy London, or Clifton Beach in Cape Town?'

'No question,' he replied, 'South Africa all the way.'

'Oh, I don't know, this fog is quite atmospheric, in a Gothic sort of way. You feel as though Jack the Ripper could leap out at any moment.

'Delightful.'

'You're all right. You don't look much like a hooker.'

'Good thing Alex went clubbing, though.'

'Oi!' I said, giving him a playful punch on the arm. 'But seriously, are you really sure you want to come back to England? Aren't you going to miss all the sunshine and the adventure?'

'The sunshine I'll miss. The adventure, not so much.'

'Are you okay, Aidan?'

'I'm knackered, Nic. I'm completely and utterly exhausted. And I've been offered a good job – assistant director of documentaries and features at Cannon TV. I'm actually going to be earning a living wage for the first time in my life.'

'That's brilliant, Aidan. I'm just, well, a bit surprised, I suppose. Can't quite picture you sitting behind a desk all day.'

He puffed out his cheeks and sighed. 'You know what? I'm looking forward to sitting behind a desk. I've just . . . had enough, you know? Since I left Kinshasa, I've never drunk so much in all my life. For weeks I couldn't sleep unless I drank enough to make myself pass out . . .'

'Jesus, Aidan. I'm sorry.' He slipped his arm around my shoulders and pulled me closer.

'It was awful. I can't explain it. I've been in some shitty places, but the Congo was just . . . soul destroying. You wouldn't believe it, Nicole, you wouldn't believe what's been happening there . . . I mean, you should believe it, because we're out there reporting it, but you know what it's like. The wholesale rape and slaughter of women and children somewhere in the middle of the jungle doesn't sit so well on the front pages as Kosovo or the euro or Y2-fucking-K, does it? No one gives a shit.'

'That's not true, Aidan, it has been reported . . .'

'You've no idea, Nic. You've no idea.' He passed his hand over his eyes, shook his head, as though trying to dislodge the bad memories. 'There are girls, little girls, ten or eleven, who've been gang raped by soldiers, it's just another weapon, a cost efficient way of destroying the enemy. It makes you want to fucking weep. Because when it's over, when they're done, if these women are left alive, they're ruined. They're just finished.'

His hands shook as he tried to light his cigarette. I placed my hands on his to steady them. He smiled and took a deep drag.

'I've had enough. The whole thing has been doing my head in. And you know what? I've been doing this so fucking long that I've started to forget that there are people, plenty of people in fact, who live their lives and do their jobs without being in constant bloody fear of getting their heads blown off. I want a life like that. I can't explain it to you, I really can't, how fucking exhausting it is, just always being afraid.'

'Aidan,' I said, squeezing him tighter, I had no idea what to say, I'd never seen him like this, vulnerable like this, I'd never felt protective of him before.

'Plus, I'm getting old.'

I seized the opportunity to lighten the mood.

'That's right, you're in your thirties now. Bloody ancient.'

'It's depressing, I can tell you.'

'I know, I'll be twenty-three in May. That's mid-twenties! I'll no longer be in my early twenties! It's horrible.'

'Yeah, but you're just as beautiful as you were the first time I saw you,' he said, turning to face me, running his thumb from my cheekbone to my lips.

I pushed him away. 'I was fourteen the first time you saw me, you pervert.'

'But I thought you were sixteen.'

'I still reckon that makes you a pervert.'

We walked on to Southwark Bridge, where we crossed the river. We walked on, past the Globe, past the imposing edifice of the Bankside Power Station, not quite yet the Tate Modern; we found ourselves a bench and sat down, huddled together for warmth, looking out across the river.

'It's not the only reason,' Aidan said to me. 'Those aren't the only reasons.'

'What aren't the only reasons for what?'

He flicked his cigarette butt over the guard rail, watched the shower of sparks descending into the black.

'The job, Congo, my being a knackered alkie. They aren't the only reasons I wanted to move here.'

I could feel my pulse start to race.

'I was thinking, you know, if you want, that maybe . . .'

'Maybe?'

'I don't know. We could, you know, make a go of it. You and me.'

It was the most awkward romantic proposition I'd ever had. It was funny, actually: this was Aidan, the one who'd always been so smooth, and here he was coming off like a thirteen-year-old boy. I smiled at him.

'I don't know, Aidan, I'm not sure—'

'I want to be with you, Nic. I think about you all the time. I've missed you.'

And there he was, all smooth again. It was strange, this was exactly what I'd wanted to hear, and yet the moment he said it, it sounded like a line. Like a lie. I pulled away from him a little, sat up straight.

'You wouldn't have known it, from all the times you called me.'

'I'm sorry, Nic, you know what I'm like. When I'm working . . . I just get caught up in stuff.'

'That's not an excuse, Aidan.' I felt pissed off with him all of a sudden, I could see myself, see *us*, through Alex's eyes and I didn't like it. 'I was really messed up after last time. This thing you do, dropping in and out of my life whenever you feel like it – it messes with my head.'

'I know, and I'm sorry, but it won't be like that any more, I promise you . . .'

'Don't make promises. And don't move back here to be with me, because I'm not even sure that's what I want. I can't count on you. I can never rely on you. All you ever do is let me down.'

I got to my feet and started walking away.

'Where are you going?' he called after me.

'Blackfriars. I'm going to get the tube home.'

He walked behind me all the way, and followed me down into the bowels of the underground. He sat next to me in the tube carriage, holding my hand, not saying anything. I didn't have the strength to tell him to let me go. I didn't want to. We walked back to the flat in silence; the rooms were in darkness, Julian and Alex were still out. It was just after three. We didn't turn on the lights, we undressed each other as we moved through the flat, from hallway to living room to hallway to bedroom.

* * *

I woke just after seven, slipped out of bed, moving silently through the house, picking up our clothes as I went. Alex and Julian's bedroom doors were both closed. I hadn't heard them come in. I put on the kettle and made two cups of coffee, white for me, black and sweet for Aidan.

I went back to the bedroom, nudged Aidan awake with my knee, handed him his coffee and gave him his marching orders.

'You need to go,' I told him. 'I don't want you here when Alex gets up. She's just going to give me a hard time.'

'It's none of her business, Nic,' he protested sleepily, slipping his hand under the oversized *Cure* T-shirt I was wearing. One of Julian's cast-offs.

'Well, I want you to go anyway. I need to think about things and I can't think straight when you're in the room. Never have been able to.'

He grinned at me, lazy, lascivious, infuriating. Irresistible. An hour later, I walked him downstairs to his bike and kissed him goodbye. The street was deserted; no one else yet out of bed on the first day of the new year (not the new millennium). We were alone again.

'I'll ring you later,' he said to me as he swung one long leg over the bike.

'Don't,' I said, enjoying for the first time the feeling that I had some power, some control over the relationship. He was staying, I didn't need to panic, I could call the shots. He reached out, placed his hand on the back of my neck and gently pulled me towards him. He kissed me, long and deep.

'I love you, Nic,' he said. 'I mean it, I'm in love with you.'

My heart stopped. He smiled, pulled on his helmet and rode off down the road. That feeling of control hadn't lasted long.

Back upstairs I went into the kitchen to make myself another cup of coffee. I couldn't get to the kettle, however, because there was a naked man standing in front of it, his back to me.

'Hi,' I said.

'Oh, hello,' he replied, turning to face me. He was holding a tea towel with a picture of the Queen's head on it in front of him. A Sex Pistols tea towel. Julian had found it somewhere. 'I'm Karl,' he said. A German accent.

'Nicole,' I replied.

'I've heard a lot about you.' He didn't appear to be in the slightest bit embarrassed about his nudity. A Germanic thing, perhaps.

'You were at Fabric last night, then?'

'That's right. It was a lot of fun.' He was handsome, in good shape, with a tattoo on his washboard stomach that was partially obscured by the Queen's face. I couldn't, on such a cursory inspection, figure out whether he was with Alex or Julian, and didn't want to offend him by asking. The kettle began to whistle.

'Would you like some coffee?' he asked me, turning once more to display his perfect backside.

'I'm all right, actually.' I couldn't quite bring myself to force him to put down that tea towel. 'I think I'll just get myself some juice.'

I went back to bed. When I woke again, the sun was streaming in through the window, the sky an icy blue. I pulled on the *Cure* T-shirt and some trackie bottoms and poked my head around the door. I could hear muffled laughter coming from Alex's room. I crept up to the door, listened for a second. I could hear Alex's voice, and Julian's. No one else's. I pushed the door open; the two of them were lying on the bed, Alex up against the headboard, Julian with his head resting on her tummy.

'There you are at last!' Jules said as I stuck my head around the door.

'I was too scared to come out of my room in case I ran into any more naked men,' I replied. 'Which one of you was responsible for him?' Then, in a lower voice I asked, 'Shit, he's not still here is he?'

'No he is not,' Julian replied, 'and oh my god you need to get your gaydar seen to.'

'Yours then?'

'Of course. I thought you saw him naked? Straight boys don't have bodies like that. Straight boys don't have piercings like that.'

'I didn't noticing a piercing,' I said.

'Well, you probably didn't see him quite as close up as I did,' Julian replied archly.

I blushed. 'It was probably obscured by Her Royal Highness.'

'A queen hiding behind the Queen,' Julian remarked. 'How apt.'

'Well, he was very pretty.'

'Wasn't he?'

'And you, miss?' I said, turning to Alex. 'How did you fare?'

'Well, I got three numbers – one from a *professional* rugby player – but came home alone because I have some dignity and self-respect and am not a total slut like the pair of you.'

'I am not . . .' I started to protest, but they both started laughing.

'Oh, we saw your underwear strewn all over the place last night,' Julian said. 'Strumpet.'

'Where is he anyway?' Alex asked. 'Waiting for breakfast in bed?'

'I kicked him out first thing, actually,' I replied, giving Alex a triumphant look. 'Without so much as a bacon sandwich. Told him I needed time to think about things. Told him—'

But Alex was no longer listening. 'Bacon sandwich!' she exclaimed, shoving Julian off her and jumping to her feet. 'Please, please, please tell me we have bacon.'

Chapter Nine

28 December 2011

I leave the Ashton Guest House just after nine and drive back to Dad's, picking up coffee and muffins from Starbucks on the way. Dad greets me at the door looking brighter, healthier and a good deal more cheerful than he had the previous evening. My mood lightens immediately. I was right to come; Dom must understand that. Okay, as usual I handled things badly, but he knows I'm lacking in emotional intelligence. I think it's one of the things that attracted him to me in the first place. It makes me vulnerable.

'Got something to show you, Nicole,' Dad says as he ushers me into the kitchen. There, on the table, is a notebook. On its face is printed, in my father's neat hand, 'NB, work, 2006–'. I flick open the book. On the first page a date is written: 6 March 2002. Below it my father has stuck a small square of newsprint cut from a *TV Guide*:

BBC Choice, 11.30 p.m.: Twenty-First-Century Slavery: *a harrowing look at the illegal sex traffic from eastern Europe and Africa to the UK, including interviews with trafficked women and the men who pay for their services.*

It's the listing for the first film I ever had shown on television. I flick over the next page, and the next – I'm astonished. Here, in this book, through press cuttings and reviews, my father has followed my career. I can't quite believe it, I don't know what to think. He knew all about me, he knew what I was doing and he was interested enough – proud enough – to make this scrapbook. He was just never brave enough to pick up the phone and tell me that he was proud.

I leaf through the book until I get to the centre spread: there, in pride of place is an article from *Marie Claire* which named me 'one to watch' in a piece on movers and shakers in the arts who had not yet turned thirty. Those were the days. There was a picture of me, looking solemn and austere in a black trouser suit, surrounded by prettier, sunnier creatures: actresses, composers, music producers.

That was in the summer of 2007. After that, there were just two more entries. Dad watches me flick through a few blank pages before closing the book.

'You've done ever so well, Nicole,' he says.

'Well, I started well, certainly,' I say with an embarrassed little laugh.

We sit down at the table. Dad wolfs down his blueberry muffin. I pick at mine. Apple Bran. Trying to be healthy.

'What are you working on at the moment?' he asks. A question I've come to dread.

'It's . . . it's a thing on relationships.'

'Right, right . . .' He obviously expects me to tell him more, but I don't want to.

'It's not a big deal. It's a thing for Channel Five. Bit trashy really.' He looks disappointed. I sigh. 'I don't do so much of the serious stuff these days.'

'Why's that? You were so good at it. That programme about the people traffickers, the thing you did in Albania – that was really good. That was proper, hard-hitting stuff. I remember talking about it to some of the chaps from work.'

I'm simultaneously touched and annoyed. Touched because, after all this time, all our troubles and our silences, I know that he is proud of me, proud enough to go bragging to his colleagues. Annoyed because he even needs to ask why I stopped doing that kind of work.

'Well, you know. After . . . what happened, I didn't want to travel so much any more. I wanted to stay in England. I didn't want to be travelling to Albania, Ivory Coast, Afghanistan. I wanted to be at home, with Dom.'

'Right . . .' he sounds unconvinced. 'It's a pity though, because you were doing so well.' I notice how

171

quickly we've moved from 'you've done ever so well', to 'you *were* doing so well'.

I sip my coffee.

'I'm going to New York on Thursday,' I say.

'Oh right? And is that for work?'

'No, Dad, it's a holiday. Dom and I are both going. There's a party, Karl's having a party.'

'Karl?'

'Julian's Karl.'

'Right.'

We finish our coffee in silence. I give him my muffin; I'm no longer feeling hungry. When he's finished eating, he gets up and replaces the scrapbook on the bookshelf, next to the telephone directory and a small, framed photograph. Dad and Uncle Chris, when they were young, probably in their twenties. I glance around the room. There are no other photographs on display.

I get to my feet. 'I ought to get going, Dad. Dom's expecting me back.'

'All right, then.' He looks disappointed.

'I'll come back and see you as soon as I get back from New York. Okay?'

He shrugs.

'I will.' I reach out to put my hand on his shoulder but he turns his back on me, clears the coffee cups from the kitchen table.

Now I feel anguished again, and uncomfortable, the way I had last night, that unpleasant combination of irritation and fear. Dad walks me to the front door.

'The real reason I wanted you to come here,' he says, 'was to ask you a favour.'

'Of course,' I reply.

'I want to see your mother,' he says, and my heart sinks. 'I telephoned her a few weeks ago, but that man answered and I didn't want to talk to him so I hung up. I want you to speak to her. Ask her to come and see me.'

'Dad . . .'

'It's not much, Nicole. I don't ask you for much.'

Nor I you, I think, but I don't say anything. I don't want to ask Mum to go to see him, because if I do, she'll feel obliged, and I don't want her to feel obliged. She doesn't owe Dad anything. And I'm upset, too. The *real* reason for asking me here was to get me to persuade Mum to visit? So he didn't really want to see me at all?

'Nicole?'

'She's away at the moment,' I say, not meeting his eye.

'When's she back then?'

'I'm not sure.' That's a lie, she's back this evening and I can tell from the expression on his face that he knows I'm lying.

'It's not much, Nicole. I just want to see her before . . .'

'Before your operation.'

'Before I go.'

'I'll see what I can do,' I say. I leave him standing on his doorstep.

*　　*　　*

By the time I get to the end of his road I have to stop the car because I'm crying so much I can't see where I'm going. I'm hurt, of course, but it's more than that. I just feel so angry with him, so pissed off that he missed out on my life, on my growing up, and I missed out on having a dad. And all for what? For nothing. I forgave him, I forgave him for that terrible night, the night he struck my mother, we could have got past that. Only he chose not to. He chose, when Mum threw him out, to let me go too. I still don't understand that.

It wasn't like we were never close. I can remember, when I was very small, maybe five or six, how he used to take me fishing with him. On Saturday mornings, we'd go down to Spade Oak and sit there for hours. We never caught anything and it was always freezing cold, but I remember loving it – putting worms on hooks and skimming stones and spotting birds' nests in the trees or just sitting next to him, holding his huge warm hand, waiting for something to bite. I can remember Mum telling her friends: 'She's Daddy's girl, that one. I don't stand a chance.'

I can't remember when we stopped going fishing. I can't remember when I stopped being Daddy's girl. It was when I got older, though, once I was old enough to realise how hard he was on Mum, how unreasonable he could be. I switched allegiances. And he never seemed to forgive me.

And now I'm okay, and Mum's okay, and he's alone. And the thing that kills me, the thing that hurts me most of all, is his loneliness. His loneliness is unbearable, and if it's unbearable to me, I cannot imagine what it must be like for him.

On the way back to London I stop at the Chieveley Services where I buy a bacon double cheeseburger and devour it ravenously. Should have had that apple bran muffin. I turn on my phone and listen to my messages.

Message received this morning at 8.52 a.m.

'It's me. I missed your call last night. Wasn't really in the mood to talk to you. I take it you're coming back today? Or are you planning a longer excursion? Is New York still on, or should I be cancelling the flights?'

His voice sounds whiny and sarcastic, I delete the message.

Message received this morning at 10.33 a.m.

'Hi Nic it's me.'

There are only a few people in one's life who can ring up and say, 'It's me.' Parents, siblings, significant others. I don't think ex-lovers are supposed to be on that list, but Aidan still does it.

'Ummm . . . I just wanted to have a chat. It's . . . god, what time is it? Four-thirty here. In the morning. I can't sleep. I wanted to talk about work, the job I emailed you about . . . Give me a call, yeah?'

I save the message.

Then, instead of driving back to Wimbledon Village

to get my hair done and my nails painted, I head instead for Queenstown Road in Battersea. I park the car opposite Our Lady of Mount Carmel and St Joseph Catholic Church and get out. I lean against the car door, light a cigarette and look up at the second-floor window of the converted Victorian house I am standing next to: that was our bedroom window. Me and Aidan shared that bedroom for seven months in 2002. Not seven particularly happy months, it has to be said. Despite its proximity to Battersea Park, Queenstown Road was a horrible address – still is in fact. Our flat was virtually adjacent to the railway line; the windows rattled whenever a train came past; the kitchen was home to a indefatigable intrusion of cockroaches. But all that wouldn't have mattered had we been happy.

We weren't. We moved in together at precisely the wrong moment, just when Aidan's wanderlust was starting to get the better of him once more. The nightmares that had plagued his sleep when he came back from Congo were gone, he'd weaned himself off the antidepressants, he was strong and healthy again and bored with being deskbound. We'd been talking about living together for ages, but it took us forever to find a place. We moved in just at the time when Aidan was starting to feel his feet itch. Moving in with me may have been the straw to break the camel's back: Julian always said that Aidan was the most doggedly commitment phobic person he'd ever met. He'd been amazed that our relationship, rekindled the (fake) dawn of the third millennium, lasted past January of 2001.

But it did. And we were incredibly happy most of that time. Aidan surprised me by loving the desk job at Cannon, he surprised me by renting a flat about ten minutes' walk from our place on Heneage Street (I'd imagined that he'd want to keep *some* distance between us), he surprised me by becoming an attentive, considerate boyfriend. He bought me flowers for no reason, he threw me a huge surprise party on my twenty-third birthday, he whisked me away on spur-of-the-moment trips to Rome and Copenhagen. We never ran out of things to say to each other.

He hadn't changed completely: he would still disappear, from time to time, without telling me where he was going and when pressed, would become evasive. He still drank too much on occasion. His eye still wandered – he was physically incapable of not looking at pretty girls who wandered past us in restaurants. But then, Julian was physically incapable of not looking at pretty waiters who wandered past us in restaurants, so maybe it was genetic? Aidan may not have been perfect, but I was never, ever bored with him. There was never a moment when I looked over the fence and saw greener grass. I just knew, it was right.

Aidan was my inspiration. Since that night on the beach in Cape Town, when he told me all his stories, recounted his adventures, I knew what I wanted to do. I wanted to do what he did. He was the one who showed me what it could be like, and then, years later, he was the one showing me how to do it. We never worked together, not for the same company, but we always worked side by side. He taught me how to edit, he helped me develop a director's eye. He taught me more about the way to get to the heart of a story than any boss or any course. I remember how excited I'd been back then, planning trips with him, dreaming up projects we would work on together. And he was excited about it, too. For a while, anyway.

I stub out my cigarette underfoot, take one last look up at my former home and get back in the car. Moving in together had just been a step too far. Almost from the moment we signed the lease on that horrible little flat I could feel him pulling away, backing out of the door before he even came in.

I drive back to Wimbledon, taking a circuitous route (via Harvey Nichols to look, unsuccessfully, for a dress for Karl's party). I arrive back home a little after two, welcomed with great enthusiasm by my dogs. Not by my husband. I make tea in the kitchen, waiting for him to come through to see me. He doesn't. I know he's home because the alarm's not on, and he always puts it on if we're both out. Plus, the dogs would have been outside if he'd gone out. Hang on, why are the dogs still here? Matt and Liz were supposed to take them back to Sussex . . . Oh Christ. My heart sinks.

He hasn't really cancelled the New York trip has he? He can't have done . . .

I make some tea and take it through to Dom's study where I find him typing away furiously. He doesn't turn around at first, but cocks his head to one side and raises his right hand slightly. This is code for, 'I'm not ignoring you, but I'm in the middle of a sentence and I want to finish it before I lose my train of thought.' I put down the tea next to him and kiss him on the top of the head. I put my arms around his neck and hold him until he stops typing.

He looks up at me.

'You okay?' His face is inscrutable, I can't tell if he's still angry or not.

'Dad has cancer,' I say, and he gets to his feet and takes me in his arms.

'I'm so sorry, Nic, I'm so sorry,' he keeps repeating that, over and over, and I feel terrible, because there's a reason I blurted it out so bluntly, just at that moment. I knew he couldn't be angry with me then, not when I'd just told him my father was dying.

We go upstairs together and lie on the bed, holding hands. I tell him I'm sorry about going away without saying anything.

'It's okay, you were freaked out. I shouldn't have got so pissed off.'

'Were Matt and Liz okay? What did you tell them?'

'I told them the truth. My crazy bitch wife has disappeared on me again, who knows when I'll see her again.'

'Why didn't Matt and Liz take the dogs, Dom? You're not . . . you're not thinking of not coming are you?'

'No, of course not. I just thought you'd want to say goodbye to them.' I snuggle closer to him, resting my head on his chest. 'And Matt's got a meeting in London tomorrow morning so he said he'd come back and pick them up on his way home.'

'I *am* a crazy bitch.'

'You are.'

I feel warm and safe and relieved, I try not to think about Dad, or about the fact that in a couple of hours Mum will be back home, she'll be ringing to tell me about her holiday, and I'm going to have to make a decision about what to do.

We make love, Dom dozes off, I get up and make more tea. I take my laptop from my bag and sit at the kitchen table working. If I go upstairs to the attic, I'll wake Dom up. I put on Radio 4; they're talking about the best books of the year. I'm ashamed that I haven't read any of them. When did I stop reading? Even when I was at my busiest, even when I was travelling around the world, dodging bullets, filming the aftermaths of earthquakes and tsunamis, I found time to read.

I open my resolutions file and re-draft.

1. ~~Get in touch with Aidan re job offer Talk to old BBC contacts about work~~ Email Aidan to decline job offer – ask that he no longer calls me

2. Lose half a stone
3. Stop taking the pill (or at least admit to Dom that I'm still taking it??)
4. ~~Repaint the kitchen~~ Read more! Read everything on 2011 Booker shortlist. And 2012 shortlist. When it comes out.
5. ~~Sort out things with Dad~~ Make an effort to see Dad regularly – monthly dinners?

This last one will only be possible, I know, if I grant his request and persuade my mother to go and visit him. I decide that I will tell her, as soon as she phones. She's a big girl, she can decide for herself. I'll make it very clear that I don't mind either way. It's entirely up to her. In fact, I won't wait until she calls me, I'll call her now, while my rationale is clear.

I dial her number but it goes straight to voicemail. She's probably on the way back from the airport. Feeling slightly deflated, eager to begin the process of sorting my life out, I decide to contact Aidan instead. I open the secret Hotmail account and draft a new message.

'Dear Aidan,' I write, 'it was so lovely to hear your voice again' and then I stop writing because I realise, without turning around, that Dom is standing behind me. I didn't hear him coming down the stairs, because the radio was on, but now I can tell, by the way that the dogs are looking past me and wagging their tails, that he's right behind me, reading over my shoulder.

Chapter Ten

New Year's Eve, 2001
Paris

Resolutions:
1. Send copies of *A British Tragedy*, plus CV, to BBC, Channel 4 and major production companies
2. Move house! Go east again? Hackney/ Dalston?
3. Backpack across Cambodia/Vietnam
4. Lose half a stone
5. Learn to speak French

'Une soirée sur une peniche! Nous sommes invités a une soirée sur une peniche! Une peniche sur la Seine! C'est formidable!'

Julian found it unbelievably hilarious to repeat this little phrase (A party on a houseboat! We have been invited to a party on a houseboat! A houseboat on the Seine! It's wonderful!). The rest of us had begun to find

183

it tiresome before we left Waterloo. Us: Alex and Mike (the professional rugby player), Julian and Karl (the naked German), Aidan and I. The six of us had boarded the Eurostar for Paris that morning, bound for *une soirée sur une peniche*, thrown by Bertrand et Laure, friends of Aidan's. Subjects of Aidan's in fact: they had featured in a film his production company made about the work of Médecins Sans Frontières in west Africa.

Aidan was a bit nervous about it – so nervous he'd actually tried to get out of the whole trip claiming that he didn't feel very well, but there was no force on this earth that was going to deny Julian a New Year's Eve party *sur une peniche sur la Seine*, so there we were.

I understood Aidan's nerves. He'd been invited to this party by people he knew from work. They had insisted that he bring friends, but five 'might be pushing it', he'd said to me the previous night. Plus, he just wasn't sure how we were all going to get along. Or, more accurately, how we were all going to get along with Mike, who was taciturn to the point of rudeness. And, by his own admission, he didn't 'think much of the French'.

I was nervous, too. For months now I'd been hearing about Bertrand and Laure: Aidan talked incessantly about the fantastic (and dangerous) work they'd been doing in Cote d'Ivoire and Sierra Leone, about their passionate commitment to improving the lives of people in Africa, about their radical politics, their fantastic relationship.

'It must be so amazing,' he'd said, 'to be able to

work with your other half like that, to travel together, to do everything together, to have a real partnership'. I loved it when he talked like that, because that's what I wanted, too, and that's exactly what I saw developing between us. As soon as I managed to establish myself as a director of serious work, he and I could take off around the world to film together. In my fantasies I even had us establishing our own production company: Blake Symonds Films. Or Symonds Blake Films. Or something.

Back in the real world, I was nervous. Bertrand and Laure sounded like a lot to live up to, and I was desperate to make a good impression. I'd been trying to improve my schoolgirl French in the weeks before the trip – it would be nice to be able to hold the most basic of conversations with them. At least then they wouldn't be able to see me as the typical lazy English person who couldn't be bothered to even try speaking a foreign language (although that was precisely what I was). It would make me look so parochial.

We'd all checked in to a fairly ropey guest house just off the Boulevard St Germain. Mike, in particular, was not impressed.

'We can afford better than this,' he complained as we trudged up four flights of stairs (the lift was *hors service*) to our dingy rooms.

'We're not going to be here long,' Alex said, 'we'll just be crashing here for a few hours after the party.

Then we'll go for breakfast and get back on the train. It would be a bit ridiculous to get rooms at the Georges Cinq for a few hours' kip, wouldn't it?'

'I'm not asking for the Georges Cinq, Alex,' he replied grumpily, 'but I'd settle for clean.'

Mike may have had an annoying habit of refusing to look on the bright side, but in this case, he had a point, as we discovered when Aidan and I took a quick look around our room. The windows, which looked out onto a rather drab courtyard at the back of the building, were filthy. The carpet was threadbare, the bathroom smelled odd.

'It's not that bad,' I said, unconvincingly.

Aidan shrugged. 'Seen worse,' he said, but it wasn't an auspicious start to our trip.

Not wanting to linger too long in the hotel, the six of us dumped our bags and met downstairs in the lobby. Mike wanted to go for a drink. Alex wanted to go shopping at Galeries Lafayette. Julian and Karl fancied the Musée Rodin.

'What do you feel like doing?' I asked Aidan.

He shrugged. 'I'm easy,' he said, but he didn't seem it. Quite the opposite: uneasy summed him up perfectly. I slipped my hand into his.

'Well,' I said, consulting my map, 'why don't the arty boys go to the Musée Rodin, Alex and I will go on a brief shopping spree and we can all meet up afterwards for a drink?'

'Sounds good,' Julian said. 'Where shall we meet?'

'How about the Marais?' Karl suggested. 'Lots of good bars there.'

'Isn't that the gay bit?' Mike asked. Julian flinched, but didn't say anything.

'It's a bit out of the way,' I said diplomatically, 'given that we're going to have to come back here afterwards to change for the party.'

'Look, there's a bar on the corner there, just down the road,' Mike pointed out. 'That'll do.' We all looked over at a rather sorry-looking café tabac with a tatty red awning.

'Oh hell no,' Julian said. Mike gave a sigh of irritation. Aidan yawned.

'Buddha Bar, Place de la Concorde,' Alex said decisively. 'Look,' she went on, pointing at the map. 'It's about twenty minutes' walk from the Rodin place and five minutes' walk from Hermès. Perfect. We'll see you there at six.'

Alex, Julian, Karl and I headed off towards the metro station, leaving Aidan and Mike standing awkwardly on the pavement, unsure of what to do next. It was perfectly obvious to me that Aidan would have preferred to go to the art gallery with Jules than spend the afternoon drinking with Mike. He was being weirdly polite. It really wasn't like him.

And, as Alex and I discussed as we tried on dresses at Galeries Lafayette, it wasn't a very good idea.

'They're going to be pissed by the time we leave for

the party,' Alex said. 'God, I hope Mike's not going to start up on the cheese-eating surrender-monkey business. He's not really all that keen on the French, you know.'

'So I've gathered.'

'And what's up with Aidan, anyway? He was so quiet on the way over. Not his usual self at all.'

'He's just nervous, I think.'

'Thinks we're going to show him up in front of the great Laure and Bertrand?'

'Something like that.'

Drinks at the Buddha Bar were subdued. Thankfully, Aidan and Mike had not had too much to drink (they'd spent a couple of hours 'wandering aimlessly', according to Aidan). Karl chatted enthusiastically about the Rodin Museum; Julian was quiet. Still annoyed about the 'gay bit' comment from Mike, probably. All in all, the trip was not shaping up to be the carefree funfest I'd been hoping for.

Still, there was the main event to come, and I was delighted with my purchase from Galeries Lafayette for the purpose: a pretty sixties print dress and Mary Janes. *Très chic*, I thought. Back at the hotel, Aidan watched me getting dressed.

'You look very cute,' he said, when I was done, coming up behind me and slipping his hands around my waist. I'd been aiming for drop-dead gorgeous, but cute was okay. He kissed me on the top of the head. 'You look lovely.' That was better, only when he said it he looked sad, almost mournful.

'Are you all right, Aidan?' I asked, turning to face him, kissing his neck.

'I'm fine, Nic.' He didn't sound it.

We set off for the party. Alex looked ravishing in a very short black dress that showed the tops of her stockings when she bent over.

'You may as well not bother with a skirt at all,' Mike grumbled.

'I think she looks hot,' Julian said.

'Yeah, well, it's not you I'm worried about,' Mike replied, casting menacing glances at any passing Frenchman who looked in Alex's direction.

Julian opened his mouth to say something but Karl squeezed his hand, shaking his head almost imperceptibly. We descended into the metro in silence.

We took the train from Saint Michel-Notre Dame to Champ de Mars-Tour Eiffel, emerging into the chilly night in the shadow of the Tower itself, illuminated by thousands of white lights. The unease, the awkwardness which had settled over us all dissipated, and we stood and gawped, excited at last, thrilled by the beauty of Paris at night.

We walked along the river to the Quai de Grenelle where Laure and Bertrand docked their houseboat. As we approached we could see the lanterns strung up on the deck at the rear of the boat, we could hear the chatter of French voices in the night. I gripped Aidan's hand, my nerves all of a sudden in overdrive. Aidan led us across the gangway onto the boat; as I stepped down onto the deck, I slipped. He caught me.

'Steady on,' he said with a smile. Good start.

We descended into the cabin of the boat, a long, narrow room with a low ceiling, a fireplace at one end, low slung benches on either side, bright African prints adorning the walls.

'Christ, you can barely stand up in here,' Mike muttered, stooping to avoid smacking his head on a beam as we entered.

The cabin was hot and crowded, a thick fug of smoke hanging over the heads of the guests, most of whom seemed casually attired in jeans and tailored jackets or crisp, sheath-like dresses. By contrast I felt garish, overdressed.

'*Salut*, Aidan!' a voice called out from the crowd. A stocky, deeply tanned man with a shock of wiry dark hair emerged from the throng, holding his hands out in greeting.

'*Bonsoir*, Bertrand!' They embraced, Bertrand kissing Aidan on both cheeks.

He turned to me. 'And this is Nicole?' he asked, turning to kiss me, too. Dishevelled, unkempt and friendly, he wasn't the suave, stand-offish Frenchman I'd been expecting. I felt incredibly relieved.

The six of us lost ourselves in the party. Julian and

Karl were talking property with a couple of goatee-bearded hipsters in one corner (Paris, London or Berlin – where was the best place to buy?); Alex and I found ourselves chatting to a couple of incredibly charming French theatre actors; Mike skulked in a corner, drinking a beer. Aidan disappeared into the crowd.

It was only when I realised that I hadn't seen him for well over an hour that I decided to go looking. I weaved my way through the party guests, from one end of the boat to the other, but there was no sign of him. Back I went, all the way to front to aft. I found him outside on the deck, talking to a small, slight woman wearing jeans and a black vest with a silver chain around her neck and large silver rings on her delicate fingers. They were sharing a joint. When Aidan spotted me, he waved me over.

'Hi, Nic, come and meet Laure,' he said.

The woman turned. Her dark hair was cropped close to her head, she had enormous dark eyes and elfin features. The skin on her shoulders and breastbone was lightly freckled.

'Hello,' she said, holding out her hand. 'Nicole? It's nice to meet you.' She looked me up and down, turned to Aidan, raised an eyebrow and smiled. *'Elle est mignonne,'* she said. She's cute. My French wasn't great, but I understood that much. There was something in the way she said it I didn't like. Aidan grinned a little sheepishly and looked away. We chatted for a minute about the programme Aidan had been making about them, which was due to air in a few weeks. We talked about her next posting – there was a possibility she and her husband might go to Afghanistan, though she was desperate to avoid that, not wanting anything to do with the Americans' 'dirty war'. Then she asked me what I did for a living. I told her I was freelancing as an assistant producer, though I really wanted to direct.

'You follow in Aidan's footsteps?' she said with a laugh.

'Not exactly,' I replied, 'he was a cameraman.'

She turned to Aidan. 'And is she any good?'

Aidan looked embarrassed. My hackles were rising.

'She's great, actually.' He put his arm around my shoulders, steering me back towards the cabin. 'In fact,' he said, 'there's someone here you should meet. Simon Carver, the head of programming at Breakthrough. You remember I mentioned him before? Well, I sent him the film you made, the one on the British relatives of 9/11 victims, the *British Tragedy* thing . . .'

'Aidan!'

'Well, someone had to get it out there. You've re-edited it a hundred times, you've been dragging your heels for weeks. In any case, he was impressed. He wants to meet you.'

As we climbed back down to the cabin, I glanced over my shoulder at Laure, who was watching us leave. I caught her eye, but she didn't smile.

'She seems nice,' I lied, as I allowed Aidan to lead me back into the crowd. He didn't reply – whether he was embarrassed by her rudeness or he hadn't heard what I'd said I wasn't sure.

We found Simon Carver at the other end of the party, leaning against a long wooden table that served as the bar. Large and overweight with a face turning from pink to puce, you could have picked him out as English in this crowd from a hundred paces.

'Ah-ha!' he boomed when Aidan introduced us. 'The next Nick Broomfield, the next Michael Moore. Only *much* better-looking.' I blushed to my roots, more thanks to the Broomfield comparison than the compliment on my looks. 'Come and sit here next to me,' he said, patting the space next to his ample arse, 'and tell me what you want to work on next.'

I inched forward and leant, as lightly as I could, against the table. I wasn't sure it would bear my weight as well as his.

'Well . . .' I said, my mind immediately going blank, wishing Aidan had given me a little more warning. 'There's a short film I've been working on in my spare time. It's about the illegal sex traffic industry.'

'Spicy.'

'Not really. I volunteer at a refuge, and I've met some women who are prepared to talk. It's fairly horrific really.'

'Strictly post-watershed, eh? They attractive these women?'

I was tempted to tell him to piss off, but this was Simon Carver – head of programming at Breakthrough

Productions. He might be a misogynist arsehole, but he was an influential misogynist arsehole. Through gritted teeth, I told him about my idea.

Three-quarters of an hour later, I had my first-ever commission. A thirty-minute film, to be completed by the end of February, for which Breakthrough would provide a small budget. Carver obviously couldn't guarantee that it would show anywhere, but it was paid work, with a respectable company. It might lead on to other things, it might even lead to a proper job. This could be it! This could be my big career break.

Ridiculously excited, I went in search of Aidan to tell him the fantastic news. I found Julian first.

'You're not going to believe this!' I squeaked at him. 'I'm a director! I'm going to be a director!'

The two of us commandeered a bottle of red and toasted my imminent directorial debut.

'This is amazing, Nic! I'm so proud of you,' Julian gushed at me, downing his first glass and pouring us each another.

'Lucky for me I've got contacts,' I said.

'Oh, bullshit. You totally deserve this. The guy's seen your film and he loves it – he's not commissioning you because you know Aidan.' Julian put his arms around me, squeezed me tight and lifted me off my feet. 'This is so exciting! This is so bloody exciting!'

Light-headed, intoxicated with the wine and buoyed by Julian's genuine delight, I went once more in search

194

of Aidan. I spotted him back near the bar, talking to a small group of people, including Laure and Bertrand. I was just about to go bouncing up to him, to fling my arms around him, to thank him for sending Carver my film, for his confidence in me, when I stopped. I watched him as he talked animatedly about something, then Laure replied, and I noticed something odd. Something off. Aidan, who looks everyone in the eye, wouldn't look at her. When she spoke, he was obviously listening, but he was looking at his feet or over her head. And then I noticed, as she turned away to pour another drink for her friend, that he placed his hand in the small of her back, and I knew. She looked up at him, she smiled, and I knew. And at that moment, he saw me. He saw the look on my face, and he knew that I knew.

Fresh air. I needed fresh air. I pushed my way through the hip, hot and happening Parisians, and climbed out of the stifling cabin onto the deck, feeling as though my legs would buckle beneath me. There was no one else out there, it was almost midnight. Everyone else was below, waiting for the countdown, the kisses, the champagne. There would be none for me. There would be no Blake Symonds Films, there would be no perfect partnership. And suddenly everything became so very clear to me. It was obvious, really – how could I have been so stupid? It wasn't the miserable flat in Battersea that was making Aidan unhappy, it wasn't the constant noise of trains, the cockroaches, it wasn't even the commitment thing. He just didn't love me any more. Pure and simple. He'd fallen in love with someone else.

He found me leaning up against the railing on the deck, gulping deep breaths of cold air, biting back tears. He put his hand on my shoulder, trying to turn me to face him, but I shrugged it off. I couldn't look at him.

'Nic, I—'

'How long?'

'Nicole—'

'How long has this been going on, Aidan?'

'I didn't mean for it to happen.'

'Are you in love with her?' I asked the question, though I didn't want to hear the answer.

'We didn't mean for it to happen.'

I started to cry

'I love you,' I said, my voice husky with tears.

'I'm sorry.' He took me in his arms, pulled me away from the railing, turned me around to face him, held me tight. 'I didn't mean for it to happen. I'm so sorry, I'm so so sorry.'

I pushed him away, started up the steps to the gangway, slipped. Again. This time he didn't catch me. He tried to help me up, but I pushed him away a second time. I staggered to my feet, half blind, desperate to get away, to be anywhere else but here.

On the quai, I stopped for a second, disoriented, not sure which way I should be walking. I wasn't sure I'd find the hotel on my own. I wanted to be sick. I could feel the mix of champagne and the cheap red wine rising in my gullet. That was it, I was the drunk girl, throwing up outside at the New Year's Eve party. This was not what I'd imagined for New Year's Eve in Paris, this was not the impression I'd wanted to leave on sweet Bertrand and hateful Laure.

Laure, with her perfect skin and her skinny arms, her insouciant French style, her supercilious looks. I hated her. I hated her. I wanted to go back into the party, tell her husband, her lover, whatever the fuck he was, that she'd been cheating on him – with a man he counted as a friend. I wanted to tell him that their partnership meant nothing. But what would be the point? He probably already knew. They were probably one of those nauseating French couples who had a completely relaxed attitude to adultery, for whom sexual jealousy was an absurdity. They probably came home from their respective lovers and compared notes in bed.

I knew I wasn't getting back onto that boat, I didn't have the guts and I didn't want to give the patronising, smug bitch the satisfaction of showing her how crushed I was. I started to walk away, heading back towards to the sodding Eiffel Tower and all of a sudden all I could hear was Julian. Julian yelling at Aidan. I turned back. He was standing on the deck, with Karl at his side, Karl pulling at his arm, trying to get him to walk away, but he wouldn't. He was up in Aidan's face, shouting at him.

'This is the last fucking time, Aidan. This is the last time you break her heart. You stay away from her. Do you understand what she means to me? You break her heart; you break mine. We're done, you and me. I don't want to see you any more, not after this.'

Then Aidan was grabbing his arm, trying to say something, but Julian shouted. 'Will you fucking grow up? Will you ever grow up?'

I started to walk away again, but Julian caught up with me, grabbed me violently and pulled me into his chest. We stayed like that for a moment and then, with his arm firmly around my shoulder, he marched me away from the boat.

We walked in silence for what seemed like ages, me stumbling along beside Julian on the cobbles, him holding me up. From the apartments on the riverside and the boats on the quai we could hear the sound of people carousing, the cheers as the clock struck midnight. People greeted us as we passed, wishing us *bonne année*. I attempted to reply, Julian said nothing.

'Where are we going?' I asked him eventually. 'What about Karl? And Alex?' He stopped marching for a second, looked around.

'There,' he said, and pointed up a side street to a bar fifty yards or so up the road.

Le Rendezvous, a tiny dive stinking of stale beer and Gitanes was not a place I would have picked to celebrate the arrival of the new year. In fact, it appeared it wasn't a place anyone would have picked to celebrate the arrival of the new year, since apart from a sullen barmaid and a couple of drunks at the bar, we were the only people there. Still, I didn't care: it was warm and I could sit down. My feet were killing me.

Julian ordered a pitcher of red from the girl behind the bar. We sat in the corner and toasted the occasion.

'Happy New Year, Nic,' Julian said, clinking my glass. I burst into tears again. When I'd finished crying, and had been to the (disgusting) toilet to clean myself up, I sat back down at the table, smiled my brightest smile and said, 'Okay. I'm done. No more tears. For tonight anyway.'

Julian looked relieved, but he just slid his hand over the table and covered mine. 'You cry all you want, sweetheart. Not that he deserves your tears. He doesn't deserve anything from you. Shithead.'

'What about the others? We just left without saying anything.'

'It's okay. I told Karl we were leaving, I said that he should find Alex and they should go straight to the hotel when they were ready to leave.'

'I'm sorry, Jules . . .'

'For what?'

'Ruining your perfect *soirée sur une peniche*.'

'You didn't ruin it, Nic. Aidan did. Anyway,' he said, pouring us each another glass, 'the night isn't ruined. It's not over yet.'

I raised an eyebrow, then raised my drink.

'To us,' Julian said, clinking his glass against mine. 'You and me, Nic. We never need anything more than you and me.'

'And Alex,' I said, 'and Karl.'

'But not Mike . . .' Julian said, and we both started to giggle, and found we couldn't stop. Tears streaming down our faces, we laughed hysterically. The sulky barmaid and the drunks eyed us with disdain. We didn't care. Eventually, when we had regained our composure, Julian said, 'I love Karl, and I love Alex, but you're the most important thing in the world to me, Nic. As long as there's you and me, everything will be fine.'

The barmaid started putting chairs on tables just after three, at three-thirty she opened the door and pointed to it. We left. We walked hand in hand along the Seine, stopping to admire the Place de la Concorde on the other side of the river. Its obelisk illuminated, it looked as though it were made of gold. We walked all the way along the Quai d'Orsay (I, abandoning all pretence of dignity and self-respect, took off my shoes and walked in stocking feet), swapping New Year's resolutions as we went.

'Well, I've got my film commissioned,' I told Julian, 'so I can chalk that one off.'

'You see!' Julian said, squeezing my hand, 'in a few years' time we won't remember this New Year for *him*, we'll remember it as the start of your brilliant career.'

'Let's hope so. In the meantime, I suppose I can put finding somewhere to live as number one. Not so much a resolution as a necessity.'

'Move in with us!'

'Into your love nest? I think not.'

'Temporarily, anyway.'

Knowing I had the offer, knowing I wouldn't have to sleep another night in the flat in Battersea, made me feel a million times better.

'I resolve to try and do some more serious work,' Julian said. 'I'm tired of snapping models in their scanties. Even male models. It feels kind of soulless.'

We were walking along Quai Voltaire. We passed number nineteen, a hotel that, according to Julian's guidebook, had welcomed Oscar Wilde and Baudelaire among others. Across the river, you could just make out the pyramid of the Louvre.

'Oh my god, wouldn't you just love to live here?' Julian sighed dreamily.

'Nope, I've gone off Paris. And the French. In fact, I'm crossing number five off my list, too. I think I'll learn Italian instead.'

We turned down Boulevard Raspail, the last leg of the journey home. A car passed us, honked its horn, shouted something inaudible. God only knows what we looked like. I didn't care.

'There's another resolution you need to make,' Julian said, dropping my hand and putting his arm around me instead. He pulled me closer so that my head rested on his shoulder.

'I know. I'm done with him now. I won't see him any more, won't even speak to him. He's out of my life now.'

'Mine too.'

'You can't cut him off, he's your cousin. Plus, you love him, and he's been good to you.'

'I don't care, Nic. You mean more to me than he ever will.'

We slept for a few hours in Julian's room, me sandwiched in between the two boys. I couldn't face going back to my room, couldn't bear to hear his excuses, his self-justifications. Couldn't bear his pity. I needn't have worried, though. When I woke, just after nine, and went back to my room, I discovered that the bed was still made, it hadn't been slept in, and Aidan's things were gone.

Chapter Eleven

28 December 2011

I hit delete, too late.

'I didn't know you two were talking these days,' Dom says, moving past me into the room. He reaches for the bottle of Scotch on the kitchen counter. It's four o'clock in the afternoon. He pours himself a glass, downs it in one, pours another. 'There's just so much I don't know, isn't there, Nicole?'

He puts the drink down and turns to face me, his arms folded across his chest, a look of resignation on his face. Here we go again.

'If we're going to go over that old ground, you'd better pour me one of those, too,' I say, closing my laptop. He doesn't move. 'But before we get started, can I just tell you that I'm *not* talking to Aidan? He rang me, a couple of times, he left messages, something about a job. I haven't rung him back—'

'But it has been *lovely* to hear his voice . . .' Dom's voice drips sarcasm.

'It has. He's an old friend.'

'Ha!'

'He is, Dominic,' I shout, getting to my feet. Mick, who's been sleeping under the table, lets out a little whine and retreats to the laundry room. He hates it when I raise my voice. I pour myself a drink – if Dom's going to be like this, I'm going to need it. I continue, more calmly: 'I know there's been other stuff between us, but I've known him half my life, more than half my life. And he's—'

'Julian's cousin, yes, I know. He's the only person who could possibly understand how you feel. Unless, of course, you count me. Unless you count Alex . . .'

'Oh right, you can say her name now can you?' Silence. 'And you *don't* understand how I feel, and neither did she.'

Dom sits down at the other end of the kitchen table.

'You know what, Nic? It doesn't really bother me that you're talking to Aidan. It bothers me that you didn't tell me he'd been in touch. It bothers me that you couldn't talk to me about your dad being ill before running away to see him. This is supposed to be a marriage, a partnership. We're supposed to be on the same side. I thought – after everything – that we'd agreed that we would talk to each other, that we wouldn't keep secrets.'

I gulp down my Scotch, it burns in my chest. 'Okay,' I tell him. 'Fine. You want honesty? I can do honesty.' I rattle off the facts: 'Aidan rang me, he left a message on my phone. He's running a production company in New York now, he has a project he thinks would be perfect for me. It's a film about the role of women in the Libyan uprising. He doesn't have a director because the person who was supposed to do it is having a nervous breakdown or something. He needs someone to start in January. And I want to do it.' Dom says nothing, just raises his eyebrows and passes a hand over his mouth. 'Because I hate doing what I do now, Dom. I *hate* it. It's pointless, it's trash, I hate it.'

'So you want to go running off to Libya?'

'Oh, I'm not finished,' I say. The alcohol is burning in my belly now, it feels like courage. 'Since we're being honest, I should tell you that I've been talking to Alex. Well, emailing Alex. For months now. She's supposed to be getting married again. Only the guy she's with is cheating on her. She wanted my advice. Knowing, of course, that I have some experience in that area.' He breathes in sharply; that punch landed. I've hurt him. It doesn't feel good, it feels awful. I can't believe we're doing this, the day before we're due to go on holiday.

'I'm sorry,' I mutter, and leave the room. We retreat, wounded, to our respective corners, him to his study, me to mine.

Later, he calls up to me. 'I'm taking the dogs out. You want to come?'

An olive branch.

It's dark outside, so we don't go onto the common. We walk along the road up towards Wimbledon Village, the dogs on leads. I take Marianne, he takes Mick. Dom takes my hand, he sings to me: 'You can't always get what you want.' An old joke, but it seems to have resonance now.

'Do you really want to go off around the world again?' he asks me. 'Staying in fleapits, getting jabs, popping malaria pills, getting ill all the time, getting shot at all the time, feeling afraid . . . Do you honestly want to go back to all that?'

'This is an opportunity, Dom. To do something worthwhile again. And to be honest, I feel stifled here. I need to get out there again.'

'I didn't know I stifled you.'

'You don't,' I say, squeezing his hand tighter. '*You* don't stifle me, I just . . . feel stifled.' Why can't I explain this to him?

'In any case, you can do worthwhile stuff here. You don't have to go to Libya to film something real. There are plenty of awful, gritty, hard-hitting stories right here in good old Blighty, you know? There's no reason you have to work on the kind of crap . . . on the kind of stuff you've been doing for the past few years.'

I ignore the slur on my work. It's a fair comment. 'I know that, Dom, but I've got the commission for this job, and it's with a really good production house. That's a big deal. I don't have the contacts I once did.

The industry has completely changed over the past few years, everyone I knew has moved on . . .'

We reach the end of the high street and turn right, it's a mini-circuit we do when we've left it too late to take the dogs on a proper walk. Dom lets go of my hand and walks on ahead.

'When did he ask you?' he calls back over his shoulder. 'When did Aidan offer you the job?'

'A couple of weeks ago.'

'Why didn't you say anything?'

'Because I wasn't sure what I wanted to do.'

'And you didn't think I'd be able to help you make a decision?'

'Not really, no. Not when it comes to this. Not when it comes to him. And not when it comes to the question of me spending time elsewhere.'

We complete the rest of the walk in silence. When we get home, I feed the dogs, wash my hands, open the fridge and stare mournfully at the leftovers. I really can't justify getting takeout again. Behind me, Dom is opening a bottle of red wine.

'I'm not sure all this alcohol is going to help us sort this out, Dom,' I say, trying to sound jokey.

'Did you honestly think we were going to get anything sorted out? Because I thought you were just going to do whatever you wanted to do, having made the decision yourself, without discussing it with me.'

I feel like I've gone back in time. It's two years ago, and we're going round and round in circles. He's hurt and angry because I won't open up to him, won't tell him exactly how I'm feeling; I'm frustrated because I don't want to have to explain everything. He's my husband, he should get me – I shouldn't have to spell everything out.

I take the bottle from him and pour myself a glass of wine.

'What do you want for dinner?' I ask him. 'Shall we eat the rest of this bloody turkey or shall we give it to the dogs?'

'Turkey curry?' he says, the ghost of a smile playing on his lips. I reach over to the spice rack and lob him a jar of ground turmeric.

We chop vegetables in companionable silence. I'm flooded with relief; the argument is over. I shouldn't have told him I felt stifled here, even if it's true. He's right, I don't need Aidan to kick-start my career; there's no reason I can't start over all by myself, in London. It's just the thought of it: heading off on my own again, into the unknown, a small bag packed, a cameraman at my side, not really knowing what's going to happen or how things will turn out. It's intoxicating.

'What are you smiling about?' Dom asks me, tossing the remainders of the turkey, cut into chunks, into the pan.

'Nothing,' I say, regretting it the moment the words leave my lips. Dom raises his eyes heavenward.

'Why can't you just say it? Just tell me?'

'All right, I was thinking about work. About how much I'd like to get my career back on track. That's all. I wasn't thinking about Aidan.'

'I didn't say you were.' He picks up the pan, jiggers it about, coating the turkey in spicy, creamy goo. There's a long, dangerous silence. This argument is not over. I was an idiot to think it was over. Dom takes a sip of wine, he takes a deep breath. Here we go.

Round two.

'What about the baby?'

'Dom . . .'

'You said you wanted to try.'

Not exactly true, this. He said he wanted to try and I said all right, I'd stop taking the pill. Only I haven't. Not yet. But I don't correct him.

'I did, I do. But I'm thirty-four, Dominic. There's plenty of time.'

'We don't know that . . .'

'Well, no, of course. We don't *know* anything. But there's no reason to think we'll have trouble. We're both healthy, we're not overweight – not by much, anyway, we don't drink too much, we don't smoke—'

He snorts.

'Oh, for god's sake. One cigarette every now and again . . .'

'Every now and again? There was half a pack in the glove box when I took your car in to be serviced before Christmas. It was gone when I looked this afternoon.'

'Oh for fuck's sake!' I throw the knife I've been chopping with into the sink. The dogs scarper. I storm out of the room, then turn around and storm back in. 'I can't believe you! You're counting my fucking cigarettes now!'

'Stop swearing at me.'

'Oh, god! Don't smoke, don't swear, don't talk to your friends . . . I was stressed, all right? I'd just found out that my father has cancer . . .'

'Stop using that, Nicole. It's ugly.' He's right, and I feel ashamed. 'In any case, I would have thought that finding out your father had cancer would be a very good reason not to smoke.' He takes another deep breath, reaches over to me and takes my hand in his. 'Do you want to have a baby, Nic?'

'I'm not sure.'

'Not sure about now? Or not sure at all?'

'I don't know.' I really don't know. I know that I don't want to have a baby right now, I just don't feel that urge that other women do. Does that mean I'll never want to have one? Or is it worse than that? Is it just that I don't want to have a baby with Dom?

'We don't have to decide now, Dominic. There's plenty of time.'

'Is there?' He looks at me sadly, then turns away. 'I would have thought you of all people would know that no one ever has as much time as they think they do.'

My mobile rings. Saved by the bell. It's Mum.

'Hola!' she greets me. '¿Cómo estás?'

'Well, hello. How was Costa Rica?'

'Wonderful, darling. Wish you and Dom could have come. It was just lovely. Fantastic weather, gorgeous beaches . . . I missed you.'

I take the phone into the living room and pace up and down while we chat, about Christmas, her holiday, Charles's dodgy knees. 'We climbed the Arenal volcano on our last day. Bad idea. I thought we were going to have to get a stretcher to get him down.'

Eventually, once the small talk and holiday chatter run out, I know I'm going to have to tell her.

'Anyway, darling, I should go. Charles has made shepherd's pie.'

'Okay. Mum . . .'

'Is everything all right, darling? You sound . . . I don't know. A bit sad.'

'I'm fine, Mum. I'll give you a call soon.'

I end the call and sit down on the sofa. Dom comes and sits next to me, and places his arm around my shoulders. 'You can tell her tomorrow,' he says.

We eat dinner in the living room, watching the news. A flood here, a train crash there. Kate and Wills are opening something, Lindsay Lohan back in rehab. It blurs before my eyes, I can't concentrate on anything.

'I think I'll go upstairs and do some work,' I say to him, getting to my feet and picking up the plates. 'That was delicious, actually, thank you. Much better curried than roasted.'

'I'm a better cook than my mother.'

'You are.' I kiss him on the forehead, go into the kitchen and fetch my laptop.

Upstairs, sitting on our bed, I log into my Hotmail account, discard the message I'd been composing to Aidan, and email Alex instead.

Do you regret not having a baby?

With Mike? No. But I do want one. Though with the way things are going at the moment I'm starting to think it's going to be just me and the turkey baster. Why? Something to tell me? Omfg, are you pregnant?

No. But Dom wants us to try. He doesn't want to wait any more. He thinks I stopped taking the pill two months ago.

Nicole, you can't lie about stuff like that.

Annoyed, I ignore her last message and open a new browser window. I go to the BBC news page and read about the news I just watched on television. I still don't take it in. I hate it when Alex gets self-righteous. She has no right to come over all self-righteous with me. Still, once I'm done with the news, I check my messages again and read her latest:

Nicole? Have you gone away again? Don't be pissed off. If you don't want a baby right now, you just have to tell him.

Problem is I don't know what I want.

I wish we could talk properly. I wish you would let me come and see you.

I should just tell her. I'm going to be in New York tomorrow. I'll meet you at the Plaza, for cocktails. But I don't.

Have to go, Alex. Talk soon.

I open my resolutions file, yet again.

1. ~~Get in touch with Aidan re job offer~~ ~~Talk to old BBC contacts about work~~ ~~Email Aidan to decline job offer – ask that he no longer calls~~ Ignore Aidan, talk to old BBC contacts about work
2. Lose half a stone
3. ~~Stop taking the pill – or at least admit to Dom that I'm still taking it~~ Tell Dom I'm still on the pill and am not ready for a baby
4. ~~Repaint the kitchen~~ Read more! Read everything on 2011 Booker shortlist. And 2012 shortlist. When it comes out.
5. ~~Sort out things with Dad~~ Make an effort to see Dad regularly – monthly dinners?

I hear Dom coming up the stairs, so I close the file, close my Hotmail account and click on the file containing my notes from the meeting with Annie. Have I always been so secretive? Dom pops his head around the door.

'You want tea, love?'

'I'm all right, cheers,' I reply, picking up the half-full wine glass which is on the bedside table.

'You going to pack tonight?'

'I was thinking of leaving it until the morning,' I say.

'We need to be at the airport at nine, Nic. That means leaving here at seven-thirty.'

'Eight.'

'Seven-thirty.'

'Geez, all right then.'

I pull a chair over to the wardrobe and climb on top of it in order to get the suitcases from the top shelf. As I pull my case out, I manage to shift one of the boxes that we packed back into the cupboard on Boxing Day. It comes crashing to the ground, its contents spilling out onto the floor. As I clamber down to pick everything up, Dom comes running into the room.

'Are you okay?'

'Fine, just clumsy.'

He gives me a hand collecting together the papers and photographs. Once we're done, I notice a little strip of paper under the chair I'd been using as a stepladder. Dom and I both go to pick it up at once, we bang our heads together, we start laughing. He gets to the bit of paper first. It's the photo strip, the one I noticed on Boxing Day. Me, Julian and Alex in 1999. We got it done at Aldgate East Station, a few days after we moved into the flat off Brick Lane.

'That's weird,' Dom says, placing the strip back into the box.

'Don't,' I say, 'don't put it away.' I take it from him and put it in my bedside table drawer.

'How cold is it in New York, have you checked?' Dom asks me as he pulls his own suitcase out of the wardrobe.

'The BBC claims that it's quite mild for this time of year – around seven or eight degrees, I think. But their weather forecasts are rubbish, so who knows?'

'You could always ask someone who lives there. You know, Karl, or maybe . . . I don't know . . . Alex?' Dom says, giving me a half-smile. I smile back, but I don't say anything. 'Are you going to see her?' he asks. 'Will she be at the party?'

'No, Karl didn't invite her.'

'But if you've forgiven her, Nic, why don't you let him know? You could see each other again. It's been . . . such a long time.'

'Two years. And I haven't forgiven her, Dominic. I just can't live without her. I can't live without them both.'

Chapter Twelve

New Year's Eve 2003
London

Resolutions:
1. Pitch three-part series on refugees to BBC
2. Organise killer hen-do for Alex
3. Lose half a stone
4. Organise North Korea research trip
5. Try a relationship with a grown-up. You are too old for bad boys on bikes.

Talking of being grown up, I was *'cordially invited'*, the embossed white card read, *'To a housewarming/New Year's Eve Party at Number Six, Tabard Wharf, the brand-new and exclusive digs of Messrs Karl Schnelle and Julian Symonds. Drinks from 6.30.'*

It was very grown up. Very civilised. Not exactly rock and roll. Particularly as there were only six of us in attendance: the hosts; Mike and Alex; me and my new boyfriend, Dominic.

'I think we could do with a nice, calm New Year's Eve,' Julian said to me when I asked him when we'd become so incredibly boring. 'Plus, Alex and Mike are skiing in Verbier until the thirtieth, so they're going to be all partied out. And you must be knackered, too.' It was true, I'd only just returned from filming in Russia. 'Plus, I'm off on the third, so . . .'

'Off where?'

'I'll tell you on the night.'

Julian and Karl, who had been renting a flat together in Camberwell for a couple of years, had finally taken the next step. They had made the big commitment. They had got a mortgage. And it must have been a pretty big commitment, because they used it to buy a warehouse conversion just around the corner from Borough Market with a glimpse, just a sliver of a glimpse, of the Thames. It was the *dernier cri* in urban industrial chic. They even had a lift.

'It's like living in Manhattan,' Alex said as they welcomed us into the flat.

'That's the idea,' Karl replied. 'Since I can't persuade him to move to New York, I can at least pretend.' Karl had been agitating for a move to Manhattan for ages; but Julian, who had always dreamed about New York as a teenager, was refusing to live in a country run by George Bush.

'Because Tony Blair is so much better?' Karl argued.

We were sitting on reproduction Corbusier sofas in the middle of Julian and Karl's vast open-plan living

218

area drinking champagne ('It's not a living room,' Julian told me with a wry little smile. 'It's a living space. There are no rooms in this apartment. Oh no. There are spaces.') Dom, who I'd only been seeing for a couple of months, perched on the edge of the sofa next to me, his back ramrod straight. Alex watched him with an amused expression on her face, every now and again she and Julian exchanged a look. I knew what they were thinking. Well, I could imagine what they were thinking, anyway. They were sizing up the new boy, taking in his sandy blond hair and fair skin, checking out the neatly pressed chinos and the jumper from The Gap (fashion wasn't really Dom's thing), judging his diffident manner, comparing and contrasting. At least that's what was going on in my head.

'So Jules,' I said trying to get them to stop smirking at each other, 'where are you off to? You said you were going somewhere in a couple of days.'

'Oh yes, where is it this time? Paris? Milan? The Bahamas?' Alex asked.

'Monrovia, actually,' Julian replied.

Alex looked at him blankly.

'It's in China,' Mike told her, patting her on the knee.

'Not Mongolia, Monrovia.' Now Mike looked blank. 'Liberia. West Africa.'

'Liberia?' I repeated, stunned. Julian was going to *Liberia*? Julian couldn't possibly go to Liberia.

'You're doing a fashion shoot in Liberia?' Dom

219

asked, incredulous. 'Isn't that a bit . . . insensitive? I mean, the war's barely over.'

'It's not a fashion shoot,' Julian said with a smile. 'I'm doing a reportage piece for *Time*. I've wanted to move out of fashion for ages. I've done some photojournalism here – I got a really good response to the shots I did on the anti-war demo.'

'Those were great,' Alex conceded, 'but still – *Liberia*? Not Paris? Not Milan? Are you sure? I just don't think I can picture it . . .'

'He'll do great,' Karl said, putting an arm around his boyfriend's shoulders. Julian gave him a peck on the cheek, then looked over at me, smiling reassuringly.

'I think I'll be all right,' he said. 'I've been wanting to do something more challenging for ages, wanting to stretch myself . . .'

I smiled thinly at him. 'Well, Liberia's certainly a stretch,' I said.

Karl went into the kitchen 'space' to finish preparing the starter (Jerusalem artichokes, porcini mushrooms and parmesan 'hats', apparently). I volunteered to help. He did a brief double take, but then smiled and thanked me.

'You're worried about him,' he said to me once we were out of earshot of the others.

'Aren't you?'

'Yes, but this is what he wants to do, Nicole. Do you not think he worries about you all the time? A

220

woman, running around filming people traffickers and drug-crazed boy soldiers?'

'But I'm tougher than he is,' I said. 'Plus, I don't think he really does worry. He's never said so.'

Karl, who was shaving porcini mushrooms into wafer-thin slices with a mandolin, stopped and looked up at me, an expression of disbelief on his face.

'You think because he never says anything he doesn't worry? He never says anything because he doesn't want to upset you, he doesn't want to make you feel bad. He's proud of you. He admires you. He supports you.' He went back to his mandolin and his mushrooms and – without looking at me – added: 'You might want to do the same.'

Chastened, I returned to the living space, giving Julian a kiss on the top of the head as I reclaimed my seat.

'Congratulations, Jules,' I said, and he beamed up at me.

'Thanks, Nic. I'm really excited about it. You know I've been wanting to do something like this for ages and this opportunity . . . well, it just came up.' There was something odd about the way he said this, something in his expression which gave me pause, but I didn't have time to say anything. 'You've just been doing so well,' he said, squeezing my hand, 'and I'm jealous! I want some of that. I want to do be doing something more . . . meaningful. You know?'

It was true that I had been enjoying a pretty stellar year or two. After the sex trafficking film I'd made for

Simon Carver's firm, I'd lucked out on *Boys' Club*, an award-winning piece on sexism in the workplace, partly based on personal experience. After that, the work just kept on coming. I'd been to Uganda to produce a film on the child soldiers of the Lord's Resistance Army, I'd made an Unreported World feature on the futility of the war on drugs, and most recently I'd been in Russia researching a film on Chechen separatists. It had been an exhausting, exhilarating, mind-blowing time; I'd barely stopped to catch my breath.

'So, what's the focus of your Liberia story?' Dom was asking Julian. 'Do you have a specific idea in mind, or do you just go out there and see what happens? I'm not really sure how this kind of thing works.'

'There is a specific angle,' Julian said.

'Which is?' Alex prompted.

Julian looked shifty for a moment. 'I'm going to visit a couple of centres which are helping kids who've been traumatised by the war.'

'That sounds interesting. Is that UNICEF or World Health?' Dom asked.

'It's uh. . . . with MSF,' Julian said, swallowing the last part of the sentence so that we could barely hear him.

'With whom, sorry?' Dom asked.

'MSF,' Julian said again. He was looking at his shoes. So that's why he looked shifty before.

'MSF?' Mike asked. 'What's that?'

'Médecins Sans Frontières,' I said, getting to my feet. 'It's a French medical charity.'

I stood there for a second, not knowing what to do. I wanted to get away from everyone, but I couldn't leave the room, since there was no room to leave. I couldn't just go and stand in the corner, so in the end I just went to the loo and sat in there for a while, feeling betrayed.

After about five minutes, there was a soft knock at the door

'It's occupied,' I said.

'Nic, please come out.' Julian.

'Go away,' I said. I was behaving like a child. I unlocked the door.

'Come on,' he said, and took my hand. He led me out of the flat, to the end of the corridor and out onto a fire escape. There was a narrow, iron spiral staircase that led up to the roof.

'Christ, it really is like New York,' I said, clinging onto the guard rail, trying not to look down.

Julian and Karl had already colonised their corner of the roof, cordoning it off with pot plants and placing a couple of deckchairs in the centre. He and I sat down, side by side, looking out towards the river. It was a mild night for December, the clouds low and the smell of rain in the air.

'It's amazing up here when it's clear,' Julian told me. 'You can see the top of the Eye, Canary Wharf . . . Not tonight, though.' He lit a cigarette. 'It's not with her,' he said eventually. 'She doesn't even work for MSF any more.'

'It doesn't matter,' I said. 'I was being childish. It's not like it matters in the grand scheme of things, does it?'

'It matters to me. It was Bertrand who organised access for me. I saw him a couple of months ago when he was over in London. Poor fucker, he's a shadow of his former self. Don't think he's over it . . .'

'Sorry to hear that.' I took the cigarette from Julian's hand, took a drag and handed it back to him. 'How are the happy couple, anyway? You heard from him?' I couldn't stop myself from asking the question even though I didn't want to know the answer.

'Laure left him for some Spanish bloke.' I felt a surge of adrenalin, an ignoble rush of delight.

'When? Why didn't you tell me? Have you seen him?'

Julian sighed and flicked the cigarette butt over the edge of the building.

'Because it's been two years, Nic, and I really hoped that you no longer cared.'

'I don't care.'

'Of course you don't.' He draped an arm around my shoulders and pulled me closer, kissed me on the head. 'I saw him two months ago, when my grandmother died. He was at the funeral. I don't know when they split up, he didn't seem to want to talk about it.' He finished his cigarette and crushed the butt beneath his foot. 'Shall we go back down? Your boyfriend will be wondering where you've got to.'

* * *

224

We climbed back down the fire escape and made our way to the dining space where Karl was serving the starter. Dom took my hand and kissed me on the cheek.

'Everything all right?' he asked.

'Everything's fine,' I replied. He pulled out a chair for me to sit down. I could feel Alex and Julian's eyes on us again.

'Remind me how you two met?' Alex said to Dom.

Dom looked sheepish. 'I was a fan,' he said, giving me a shy smile. 'I'd watched that Channel 4 programme Nic made last year, the *Boys' Club* one. Anyway, I thought it was very interesting – it's kind of my field, employment issues, that kind of thing – and then I saw an interview with her in the *Independent* and they had this picture . . .'

Julian started laughing 'Oh god, the one where she's wearing that . . . er. . . . rather fitted top?'

'Oh shut up,' I said, giving him a kick under the table. I could feel the colour rising to my cheeks.

'That's the one,' Dom said. 'I thought she was gorgeous. And would you believe it, a couple of weeks later I'm at a dinner party thrown by an old mate from college, and there she is. He'd been a consultant on the programme.'

'So it was fate,' Alex said with a smile.

'I don't know about that,' Dom replied, 'but the moment I saw her, I was finished. Love at first sight.'

Alex and Julian laughed, Karl whistled, Mike stifled a yawn. I went from a gentle blush to puce.

*   *   *

After dinner, in the kitchen space I found Alex and Julian in the corner, gossiping in hushed tones. They fell silent as I approached. Alex handed me a glass of champagne.

'So, rebound man seems nice,' she said with a cheeky grin.

'He's not the rebound man!' Julian said, feigning outrage. 'Didn't you hear? It was love at first sight!'

They both giggled, peering through an archway to get another look at Dom, who was attempting to engage Mike in conversation. At just five foot eight and slight of build, he looked almost childlike, dwarfed by Mike's six foot something rugby player's frame.

'Honestly,' Alex said, 'he's *so* sweet.'

I rolled my eyes at them. 'He is sweet, and he is not a rebound man. It's been two years since I split up with Aidan.'

'And since then you've had how many relationships?' Julian asked. 'Oh, right, that would be none at all.'

'Bollocks!' I said, a little too loudly. Mike and Dom looked up from the table where they were having a rather stilted conversation about the prospects for Warwickshire in the county cricket championship. 'There was Heath . . .' I whispered.

'I said relationship, not one-night stand.' Julian corrected me.

'. . . and Peter . . .'

'. . . whom we never met. I'm still not convinced he actually existed,' Alex said.

'What about Clive?'

The two of them burst out laughing.

'Oh my god, Clive!' Alex exclaimed, snorting with mirth. I knew I shouldn't have mentioned Clive. 'Clive with the slip-on shoes? He was brilliant. Wasn't he a trainspotter?'

'A planespotter, actually. It's entirely different.'

'Didn't he take you to Heathrow for your first date?'

'It was the Renaissance Hotel, actually. In Hounslow. It's one of the *premier* plane-spotting hotels in Europe.'

Alex and Julian clung to each other, helpless with mirth.

'All right, all right,' I said, stifling my own giggles. 'I'll admit, Clive was a bit of a low point. And okay, I haven't had any real relationships since Aidan. But that does not make Dom a rebound man. He's kind, funny and attractive. He's a grown-up.'

Alex yawned.

'Don't be rude about him, Alex. You might just be looking at my future husband in there.'

'Yeah, right,' she said with a wry smile. She grabbed another bottle of champagne from the fridge and sauntered off into the living space, singing 'Inbetweener' as she went.

'He's not a prince, he's not a king, he's not a work of art or anything . . .'

'Shut up, Alex,' I warned her, beaming at Dom who was now discussing Gus Van Sant's latest film with Karl. Mike was reading text messages on his phone.

Mike was a bit of a mystery to us all. It was true that Alex and I had never had similar taste in men, but in the past at least I'd understood the attraction. However, with Mike it was a source of persistent amazement to me – and to Julian – that he was still around. He had his good points, of course. He was good-looking, he had lots of money, he drove a very nice car, he lived in a flat in Chelsea. I could see how he'd be attractive for a brief fling, but more than that . . . I just didn't get it.

Alex knew I didn't get it, and we'd agreed to disagree on the subject.

'He treats me well, Nic. He'd do anything for me,' she told me. I believed her: he did treat her well, he bought her great presents, he paid for expensive holidays like the skiing trip they'd just been on to Verbier. But I never saw them laughing together. Plus, I couldn't bear the way he felt it necessary to slap her on the arse every time she walked past him. Or the fact that he read the *Daily Mail*, and voted Tory and was forever complaining about 'bloody immigrants' despite the fact that he was about to marry one. The wedding was to take place in April and I was maid of honour. So I just had to grin and bear it.

I had to grin and bear the wedding chatter, too. Over dessert we'd covered dates for the final three (three!) fittings for my bridesmaid's dress ('Just in case you put on weight,' Alex explained. 'Or lose it,' she added diplomatically); the choice of vehicle to carry Alex to the church ('Classic Roller or something more sporty? Or should I just go full-on princess and get a horse-drawn carriage?'); and had a lively debate on the pros and cons of a tian of prawn and crab versus classic smoked salmon as a starter. Now she'd moved onto speeches.

'I think Nicole should make a speech,' she announced, as I choked on my wine.

'No . . .' I spluttered. 'I really don't think that's a great idea.'

'Women don't make speeches,' Mike said. 'It's not traditional. And women are never very funny, are they? How many great comediennes do you know?'

'I think they're just called comedians now,' Julian said. Mike harrumphed.

'Mike's absolutely right,' I said, to looks of amazement from Julian and Karl. 'Women should be seen and not heard. They've no place giving speeches at weddings.'

'You're just chicken,' Alex muttered.

'I'm a traditionalist,' I retorted, prompting disbelieving laughter all round. 'But I tell you what, if you move the wedding to Cape Town, rather than Sussex, I'd be prepared to cast aside my conservatism and write a few lines . . .'

'Exactly!' Julian said. 'I can't believe you're getting married in some cutesy English village rather than giving us an excuse to go on holiday to South Africa.'

'Yes, well,' Mike said gruffly, getting to his feet, 'not everything about this wedding revolves around Alex's friends.' And with that he headed off in the direction of the bathroom.

Alex pulled a face. 'He's a bit touchy about the whole Sussex thing. *Everyone's* been complaining that we're not going to South Africa. I think he's feeling a bit hurt.'

'It's understandable,' Karl said diplomatically. 'If I were going to get married, I'd probably want to do it in my home town.'

'If you were to get married?' Julian asked him with a smile. 'Not very likely, is it?'

'Well, maybe not a full church wedding, but they are going to allow civil partnerships here shortly, aren't they? So why not?'

Julian sighed dramatically. 'Christ, I always thought one of the great things about being gay is that you don't have to get married. Why would we want to pretend to be heterosexual? It's a horrible way to live. Homos have much more fun.'

Alex and I exchanged a familiar glance: a look of affection, tinged with just a touch of envy. We'd spoken about Karl and Julian's perfect relationship before. It couldn't be improved upon. They never tired of each other; they never bickered. They backed up each other. They adored each other. And, so Julian told me, they had great sex together. They were absolutely right for each other. It was incredibly annoying.

* * *

At a few minutes to midnight, Karl opened yet another bottle of champagne, poured us each a glass and tinged his flute with a fork.

'Right. Since we're not allowed to share our resolutions because that's Julian and Nicole's thing and they're completely weird about sharing their little ritual, despite the fact that *everyone on the planet does it*, I think that to ring in the New Year we should all say something we're grateful for.'

'Like Thanksgiving?' Mike suggested.

'Exactly.'

'I'll go first then,' Mike said, getting to his feet. He cleared his throat and raised his glass, turning to face Alex. 'It's pretty simple, really. And pretty obvious. I'm thankful that the most beautiful girl in the world has agreed to marry me.' Alex smiled coyly and fluttered her lashes at him 'And the thing is, the thing people don't realise, is that her beauty isn't even the best of her. She's generous and kind, she's going to be a great mum . . .' There was a little 'oooh' at this point from Julian and Karl. 'And I love her, and I'm so happy we're going to be together. That's it.'

And in that moment I caught a glimpse, as I occasionally did, of how lovely Mike was with her, and of how much he loved her, and I chastised myself, yet again, for allowing my liberal feminista sensibilities to prevent me from embracing my friend's husband-to-be.

Alex, wiping a tear from her eye, got to her feet next. 'Can I be grateful for two things?' she asked.

'She's so greedy,' Julian tutted.

She giggled. 'I'll be brief. Number one, I'm thankful for my amazing husband to be . . .' she held out her hand to him and he kissed it, '. . . and number two, I'm thankful for my bloody amazing job!' Alex had just been promoted to the head of marketing at Scribe, the little publishing house where she worked, quite an achievement for a twenty-six-year-old. 'I really am a very lucky girl.'

Julian was next to his feet. 'I could go on about new opportunities and new horizons and of course I'm thankful for that, but obviously the two things in the whole world I am most thankful for are the love of my life, who I found three years ago today . . .' he stopped to give Karl a kiss, '. . . and the best friend I'll ever have, who I found thirteen years ago today. Lucky for some,' he said, raising a glass to me.

Karl went next. 'Well, I know I'm supposed to say I'm thankful for Jules because we're all being all lovey dovey and things, but really right now I'm most thankful for my fabulous new apartment,' he said with a grin. Everyone gave a little cheer. 'And of course for the fact that I sold four paintings this year, which is four more than I sold last year.'

There was a little round of applause and then silence fell as Dom got to his feet, blushing before he even started speaking.

'Dom shouldn't have to do this,' I objected, 'he doesn't even know you all.'

232

'Oh yes he should!' came the chorus from the rest of them.

'I'm grateful for the opportunity to spend the evening with you all,' Dom said diplomatically, 'and of course I'm grateful to have met Nicole. And for Radiohead. *Hail to the Thief* is a fucking work of genius.'

I breathed a sigh of relief as he sat down. I wasn't quite ready for another declaration of love.

And then it was my turn. 'Well,' I said, feeling faintly ridiculous as I got to my feet, 'I'm thankful for us. For all of us. It feels like . . . things are coming together for us all. We have good jobs, we have great lovers, some of us have fabulous apartments . . . so I think that's plenty to be thankful for. And now I think it's almost midnight so I think we should all drink our champagne and snog and stop being so fucking cheesy!'

And with that we counted down to midnight, and more champagne corks popped, and cheesy or not I did feel like things were coming together for us, for Julian, Alex and me. And for the tiniest fraction of a second that made me nervous. And then Dom kissed me and I forgot all about my nerves and realised that for the first time in ages I didn't really have anything to worry about.

After midnight, Julian grabbed a blanket from the mezzanine that served as the bedroom space, and he and I snuck away, back up to the roof, to exchange resolutions.

We sat side by side on the deckchairs, the blanket draped over our knees.

'Well,' Julian said, 'obviously I'm going to quit smoking.'

'And I'm going to lose half a stone.'

'I'm going to start keeping a journal.'

'Oh a *journal*. Not just a diary.'

'A journal, darling. To form the basis of my memoirs.'

'Excellent. And I am finally going to get my refugee pitch ready for the BBC.'

'That's brilliant, Nic, it's about time.'

There was a noise behind us, a clattering, as someone else climbed up the fire escape. Then there was a thud, the sound of someone falling, followed by soft cursing.

'Jules? You up here?'

My stomach did a little flip. I'd know those soft Glaswegian tones anywhere.

'Julian?' the voice called out again.

'Oh shit,' Julian said, getting to his feet. 'I'm over here.'

I turned around and saw Aidan swaying through the darkness, a hip flask clutched in his hand.

'Happy New Year,' he said when he saw us, raising the flask to his lips, before breaking into a tuneless version of 'Auld Lang Syne'.

Even in the firelight, I could see he didn't look good. Paler, thinner, haggard almost. Even more dissolute than usual. He smiled at me.

'Hello, Nic,' he said. 'You look pretty. Don't I get a kiss?'

'I'm going back down,' I said to Julian. I climbed over the pot plants and pulled my arm away when Aidan tried to grab hold of me as I went past.

'You never wrote back!' He called out after me. 'You could have at least replied.'

After Paris, I'd seen him only once, when I went back to the flat on Queenstown Road to pick up my stuff. He tried to talk to me then, but I refused, I ignored him as best as I could and when he wouldn't let me be, when he insisted that we talk, I screamed at him and shoved him out the door. A couple of months later he wrote to me, telling me how sorry he was, how much he'd loved me, how – as he'd told me on the boat that night – he'd never meant to fall for someone else, he'd never meant to hurt me. He told me how I'd always hold a special place in his heart. That made me gag; he could at least have tried to avoid cliché. I never wrote back to him. I didn't think he deserved it. I kept his letter though, and every now and again, when I was feeling low or had had too much to drink, I got it out, just to torture myself. Like picking at a scab, I wouldn't let the wound heal.

Downstairs, Karl was hovering near the front door looking nervous.

'I didn't know what to do,' he said to me when he saw me. 'I'm sorry, Nicole, but I couldn't exactly tell him Julian wasn't here . . .'

'It's okay,' I said, giving him a hug. 'He's just a bit pissed. I'm sure he'll leave in a bit.' Dom was sitting on the sofa, looking at me questioningly. I shook my head as I approached.

'It's nothing,' I said, but my hands were shaking as I picked up my glass of wine. I looked over at Alex who mouthed, 'Okay?' at me.

There was a clattering from outside, they were coming back down.

'I'll put some music on, shall I?' Karl said brightly, and everyone agreed, a little too enthusiastically. Outside, in the hallway, I could hear Julian trying to persuade Aidan to leave.

'We'll talk tomorrow, okay? Later today, whatever.'

'But I want to see your new gaff . . .'

'Not now, Aidan. It's not a good time.'

'Just a quick peek . . .' And there he was, reeling through the door. 'Fucking hell Jules! What did this place cost? It's a fucking palace!' Craning his neck to get a look at the height of the ceilings, he stumbled into the room, knocking over a lamp as he went. Julian put an arm out to steady him, he brushed it away. 'All right, Karl!' he called out, 'All right there, Alex? And er . . . I don't think we've met?' he said, holding out a hand to Dominic.

Dom got to his feet, introduced himself, shook Aidan's hand. Aidan was standing there, swaying slightly, trying to focus.

'You the new guy are you?' he asked Dom. My heart fell ten storeys.

'I'm sorry?' Dom replied politely.

'It's okay, it's okay,' he said, waving a hand in Dom's direction. 'You've done well, mate. You're a lucky man.' Dom gave me a quizzical look; I just shrugged helplessly.

'All right, Aidan, I think that's enough . . .' Julian said, grabbing his arm and pulling him towards the door.

I went immediately to Dom's side and slipped my hand into his, whispering 'Sorry' into his ear.

'So that's the ex is it?' he asked softly. 'Seems . . . interesting.' He was smiling but there was a tautness about his jaw and a colour to his cheeks that betrayed his irritation.

'He's just drunk,' I said, slipping my arms around his waist.

'Aah, look at that. Aren't you two cute?' Agonisingly, Julian still hadn't managed to manhandle Aidan out of the flat. He was standing in the doorway, looking back at us. 'I mean it, mate. You're a lucky man. She's gorgeous, isn't she? Isn't she gorgeous?'

At last Julian pushed him out of the door and closed it behind him.

Chapter Thirteen

28–29 December 2011

We're in bed by eleven. Dom falls asleep with *The Economist* on his chest at about eight minutes past. I have terrible sleep envy with Dom: he passes out almost instantly and will sleep a solid eight hours without waking every night. The sleep of a man with a clear conscience, I suppose. No surprise then that it always takes me ages to drop off, and once I do I always seem to wake up forty minutes later busting for a pee.

I try to read for a while, but I just keep getting to the end of the page and realising that I have no idea what just happened, because I'm not really reading, I'm running over the events of the day in my mind. Dad, Mum, the argument with Dom . . . I turn off the bedside lamp, roll onto my side and lie there in the dark, watching him sleep. I love him so much, the thought of anything happening to him, just the thought of him being sad or hurt, makes me feel physically ill, and yet I still don't feel that I love him like I ought to. Can you just make a decision to love someone the right way? Is it just a force of will? If I could just let go of everything else, I could be happy. Happy enough, anyway. Contented. Isn't contentment enough to be getting on with?

A little after midnight I give up. Sleep isn't coming. I creep downstairs and pour myself a Scotch. I sit in the kitchen with the lights off, sipping my drink. I finish it and pour a second. I listen to the two answer-phone messages from Aidan; the one from before Christmas and the one from yesterday. I notice that there isn't much whisky left in the bottle, so I decide that I may as well finish it off. I click on Aidan's message again, I go to 'options'. Return call? I click yes. I let the phone ring twice, end the call and switch off the phone. Why didn't I hide my caller ID? Idiot that I am.

I pour the rest of the Scotch down the sink and go back to bed.

At two-fifteen, sleepless and desperate, I get up again. I take my laptop downstairs and read through my emails from that afternoon. Spam, mostly, plus a message from Play TV, the production company behind Betrayal. It was from the head of factual and features, the subject line read *Sex it up!*

Hi Nicole, hope you've had a pleasant festive season.

Just wanted to say, that I've seen the preliminary notes and interview footage on *Betrayal* and, while I think you're heading in the right direction, it needs sexing up. This Annie woman is a great case study — but we need the sister in the programme too — what does she look like? Hopefully a bit less mousy. We need to get the husband involved, stoke things up a bit. Which one was better in bed? At the moment it's just a bit too worthy, it needs spicing up. We're not making Dispatches here, this is for Channel 5.

Other than that, great. I'll talk to you in the New Year.

Best wishes,
Paul.

I hit reply.

Dear Paul,

I had a very pleasant Christmas, thanks very much.

Regarding *Betrayal,* I find your suggestion that we try to play the sisters off against each other and goad the husband into revealing the sordid details of their sex lives repellent. You can take your stinking programme and shove it up your arse.

Best wishes,
Nicole.

I move the cursor to the 'send' button, let it hover there a moment. Then I move it on to 'discard message' and click. If only. If only I had the courage. I'm pretty sure I used to. The old Nicole wouldn't have hesitated to tell that idiot where to go.

The old Nicole wouldn't even have considered getting involved with this kind of project. The old Nicole had principles, and stuck by them, even when she risked losing everything. The old Nicole once told her boss to go fuck himself. She'd said it loudly and clearly, in front of the entire office.

This was in the summer of 2002. I was still working for Breakthrough, the company that had given me my first big break, via Simon Carver, the man I met on the boat on that awful night in Paris. We were working late, just me and my fellow assistant producer and all-round dogsbody, Joanne. The two of us were in charge of organising a trip to Gujarat in India – the company was producing a film about Muslim–Hindu violence in the province. It was up to us to book the air tickets, organise cars, drivers, translators, handlers – that kind of thing. As was always the case, we'd been assigned this task at the very last minute and were racing against time.

We were just considering whether we'd earned the right to order ourselves a pizza on expenses when an inebriated Simon came thundering into the office, his face ruddy with drink. He'd been in the pub for a good few hours, watching England play Sweden in the World Cup.

'Absolutely fucking useless,' he'd bellowed as he came through the door. 'Every single bloody last one of them.'

Jo and I exchanged amused glances.

'Not a great match then?' she asked him.

'Bore draw. Bunch of overpaid, overrated wankers . . . Bring me a drink, will you Jo? There's a bottle of Chenin blanc in the fridge in the kitchen.'

There was always wine in the fridge in the kitchen, and Scotch in the cupboard, a bottle of vodka in the freezer . . . Simon functioned best when lubricated. Or so he said. From my desk under the bank of TV screens in the centre of the open plan section of the office, I watched Jo, a diminutive blonde with a perfect hourglass shape, carry a glass of wine into Simon's office. He was sitting at his desk, slouched forward with his chin propped up in his hands, glowering at the screen of his PC, directly in my line of vision. I watched as Jo approached with the wine, which she placed on the desk next to his elbow, I watched as casually, lazily, he reached out his left hand and groped her on the arse. I saw her react, shocked and angry, pushing away his hand and then I watched as he got to his feet, shoved her hard against the desk, his face inches from hers. I couldn't hear what he said to her. She wriggled away from him and ran out of his office and out of the room.

The next day, I went with Jo to make a formal complaint to Gerry Marsters, the company's chief executive. He listened to us, nodding his head gravely, expressing shock and sympathy in all the right places; and then he told us that Simon had already spoken to him about it, and he had apologised, and he was prepared to apologise to Joanne, but that would be the end of it. There would be no further disciplinary action. Jo and I were so utterly gobsmacked, we didn't even protest. We left the office and went to the pub for lunch.

'Apparently they went to Harrow together, Simon and Gerry. And they shared a house at Cambridge,' Jo told me. 'I should've known I'd never get anywhere with him.'

'Sodding old boys' network,' I muttered, gulping down my gin and tonic. 'You'll have to sue.'

Jo looked uneasy. 'I'm not sure I can afford it, Nic. And even if I won, that kind of stuff . . . well, it doesn't look great on the CV, does it?'

'You could at least threaten to sue,' I suggested. 'Maybe then Gerry will actually do something about Simon.'

'That might work,' Jo said, but she looked doubtful.

She was right to be doubtful; it didn't work. Gerry laughed at the suggestion of a lawsuit.

'You go ahead, love, if you want to. Good luck with that. Just don't expect to be hired to work in TV again. Little girlies who cry sexual harassment just because someone patted them on the arse aren't particularly attractive to employers . . .'

'It was not a pat on the arse,' I protested, 'there was a lot more to it than that.'

'Says you, the other junior AP. That's not the way Simon tells it.'

'This is unbelievable,' I said.

Gerry shrugged. 'You girls are going to have to toughen up if you want to work in the media,' he said. 'This is not a knitting circle. This is the real world. Jobs are hard to come by.'

Jo trooped sadly out of Gerry's office, I followed to the door, where I stopped, turned around and said, in a loud, clear voice: 'I don't care how hard jobs are to come by, actually. This is bullshit. You – and Simon – can go fuck yourselves.'

Jo was 'let go' a few weeks later. She and I managed to talk our way into work at a rival production house where we made *Boys' Club*, an hour-long documentary on sexism in the workplace which was shown in prime time on Channel 4. We got lucky, managing to get an interview with the best-known (only well-known) female hedge fund manager in the UK who laid into some pretty high-profile people in an extraordinarily candid interview. She'd just had her fourth child, she wasn't planning on going back to work. and my god did she enjoy burning her bridges. The programme caused a huge fuss and ended up winning the award for best one-off documentary at the BAFTAs. It put me on the map. It put Jo on the map, too: she was pictured at the awards ceremony throwing a glass of

245

champagne in Simon's face, her pretty face was then plastered all over the newspapers, and a few weeks later she was offered a presenting job by some US station. Now she lives in Beverley Hills.

Smiling at the memory, I make myself a cup of tea and drink it standing at the kitchen window. It's almost five o'clock, still pitch black outside. But I won't be able to take the dogs out for a week after this, so what the hell. I creep back upstairs and fetch an old pair of jeans from the closet. Dom is still sleeping peacefully, in exactly the same position he was when he first dropped off. Unbelievable.

Back downstairs, Mick and Marianne don't even get excited when they see me putting on my wellies. They just look at me, sleepy, disbelieving. Surely she can't want us to go out at this hour? But with a bit of coaxing I get them up and out and the three of us walk down the lane in the freezing dark, our breath clouding the air.

We walk out onto the common. I stumble a couple of times, I can't really see where I'm going, and I'm afraid, but there's something exciting about the fear. I remember it now, how I used to enjoy that adrenalin surge, that twisting knot in the pit of my gut, blood roaring in my ears as my heart rate soared. Somewhere in the gloom to my left I hear a noise and I jump, stumble, turn back, start to run, the dogs racing ahead of me. Then I stop and look around. I can't see anyone.

Why would anyone be out on the common at five in the morning in December? But still, the fear's not quite so intoxicating now, so I take the dogs back home.

There are still two hours to go before we have to leave for the airport and I can't settle. I've finished the packing, there's nothing else to do. I can't bear just sitting around doing nothing, so I write a note for Dom, get into the car, drive to a service station on the A3 where I buy two coffees, then drive down to Cobham. It takes less than twenty minutes at that time of day. I park my car in the street outside Mum's house and ring her mobile.

'Nic, what's wrong?' she says when she picks up. Calls at that time of day are always bad news.

'Nothing,' I say. 'Sorry. I'm outside in the car. Can you come out? I need to talk to you.'

'Have you had a row with Dom?'

'No, it's not that.'

'We don't have to sit in the car. You come in.'

'I don't want to wake Charles.'

'He had three-quarters of a bottle of red wine and a couple of super-strength painkillers before he went to bed last night. He wouldn't wake up if the house fell down.'

We sit in the kitchen drinking coffee from Styrofoam cups. Mum takes a couple of sips and pulls a face.

'This is revolting. I'll make us a proper pot.' You'd have thought that thirty years of working in NHS hospitals would have immunised my mother to crap coffee, but no. She still demands the good stuff.

'You look great, Mum,' I say, and I mean it. She's tanned and slim, glowing with health.

'You look tired,' she replies.

'Thanks.'

'Sorry, but you do. And since you're turning up on my doorstep just before six in the morning I'm assuming you're having trouble sleeping again.' I nod. 'Anything particular you're worrying about?'

I take a deep breath. 'There is, actually Mum. It's Dad.'

She sits back down and takes my hand, an expression of concern furrowing her brow. 'He's been in touch, has he? Was he unkind?'

'No, it's not that. Nothing like that. He's ill, Mum. It's cancer.'

Mum doesn't say anything, she gets to her feet, goes over to the kitchen counter, pours us each a cup of coffee. It smells rich and comforting, and I'm suddenly overwhelmed by how relieved I am to be in my mother's kitchen again, and by the time she places the mug of coffee down in front of me, I've started to cry. She sits beside me with her arms around me, stroking my hair, saying, 'I'm so sorry, love. I'm so sorry.'

'It's bloody ridiculous,' I sniff. 'I shouldn't be this upset. I hardly know the man any more, I've barely seen him since he left us.'

'He's your dad,' she says. 'Of course you're upset. And he didn't leave us, you know. I threw him out. He didn't have any say in the matter. And I'm not sure he ever got over the shame.'

I blow my nose noisily. 'Well, he wants to see you. I went to see him and he asked me if . . . he asked me if I would talk to you. I think he wants to . . . I don't know. I don't even know if he'll apologise. He might just want to have a go at you again . . .'

Mum sips her coffee thoughtfully.

'What do you think I should do?' she asks me. 'Do you want me to go?'

'No! I mean . . . I don't want you to go because you think I want you to. I don't want you to go unless you want to.'

'Maybe we could go and see him together? After you get back?'

'I think he's worried he might not make it through the operation.'

'What kind of cancer is it?'

'Prostate. Apparently it's not particularly advanced, but they need to operate . . .'

'That's a simple op, Nic, believe me. They have very high success rates. Anyway, you know what your dad's like – he's not exactly Mr Glass Half Full, is he?'

'That's true.'

'I'm perfectly happy to go to see him, but I'd be a lot happier if we did it together.'

'That's brilliant, Mum, thanks.'

We drink some more coffee, she asks me about the New York trip.

'You looking forward to seeing Karl?'

'Can't wait.'

'How long's it been since you saw him last?'

'God . . . it's been ages. Our wedding, I suppose. I haven't seen him since our wedding.'

'And how is Dominic?' There's a slight edge to her voice when she asks this. Not so long ago, she'd always ask, 'How's my lovely son-in-law?' or at least 'How's gorgeous Dom?' Now it's 'How's Dominic?' and I can always tell she isn't really all that interested in how he is, she's just doing it out of courtesy. My mother is a lovely, forgiving person but when it comes to me, to my feelings getting hurt, man can she hold a grudge.

The sky is just starting to turn from black to grey. It's three minutes to seven. Time to go. I kiss Mum goodbye at the front door.

'Have a lovely trip, darling,' she says. And then, 'Oh, by the way, should you speak to Charles, please don't mention anything about your dad. About me going to visit, I mean. He wouldn't understand. There are some things I think it's best I just don't tell him.'

Like mother, like daughter.

* * *

I break the speed limit all the way home, arriving back at twenty past seven. Dom is pacing anxiously in the kitchen

'Jesus Christ, Nicole,' he says as I walk in the door. 'Cutting it a bit fine aren't you?'

'I'm sorry,' I say, kissing him as I hurry past. 'I had to see Mum. I couldn't leave without seeing her.'

'Okay then, but hurry. We need to leave in five minutes.'

I shower, dress, kiss the dogs goodbye. Twenty minutes later, with Dom working himself into a frenzy, we're ready to go. We argue over who's going to drive.

'You'll drive too fast,' Dom says. 'You drive like a maniac when you're in a hurry.'

'You won't drive fast enough, Dominic. You drive like an old lady even when there's an emergency.'

I drive. Dom clutches at his seat belt, ghost braking all the way from Wimbledon to Heathrow.

After check-in and security, Dom goes off to WHSmith to stock up on reading material. I sit in Costa Coffee and scribble down a new set of New Year's resolutions on a paper napkin.

1. Organise fortnightly dinners with Dad
2. Lose half a stone
3. Ask Dom to wait (at least) one year before trying for a baby

4. Read everything on all Booker shortlists. And
   War and Peace
5. Stop making awful television programmes

Next, I make two phone calls. The first is to my father.

'How are you feeling, Dad?' I ask when he answers.

'About a hundred and three,' he replies. He sounds exhausted.

'I hope I didn't wake you.'

'No, no. I've been up for hours. Pain in my gut. Indigestion I think.'

'Well, I just wanted to say bye. I'm at the airport now. And I also wanted to tell you that I spoke to Mum, and that she said she would come and visit you . . . after New Year. When I get back.'

'All right.' He sounds disappointed.

'Is that okay? She's just . . . she's got a lot on over the next few days.'

'I see.'

'I'm sure it'll go fine, Dad. Try not to worry too much.'

'Okay, love. Have a good trip.'

'Thanks.'

'All right then. Thanks for speaking to your mum.'

'That's okay.'

'I love you, Nicole.'

The words sound so strange coming from him, I can't remember the last time I heard him tell me he loved me. I realise in that instant how frightened he must be, and for a moment I can't say anything because I don't want to start crying again.

'Nicole?'

'I love you too, Dad. It's going to be fine. I'll see you next week.'

The second call is to Annie Gardner. I get through to her voicemail and leave a message: 'Annie, it's Nicole Blake here. This is going to sound a bit odd, but I'm phoning to advise you not to take part in the *Betrayal* series. I know that I'm the one who's been trying to convince you to do it, but I'm starting to get the feeling that the programme is not going to be helpful to you, it is not going to portray you in the best light. I'm concerned, in fact, that it could make your situation worse, and I'd hate for that to happen. If you do decide to go ahead, you should know that I am no longer going to be involved. If you have any questions, don't hesitate to call me. I'm going away for a few days but I have my mobile with me and I'll be checking emails. All the best. Happy New Year. Bye.'

As I hang up I'm flooded with a sense of relief, as though some oppressive weight has suddenly been lifted from my shoulders. I'll be in breach of contract and they'll be entitled to ask for my salary back. They could even sue me, though I doubt they'll bother. Of course, my name will be mud and I won't be offered any more work by that production house and possibly many others. I don't care. For the first time in ages I feel like I'm doing the right thing in my professional life.

Dom approaches carrying two plastic bags stuffed full of newspapers and magazines for the flight.

'Can I borrow your laptop?' I ask him. I haven't brought mine. 'I need to send an email.'

'Sure. To anyone in particular?'

I hesitate.

'Nicole . . .'

I take a deep breath. Please god, don't let this be the start of another argument. 'I don't want to do the programme,' I tell him. 'The *Betrayal* one. I'm going to email Paul Ronson to tell him I'm pulling out.'

'Good,' Dom says, unfolding the *Financial Times* on his lap. 'That kind of shit's beneath you.'

'You don't mind?' I'm impossibly relieved.

'Course I don't. We don't need the money, it's not like you *have* to work. We're fine on my salary at the moment.'

He's missed the point.

'You know that I want to work, right? I'm not quitting because I don't want to work, I just don't want to do *that* kind of work.'

'Yes, I know that,' he smiles at me and reaches out his hand to massage the back of my neck. He reads for a while, and then an idea occurs to him, and he looks up at me, an expression of concern on his face. 'This isn't about the offer from Aidan Symonds is it?

254

You're not quitting because of that? You're not taking him up on his offer?'

'No,' I say. 'I'm not taking him up on his offer.'

We board the plane and are ridiculously delighted to discover we've been allocated the emergency exit seats. We stretch out our legs, kick off our shoes and wriggle our toes, to the irritation of the man across the aisle one row forward, who is at least six foot four. At five five, I should offer to swap places with him, but Dom is ordering champagne and holding my hand, so sod him. This is our holiday, the trip I've been looking forward to for weeks and weeks. I feel giddy, honeymoonish. I've sorted things out with Dad, and with Annie Gardner, I've made a decision about Aidan, and about the baby – all my ducks are in a row. Bring on New York!

Chapter Fourteen

New Year's Eve 2005
Oxfordshire

Resolutions:
1. Set up my own production company
2. Buy a flat in London
3. Lose half a stone
4. Go on a road trip with Alex and Jules
5. Write to Dad

With Dom at the wheel and the weather filthy, it was a long, slow drive to Henley and my mood darkened with the skies as we approached. I was exhausted. I'd been travelling almost non-stop for four months and since I'd come back I'd been doing thirteen-hour days in the editing suite. The last thing I felt like doing was spending New Year's Eve at the Griffiths' country pile.

Not that I wasn't looking forward to seeing Alex. I couldn't wait to see Alex – and Julian, of course. Our paths had barely crossed over the past year. Either I was working or Julian was working or Alex was on holiday . . . we just never seemed to be in the same time zone any more.

It was just that it had been made clear to me that this was very much Mike's party, rather than Alex's affair.

'He's been moaning about the fact that we always do whatever I want to do on New Year's,' she explained when we spoke on the phone at Christmas. 'So this year it's his baby. Well, not that he actually organised the thing, he's paid some party planner to do it. Karen. Vile woman. I'll tell you about her when you get here. But it's mostly his friends. Plus you and Jules.'

Alex and Mike bought the place in Henley a few months after they got married. It was huge – six bedrooms, I think – and had a lovely garden sloping down to the river, but it wasn't what I'd have chosen, had I had a few million quid to spare. It was newly built, 'the kind of thing a footballer would buy', as Julian put it after the first time we went to visit.

'Or a former rugby player,' I pointed out.

'Will you two stop being such awful snobs?' Karl scolded us. 'There's nothing wrong with it. You two are just determined to dislike everything that Mike touches or has anything to do with. It's not very charitable, is it? Do you think Alex doesn't notice?'

I had promised myself at the time that I'd make a greater effort with Mike, but in reality I'd barely seen

258

them since. Alex and I emailed, of course, but our missives tended to be fairly cursory: are you okay, where are you, when are you next in London, let's meet up soon. I really didn't have any idea what was going on in her life.

As we pulled up to the electric gates at the bottom of Alex and Mike's driveway, Dom leaned over and squeezed my leg.

'It'll be fun,' he said reassuringly. 'Stop looking so worried. You never know, something unexpected might happen.'

'What's that supposed to mean?' I asked him, mildly alarmed. I'm not all that big on surprises. He just grinned and pressed the intercom button.

'Yes?' came the crackly response.

'It's . . . um . . . Dom and Nicole.'

'Sorry? Mister?'

'*Mister* Dominic Taylor and *Ms* Nicole Blake,' Dom yelled. He shot me an amused glance, I raised my eyes to the heavens.

The gates slid open ever so slowly, making an ominous grinding sound.

'You'd think we were visiting Buckingham Palace,' I grumbled.

'Now, now,' Dom said with a wry little smile, 'one has to protect oneself from the criminal gangs roaming the streets of Henley-on-Thames.' He accelerated gently up the driveway, bringing the car to a halt in front of the house's grandiose entrance.

Mike came out to greet us, his arms outspread.

'Hey, guys!' he called out, 'welcome!' He greeted Dom warmly and gave me a kiss on the cheek. 'You okay? Journey all right? Traffic not too bad?' He fussed around us, helping taking the bags out of the back of the car, clapping Dom chummily on the back, complimenting me on my suntan. This was Mike in host mode, making an effort. He made no mention of Alex.

He showed us up to our room, a small guest bedroom at the front of the house overlooking the driveway. We'd been downgraded. Last time we visited we had an ensuite with a view of the garden and the river.

'You two get settled and changed, and come downstairs for a drink,' Mike told us. 'Unless you'd like me to bring something up to you?'

'That's fine, Mike. Is Alex around?' I was surprised she hadn't come out to say hello.

'Somewhere,' he said cheerily and pulled the bedroom door closed behind him as he left.

I showered and changed into my party dress, a rather tired-looking LBD bought the previous Christmas. I hadn't had time to do any shopping. Or get a haircut, or my nails done. I looked at my reflection in the mirror with some disdain. Dom came up behind me and slipped his hands around my waist.

'You look lovely,' he murmured into my hair.

'I look old and tired and very last year,' I said, turning to kiss him, 'but thanks anyway.'

'Hey, at least you don't look like you ought to be serving canapés,' he said, pulling away from me and indicating his own garb. It was true: Dom was not one of those men who can effortlessly pull off black tie.

'Well,' I said, 'maybe you *do* look a bit more waiter than James Bond, but at least you look like the kind of waiter the sluttier posh girls will want to grab and drag into the library for a quickie.'

'Darling, you say the sweetest things.'

Hand in hand, we descended the stairs and made our way into the living room, already crowded and hot, filled with loud men in penguin suits and women with big hair wearing Gucci. Dom and I clung to each other, feeling out of place.

'Everyone seems kind of . . . old, don't they?' I whispered to him.

'I think they're just grown-ups,' he whispered back.

'I didn't realise these were the sort of parties I'd be going to on New Year's Eve until I was like . . . thirty or something. Are we already too old for clubs and drugs?'

'Never,' Dom replied, grabbing a couple of glasses of champagne from a passing waiter and handing one to me. 'Give me an E and a whistle over this shit any day.'

'I'm not sure people still have whistles at clubs, Dom. Where the fuck is Alex?'

* * *

We mingled. We mingled awkwardly. Mike's friends appeared to be a collection of stockbrokers and former rugby players, all of whom now worked in the City. Their wives, manicured to within an inch of their lives, were art history graduates who worked in public relations or at auction houses. Conversations tended to go like this:

Former rugby player turned City boy: 'So, Dom, what do you do?'

Dom: 'I'm a solicitor.'

City boy: 'Oh, right. Yah. Corporate law, yah?'

Dom: 'Labour law, actually. Employment issues.'

City boy: 'Right, right. You on the side of the good guys, or the bad? Hope you're not the kind of guys bringing all these sexual harassment suits, are you?' Then, in a girly voice, 'Oh, Mr Judge, my mean boss made me go to Spearmint Rhino. Can I have six million pounds please?'

Dom mutters something incomprehensible, the two of us slink away.

Still, Dom's conversations lasted longer than mine. Whenever I told anyone I made television documentaries for a living, they just looked at me blankly and walked away.

'A lot of ITV watchers, I reckon,' Dom said.

'Where the fuck is Alex?' I said.

After about half an hour of painful socialising, I left Dom gamely attempting to engage one of the Gucci girls in conversation and went in search of Alex and Julian. There was no sign of either in the living room, so I wandered back through the house. No sign of them in the kitchen, either, or in the conservatory which led off it. On the opposite side of the house, I remembered that there was a study, which Mike referred to as the library despite the fact that it didn't appear to have any books in it aside from his collection of John Grishams. The door, which led off the entrance hall, was slightly ajar. I pushed it open a little further and peeked in. I could see Alex standing at the opposite end of the room, dressed in a very short white dress, pouring herself a drink. Mike was standing off to the left, his back to her, looking out of the French doors.

'You might want to go easy,' he was saying. 'After all, you did start at three.'

'I did not start at three,' she snapped back at him, 'I had one glass of wine at three.'

Her voice sounded thick with alcohol, as she turned I could see she was a little unsteady on her feet. She was heavily made up, her lips a deep scarlet. Her mascara had run a little on one side, she looked as though she'd been crying.

'Well, you look pissed to me,' Mike retorted, turning to look at her. 'Christ's sake, Alex. I don't know what to do with you.'

'You don't know what to *do* with me?'

'You don't even try.'

'I am trying. I *am* trying.'

I inched backwards, not wanting to witness this and yet unable to tear myself away.

'Well, it doesn't look like it to me.' Mike put his own glass down on the desk and took a couple of steps towards the door. I inched back further. 'You know what, Alex,' he said, 'I think it's a good thing you haven't been able to get pregnant. Jesus, just look at you. What kind of mother would you make?'

He started walking briskly towards the door and I leapt back, stepping on the foot of the person standing behind me as I did.

'Ouch,' the person said. I turned around and there he was. Again. As he always seemed to be, on my every New Year's Eve: Aidan.

'And what are you up to?' he asked me with an amused look on his face. 'Who are you spying on?'

'Shhh . . .' I hissed at him, pushing him away from the door to the study. 'We have to get out of here!' I shoved him out of the front door and onto the porch, closing the door quickly behind us.

'You know, if you wanted to get me alone, you only had to ask . . .'

'Oh, get over yourself. I just didn't want Mike to see us. He and Alex were having a fight – I overheard them.'

'Oh dear, trouble in paradise?'

'I'm not sure it's ever been even remotely utopian around here,' I said. 'God, he's awful.' I pushed the door open just a fraction and peered in. 'I think he's gone. I have to go and talk to Alex.'

'Hang on,' Aidan said, reaching for my hand. 'You haven't even said hello.'

I turned to look at him, pulling my hand away and trying to ignore the fact that despite his stubble and usual casual dishevelment, he still managed to look more James Bond than waiter in his tux.

'Hello, Aidan,' I said. 'I have to go and speak to Alex now.'

Alex was no longer in the study. I couldn't find her in the living room or out on the terrace, where the smokers gathered in huddles around patio heaters. This was where I found Julian and Karl, both wrapped in expensive-looking black coats, easily the best-looking men at the party.

'Have you seen Alex?' I asked Jules after we'd kissed our hellos.

'Not since we got here,' Julian said, shooting a nervous glance at Karl. 'We think she might have been a bit . . . you know . . .'

'Pissed.' Karl finished his sentence.

'I think she and Mike are having some kind of problem,' I said. 'And why the fuck is Aidan here?'

'Aidan's here?' Julian looked incredulous. 'I thought he was in New York. What's he doing here? Alex doesn't even like Aidan. And Mike *loathes* him.'

'Well, he's here.' I took a quick toke off Julian's cigarette. 'I really have to find Alex.'

*   *   *

I found her upstairs in the master bedroom, snorting a line of coke off the dressing table.

'There you are!' she said when she saw me. 'At last! At long last!' She flung her arms around my neck and held onto me tightly. 'Thank god you're here.' She pulled away and held out a rolled up fiver. 'You want some?' she asked.

'I'm all right, thanks. Are you okay? I've been looking for you for ages.'

We kicked off our shoes and sat on her bed.

'How was Pakistan?' she asked me. 'You were doing that thing, the thing on refugees? On the Afghan border? That was it, wasn't it? Tell me about that.'

'Alex, that was ages ago. I told you about that, we finished it in May. It was on the BBC a few months ago. I sent you an email.'

'Oh god, yeah. Sorry.' She looked embarrassed. 'My head . . . all over the place at the moment. So, where have you been?'

'I was in Indonesia for a while . . .'

'Of course, the bombing thing. Okay. How was that?'

'It was . . . difficult. After that, I went to Vietnam . . .'

'Oh, how lovely.'

She looked distracted, scattered. I took her hand.

'Alex, are you all right?' I asked, and she started to cry.

Julian found us a few minutes later, me sitting on the bed, Alex lying with her head in my lap. He came into the room and shut the door behind him. He had a bottle of champagne in one hand and three glasses in the other.

'I thought we could have our own party,' he said. 'I don't seem to be getting the greatest vibe down there.'

'Oh Jesus,' Alex said, sitting up and wiping her eyes, smearing mascara everywhere. 'Mike's friends are bloody awful. There are more homophobes per square inch down there than at a Texan church fete. Sorry, Jules.'

He grinned at her, put down the champagne and plucked a Kleenex from the box on the dressing table. He wiped the black smudges from her face. 'Don't worry about it. Karl's quite enjoying himself, baiting them. He's turned the camp up to ten, you've never seen anything like it.' He poured us all a glass of champagne, we clinked glasses and he said: 'So, come on, Alex, are you going to tell us what the fuck is going on?'

Things had been good, Alex told us, for about three months after the wedding. Then Mike wrecked his cruciate ligament when he twisted his knee in the scrum. The doctors told him to retire, he wouldn't play professionally again.

'He was in a pretty bad way,' Alex said. 'He just sat around the house, drinking all the time, picking fights with me.'

Things got better for a while, she explained, after one of his old school friends fixed him up with a job as a financial adviser. 'He sells insurance, really,' she explained. 'But he calls himself a financial adviser.' Relations deteriorated once again, however, when Mike decided that it was time for them to start having children. 'Harry, his best man, do you remember him? Well, his wife had a son and so did Stephen's wife, and so Mike, not wanting to be left out, thought we should start trying.'

'And how do you feel about this?' I asked her.

She shrugged. 'I don't know. I do want to have children, of course I do. You know I do. But I'm twenty-seven . . . I don't know. I hadn't really planned on having them until I was in my thirties.'

'You should tell him that then,' Julian said, topping up our glasses.

'I did, and we just argued about it, so in the end I just gave in . . .'

'Alex, you shouldn't let yourself get bullied into doing something you don't want to,' I said.

'But I *do* want to,' she said, a little crossly. 'I'm not like you, I'm not obsessed by my career. I do want kids. It's just a timing issue.'

'Okay,' I said, chastened.

'Anyway,' she went on, her eyes welling up again, 'it doesn't bloody matter because we've been trying for bloody ages and I just can't seem to get pregnant. I don't know what's wrong with me.'

'There's nothing wrong with you!' I said. 'For some people it just takes time.'

She sniffed. 'Mike says it's because I drink too much.'

'That's bullshit,' Julian and I said in unison.

'No!' she wailed 'It's true. It is true. I have been drinking too much, especially since I stopped working . . .'

'Hang on, what?' I asked, disbelieving. 'You stopped working? When? Why?'

For the past two years Alex had been running the marketing department at up-and-coming publishers, Scribe. She *loved* her job.

'I quit a couple of months ago,' she said, draining her glass and holding it out for Julian to refill. 'We decided . . . I decided that if I was serious about getting knocked up, I should have as little stress as possible.'

Julian and I exchanged the briefest of looks. Alex noticed. 'It was my decision!' she snapped, getting to her feet. 'Don't look like that. I chose this. I want this.' She slipped her feet back into her stilettos and wobbled towards the door. Then she turned to us and said, 'I know what you're thinking, but you don't understand. You're not married. Marriage is different.' Julian opened his mouth to say something but thought better of it. 'Come on,' Alex said, smiling now, her moods changing as quick as clouds scudding across a summer sky, 'Let's go back to the party. Oh! I should warn you, Nic, that I invited Aidan. I bumped into him in London last week and, well, you know how Mike can't *bear* him. I just couldn't help myself.' She teetered off down the corridor, straightening the seams of her stockings as she went.

Back downstairs I looked in vain for Dom, but found myself trapped in conversation with some of the Gucci wives ('Meribel this year? Or Vail?'). Eventually I managed to extricate myself and fought my way through the braying mob to the terrace, where I was horrified to see Dom standing under one of the heaters, talking to Aidan. Could this party get any worse?

I made my way over to where they were standing but, instead of just going up and interrupting, I let my curiosity get the better of me and hid behind another group of people while eavesdropping on their conversation.

'I owe you an apology,' Aidan was saying, 'for the last time I saw you. I can't really remember, but I think I behaved like an arsehole.'

'You did,' Dom replied, 'but only briefly. I wouldn't worry too much about it. And I understand, I do. I'd definitely go off the rails if I messed things up with Nicole.' Aidan shifted uneasily from one foot to another. Ignoring his discomfort – or perhaps enjoying it – Dom went on: 'It would kill me to see her with someone else,' he said. 'I'd hate it.' Aidan nodded, he looked at his feet and then glanced around, searching desperately for someone to rescue him from this conversation. I obliged.

'Hello!' I said, a little too loudly, a little too brightly. 'Enjoying the party?'

Dom slipped his hand around my waist and kissed me on the mouth for longer than was strictly necessary. Marking his territory. I pulled away. Aidan just stood there, smiling awkwardly.

'Yeah, it's all right,' he said.

'Liar,' I replied, and he laughed.

'Is Alex okay?' he asked me.

'I don't know.'

'Why?' Dom asked, seemingly miffed at being left out of the loop. 'What's going on?'

'Things are a bit difficult with her and Mike,' I said. 'She was upset earlier . . .' I got the feeling that he wasn't really listening, he was watching Aidan, who was looking at me.

'I saw the Pakistan programme,' Aidan said to me. 'They had it on BBC World over in the States. It was great, Nic. Amazing work.'

'Thanks,' I said, and I could feel myself colour. Praise from him meant a lot, and not just because of our history. Aidan was the one who first made me want to get into TV, his opinion meant the world to me. For a second, we just stood there, looking at each other, until I started to feel a little dizzy and I turned to Dom and said, 'We should go inside. It's freezing out here.'

I realised that I had barely eaten anything all day, so I went in search of canapés while Dom chatted to one of Mike's less objectionable friends. At the far end

271

of the room was a table covered with a linen cloth and on it were trays laden with various goodies: I joined Julian and Karl at one end of the table and began making my way along. By the time we reached the other end of the table I was clutching a plate laden with quails' eggs and cherry tomatoes, smoked salmon with caviar on toast, duck parfait with daubs of caramelised orange on top. Karl gave me an amused look.

'Did they not feed you in Vietnam?' he asked. 'Because when we went there last the food was fabulous. Just fabulous. Do you remember the beef noodle soup in Hué, Jules? God, to die for.'

I was trying to listen to what Karl was saying, but I was finding it difficult to concentrate, because standing behind him were a group of chinless idiots, exaggeratedly imitating his speech and actions, sniggering like schoolboys. Julian had noticed them too. He shot me a look.

'Let's move outside,' I said to him, quietly.

'No, fuck 'em,' he mumbled through a mouthful of foie gras. 'It's freezing out there. I'm not moving on their account.'

Karl carried on chatting, oblivious. I gave the City boys my iciest glare, but they didn't let up.

'So,' one of them piped up, addressing Julian. 'You've been to Vietnam, have you?' he asked. The man had a shiny pink head and no chin. 'Meet any lady boys?'

272

'That's Thailand, you ignorant fuck,' I replied.

'What did you say?' the chinless wonder responded, shocked.

'Watch out for that one,' his friend chortled. 'She's a feminazi.'

'I called you an ignorant fuck,' I repeated in a loud, clear voice. I could feel Julian's hand on my arm, an attempt at restraint; I ignored him. 'Is there a word there you'd like me to spell for you?'

'You watch your mouth, bitch,' the chinless man growled.

I was about to reply to this, but I didn't get a chance because all of a sudden my opponent was on the floor, a trickle of blood oozing from the side of his fish-like mouth. Aidan was standing at my side, clenching and unclenching his right fist.

'Don't speak to her like that,' he said quietly, then he turned on his heel and started to walk away, only to be confronted by an irate Mike, who grabbed him by the lapels of his jacket.

'Get out of my house, you fucking oik,' he snarled at him.

Aidan calmly removed Mike's hands and replied, 'With pleasure.'

Across the room I could see Alex watching the scene unfold, her face without expression. I glanced around to find Dom, but he was nowhere to be seen.

I followed Aidan to the front door and out onto the porch.

'And there I was thinking you'd been acting all grown-up tonight,' I said with a smile.

'Hey, I was defending your honour.'

'Thank you.'

'Did he seriously just call me an oik?'

When we'd both finished laughing there was a long awkward silence, and then we both started speaking at once.

'Well I suppose . . .' he said

'I was in New York . . .' I said.

We laughed. 'You first,' he said.

'I was just saying that I was in New York a couple of months ago. I thought about looking you up, but . . . you know. I wasn't sure.'

'You should have done.'

'Things are going well there?'

'Great, really great.' We walked down the steps into the driveway, where Aidan's motorcycle was parked. He lit a cigarette and offered me one, which I took.

'Julian said that you'd been promoted?'

'Yeah, I'm a commissioning editor now. I've gone all respectable.'

'I'm glad it's going well.'

He was leaning against his bike, just looking at me, those impossible green eyes locked on mine. 'God,' he said, reaching out to brush my hair from my face, 'I've missed you.' I pulled away from him.

'Aidan . . .'

'Sorry,' he said. 'I'm sorry. I didn't mean . . .'

274

'I know.'

We stood there, awkward and uncomfortable again, then started to laugh.

'I should go back inside,' I said, crushing my half-smoked cigarette under my heel.

'Yeah. And I should probably get out of here before I get my head kicked in.'

'Good plan.'

Another awkward moment, and then he leaned forward and gave me a peck on the cheek.

'It's good to see you, Nic.'

'You too.' I wanted to say something else to him, but I wasn't quite sure what, so I just turned and started to walk away. I was almost at the front door when he called out to me

'Nicole!'

I turned around. 'What is it?'

'It's . . . nothing.' He swung his leg over his bike, then he shook his head and said: 'It's just . . . It was the most stupid thing I ever did, you know that?'

'What was?' I asked him. 'You're going to have to narrow it down for me, Aidan, the list of stupid things you've done is a long one . . .'

'Letting you go. It was the most stupid thing I ever did.' He gave me a sad smile. 'I hope you're happy. I mean it. You deserve to be very happy,' he said. He put on his helmet, kicked the bike into life, and he was gone.

*   *   *

I found Alex and Dom in the kitchen. She was perched on the kitchen counter, her shoes off. Dom was leaning against the fridge, drinking a beer.

'Is he all right?' Alex asked me.

'Is he gone?' Dom said.

'Yes and yes,' I replied, avoiding Dom's eye.

Alex was red-eyed, she looked exhausted. 'Happy New Year,' she said.

'You missed the countdown,' Dom added. I looked at my watch, it was six minutes past twelve. I'd spent midnight on New Year's with Aidan again.

'Sorry,' I said, and gave him a kiss.

Alex hopped off the counter and put her arms around me, hugging me tightly.

'Well,' she slurred into my neck, 'it's been a fucking fabulous evening, but I think I've had just about enough. I'm off to bed.'

She bent down and picked up her shoes before weaving her weary way out of the room.

'Jesus,' I said. 'What a bloody night.'

Dom didn't say a word, he was just looking at me, his expression inscrutable.

'Is Julian all right?' I asked him.

'Yeah, he's fine. He and Karl went off to bed. He said to say he'd do resolutions with you in the morning.'

'Thanks,' I said, slipping my arms around his waist and pulling him closer to me. 'I'm sorry I missed the countdown.' I kissed him, longer this time, a proper kiss.

'You can't help yourself around those Symonds boys, can you?' Dom asked as he broke the kiss. 'Julian, Aidan, you just go running . . .'

'That's not true.'

'You might want to pay the same attention to Alex, Nic.'

I pulled away from him. 'What do you mean? I care about Alex. You know I care about Alex. And I know she's having a hard time, I spoke to her earlier—'

'Hey,' he said, pulling me back towards him, 'don't be defensive. I know you care about her, I know how much you love her. I'm just saying. She seems . . . really lonely.'

'Did she talk to you?'

'A little. She misses you.'

'I miss her, too. I know I should see her more, but it's not always easy when I'm spending half my life on the other side of the world.'

'True.' There was a little pause, and then he said, 'Maybe you should try spending more time in England. Let work take a back seat . . .'

I sighed loudly. 'Oh, we're back to this, are we? This is not about Alex, is it? This is about *you* wanting me to travel less . . .'

He smiled, a guilty little smile. 'It's about Alex *and* it's about me.'

We snuck away from the party and up to our room. I was fidgeting with the hook at the top of my dress,

Dom came up behind me, undid it and slowly unzipped me. He slipped his hand inside the dress and around my body, pulling me up against him.

'I've been meaning to ask you something . . .' he said softly, turning me around, kissing me on the mouth.

'Oh yes?'

'I want you to marry me,' he said. 'Will you marry me, Nic?'

I was so shocked by this that I actually jumped. I literally gave a little leap into the air.

'What?' I asked him, half-laughing. 'Are you serious?'

'Of course I'm serious,' he replied. He looked a little wounded by my reaction, so I took him in my arms and kissed him.

'We've only known each other two years, Dom,' I said to him. 'Don't you think it's rushing things a bit?'

'I knew the first time I met you I wanted to marry you, Nicole. I can't even remember what my life was like before we met, and I don't want to think about a life without you.'

'Dominic . . .' I kissed him on the mouth again and began to unbutton his shirt. 'I love you. I do, but you were at that party tonight. Tell me honestly, which couple would you rather be: Karl and Julian or Mike and Alex?'

'Mike and Alex aren't unhappy because they're *married*, Nic. They're unhappy because they're unhappy. We wouldn't be unhappy.'

'I like how we are now.'

'What about living together then?'

'But I've been thinking about buying a place of my own,' I told him.

'We could buy somewhere together,' he pointed out.

'I think I need the security of my own place, Dom. Plus, buying a house together is a huge commitment.'

'Nicole, I just asked you to marry me. I *am* committed.'

Later on, just as the sky outside was turning black to charcoal, he asked me: 'Do you still love him?' He was talking about Aidan.

'No,' I replied. 'I don't think so.'

'I can wait, you know. Even if you do still love him, you won't for ever. One day, you'll look at me the way you look at him. I know you will.'

Chapter Fifteen

29 December 2011

I fall asleep without even finishing my champagne, waking at the exact moment the pilot tells us he's switching on the fasten seatbelt sign as we are about to start our descent. This is the way to travel.

'Did I snore?' I ask Dom sleepily.

'Like a buffalo in need of nasal decongestant,' he replies.

'Oh god, really?' I ask, looking around to see if the people sitting around me are giving me evils.

'Not really. You snuffled occasionally.'

'Did you sleep?'

'Nope. Read all the papers though. I am very well informed. I will have lots of fascinating things to say to everyone at the party on Saturday. Actually, I'm shattered. Looking forward to an early night,' he says, and gives my knee a squeeze.

I don't want to have an early night. We're in New York! I want to go out, feel the buzz. I don't say anything. I'll find a way to convince him later.

*   *   *

281

We grab a taxi outside JFK. All along the drive into the city, along the Long Island Expressway, past all those tatty houses with the stars and stripes hanging off their porches, through the tunnel and up into Manhattan, the butterflies in my stomach agitate, they swarm and circle. I can't stop smiling. New York! It's a gorgeous day, cold and still, the sky an icy blue. Pale winter sunshine becomes dazzling as it reflects off the tops of the skyscrapers. We traverse Manhattan, turn down 8th Avenue and on to West 29th Street, stopping outside the Ace Hotel.

It's a little after three in the afternoon but the lobby is buzzing, just as Karl told me it would be.

'You must stay at the Ace,' he urged when he first invited me. 'It's fabulous and not horrendously expensive. And very cool. Some of the best people-watching in town, and believe me, in Manhattan, that's saying something.'

The lobby is a long, open space with sofas and tables in the centre of the room and a bar at the far end. Hipsters abound.

'Christ, it's loud in here,' Dom mutters as we make our way to the reception desk. 'I hope our room isn't on the first floor. We'll never get any bloody sleep.'

I smile at him through gritted teeth. There was a time when I used to find his curmudgeonly young fogey act amusing, but not now. And I know why he's being grumpy. It's not just because he got no sleep on the flight. It worries him that I'm obviously so excited to be here, that New York exhilarates me in a way London doesn't seem to these days. To Dom, New York looks like competition, and he wants to put the competition down.

We check in. To Dom's relief, we are not on the first floor, in fact we're on the fourteenth. From our window we can see the Empire State Building, just a few blocks away, rising into the sky like a rocket ready for take-off.

'It's quite small, isn't it?'

'The Empire State?'

'The room.'

'I think it's lovely.' There's a double bed and a leather sofa, and bright abstract paintings on the walls. 'Shall we have some champagne?' I ask him. I'm desperate to get him to lighten up and enjoy this, because if he doesn't I'm going to be tempted to punch him in the face.

'It'll be hellish expensive if we take it from the mini-bar . . .' he says.

'Dom, come on.'

'Okay. Sorry. I'm just a bit tired.'

'I know. We'll drink some champagne, watch some TV . . . who knows, you might even get lucky,' I say, giving him a coy little smile.

We drink the champagne, but we don't watch TV.

* * *

Later, in the shower, I plan our night out.

'Karl reckons we must have a steak at the Breslin,' I tell Dom as he soaps my back.

'Where's the Breslin?'

'Downstairs.'

'That sounds perfect.'

'And after that we could go to Flute, for more champagne. That's not very far away. Or there's the Russian Vodka Room . . . You'll love that, more vodka varieties than you can shake a stick at.'

'Or we could just come back up here and have more sex,' Dom says, his hands wandering.

'Dom, we're only here for four nights . . .' I say, wriggling away from him. 'I don't want to spend the entire time in our hotel room.'

Dom puts on jeans, jumper and tatty trainers. I put on a dark red wrap dress, my highest heels and the Marc Jacobs coat I got on sale last winter. I am dressing to impress. I am pointedly dressing to go out on the town.

The Breslin is packed, four deep at the bar, forty minutes' wait for a table.

'We could always order room service,' Dom says hopefully, but I'm already wading into the throng on my way to the bar. A charming, goatee-bearded man lets me push in front of him.

'Just go for it,' he says to me. 'Don't be British. Just get in there.'

This is what I want! I want to have conversations with random strangers in bars, I want to get stoned with artists who live in Williamsburg and date European models with unpronounceable names. That's what you're supposed to do when you're in New York. You're not supposed to spend the whole time in your hotel room with your husband. I smile up at the goateed man, but he's not looking at me, his eye's been caught by someone else.

I emerge a moment or so later with a couple of dirty Martinis and join Dom who is skulking by the window.

'Apparently it's going to snow tomorrow,' I say, handing him a drink. 'I hope it's a proper snowfall. I've never seen New York in the snow.'

'I have to get some work done tomorrow,' Dom says.

I am trying very hard not to be annoyed with him, but it's getting difficult, all the more so because I get the feeling that he's deliberately trying to annoy me, although I'm not entirely sure why. I think, perhaps, he doesn't want me to have *too* much fun in New York. I turn around, hop up on a stool and survey the room. I smile, I can't help it, there's something about this place that makes the pulse race. Dom isn't going to bring me down.

He cheers up over Shibumi oysters and the enormous (eye-wateringly expensive) rib-eye we share. It is unbelievably good, rare and succulent and tender on the bone. We can't finish it, so we ask for a doggy bag.

'That will make an excellent midnight feast,' Dom says, stifling a yawn. It's barely nine-thirty and I can tell he's agitating to go to bed.

'I'm not tired, Dom,' I say pre-emptively.

'That's because you slept the whole way over on the plane.'

'I know, but I'm not tired. I don't want to go to bed now.'

'We don't have to go to sleep straight away,' he says, raising one eyebrow, just like Roger Moore. Usually I would find this funny and charming, but now it's annoying. I want to go out.

'I want to go out,' I say. I can almost feel my lip plumping out.

'Nic, I'm exhausted.'

I sigh. 'Fine, you go up to bed, I'm going to go for a little wander round the block, then I'll maybe have a glass of wine in the bar down here. Okay?'

'Okay. Why don't you just have a glass of wine? Don't go wandering about.'

'Dom, it's the centre of Manhattan and it isn't even late. There are mobs of people around. I just want to get out and about for a bit. I'll be fine by myself.'

He kisses me goodbye at the elevator.

'If you're going for a walk, don't you want to change into more comfortable shoes?' he asks.

'I'm fine,' I say, but I want to scream, 'No! I don't bloody want to change into comfortable shoes! This is what you're supposed to wear in Manhattan! Have you never seen *Sex and the City*?'

'Shouldn't you take a map?' he asks.

'I have my phone.'

I pull away from him, I'm desperate to get out there. Sometimes I think he forgets that I used to face greater challenges than walking down Broadway in high heels; I've been to the Congo and North Korea, I was in Lebanon during the last Israeli invasion, I was in a car that came under fire in Basra. He forgets that I used to be fearless. Perhaps it's about time we both remembered.

I walk south on Broadway, through Union Square, past Grace Church, I cross over onto 4th Avenue and into the East Village. My feet are killing me (yes, all right, he was right, I should have changed my shoes), so I stop for a drink at a tiny place that doesn't appear to have a name. I sit at the bar and order myself a Martini. My phone is buzzing in my handbag. There's a message from Dom.

Hope you're having fun, don't go too far, see you soon x

I look at the map of New York on my phone. I am about nine or ten blocks from Alex's apartment. I knew she lived down this way, but I didn't know I was this close. I sip my drink, weigh up my options. It's not quite ten-thirty. I could go back to the hotel and sit in the bar and people-watch. I could go to bed. Or I could hop in a taxi and visit my former second best friend in the whole world.

Outside, I hail a cab and ask the driver to take me to the corner of Mulberry and Grand.

'I know it's not very far,' I say in the best Queen's English. 'But my feet are hurting and I don't really know my way around.'

The taxi driver is totally charming about it.

'That's okay, I know what you ladies are like with your heels, my wife's the same.'

'Thank you,' I say. 'If I did this to a taxi driver in London, he'd bite my head off.'

He laughs. 'Lady, this ain't London.'

Alex's apartment building is modern and faceless. There is no concierge. I realise that I don't know the number of her apartment, and I suddenly feel incredibly relieved. I can run away now. I've had the thrill of coming here, of contemplating what it would be like to see her again, what I would say, how she would react, but I don't actually have to go through with it. Then I notice that some of the buzzers have names next to them, and there, in type so faded it is almost illegible, is A. Rose.

My hands are shaking as I go to press the buzzer. I chicken out, turn around and start to walk down the street, looking for another taxi. Then I turn around again and go back to the apartment block. This is ridiculous. She's probably not there anyway. I press the buzzer.

By the time the intercom crackles into life I realise that I have been holding my breath, and exhale loudly.

'Go away, Aaron,' a voice is saying to me. 'I'm not bloody interested.'

'It's Nicole,' I say in a small, croaky voice.

'What?'

'It's Nicole.'

Silence. Then, 'Who?'

'Alex, it's Nicole.'

There's a buzz and a click as the door opens.

'Fifth floor,' she yells through the intercom. 'Number thirty-two.'

Once in the lift, I realise I am desperate for a pee. Why didn't I go back at the bar? I try not to think about it, focusing instead on what I'm going to say. What am I going to say? Why didn't I think about that back at the bar?

The doors open and Alex's arms are around me before I even have time to step out of the lift. She's sobbing, squeezing the breath out of me, saying, 'You're here, you're here, you're here.'

'Alex,' I say, pushing her back so we can both get out of the lift before the doors shut again, 'I really need to go to the loo.'

Her apartment is tiny, just two rooms – a bedroom and living room-slash-kitchen – plus a bathroom. It is also beautiful, with enormous windows looking out onto the street and huge, dramatic black and white photographs on the walls. The pictures are familiar to me; I know them all. I try not to look at them.

When I get back from the bathroom we sit down on the white sofa which faces the windows. Alex pours us each a glass of red.

'You're here for Karl's thing, aren't you?' she asks me.

'That's right.'

'I thought you would be coming, but then you didn't say anything, so . . . I'm not going. I wasn't invited. Well, I kind of was, but I thought it was probably polite to say no.' She smiles at me and wipes her eyes. I'd forgotten how beautiful she is.

'You're thin,' I say, squeezing her thigh.

She laughs. 'You know what misery does to me,' she says, and we both start crying and it's a long time before we stop.

We talk about work (she is now earning a fortune as director of sales at Dylan Publishing), her break-up with Aaron (surprisingly liberating), her sisters (all married, happily, with children). She asks me about my work (I'm evasive) and about the dogs. We're avoiding the real stuff, but by the time we finish the first bottle and open the second, we get to it.

'How are things with Dom?' she asks me.

'They're all right,' I reply. 'Sometimes it's really good. Sometimes it isn't. Sometimes I feel like I settled.

That's just the way it is. I imagine most people feel like that at some point in their marriage.'

She reaches for my hand. 'I haven't forgiven myself,' she says. 'I never will.'

'Don't worry, neither will I,' I reply, and we both start laughing. 'Honestly, Alex, I don't know that it hurt the marriage all that much. I mean, it did for a while, but I'm not sure that we'd have been any happier even if you haven't slept with my husband.'

'Sometimes I wake up and I think: did I dream that? I would never have done that. I would never, ever have done that.'

'In the end, it was worse for you and me than it was for me and Dom. The damage done to us was much worse.'

'I still don't know why I did it, how I came to be in that state . . .' She's crying again, and I put my arms around her.

'I know why you did it,' I say, as she sobs into my shoulder. 'You were heartbroken. You were messed up and lonely and I wasn't there. I was never there. You were drunk, you were desperate. I understand,' I say, and I'm amazed, even as I'm saying it, by how calm I sound and by the fact that I mean it. I *do* understand. I just didn't realise it until now.

'We should go out,' I say to her getting to my feet. 'Otherwise we're just going to sit here, weeping and being maudlin.'

'That is a very good idea,' she says. 'Plus you look

amazing. That dress should not be wasted on my flat. And there is a very cool little place down the road, the Mulberry Street Bar, which does this blackberry Martini thing which will blow your fucking mind.'

In five minutes Alex had changed out of her 'sweats', as she now calls them, and into skinny jeans and an incredibly beautiful shearling-collared leather jacket.

'The most expensive thing I ever bought,' she whispers to me as she slips it on, 'aside from my car and the house on Shelter Island.'

'You bought a house on Shelter Island?'

'Well, I bought a third of a house on Shelter Island. Aaron bought two-thirds.'

'And now?'

'And now either he buys me out or we sell it or we could be incredibly civilised about the whole thing and keep it, but just agree to use it at different times. And although I would dearly love never to have to see or speak to the fucker again, I'm tempted to go with the civilised option. It is a lovely house.'

We've arrived at the Mulberry Street Bar and we press our way through the throng, miraculously finding ourselves seats at the back bar. The bartender greets Alex with enthusiasm, kissing her on both cheeks. Our Martinis are set in front of us almost immediately. From along the bar we receive dirty looks from a group of women who've clearly been waiting ages to be served. This is what it's like to hang out with Alex.

We clink our glasses and Alex looks as though she's about to burst into tears again, so I lean forward and give her a kiss on the cheek.

'It's okay,' I say. 'I really think we're going to be okay. Will you come to the party on Saturday?'

She shakes her head. 'I don't know. I'm pretty sure that would ruin Dom's evening.'

'Oh crap,' I say, and realise I've forgotten all about him. It's almost midnight – if he's still awake he'll be wondering where the hell I am. There are no messages on my phone, though, so perhaps he's fallen asleep. I don't want to call, I don't want to risk waking him up, I don't want to have to explain where I am. I put the phone away.

'Never mind Dom,' I say. 'He'll get over it. You should come to the party. You ought to be there.'

She smiles but doesn't say anything. We drink our drinks and fall into companionable silence. It's strange how easy it is to be with her, after all this time, after everything.

'They filmed a scene in *Godfather III* here,' Alex says all of a sudden.

'I'm not really sure that's something you should advertise,' I reply.

'And a scene from *The Sopranos*.'

'Oh, that's much better.'

We start giggling at exactly the same time, we're thinking of the same thing.

'Do you remember that fancy dress party, Nic?'

'You were Adriana and I was Carmela. Oh my god, that wig.'

'Those shorts I was wearing . . .'

'And Mike with the grey stripes in his hair like Paulie . . .' We laugh uncontrollably. I spill my Martini into my cleavage and down my dress, the barman kindly brings me another drink. The girls along the bar frown at us.

'Do you ever speak to him?' I ask Alex. 'Mike, I mean.'

'Not since the divorce came through. That was . . . god, when was that? August . . . no September 2008. He told me I was the biggest mistake he'd ever made, and that he sincerely wished he'd never met me. I told him the feeling was mutual. It was delightful.'

Now we're back on dangerous ground, and I know I probably shouldn't go there, but I owe her an apology.

'I'm sorry, Alex, about how I behaved.'

'It's okay.'

'No, it isn't. I was never around when things went wrong with you and Mike, I knew you were having a terrible time and I didn't do anything about it.'

'You were working,' she says, but she doesn't look up at me.

'And then after . . .'

'You don't have to apologise for that,' she says, taking my hand in hers.

'I know that I hurt you,' I say.

'Well, everyone was hurting everyone else, weren't they? None of us come out of it covered in glory, do we?'

She looks at her watch. 'It's twenty past twelve,' she says. She has tears in her eyes again, and so do I.

'December thirtieth.'

She raises her glass and I raise mine. 'To Julian.'

Chapter Sixteen

New Year's Eve 2007
Snowdonia, Wales

Resolutions:
1. Look into financing for series on 21st-century warfare
2. Take Alex away for a spa weekend
3. Lose half a stone
4. Go to Ibiza with Jules and Karl this summer
5. Look into buying a flat in Barcelona? Or Berlin?

A cottage halfway up the side of a Welsh mountain in December might not appeal to all comers, but to me it sounded like heaven. I'd spent eight weeks, eight sweltering, feverish, frightening weeks in Kinshasa, and the idea of being somewhere cold and quiet and completely free of gunfire was absolute heaven.

There were six of us going, including Dom and I: the others – Matt and Liz, Peter and Katy – were all solicitors, but even that couldn't dampen my mood. All I could think about were the long, bracing walks I was going to take over blasted heaths, the nights curled up with Dom and a good glass of red in front of the fire, the snowball fights on the front lawn of the crumbling stone cottage I envisaged in my head.

I had invited Alex to come with us, but she declined.

'We're thinking of going to South Africa,' she told me.

'We?'

'Well, maybe just me. I'm not really sure what's going on at the moment.'

She and Mike were still having problems, and they were getting worse, rather than better, from what I could gather. Not that I'd gathered very much – she and I hadn't spoken much since we'd gone on holiday together in April. These days, whenever she phoned me I got the feeling that she'd just opened her second bottle of wine. I'd come to dread her calls.

Not so Julian's, which were rare indeed now that he spent most of his time in warzones. He rang me on the morning of the 28th, just as Dom and I were leaving the M1 and joining the M6 on our way to Wales.

'Hello!'

'Jules! I didn't expect to hear from you today. How's it going? Are you okay?'

'I'm on the sat phone. Probably won't get another chance to call you until I'm in Pakistan.'

'That's okay, I'm going to be in deepest, darkest Wales, so I'm probably less likely to have signal than you are. Where are you, anyway?'

'About a hundred miles from the border, I think.'

'Is it okay there?'

'We're in convoy with the Yanks, so I'm surrounded by marines. I'm feeling pretty safe right now,' he said. 'Not to mention a little bit turned on,' he added, *sotto voce*.

'When are you coming home?'

'Not exactly sure. Once we're in Pakistan we'll drive south to Karachi, then I'll get a flight home from there. I'm hoping to be back within the week. How long are you in Wales?'

'Just until New Year's Day.'

'Excellent. I can't wait to see you. I was thinking . . .' the line crackled and screeched, white noise and static.

'Jules?'

'Can you hear me?'

'I can now.'

'I was thinking we should do another road trip. Will you have time, maybe in the spring?'

'Definitely.'

'What about Alex?'

'I don't know. But I think we should persuade her. I think an intervention might be in order.'

'That bad?'

'I think so.'

More crackling.

'So that's my first resolution,' Julian was saying. 'Road trip. Number two . . .'

'Quit smoking?' I interrupted.

He laughed. 'You know me so well. Three: take Karl to Zanzibar for his birthday.'

'That sounds a bit honeymoonish . . .'

'Oh, don't you start. He's really on one with this civil partnership bollocks. Four . . .' the line crackled again, more loudly this time, there was some beeping, and then it went dead.

'Julian? Jules?' I called out, vainly of course. 'Maybe he'll ring back,' I said to Dom, slipping the mobile into my pocket, but he didn't.

With Dom at the wheel most of the way, London to the Snowdonia National Park took the best part of the entire day. It was dark by the time we arrived, I was dozing in the passenger seat. Dom gave me a kiss on the cheek to wake me, I opened my eyes and looked out on paradise: a log cabin, blanketed in three to four inches of virgin snow, and not another building in sight, no other lights visible unless you counted the stars.

The front door flew open and there stood Matt wearing a bright red woolly jumper with a Christmas tree on it, a shot glass in each hand.

'Welcome!' he called out to us. 'Schnapps?'

The others had been there for a good few hours, a

fire was roaring in the hearth, the smell of a roasting chicken filled the cabin.

'You see,' Dom said to me, 'there are advantages to my refusal to drive at a million miles an hour.'

'I don't ask you to drive at a million miles an hour, Dom, I just point out that it is generally not thought of as a particularly grievous crime to break the speed limit every now and again.'

We spent the next couple of days exactly as I'd hoped we would: messing about in the snow, going for long, freezing walks, hanging out in the pub playing pool or sitting in front of the fire playing Scrabble. There was, as we'd predicted, no signal for our mobile phones, there was no TV, no Internet, we were isolated, cut off from the world. It was peaceful in all senses: quiet and harmonious. No one argued, except maybe a little about politics, and even then they were good-natured discussions: whether Gordon Brown's premiership meant a return to Labour's roots, Barack Obama's prospects versus Hillary Clinton, whether or not it was acceptable for adults to read Harry Potter books in an entirely unironic fashion.

It was a little bubble of middle-class niceness. There were no sexists, no homophobes or racists, no drunk ex-boyfriends, no tear-stained break-ups, no black eyes or bloody lips: it was one of the calmest New Year's Eves I'd ever spent. Everyone mucked in. No one shirked washing up duties. If I'm honest, everyone was so bloody nice it almost made me want to throw things, but that isn't a reasonable reaction, is it?

All six of us, under the direction of Katy who was an amazing cook, helped prepare a four-course feast: a pear and Roquefort salad, followed by a roasted rack of lamb with rosemary and crushed potatoes, possibly the most heavenly panna cotta I have ever tasted, followed by a board of cheeses (all Welsh) which Katy had found at a market in a place called Rhiwbryfdir the previous day.

At midnight, we sat out on a little terrace at the back of the cabin, wrapped in thick woollen blankets, toasting the New Year with chilled champagne, as a light dusting of snow began to fall over the mountain above.

'Bet you've never spent a New Year anywhere quite as beautiful as this, have you?' Dom asked, and immediately my mind jumped to the beach in Cape Town, but I just said, 'No. Never.'

Later, in bed, he asked me to marry him again. It was the third time – it had become our New Year's ritual. And for the third time, I said no.

The first time he asked me, back at Alex's place in Oxfordshire, it had been a total shock. The second time he asked me, I couldn't claim to be surprised.

'I'm not ready, Dom,' I told him. 'I'm twenty-eight. And I think people who marry very young often live to regret it, you know?'

'Twenty-eight is not that young, Nicole.'

'Well, you're not helping your cause by calling me old.'

That New Year, when he asked me for the third time, as we lay in the four-poster in the log cabin in Wales, I said no again.

'I can't settle down now, Dom. There's too much to do!'

Blake Productions, the TV company I'd set up, had until this point been making worthwhile but very minor films which aired in the middle of the night on unwatched cable channels, but had just been commissioned to make its first really major documentary, due to air in a prime time slot on BBC One.

And then there was the road trip, mark two. That April, Alex, Jules and I had taken three weeks off to drive the length of the Atlantic coast of Europe: starting out in Cherbourg, we drove south along the French coast, across the border to the Basque country, around the coast of Portugal and back into Spain, up the Costa le la Luz, finishing up in Tarifa. And since Jules had mentioned a second road trip to me on the phone a couple of days previously, I'd been thinking about it. We could aim bigger this time.

'We could combine work and holiday,' I told Dom. 'I'd love to work with Jules. We could film it, or do a blog or something: but it would need to be a big trip, something amazing, like Cape Town to Cairo.'

'You can't do Cape Town to Cairo, Nicole, because that would entail driving through Sudan, which is much too dangerous.'

'Says who?' I asked him, and he hugged me closer.

'Says me. In any case, all this is beside the point. You're making excuses.'

'I am not.'

'Why do you think that you can't be married *and* have a successful career or go on holidays with your friends? What do you think is going to happen? That the moment we walk down the aisle you'll find yourself chained to the sink, barefoot and pregnant? Marriage doesn't have to change who we are, Nic.'

'So why do it then? What's the point?'

'If I have to explain *that* to you, then you really aren't ready.' He rubbed the small of my back and kissed my neck. 'It's okay. One day you will be ready. And I'll be here.'

At 4 a.m. I woke with a start from a bad dream I couldn't properly recall. Dad was in it, and so was Alex and so was Julian. Something in my heart felt heavy and I wanted to talk to someone, to Mum, to make sure everything was okay. I got up and stumbled through the house in the darkness searching for my handbag. Eventually I found it, I turned the phone on, but there wasn't any signal. I knew there wasn't any signal. Still, I spent ages wandering around the house, holding the phone above my head, bashing into furniture, I even pulled on a pair of wellies and went outside into the snow, but not a single bar appeared on the display. Eventually I went back inside and slept fitfully until dawn.

We had to leave first thing in the morning. Dom was in the middle of an important case and they wanted him in the office that afternoon. In fact, they'd wanted him in the office that morning and the day before and the day before that, but he refused.

'Sometimes,' he said pointedly, 'you just have to let work come second. Otherwise it takes over everything.'

'It's not the same for you,' I replied. 'You don't run your own business. It's different when you're self-employed.'

'Not really,' he said. 'It's just about priorities.'

We hit the A5 at about nine in the morning, and almost the second we did, my phone started beeping. And beeping. And beeping. I had twenty-two missed calls: almost all of them from Alex, plus one from my mum and a couple from Karl. There were text messages from Alex, too, I read a couple of them.

Nic, are you in Wales? Need to talk to you.

It's urgent, pls call.

My heart sank.

'Oh god,' I groaned. 'I'm not sure I can face this just yet.'

'What's that?' Dom asked.

'It's Alex. She's been calling and calling. So either she's been hitting the booze pretty heavily or she's having more problems with Mike or – most likely – some hideous combination of the two.'

Dom squeezed my leg in sympathy. 'You don't have to call her back right away. It's only just after nine – there's no way she'll be up yet,' he said.

'No, you're right,' I replied, 'I'll ring her when I get back to London.'

I wasn't being entirely straight with him: the last missed call had been an hour before, so I knew she was awake. I turned the phone down to silent and slipped it back into my bag. Just a few more hours of peace, I told myself. Then I'll deal with it.

By the time we got onto the M6 we'd got thoroughly bored with the Kings of Leon album we'd been listening to all weekend, so Dom turned it off and tuned into Radio Four instead. It was almost bang on ten o'clock, the news headlines. Eight people were reported dead in fighting between the Fatah and Hamas factions in the Gaza Strip. More than one hundred people were thought to have been killed during rioting following the disputed presidential election in Kenya. And then:

'The British photojournalist killed in Afghanistan on Sunday has been identified as Julian Symonds of London. Mr Symonds, who was thirty-one, and an American journalist, Brian Hicks, were killed when the US military vehicle in which they were travelling was hit . . .'

I turned off the radio and covered my eyes with my hands, listening to my breathing, quick and shallow.

'Oh, Jesus Christ,' Dom was saying, 'oh my god, Nicole . . .'

I looked at him. His knuckles were white on the wheel. This wasn't real. I looked at the radio dial. It wasn't true. It wasn't true.

'Nicole? Nic?' Dom had his hand on my leg, squeezing hard. Then he reached for the radio dial again and before I could stop him he turned it back on.

'. . . Symonds and Hicks were travelling in military convoy from Kabul to the Pakistan border when their vehicle was hit by an IED. Four US service personnel, who have not yet been named, were also killed in the attack.'

It wasn't true. It wasn't true.

'Stop the car, Dominic. Stop the car stop the car stop the car.'

'Nic, I can't, there's no hard shoulder, I can't stop here.' He was holding the steering wheel with one hand, reaching for my arm with the other.

'Jesus Christ, stop the car, I have to get out Dom . . .'

I was sobbing now, I undid my seatbelt and started to open the door.

'Jesus, what the hell, Nicole?' Dom yelled. He swerved onto the edge of the motorway, drove right off the road and onto the grass verge. I got out of the car and threw up. I sat down on the grass and put my hands over my ears and tried to drown out the noise of the traffic.

On Sunday. They said he was killed on Sunday. He'd been gone for two days and I didn't know about it. What was I doing? Messing around in the snow or helping make dinner or having some polite fucking conversation about Labour party politics? Is that what I was doing when he was dying, thousands of miles away from his family, from Karl, from me?

The police came. I don't know if they just happened upon us or whether someone called them because we had stopped illegally, but they weren't particularly sympathetic. Dom tried to explain, that I was distraught, I'd been ill, but they just issued us a ticket and told us to get moving.

I lay down in the back seat of the car. I covered my head with my coat and closed my eyes. I couldn't stop trembling, my teeth were chattering in my head, but I wasn't cold.

'Do you want to call Alex now?' Dom asked me. 'Nicole?'

'No.'

'Maybe you should.'

'I don't want to talk to her. I don't want to talk to anyone. Not now.'

I stayed like that, covered up on the back seat, all the way back to London.

Chapter Seventeen

30 December 2011

I'm walking the streets of Manhattan, alone. Dom is in the hotel, working. He was asleep when I got back last night, so he doesn't know about Alex. I will tell him, I just didn't want to do it this morning. He was in a good mood (sex followed by breakfast in bed always does the trick) and I didn't want to spoil it.

I'm walking up Madison, on my way to Barney's. The weather's changed overnight, the sky no longer bright and crisp, it's dirty grey and ominous. You can smell the snow in the air. The thought of a snowstorm puts an inch or two of extra spring in my step. Dom and I have made plans to meet up later: he's going to work until mid-afternoon, then we're going to meet up at the Met for culture followed by cocktails. Maybe after that we can go ice skating at the Rockefeller Center, or take a walk in Central Park. I'll tell him about Alex then.

I can't afford anything in Barney's. Well, maybe a

scarf or a pair of sunglasses, but even that would be pushing it and I can't really turn up to Karl's party in sunglasses and a scarf.

Plus, everyone in Barney's is scarily attractive – it's as though a pack of models has been let loose on those cool white marble floors. Even in my skinniest jeans and my rocking Jimmy Choo biker boots, I feel dowdy and out of place. I scuttle out and continue along Madison Avenue, past Calvin Klein, Cartier, Chanel and Chloé. I am too afraid to enter any of these places, but the sight of the cerulean crêpe de Chine dress in the window of Giorgio Armani is too much for me to resist. I overcome my fear (I've been to Iraq, for Christ's sake, how can I be intimidated by shop assistants?), suck in my stomach, straighten my back and in I go.

The shop assistants are delightful. They are unfailingly polite, they ooh and ah when I put on the dress, they recommend shoes and jewellery to go with it. The dress is gorgeous and it looks fantastic on: it hangs beautifully, it clings in the right places, it's flattering and elegant. Perfect. And just a shade under a thousand dollars. I don't give myself time to back out, I just slide my credit card over the counter and bite my lip: Dom is going to bloody kill me. I just won't tell him what it cost.

I leave the shop feeling dizzy and guilty and delighted. I love the dress. I'll wear it a hundred times. That way it only cost ten dollars per wear. Less in fact. A bargain. Hell, at least I didn't get the heels they were suggesting to go with it which cost $400. It could have been a lot worse.

I'm walking quickly, not looking in the shop windows – I don't want to spot something I like even more for half the price, I don't think I could bear it. I need to get off Madison Avenue. I turn right and walk up a block, cross over Park and onto Lexington Avenue. I'm at the corner of Lexington and East 70th, an address which rings a bell for some reason. I've seen it somewhere recently, only I can't think where. It takes me a few moments to figure it out, and then it comes to me: it was on the letterhead at the top of an email I received. The offices of Zeitgeist Productions are at the corner of Lexington and East 71st – one block up. Aidan works *one block away* from where I am standing. I can't help myself, I have to go and just have a look.

Butterflies fluttering in my stomach, I walk past the glass doors to number 502. I stop for a moment to examine the list of names engraved into a chrome plate on the side of the building: Markowitz & Brown, Parker Prince Publishing, Zeitgeist Productions. They're on the tenth floor. I step back onto the pavement, craning my neck to get a proper view of the place where, had I the courage or the recklessness, I could work for a while. It's a far cry from the attic office with a view of Wimbledon Common. A snowflake lands on my eyelid. The snow is coming, it's time to get inside.

I walk north for a couple of blocks before ducking into a tiny Italian café, its windows all steamed up, not a table free in the place, just one spot left at the counter next to the window. Elbowing a determined-looking young woman in a power suit and heels out of the way I grab the last seat in the house, signal to the waiter and order myself a glass of red. I eat an enormous bowl of linguine with the most delicious meatballs I have ever tasted while watching the world rush by outside the window. It's better than theatre.

I finish lunch around two and start heading back south towards the Met. The sky is gunmetal grey now, it looks as though a storm is coming. I'm just passing the Zeitgeist offices again, on the other side of the road this time, when I spot him. Aidan, standing just outside the office building, talking to a woman with red hair. They're laughing about something. The woman gives him a kiss on the cheek and turns to go. I just stand there, transfixed. He's wearing jeans and a leather jacket with the collar up. He looks tanned and lean. His hair is shorter, but other than that he looks exactly the same. He turns to go into the building, and I feel weak, faint almost. I want to call out to him, but he'll never hear me at this distance, not over the noise of the traffic. Why does every driver in New York have to lean on their horns all the time? He's almost gone, and then, all of a sudden he turns back and looks at me, directly at me. He just stands there, stock still, staring at me. I don't know what to do, so I raise my hand in a half-hearted wave. He waves back.

It seems to take an age for him to cross the road to where I'm standing. I'm in the middle of the pavement – the *sidewalk* – blocking the flow of impatient New Yorkers who push past me on their way back to their desks, carrying their salt beef sandwiches, their cups of steaming soup. I can't move, I'm rooted to the spot, all I can do is watch him walk towards me, that languid movement so familiar; the way he cocks his head to one side when he smiles, it stops my heart. Aidan.

'When I offered you a job I didn't actually expect you to just turn up on my doorstep,' he says as he reaches me. 'I thought you'd at least call first.'

'I was just . . . in the neighbourhood,' I say and we both start laughing.

'Right.' He looks down at the Armani bag in my hand and says: 'Just doing a bit of shopping, were you?'

'Exactly.'

'Well, it's certainly a good neighbourhood for that.' We stand there, smiling stupidly at each other, buffeted by the passers-by, until he says: 'Do you have time for a coffee?'

The snow is falling harder now, so we duck into a bar just around the corner from Aidan's office where we order two coffees and two whiskies. Just to warm us up. We sit in a snug in the corner, raise our glasses and clink.

'So, what's going on, Nic?'

'I'm just here for a few days. Karl's having a party for New Year's Eve.'

'Oh, yes. He mentioned.'

'You're going?'

'I wasn't planning to. I no longer feel very festive this time of year.' He sips his whisky.

'I know what you mean. But seeing as it's Karl, I thought . . . Well. I never see him any more, you know?'

'Oh, I know. I think it's great you're going. He'll be so happy to see you. And it has been four years . . . It doesn't seem like four years though, does it?'

I shrug. 'I don't know. It does and it doesn't. It hurts like it happened yesterday, but I feel like I haven't seen him in a centenary. Every now and again I have to get a photograph out because I feel like I can't remember what he looks like.' I look up at Aidan. 'I suppose you don't really have that problem.'

'You always said we looked the same. I could never see it. He was much better-looking than me.'

'Much, *much* better-looking,' I say, and he laughs. 'Also kinder, funnier, more intelligent . . .'

'Yes, all right.' He looks away as he says this, so I'm not quite sure but I think he has tears in his eyes. 'I fucking miss him, Nicole.'

'I know.'

Aidan is sitting with his back to the window. He gets up and moves his chair around to my side, so

316

we can sit together and watch the snow, which is really coming down now, a blizzard.

'I'm supposed to be in a meeting with a new director in ten minutes,' Aidan says.

'And I'm supposed to be meeting my husband at the Met in half an hour,' I say.

He looks at me and grins, a cheeky, let's-play-hooky grin. 'I'll cancel if you'll cancel,' he says.

'Won't you get into trouble?' I ask him.

'With whom? I'm the boss.'

'That's right, you are. I can't believe you're the boss. You're way too irresponsible to be the boss of anything.'

Aidan rings his office and makes his excuses while I ring Dom.

'The weather's horrendous,' he says before I can say anything. 'Shall we do the Met tomorrow instead?'

'Okay.'

'Are you on your way back?' he asks.

'I'm in Bloomingdale's,' I lie. 'I haven't found a dress yet.'

Aidan goes to the bar and orders two more whiskies. When he sits back down next to me and slips his hand into mine a jolt of electricity goes through me. Sense memory. I remember what it feels like to hold his hand. I remember the last time we held hands like this. He was waiting outside my flat in Brixton the day I came back from Wales, after I heard. He was sitting outside on the steps, his head in his hands. I got out of the car and walked towards him, we were

317

both crying. Neither of us said anything, but he took my hand and we walked up the steps together, into the house. Dom followed behind us. When I realised Dom was still there, I dropped Aidan's hand, and I didn't touch him again. I haven't touched him since, not even at the funeral when he looked as though he needed someone to hold him up, and when I wanted more than anything to be that someone.

The snow stops falling. We finish our whiskies.

'Shall we go for a walk?' he asks me.

It's quiet outside, everyone has taken refuge inside shops or offices. Taxis roll by slowly, all of Manhattan is muffled by the thick carpet of snow. We crunch along the street, heading in the direction of the East River. All of a sudden, Aidan asks me, 'Have you walked the High Line?'

'Is that a euphemism for something?'

He laughs. 'No, the High Line. It's this old elevated freight railway that was built in the thirties. It closed down years ago, but it's now been reopened as this kind of long, narrow public park thirty feet up in the air. It's kind of cool. You really ought to see it when the wildflowers are out, but it should be fun in the snow, too.'

'That sounds good.'

'Let's go then.'

Aidan hails a cab and asks the driver to take us to West 20th Street by way of the park. As we drive

through picture postcard perfect Central Park blanketed in white, deserted and silent, I feel giddy, drunk
on more than a couple of whiskies. I'm transported
back in time, I'm nineteen again, on the back of Aidan's
bike, riding off into the sunset. I have to pinch myself,
to dig my nails into my palms and remind myself that
I'm not nineteen, I'm thirty-three, I'm a married
woman with a husband who's waiting for me in a
hotel room across town. I can't run away and have
adventures any more.

'What are you smiling about?' Aidan asks me.

'Nothing,' I reply. I didn't realise that I was.

'You've got that look,' he says, 'the one you get
when you're about to do something reckless. Are you
about to do something reckless?'

'I am not,' I say. 'My reckless days are over.'

'That's a shame. You were always fun when you
were reckless.'

The taxi drops us at the corner of West 20th and
10th, where a metal stairway leads up from the pavement. Taking care not to slip on the icy steps, we climb
to the top and begin walking south along the line.

To our right, we look out across Chelsea Pier and
the Hudson River towards Jersey, dimly lit in the
distance. We reach 10th Avenue Square, a kind of
mini-auditorium where you can sit and watch the
traffic whizz by underneath by way of a viewing
window. We stand up against the glass, watching taxis
slushing past.

Aidan's BlackBerry beeps. He gives its screen a cursory glance, then turns it off. 'Just work,' he says.

'Call them back.'

'It can wait. Speaking of work, you never got back to me about the Libya job. It's a great opportunity, Nic. I think you'd be perfect for it.'

'I know, I was going to call you. I can't do it, I'm afraid. That's not the kind of work I do any more. I can't leave London for months on end, that's not what my life is like now.'

'Why isn't it? It's not like you have kids . . .' This sentence hangs in the air, like an unanswered question.

'I have dogs,' I reply. 'And I have Dominic.' I realise as I say this how ridiculous it sounds.

We walk on in silence. Suddenly, Aidan stops, he turns to me and says: 'You're going to be pissed off with me.'

'Well, that makes a change . . .'

'I have to say this, though.'

'Say what?'

'You need to start living your life again.'

'What does that mean? I am living my life. Here I am. This is my life. I'm living it.'

'You know what I mean.'

'I don't.'

'Okay. After Julian died, you opted out. You stopped working—'

'I still work.'

'Oh, come on,' he says, exasperated. 'You stopped *really* working, you stopped playing . . .'

'Playing?'

'You stopped having fun.'

'I was grieving, Aidan.'

'I know, and it seems like you still are. He's been gone four years, and you're still the quiet, withdrawn, sad person you turned into after he died.'

'How would you know, Aidan?' I ask him crossly. 'You haven't seen me since he died.' The annoying thing is that he's right. Why is he right? How does he know?

'I hear things,' he says. Alex, of course. Alex and Karl, telling tales behind my back. How I'm not the girl I used to be. 'Listen, Nic, I don't want to piss you off, I really don't, but it just feels like it's a waste. You know? Do you remember how you were always making plans?' Aidan asks me. 'You were going to visit all seven continents, drive across Africa, run the Marathon des Sables, meet the Dalai Lama, live in a flat with a roof garden in Rome, run your own company . . .'

'I *had* my own company . . .'

'Yeah, you had, past tense. You wound up every-thing when Jules died.' He shakes his head sadly. 'You and Julian, with your New Year's Resolutions . . .'

'I still make New Year's Resolutions.'

'Yeah? And what are they this year?'

I hesitate. I don't want to tell him, not just because

the whole New Year Resolution thing was very much *our* tradition, mine and Julian's. Yes, I know everyone does it, but it still feels like it was peculiar to us. I don't want to tell him what I've resolved to do, I can't very well tell him about taking the pill, or about promising myself *not* to contact him, can I?

'Well?' he prompts me.

'Oh, I don't remember,' I say, irritated. 'I have to repaint the kitchen . . .'

He starts to laugh. 'You have to repaint the kitchen?'

'Oh, fuck off.'

'That's what I'm talking about. There was a time when you were planning to drive from the Cape to Cairo, or wanting to learn Mandarin. Now you're talking about repainting the kitchen.'

'That's what growing up is about, Aidan. Not that you'd know, obviously, but there comes a time in your life when you can't just think about holidays and adventures and having a good time, you have to think about . . . other things.'

'The kitchen?'

'Yes, the fucking kitchen. And marriage and kids . . .'

'So you are thinking about having kids?'

I don't want to have this conversation with him. 'I don't want to have this conversation with you,' I say. 'It's none of your business.'

'Okay.'

We walk on in silence. He reaches for my hand, and I let him take it.

'I just want to know that you're happy,' he says, 'that you haven't settled for less than you deserve.'

I drop his hand and fold my arms across my chest. 'If you're talking about Dominic, then you're way off,' I say. 'He's a good man, he's not a consolation prize. He's a good husband, he doesn't hurt me.'

'Is that right?' Aidan asks, a harder edge to his voice now. 'Is that why you and Alex stopped talking?'

'Fuck you,' I snap at him and storm off along the deserted walkway. Then I stop and turn around, I storm back again. 'You have no right, you know that? You have no fucking right to criticise my life, you have no right to question my choices, you have no right to talk to me about Alex or Dom. Especially Dom. He may not be perfect, it may not be the love affair that I had with you, but he does not break my fucking heart every chance he gets.'

'That's not fair, I never wanted to hurt you, Nicole . . .' There's hurt in his eyes, I've wounded him more than I intended, more than I thought I could. 'I know I fucked up, I know I made a lot of mistakes. Laure was one of the big ones.'

'You fell in love with her,' I say, my voice a little softer now. 'I suppose I can't really hold that against you.'

He stops walking. 'I didn't love her. I never loved her,' he says. 'I thought I did, for a while, but it turns out that it was always you.' He reaches out to me again, slipping his hand around my waist and into the small of my back, pulling me closer to him, brushing my hair back from my face. This is the point at which I should pull away, but I don't want to. I want to stay here with him, breathing in the scent of his skin, feeling his hands on me, this is where I want to be.

'I don't know what my life would have been if I hadn't loved you.' He kisses me on the mouth and I'm going back in time again, his lips on mine feel exactly the way they did when he kissed me on the beach in South Africa fifteen years ago. No other kiss has felt like that since.

'The thing I never realised, back then, was that I didn't have all the time in the world,' he says. 'It wasn't until Julian died and you got married that it occurred to me that you were gone, you were really gone. I couldn't have you. I'd always thought we'd end up together. I knew we'd end up together. You're everything to me, you always have been. It just took me for ever to realise it.'

He's saying all the things I ever wanted to hear from him and I can't stand it, it's too late. I pull away from him.

'It took you too long, Aidan.' I smile at him although I really want to cry. 'It's like what my dad said to me the other day. It's always later than you think.'

We've reached the Gaansevoort Plaza, the end of the High Line. Below is the Meatpacking District, packed with bars and boutiques. Alex and I talked about coming here, to have brunch at Pastis, just like the girls from *Sex and the City* did. We take the steps back down to street level.

'I should be getting back,' I tell Aidan. 'Dom will be wondering where I am.'

'Can I see you again before you go?' he asks.

'No, you can't Aidan. It's time we said goodbye.'

I hail a cab and leave him standing at the intersection of 8th and Greenwich Avenue. It takes all my willpower to not look back at him, to see if he's waving, or if he's already turned away.

Chapter Eighteen

New Year's Eve 2008
Lamu, Kenya

Resolutions:
1.
2.
3.
4.
5.

It was Dominic's idea to take our honeymoon over the New Year. It wasn't my choice: I was quite happy to leave it until the following summer, but Dom, who had never shown himself to be superstitious about anything up to that point, was adamant that it was bad luck not to honeymoon in the actual calendar year in which you get married, so it was our last chance.

We flew to Nairobi on the anniversary of Julian's death. I self-medicated fairly heavily on the flight: four gin and tonics and half a bottle of red. It took us a couple of hours to get out of Nairobi Airport, I spent most of that time in the toilets throwing up, then we transferred to another, smaller airport and got onto another, much smaller plane for the sixty-minute flight to Manda Island.

I was feeling better by this point, and not just because I'd purged most of the alcohol from my system. Coming back to Africa made me feel better, it always did. There was something irresistibly invigorating about the noise and chaos, the heat and space, all that blood-red earth. We landed on Manda at around five o'clock, there was nothing there but an airstrip and a little wooden hut, on which someone had hung a painted sign saying 'departure lounge'.

We – Dom and I, plus three other couples (from the looks of them, honeymooners too), and one set of exhausted-looking parents plus their two small children – were escorted to the shore and helped into two small boats, which ferried us across the narrow stretch of water which separates Manda from Lamu Island. I sat in between Dom's skinny white legs at the back of the boat, leaning against him, watching as the setting sun caught the top of the whitewashed roofs of Lamu village, and I felt at peace. Maybe this had been a good idea after all. This is exactly the sort of thing Julian would have wanted me to do on the anniversary of his death, had he been around to make recommendations.

I'd spent a lot of time that year thinking about what Julian would have wanted me to do. Mostly, I think

I'd gone against his wishes. I'm pretty sure he wouldn't have approved of my abandonment of two film projects I'd been working on for months. I doubt very much he'd have thought that marrying Dominic was the best idea. Not under the circumstances, anyway.

We got married in March. It was about as low key a wedding as is possible: just me, Dom, Mum, Charles, Dom's parents, Matt and Liz and Alex and Karl at the Chelsea Town Hall on a brisk Friday morning. I wore a pale-gold draped silk chiffon dress from Lanvin, Dom wore his best suit. We all took taxis to Petersham afterwards and had a fabulous lunch at the Nurseries. Nobody made any speeches. Everyone had a good time, except for Dom's mum who said the whole thing was so sad it made her want to weep.

Since I'd never been the sort to want to dress up like a princess, it was exactly the sort of wedding I probably would have chosen even had I not been grieving. But that wasn't really the point. It was the timing of the thing that caught everyone off guard. I could tell that even Dom was a little taken aback when, three weeks after the funeral, I told him I thought we ought to get married.

'I thought you said you weren't ready,' he said.

'I changed my mind,' I replied.

'I don't even have a ring,' he said.

'You've been asking me to marry you for three years, Dominic. How can you not have a ring?'

'I just . . . I don't know. I suppose I thought I had

at least another four or five New Years to go until you said yes.'

'I don't want a ring,' I said. 'I don't need a ring. Let's just do this quickly. No fuss, no tiaras, no brides-maids, no churches. Okay?'

He agreed, and he didn't ask more questions about why I'd changed my mind. I suppose he didn't want to press the point. Alex did.

'Are you sure?' she asked me. 'Why now? You know they say that you shouldn't make any major decisions within six months of somebody dying. Or is it within six months of winning the lottery? Something like that, anyway. I don't think this is the best time to be making life-changing decisions. Imagine what Jules would say.'

'Julian is gone,' I said, bluntly. For some reason I couldn't bear to hear her talk about him. I couldn't bear to hear anyone talk about him.

'Yes, I know Nic, but—'

'Well stop bringing him up, then. This has nothing to do with him. This is about Dominic and me. And it's time. I want to get married.'

Unlike Dom, Alex wasn't prepared to let the subject drop just like that. A few days after I'd phoned her to tell her that Dom and I were getting married, she rang me to ask me to meet her for drinks at the Duke of York off Gray's Inn Road.

'I have to see my lawyer,' she told me. 'Always a horrible experience. I'll need to get pissed afterwards.'

I didn't want to go. Getting pissed with Alex wasn't as much fun as it used to be. Plus, the weather was filthy, cold and wet, with a northern wind blasting through my corner of Brixton as though it were stuck out on some peninsula instead of being sheltered by the council blocks of the Loughborough estate.

By the time I arrived, it appeared to me that Alex had a head start; she was garrulous and louder than usual, laughing at things that weren't particularly funny. She launched into what seemed to be to be an ill-prepared 'marry in haste, repent at leisure' speech, illustrating her points with numerous examples from her own marriage, then in its spectacularly vicious death throes. I countered easily.

'One,' I told her, 'you didn't marry in haste. You were with Mike for years before you married him. And I've been with Dom for more than four years, so it's not really that hasty, is it? And two,' I went on, 'much more importantly, Dom is not Mike. Surely even you can see that?'

'All right,' she said, a look of hurt flickering across her face. Then, she asked: 'What do you mean, *even* me?'

'Nothing,' I said, crossly. I drained the rest of my drink. I wanted to leave, but I'd only just got there. Outside, it looked like the end of days, the rain hammering down, monsoon-like.

'Let's have another,' Alex suggested. She went to the bar, and instead of buying two more glasses of wine, she bought a bottle. My heart sank.

'Cheaper this way,' she said cheerily, pouring us each another glass. Then she started up on the marriage thing again.

'I know that you love Dom,' she said, 'and I'm not saying that marrying him is not the right thing to do, I just think you might live to regret a decision made in grief . . .'

'Don't talk to me about my grief, Alex,' I said, pushing my glass to the centre of the table. I'd had enough. I couldn't face this. 'You have no idea what I'm feeling. You have no idea what it's like for me.'

I got to my feet and started putting on my coat. Alex reached out to grab my hand, there were tears in her eyes. 'Nicole, don't go. I just want to talk to you. Please, Nic. I loved him too you know . . .'

'Don't do that!' I snapped, pulling my hand away from hers. 'Don't compare your relationship with him to mine, there is no comparison. You didn't have what we had.' I grabbed my handbag and walked out into the rain, knowing that I would have hurt her less if I'd stuck a knife into her chest, and having no idea why I was doing it. We'd not spoken much since.

Our little boat dropped us off at a jetty outside the Peponi Hotel, a low, whitewashed building clinging to the south-western edge of the island, surrounded by tall palms and lush lawns. A tall, white-haired gentleman with a deep tan and a Scandinavian accent welcomed us off the boat.

'*Karibu*,' he said his arms outstretched. 'Welcome to Lamu.'

We sat on sun loungers on the terrace outside the hotel bar, our fingers gently interlaced, sipping gin and tonics, watching the sun dip into the sea. A warm, salty breeze came up off the water, lulling us towards sleep. I resisted.

'I've decided I'm going to wind up the company,' I told Dom. He opened his eyes and looked over at me, a look of concern on his face.

'Really? Are you sure?'

I shrugged. 'We haven't made anything all year,' I said. 'I'm just losing money on office space and employees. I think I'm done with all that now.'

'Okay,' he said, giving my hand a squeeze. 'If you think that's best.'

'I do. Maybe I'll write instead, or . . . I don't know.'

'You don't have to work,' Dom said. 'You could just take it easy for a while.'

'I want to work,' I replied, 'I just don't feel like travelling any more. Not unless it's doing stuff, like this.' I leant over and kissed him on the lips.

'Good, I'm glad. I want my wife at home.'

I flinched at this, but I knew he didn't mean it the way it sounded, so I didn't say anything. A waiter brought us another round, with a little dish of peanuts.

'So is that one of your resolutions, then?' Dom asked. 'Winding up the company?'

'I haven't made any resolutions this year,' I said. 'It's just a decision.'

The next day, we lay on the beach in scorching sun, our pale English bodies turning gently pink in the sun. Local boys, incongruously dressed in early nineties English football strips, wandered along the shore and approached with baskets of wares to sell: samosas, cans of Coke, ready-rolled spliffs. Dom bought us two of each.

'Are you really a Manchester United fan?' Dom asked our vendor.

'Ronaldo,' the boy replied with a grin. 'Rooney, Giggs. Best team in the whole world.'

Dom looked pained and muttered something about the ubiquity of the Premiership being 'yet another thing to resent Rupert Murdoch for'. The boy just smiled at us and trotted off down the beach, humming 'Volare'.

Dom and I found ourselves a square metre of shade under a low palm, smoked our joints looking out over the shimmering sea. In our beach bag, my phone buzzed again and again. It was Alex.

'You should answer,' Dom said. 'Just say hello.'

'It'll cost a fortune from here, Dom. It'll cost both of us a fortune. Anyway. We're on our *honeymoon*. Why does she keep calling? There can't possibly have been another hideous tragedy at exactly the same time of year can there?'

'Perhaps she's just calling because it's . . . well . . . the anniversary. She probably just wants to find out if you're okay.'

'She's driving me mad.'

'She's hurt. She just got divorced, and she also lost a friend, Nic.'

'Oh, don't you start.' I got up off my towel. 'I'm going for a swim.'

In the shallows, the water was clear and warm as a bath, but it turned colder and darker blue the deeper I got. I floated on my back, eyes closed, I drifted. I was thinking about the first time I swam in the Indian Ocean. It wasn't the New Year's Eve in Cape Town, that was the Atlantic. This was eleven years ago, April or March, I think. Aidan had started his desk job in London, he was earning a decent salary at last, Karl had just sold a piece to a gallery in New York, so he was in the money, too. So the four of us – Julian and Karl, Aidan and I – decided to take a holiday in Mozambique.

We flew to Maputo and drove north to Vilanculos. I was awestruck, I'd never seen beaches like that – endless, unspoiled, completely deserted, with not a building, high rise or otherwise, anywhere in sight. We couldn't even wait to take off our clothes, let alone pitch our tents, the moment we arrived at our camping spot we just piled out of the rental car and tore down onto the sand and into the water. We bought fish from a local market and grilled it over a fire on the beach, accompanied by cheap (gut-rotting) rosé. It was heaven.

Salt tears were running down my cheeks, joining the ocean. And I could hear someone yelling my name.

'Nicole! Hey! Nicole!'

I opened my eyes and started to tread water. I'd drifted right into the middle of the channel between Lamu and Manda, the current was carrying me towards the open ocean. Drift out there and you don't come back. For just the slightest fraction of a moment the idea was tempting, the thought of disappearing out into the endless blue, but the desperation in Dom's voice brought me back to myself, and I started to swim, I started to fight.

It took me twenty minutes to get back to shore. Dom, following my progress from the land (he never was a very strong swimmer), came running to meet me as I half walked, half crawled up the beach.

'What were you doing?' he yelled, grabbing hold of me, enveloping me in his arms. 'What on earth were you doing?'

'I'm sorry,' I panted, collapsing down onto the wet sand. 'I drifted too far.'

He sat down next to me. 'That's the last time you get stoned before going swimming.'

'Definitely. Either that or we need to fashion some sort of anchor to keep me near to shore.'

Dom put his arm around my waist and kissed my

shoulder. 'If only,' he said, 'if only I could make an anchor to keep you near me.'

We went back to our room, made love under the mosquito net, drank hot sweet tea brought to us by the hotel staff. We compared sunburn. Mine was definitely worse, no doubt exacerbated by all that time in the water.

'Putting on clothes again is going to be agony,' I complained.

'We could just spend the rest of the holiday naked,' Dom suggested.

'Tempting, but do you not think we might look a little out of place at the New Year's Eve party tonight?'

'I don't know,' Dom shrugged. 'They looked to me like a pretty swinging crowd.'

In the end I wore a maxi dress with no underwear, which excited Dom no end and kept me comfortable. The party, held in the hotel bar, started out a quiet affair.

'That's the problem with these honeymoon-y places,' I grumbled to Dom. 'It's all couples, so there's no atmosphere. No one's hitting on anyone else.'

'Don't be so sure about that,' Dom replied. 'The blonde over there with the large . . . uh . . .'

'Tits?'

'I was going to say bottom, but she's fairly proportionate, I suppose. Anyway, I reckon she's been eyeing up the overly tanned chap with the tight T-shirt on.'

While other couples made stilted conversation about their weddings (size, location, quality of best man's speeches), Dom and I sat in the corner, people-watching and munching on the most delicious crab cakes I have ever tasted.

'We really ought to mingle,' Dom said after his fourth crab cake. 'We're being a bit antisocial.'

'This is our honeymoon, Dominic. We're supposed to be antisocial. In any case, I don't think they'd be terribly impressed by our registry office nuptials, do you?'

Fortunately, the handsome Danish hotelier, Michael, had invited some locals who arrived three sheets to the wind and livened the place up no end. Dom and I got talking to Bruce and Lara, originally from Devon, who ran a donkey sanctuary just outside Lamu village, and who invited us to go on a snorkelling-slash-fishing expedition on their boat the following day.

'You see?' I said to Dom. 'The key thing is to be antisocial until the interesting people show up and invite you to go out on their boat.'

'You're so much cooler than I am,' he said.

'Aren't I?'

Dom and I skipped the New Year countdown, choosing instead to go for a walk on the beach. Even at one minute to midnight, it was almost as bright as day, a full moon reflecting off the vast expanse of pale, wet sand. Apart from waves breaking far out to sea, the silence was perfect. We walked, hand in hand, for two or three miles, then turned and walked back again, awestruck by a seemingly endless expanse of inky, star-studded sky.

We rounded the beach head and were heading back towards the lights of the hotel when Dom wandered down to the water. He looked up at me with a grin.

'Fancy a swim?'

'I'm not wearing my bikini, Dominic.'

'I know,' he said, the grin turning from merely cheeky to lascivious.

Giggling like school children, we stripped off and jumped into the water. It was cooler than it had been that afternoon, it felt delicious on my hot, sunburned skin. We floated on our backs, looking up at the sky, hands interlaced.

'We should do this more often,' Dom said to me.

'Skinny dip?'

'Get away, just the two of us. And yes, we should skinny dip more often, too.'

'You reckon they wouldn't mind too much at the pool at Wimbledon Leisure Centre?'

We drifted a little further and then started back for shore. It was only when we reached the point at which our toes could touch the sand with our chins still above water when I noticed that there was somebody on the beach. Two people, actually. The curvy blonde and her husband. They were sitting about a metre or two from where I'd dropped my dress.

'Hiya!' the blonde called out. 'What's the water like then?'

'Lovely,' Dom said, shooting me a look. 'It's very nice.'

'Yeah, lovely,' I agreed. We'd reached the point at which, if I went any further towards the beach, I was going to be flashing my tits at them.

'You're braver than I am,' the blonde said. 'I wouldn't go in the water in broad daylight, let alone at night. All those creepy crawlies . . . Ugh. Have you seen the size of the crabs round here?'

Dom and I splashed around half-heartedly, waiting for the couple to get bored and leave. They did not.

'Have you been to the donkey sanctuary yet?' the woman went on. 'Poor mites. In a terrible way some of them.'

'We were thinking of going tomorrow,' Dom replied.

He and I swam around a bit more. I was starting to get cold and the couple on the beach showed no sign of leaving.

'Really enjoying it out there, aren't you?' the bloke asked.

Dom was laughing to himself.

'They're never going to leave,' he whispered.

I was getting the giggles, too.

'We're going to have to face death by freezing or death by embarrassment. Which would you prefer?'

'I say we just brazen it out.'

And so we did. Hand in hand, stark naked, the two

of us waded out of the water and up the beach as casual as you like. The blonde and her other half watched us, open-mouthed.

'The water really is lovely,' Dom said as he pulled on his boxer shorts. 'You ought to try it.'

'Maybe tomorrow,' the blonde said, her gaze averted.

'Well, we're off to bed now,' I said, and the two of us walked off towards our room, heads held high, as though flashing complete strangers was something we did every day.

Back in our room, we collapsed on the bed, laughing helplessly.

'Oh my god, did you see the way they looked at us?'

'We have to face those people at breakfast,' Dom said. 'I'm not sure I can bear to leave the room.'

'It's just like you said. We just brazen it out. Act completely natural. Never complain, never explain.'

Someone – presumably the handsome Danish hotelier – had left a bottle of champagne and a box of Belgian chocolates in our room, with a note wishing us a happy New Year. We took these goodies and climbed into the enormous stone tub in the bathroom. I lay back in Dominic's arms, my eyes closed. In moments like these, I could forget about everything. I could be happy.

* * *

I woke, as I often did, in the early hours of the morning. I wriggled out of Dominic's embrace and checked the time on my phone: it was just before four and I had three missed calls. Alex, inevitably, my mum, unsurprisingly, and Aidan.

That wasn't expected. Aidan and I hadn't spoken in months, not since he'd called me in April. He was in London for a couple of weeks, he wondered whether we could meet up. Just to talk. He was finding it a bit of a struggle, he said. I was the only person he felt he could talk to about Julian. I was the only person who would understand. I didn't tell him that I felt the same way. I didn't tell him that I couldn't talk to Alex, I couldn't talk to Dom. I didn't tell him that he was the only one I wanted to talk to, because he was the one who knew Julian like I did. I didn't say that. Instead, I said: 'I got married. A few weeks ago.'

There was a long silence on the other end of the line. Eventually, he spoke. 'Congratulations.'

'It was just a small thing,' I said, not really sure why I was explaining that. It could have been the most lavish ceremony since Charles and Diana's nuptials and he wouldn't have expected to be on the guest list.

'Okay,' he said. 'Well. That's . . . well. Brilliant. Great. Congratulations. All the best, Nic.'

We stayed on the phone for a ridiculously long time, neither of us saying anything, until eventually I hung up.

I checked the time of his call, it was about two hours

342

ago. I slipped out of bed, pulled my dress over my head and gently pushed open the door. Our room had its own little terrace, then a few steps down to a lawn, and from the lawn a few more steps to the beach. I walked down onto the sand. I sat down with my back to a palm and, my heart hammering in my chest, dialled Aidan's number.

'Hey, Nic.' I was expecting him to sound drunk, or at least to be shouting above the noise of a party, but his voice was clear, quiet and sober. 'Thanks for calling back. Wasn't sure what you were up to for New Year. Just thought I'd check in.'

'I'm on honeymoon,' I said.

'Shit. Sorry. Hang on a minute – you're on your honeymoon? First marriage didn't last long then?'

'This is my first marriage, you git. We just haven't had time to get away.'

'Where are you?'

'Lamu. Kenya.'

'Bloody hell, what time is it there? It must be . . .'

'About four.'

'Sorry, Nic. Thought you were in London.'

'That's okay. You in New York?'

'Yeah. It's just after nine.'

'Not going out tonight?'

'No, quiet one for me. Where are you?'

'Lamu, I told you . . .'

'No, I mean, where exactly? At the moment?'

'On the beach.'

343

'Really?'

'Really. I didn't want to wake Dom.'

'You didn't have to ring straight back.'

'I know.'

I was walking up the channel towards the beach head, towards the open ocean. I held the phone up above my head.

'Can you hear the breakers?'

'Not really. Maybe a little.'

I walked along a little further, holding the phone up again.

'Now?'

'Yeah, I can hear them.'

I sat down on the beach looking out across open ocean.

'I was thinking, today . . .'

'About Cape Town?'

'About Mozambique, actually. The Indian Ocean. That was the first time I swam in it.'

He laughed softly. 'I remember. You were so excited.'

'Do you remember Julian trying to climb that date palm?'

'When he fell and hit his head . . .'

'And then freaked out and insisted that we keep him awake for twenty-four hours to "monitor him" in case he had brain damage?' We both laughed at the memory.

'That was a good holiday,' Aidan said.

The sky above was beginning to brighten a little, turning from black to grey.

'I wish I didn't think about him so much,' I said.

'I wish I didn't think about you so much,' Aidan replied.

'We shouldn't talk any more.'

'I know.'

'It feels like . . .'

'A betrayal.'

'Exactly.'

'I'm sorry. I just wanted to hear your voice. I miss your voice. I miss . . .'

'Goodbye, Aidan.'

'I love you, Nicole.'

I went back to our room and slipped into bed beside my husband, slipping my arms around him.

'You're cold,' Dom croaked sleepily.

'I went for a walk,' I said.

'You're always disappearing on me,' Dom said. 'Where is it that you go?'

'Just walking. I was just walking.'

'Thinking about Julian?'

'Just walking.'

Chapter Nineteen

30 December 2011

I fight with myself all the way back to the hotel. Part of me, a big part of me, possibly more than seventy-five per cent of me, wants to tell the cabbie to turn around, to drive as fast as he can back to the street corner where he picked me up, so that I can leap out of the car and run after Aidan and catch him at the last minute, just as he's about to descend into the subway to head to who knows where, just as he's about to disappear from my life again. Just like in a film.

The rational, cool-headed part of me says, 'Don't be so bloody ridiculous. Say you did run after him, say by some miracle you did catch him. Then what? Then what happens? You go back to his apartment with him? You sleep with him, while your husband is waiting for you across town?'

The very thought makes me feel ill. I couldn't do that, no matter how much I want to be with Aidan, no matter how much he means to me. I'm not that cold; I'm not that heartless. I wouldn't be able to stop thinking about Dom, sitting there in the hotel room, watching the clock, waiting for the woman he loves to come back to him. I want to be back at the hotel, I want to get back to safety. I want this taxi to go faster. Why doesn't *this* driver lean on his horn?

When we finally get there, I leap out of the cab and run up the steps into the lobby, I press the button and wait for the lift to come. There is only one lift, which is ridiculous for a hotel this size. It takes ages, it takes for ever.

Back in our hotel room, Dom is sitting on the sofa, anxiously watching the door.

'There you are,' he says, that familiar note of irritation in his voice. 'How long does it take to buy a dress for Christ's sake? We're supposed to be meeting Karl in half an hour.'

And just like that I wish I had gone back to find Aidan.

'I'm sorry,' I say, though I don't actually feel any remorse. 'It took an age to find a cab, and then the traffic was appalling. And you know how indecisive I am when it comes to shopping.' Ridiculously, given the fact that I am lying to him, I feel put out, as though he is being unreasonable. 'I found a great dress though,' I say, holding up my shopping bag. 'Do you want to see?'

He shrugs. 'Armani?' he says, looking at the bag. 'How much did that set us back?'

I sigh. 'God, you really are determined to have a shit time, aren't you? Maybe you wouldn't be in such a crappy mood if you hadn't spent all day cooped up in this hotel room. Seriously, is this what you came to New York to do? You haven't left the room since we got here.'

'I came to New York because *you* wanted to come, Nicole, and because I wanted to be with you,' he says. 'I always want to be with you. It's just not very easy, you know? Because you're always running out the door.'

I shower and change and we hurry back down to the lobby to grab a cab to Tribeca, where we're due to meet Karl. We're not exactly fighting, but we're not exactly friends, either. We're headed for the Macao Trading Company, which, according to Karl, serves amazing cocktails in the lounge bar.

Dom grumbles all the way, but we're only ten minutes late in the end. We walk downstairs to a low-lit, high-ceilinged room flanked on one side by a long, candle-strewn bar above which are six or seven shelves of gleaming bottles. I spot Karl immediately, and start to tear up straight away. He looks wonderful. He has maintained his perfect gym-fit physique and alabaster skin, but he has grown a George Michael-esque beard, manicured to within an inch of its life, which makes him look terribly distinguished, as does the light dusting of grey at his temples. He's sitting

349

on a stool at the near end of the bar, legs crossed, reading the *New Yorker*.

'*Guten tag*!' I call out to him and he looks up, his handsome face breaking into a broad grin.

'Nicole!' he yells, leaping off his stool to the alarm of the drinkers around him. He takes a few steps towards us and grabs me, lifting me off the ground and swinging me around, bear-hugging me so tight I can barely breathe. 'Oh Nicole, Nicole! It's so good to see you, I'm so glad you're here.' He's tearing up, too. He puts me down and we both wipe our eyes and laugh, he kisses me on both cheeks and then hugs Dom, with almost as much force and enthusiasm as he embraced me.

We choose cocktails. I opt for the Westside, lemon vodka and fresh lemon juice with soda, Karl goes for a rather camp blood peach Bellini, which consists of puréed blood peaches, Campari and prosecco. Dom, much more butch, chooses a Once Daily, rum with bourbon and ginger liqueur on the rocks, with a splash of Fernet Branca.

'What the hell is Fernet Branca?' I ask.

'No idea,' Dom replies, taking a sip of his drink, 'but this is delicious.'

We find ourselves a table in the corner surrounded by assorted Chinoiserie: vases and puppets, faded pictures of beautiful Chinese girls, ancient tatty globes the very sight of which make my feet itch. Karl asks what we've been up to, we prattle on about

Christmas and swap work tales. Karl's gallery, which is just a few blocks away, he tells us, is doing quite well, recession notwithstanding.

'You should drop by tomorrow before the party, or the next day, whenever – we have this great Franko B exhibition . . .' Dom and I look at him blankly. 'Fabulous Italian artist, he's a painter but he also does performance, installations, that kind of thing. He's very interesting.' We both nod dutifully; Karl laughs. 'Philistines!' he says. 'How long are you here for?'

'Just until Monday.'

'Okay then, well apart from visiting my fabulous gallery, you must go to MoMA . . .'

'MoMA?' Dom asks.

'The Museum of Modern Art, Dom, even I know that.'

'You should go ice-skating at the Rockefeller Center, and while you're there you should go to the Top of the Rock – it's actually better than the Empire State because there are fewer people – and of course you can actually *see* the Empire State. And you *must* have pork rolls at Momofuku – they are absolutely to die for – and you should walk the High Line . . .'

'The High Line?' Dom asks, and I don't listen to Karl's answer because I'm jolted back to that afternoon and I get a pure sense memory, the sensation of Aidan's lips on mine, my stomach flips.

'You okay, Nic?' Dom asks me. 'You look flushed.'

I go to the loo and splash my face with water. I

fish my mobile from my handbag and check the call log. There's nothing from Aidan. I did tell him that it was time to say goodbye, so why am I so disappointed that, less than three hours since I saw him, he hasn't been in touch? I reapply my make-up and return to our table. Dom is at the bar, ordering another round.

As I sit down, Karl takes my hand and smiles at me.

'You look good,' he says. 'Really good.'

'So do you,' I say, reaching up to touch his face. 'I like the beard.'

He laughs. 'Not my idea . . .'

'Oh no?' I say, an eyebrow raised.

'No, a friend suggested it, he thought it would look nice.'

'A friend, eh? And who is this friend?'

Dom sits back down and hands us our drinks.

'I actually wanted to talk to you about him, about us. I wanted to see you before the party, before the . . . uh . . . official announcement. I wanted to tell you the news first of all.'

'What news is that?' Dom asks and I try to ignore the sinking feeling I'm getting.

'I'm getting married!' Karl announces raising his glass to us both.

'Bloody hell!' Dom splutters, crashing his glass against Karl's delicate champagne flute, 'Congratulations! That's fantastic, Karl. Who's the lucky guy?'

'His name's Sean, he's great, you'll really like him . . .'

'So when is this happening?' Dom asks him. 'Are you doing it here in New York?'

'We're not sure yet. When Sean first asked me it wasn't even possible because they hadn't legalised it here yet, so we were thinking Vermont or something like that, or even Germany, because you can get a civil partnership there, but now we're not so sure . . .'

I'm aware that I haven't said a word since Karl dropped his bombshell, and now they are, too, they both turn and look at me.

'Nic?' Dom says, placing his hand on my arm. 'Isn't this great?' I look up at Karl, he's looking back at me, hopeful, and so I give him the brightest smile I can and say, 'Yes, it's . . . really great. Congratulations.' All of a sudden I'm desperate to be out of there, I don't want Karl to see how upset I am, so I get to my feet and say, 'I'm really sorry, I'm not feeling very well. I have to go.'

I don't look at them as I pull my coat on, I can't bear to see the look on Karl's face. I push through the noisy crowd of drinkers and hurry up the stairs, out onto the street, into another snowstorm. I hurry along the street, half-blinded by white, looking desperately this way and that for a taxi.

'Nicole!' I hear Dom's voice behind me, 'Wait!' He catches up with me and grabs my arm, spinning me around roughly. 'What the hell are you doing? That was awful what you did back there.'

'I know, I'm sorry . . .' I stammer.

'Don't tell me you're sorry. That was fucking cruel. He doesn't deserve that. He of all people does not deserve that. Jesus Christ, I know you think your pain is greater than most people's, but do you really think it's greater than his? Do you honestly think he's suffered less than you have?' He lets go of my arm; no, he throws my arm back against my chest. 'He doesn't deserve to be happy, is that it?' He's yelling at me now, furious. 'Because you can't be happy, because you can't move on, because you're stuck in your bubble of grief, that means everybody else should be fucking miserable too, is that it?'

I feel ashamed, and not just because our unseemly little domestic is being witnessed by the hipsters waiting for their tables at Macao. He's right, what I did was awful and I can't take it back now: my first reaction to the news that Karl is getting married will always be an unkind one, there's nothing I can do about it. I turn away from Dom and walk slowly down the street, into the wind.

'Where are you going?' Dom yells, he pushes past me, blocks my path. 'You're leaving? You're not even going to go back and say sorry?'

'I can't now, Dom. Please let me go, I'll talk to him tomorrow or I'll call him later on . . .'

I carry on down the street, heading north, almost

blinded by snow. Dom stops me again, he grabs my arm again.

'Nicole, for god's sake, you can't do this. Come back inside, please. Come on – you and me, we'll go back in there, you'll apologise, we'll have a nice drink and behave like civilised human beings.'

He's right, he's right. I know he's right. If I go back there now, I can at least try to make things better. But I can't do it if Dom's there beside me, steering me back into the bar – it'll look like he's dragged me back to apologise. Which of course he has, but I don't want Karl to see that.

'I'll go, Dom. I think it's better if I go and talk to him on my own. Okay?'

It is not okay.

'For fuck's sake!' he yells at me. 'I am so bloody sick of this.'

'What?'

'You, running away from me. This isn't a partnership any more, Nicole, this isn't a marriage. This is you, in your own little world, running off to see your father, disappearing to god knows where in the middle of the night, snapping shut your laptop the second I walk into the room, having secret telephone conversations . . .' He stops, throws his hands up in the air, a gesture of resignation. 'Do you think I don't notice the way you're constantly disappearing, the way you're always sneaking around? Do you think I don't care? Did you honestly expect me to believe, for example, that you were just "walking around" last night until two-thirty in the morning?'

I did, actually.

'Where were you? Go on, just tell the truth. Just for once. Give it a try – see how it feels.' His voice drips venom. 'Were you with Aidan?'

There's an awning up ahead, a red plastic awning which affords a half yard or so's protection from the snow. I shelter underneath it, waiting for Dom to join me, but he doesn't move, he just stands there, his question hanging in the air.

'I went to see Alex,' I say. 'We talked for a while, then we went out for a drink at a bar near where she lives. Then I came back.' His shoulders slump a little, I can sense his relief, which makes what's coming a hundred times worse. 'But I have seen Aidan. I was with him today. I bumped into him outside his office . . .'

'You bumped into him?' Dom asks, incredulous. 'How fucking stupid do you think I am, Nicole? You *bumped into him* . . .' he laughs mirthlessly.

'It's the truth, I swear, I was shopping near where he works, I saw him in the street . . .'

'And then what? Then what? You were with him all afternoon? Did you go to bed with him?'

'No! Jesus, Dom, of course not. I would never do that. Believe me, please, we just walked around . . .'

'You know what?' he interrupts me. 'Don't tell me. I don't want to know. I'm really not interested in listening to your excuses. I've had enough of this. It has to stop. You have to make a choice between life with me and life with . . . them. All the others. Aidan, Alex, Julian's ghost . . . the life you had before. I'm going back to the hotel now, I'm going to get on the first flight that I can and I'm going back to London. If you're at all interested in saving this marriage, you can come with me. If not, well . . . There's nothing more I can do, Nicole.'

I stand there for a bit, under my sad little red plastic awning, wishing I had a cigarette. Wishing I hadn't told Dom that I'd seen Aidan, wishing I hadn't over-reacted to Karl's wedding announcement, wishing I could go back in time, to this morning, to sex and breakfast in bed.

I have a choice to make: I can run after Dominic and beg him not to leave, beg him to let us stay here for a couple more days, beg him to go to the party like we planned, to go ice skating at the Rockefeller Center and have cocktails at the Met, or I can go and find Karl and apologise for running out on him.

I choose Karl. I go back to Macao, but our table is empty. I search the bar for five or ten minutes, but it's obvious that he's gone. Back upstairs on the pavement, I call him from my mobile.

'Nicole?'

'I'm so sorry, Karl, I'm so sorry.'

'It's okay . . .'

'It's not okay, I don't know what came over me.'

'Are you at your hotel?'

'No, I'm outside the bar.'

'Come to my place. It's very close by. You just walk one block east and two blocks south, and you'll find me. Warren Street, number thirty-five. Apartment seven. Okay?'

'I'll be there in a minute.'

Ten minutes later I am standing outside Karl's apartment, feeling like an idiot. I press the buzzer and take the lift to the fourth floor, where he greets me as I step through the doors, embracing me as though I hadn't seen him for years, let alone run out on him twenty minutes earlier.

'I'm sorry, Karl, you took me by surprise . . .'

'It doesn't matter.'

'It does, I feel so stupid.'

'Don't feel stupid.'

'I am stupid. I want you to be happy. I'm happy you're happy.'

'I know you are,' he says. 'Come on, come inside. I want you to meet Sean.'

'Oh god, he's here? Karl . . .' I'm mortified, but short of running away again, there's nothing I can do now.

The apartment is large by New York standards, the front door opening up into an elegant hallway which leads into a living room with floor to ceiling windows looking out onto the street. The walls are covered with large, colourful paintings, some of which I recognise as Karl's own. On the left, above the open fireplace, is a stark black and white photograph, little boys, dressed in white, playing football in a dusty street. It's one of Julian's.

Karl takes my coat. While he's hanging it up in the hallway closet a slight, grey-haired man wearing jeans, a brightly printed shirt and a pair of heavy-framed specs appears from the kitchen, carrying a bottle of champagne in one hand and four flutes in the other. They were obviously expecting Dom to come with me.

'Hello,' he says, giving me a warm smile. 'Would you like a glass of sparkle?'

'I'd love one,' I say. I stand there awkwardly while the man, who has clearly opened many a champagne bottle in his life, silently and expertly removes the cork and pours us each a glass, leaving one empty.

'It's nice to meet you, Nicole,' he says, handing me one of the flutes. 'I'm Sean, by the way.'

'I guessed as much,' I said. 'It's lovely to meet you, too. Congratulations.'

'Oh yes, finally getting him down the aisle,' he said with a laugh.

'I'm sure he didn't need too much persuasion. He always was a sucker for weddings.'

Karl comes back into the living room and picks up a glass.

'What can I say? I am an old romantic.' The three

of us clink glasses and Sean invites me to sit. He is not what I expected; he has a good ten to fifteen years on Karl, not at all the twenty-something gym-bunny I imagined in my head. Why I imagined that I've no idea, but I'm oddly relieved that Karl is with someone older, someone to look after him. I feel like I ought to say something about my earlier behaviour, and I start to explain, but Sean waves away my apologies.

'Don't give it a moment's thought,' he says. 'I understand completely.'

'So,' I say brightly, sipping my champagne, 'tell me about your wedding plans. Germany, Karl said?'

Sean pulled a face. 'I'd rather do it in the States. I'm pushing for Cape Cod. Cape Cod in the spring, don't you think that would be great? Would you come over if we did it in the spring?'

'Of course, I would,' I say. 'And I'd pick Cape Cod over Germany, too.'

'What's wrong with Germany?' Karl asks. Sean and I exchange a look. I like him already.

'And how did you guys meet?'

'Sean's a sculptor,' Karl says, beaming at him proudly. 'A very good one. That's one of his,' he says, pointing to a striking bronze figure standing on a low-slung bookcase to my left. It stands next to a large framed photograph of Julian, tanned and happy, laughing at the camera. I love that he's here in the room with us. 'Sean had a show at my gallery last year and . . . well. You know.' They smile at each other, they're almost coy. It's so lovely to see Karl like this again.

'And what about you?' Sean asks me. 'I was expecting to meet your husband.'

'Oh, well,' I mumble. I can feel myself colouring. 'Um . . . he went back to the hotel. He was a bit pissed off with me about . . . earlier. I behaved badly at the bar.'

'Nonsense,' Karl says.

'Call him,' Sean says, refilling my glass, 'tell him to come over and join us.'

'Oh, I don't know . . . He was in a bit of a bad mood.'

'He'll get over it,' Karl says. You don't know the half of it, I want to say, not even the quarter, but I fish my phone out of my handbag. Just as I'm about to dial it starts to ring.

'There you go!' Sean says with a laugh, 'serendipity!'

'Hi, Dom,' I say, getting to my feet and walking over to the window. This may not be a conversation I want others to hear. 'I'm at Karl's. We were just wondering if you wanted to come over?' I bite my lip, steeling myself for a stream of bitter invective.

'No, Nic, you need to come back.'

'Please, Dom. We can talk about that other stuff later . . .'

'No, Nicole . . .'

'I want to talk about it, I do, we need to talk—'

'Nicole, forget about that. You need to come back to the hotel, okay?' His voice sounds odd, he doesn't sound angry, he sounds worried.

'Dom, what is it?'

'Your mum rang.'

'Oh, Jesus, is she all right? Is Charles all right? What's wrong?' My heart is suddenly hammering in my chest.

'She's fine, Nic, she and Charles are fine. It's your dad.'

Chapter Twenty

Resolutions:
1. Find a divorce lawyer
2. Return Alex's letters, gifts etc (except maybe the McQueen heels?)
3. Ring the cameraman who hit on me at the *Wife Swap* shoot
4. Lose half a stone
5. Start flat-hunting – contact agents in Hackney/ Stoke Newington?

I told Mum that I just wanted to stay at home, to pretend that it was just another night. It *was* just another night. What else is New Year's Eve, really? I know I've always imbued it with some great significance, but it isn't really anything special, it's just an arbitrary marker of passing time, as annoying as a birthday. But she rang to invite me round anyway.

'Why don't you just come round, love? Come and have a glass of champagne and something to eat with me and Charles? He got the new Jamie Oliver from his sister for Christmas, the American one. He's made the most delicious vanilla cheesecake. Come round and have a slice.'

'Mum, honestly, I don't want to go out. I've had a drink, anyway, I can't drive.' This was a lie, and a stupid one, given Mum's entirely predictable reaction.

'Oh Nicole, I can't bear it, you sitting there drinking on your own. It's awful. Hop in a taxi. Or I'll come there. Why don't I come round there? I'll bring some ice cream and we can watch a DVD or something.'

I didn't want to watch a DVD. I didn't want to have to talk about it, to rehash it all with her. I didn't want to eat ice cream and watch chick-flicks and live up to the broken-hearted woman stereotype.

'At the risk of sounding like Greta Garbo, I just want to be alone. Honestly. To be horribly blunt, I don't want you to come round. I'm sorry, but I'd rather just be here on my own with the dogs. Why don't we do something tomorrow? We can meet for lunch.'

'All right then,' she said, 'just don't drink too much.'

Although I'd promised myself I wouldn't drink alone, all this talk of booze had got me in the mood. I went into the kitchen and retrieved the bottle of Laurent Perrier Rosé one of Dom's grateful clients had sent to him a while back. We'd been saving it for a special occasion. The dogs followed me to the fridge, Mick standing dutifully behind me while Marianne tried to poke her nose into the vegetable drawer.

'Are you hungry, little girl?' I asked her. She wagged her tail, looking up at me hopefully. On the middle shelf of the fridge sat a honey roast ham which Dom's mother Maureen had sent to me, along with a card wishing me a happy Christmas and hoping that I would 'listen to reason' regarding the matter of her son's (understandable, in her mind) behaviour. I took the ham out of the fridge, hacked several large hunks off the bone and shared them out onto two plates. The dogs couldn't believe their luck.

I opened the champagne and poured myself a large mug. There were no clean glasses left, let alone champagne flutes. The washing up had not been done for days, the house hadn't been cleaned for weeks. Pizza boxes and foil containers from the Chinese place were piled high on the kitchen counter, a stack of newspapers that reached almost to my waist sat in Dom's study, unread and un-recycled.

I wandered into the living room with my mug and flicked on the TV, hopped through the channels mindlessly, taking nothing in. I turned it off again and turned on the stereo. I'd been listening to *Sticky Fingers* pretty much on repeat for a month. To the strains of 'Wild Horses', I slugged back my champagne and lit a cigarette.

The phone rang. For the ninth time that evening. It

was the landline, which has no caller ID so I couldn't tell who it was. It wouldn't be my mother again, she'd got wise to the fact that I wouldn't pick up the phone unless I knew the identity of the caller, so she only rang on the mobile. I couldn't say for sure who it was, but I could narrow it down to a list of two: Dominic or Alex. Who else would be calling me at ten o'clock on New Year's Eve?

The caller didn't leave a message, I 1471-ed. It was Dominic, either him or his mother, but probably him. I felt a twinge of guilt, I knew how desperately he must be hurting, how awful he must feel, but I couldn't bring myself to speak to him. I couldn't bear to listen to any more of his apologies, however heartfelt, somehow they always ended up segueing into excuses: he was desperate, he was lonely, he couldn't talk to me, he never meant for it to happen, they'd had too much to drink, they couldn't reach me so they reached out to each other. The guilt is washed away by a wave of nausea.

The worst thing, the very worst thing was that he didn't tell me straight away. He waited for months. I'd been sleeping with him for months not knowing that he had been with someone else. Better that he had never told me at all.

Alex got that one right. 'I didn't tell you,' she sobbed, when she came to see me two days after Dom came clean, 'because it wouldn't have helped. It might have made me feel less guilty, but all it did

366

was hurt you, and I never wanted to hurt you, Nic. The last thing in the world I wanted to do was to hurt you.'

'Well maybe you shouldn't have slept with my husband then,' I said, slamming the door in her face.

The deed was done, right here in this house, in September. I'm not exactly sure where. When he told me, one of the first things Dom said to me was: 'We didn't do it in our bed.' Apparently, this was supposed to make me feel better. 'Oh all right, darling, you shagged my best friend, but at least you didn't besmirch the 400 thread count sheets your mother gave us for our wedding anniversary.' I didn't ask where they *did* do it, since at the time I was too busy calling him a fucking, cheating, lying scumbag bastard, so now I find myself wondering. Was it here, on the sofa? Should I be getting the sofa recovered?

I'd been in Edinburgh when it happened, filming a particularly soul-destroying episode of *Wife Swap*. Dom and I had not spoken for two days: we'd had a terrible row before I left and I hadn't been returning his calls. More fool me.

The argument started over nothing. Dom's parents had invited us to spend the following weekend with them in Yorkshire. I didn't want to go. I told Dom that I had too much work to do, it just wasn't a good time. This was bullshit, and he knew it. I hardly had any work on at that time, certainly nothing I needed to spend my weekends researching. When he challenged me about it, I came clean.

'Okay, I don't have too much work to do, I just don't want to go. I don't feel like seeing your parents at the moment.' I was upstairs in my study, he was on the landing, we were having this conversation through the hatch.

'That's all right,' he said, conciliatory as ever, 'we don't have to go. We could do something else – why don't we invite Matt and Liz to stay? We could walk across the park to Richmond with the dogs, go to Petersham Nurseries for lunch?'

'Petersham Nurseries? That's a bit extravagant, isn't it?'

'It *is* my birthday, Nic.'

Oh shit. 'Yes, I know it's your birthday.' I'd completely forgotten about his birthday. I walked over to the hatch and climbed down the stairs. 'I know it's your birthday,' I said again. He was standing there, an amused expression on his face. He knew I'd forgotten, he thought it was funny. This annoyed me. Everything about him annoyed me, the way he made allowances for me, the way he backed down in arguments – his kindness annoyed me.

'I don't want Matt and Liz to come,' I said.

'Oh, come on Nic, it'll be fun . . .'

'I don't want them to come. I don't feel like talking to people at the moment. You just don't get it, do you?'

I pushed past him and stomped off down the stairs,

he followed at a safe distance. He caught up with me in the kitchen, where I was standing in front of the sink, glowering out of the window at the glorious sunshine outside.

'I'm trying to understand, Nicole,' he said, placing his hand gently on my shoulder.

'But you don't.' I snapped. It took an iron will not to brush his hand away. 'You don't understand. No one does. I have no one to talk to about this.'

He pulled his hand away with a sigh. We'd had this conversation a dozen times. He kept suggesting that I go to counselling.

'It's been a year and a half, Nic. And you've still not dealt with it, if anything you're getting worse . . .'

'I'm getting worse? Worse at what?'

'Don't be like that, Nic . . .'

'Like what?' I was furious with him, red-faced, blood pressure rising, my hands balled into fists, nails digging into my palms – and I wasn't even sure why. 'When do I have to be over him, Dominic? When exactly is it supposed to stop hurting? What date would suit you?'

'You're being unfair, I just want you to get help.'

'I don't want help,' I shouted at him.

'What do you want? Who do you want to talk to? Jesus Christ, Nicole, if he really is the only one you want to talk to, then just call Aidan. Go on,' he said, picking up the phone and handing it to me, 'just call him.'

'Where the hell did that come from?' I asked. I couldn't remember the last time I'd mentioned Aidan's name. He turned his back on me. 'Dominic?' Silence. 'Why did you say that?'

'I saw the letters.'

The letters. The ones I wrote to Julian, the ones in the folder on my computer desktop labelled 'Admin'.

'You *saw* my letters?' He was leaning against the kitchen counter, arms folded. He wouldn't look at me. 'You just saw them? You happened to be browsing through the admin folder on my laptop? What were you looking for, my old tax returns?'

'No, I was looking for something to help me understand what it is that is going on in your head, I was trying to help . . .'

'You were spying on me. You were invading my privacy.'

'I was *trying* to help. But according to you, according to your letters, I can't help you. No one can. The only people you want to talk to are Julian, and he's dead, or Aidan. And with him, what was it? What did you say? Oh yes, that's right.' He air quoted with his fingers. '"You can't talk to Aidan because you can't bear to hear his voice and not be able to touch him again."'

I took the train to Edinburgh the following morning, a full four days earlier than I needed to. I fumed all the way there, incapable of reading, incapable of working, I was consumed with rage and guilt. Yes, I'd written those things about Aidan, and yes, they were horrible things for my husband to read, but those letters were private. I wrote them as though I were talking to Julian, but really they were a diary, a confessional. They were never meant to be read by anyone else. And Dom had no right to read them, however noble his intentions.

In any case, I wasn't sure how noble his intentions really were. He wanted me to get better, to stop being so unhappy, of course he did. But I think he wanted that for himself as much as he wanted it for me. He wanted me to be fun again, he wanted his life to be easier. It's fair enough, why shouldn't he? But still, I couldn't help feeling that my unhappiness had become, more than anything, an inconvenience to him.

I arrived on a Thursday evening. Edinburgh, post-festival, a place with a hangover. There was a sense of normalcy returning, the English and Americans leaving, locals returning, relieved to have their city back. *Wife Swap*'s producers were putting me up in the Radisson on the Royal Mile, but that booking wasn't until Monday. In the meantime, I checked myself into an overpriced B&B on George Street. My first floor room was tiny and stuffy, the window opened only slightly, letting in no breeze but plenty of noise.

Because my room was so awful I spent most of the weekend walking the streets and parks of the city, reading my book in Princes Street gardens or in Holyrood Park, drinking endless cups of coffee at a little café on Blackfriars, ignoring my phone. Dom had been left a series of messages, ranging from the supplicating to the irate. Alex had been calling, too.

Alex and I hadn't seen much of each other lately. I'd been avoiding her and I felt guilty about it. And the more guilty I felt, the less I wanted to see her. I knew that she needed me, I knew that she'd been having a tough time with the divorce. I just felt as though I couldn't help her. I didn't have it in me. I promised myself that I would do better when I got back to London, I'd make more of an effort to see her. In the meantime, I wanted to be left alone.

I texted the pair of them. To Alex, I said: 'In Edinburgh working. Will call when I get back.' To Dominic, I wrote: 'Leave me alone. I'll call you next week.'

More fool me. Because that Sunday night, while I was lying awake in my grotty B&B room in Edinburgh, Alex and Dom were crying on each other's shoulders, seeking solace in each other's arms.

I don't know who instigated it. I'm not sure that I care. This is what Dom told me: Alex came over around eight. She arrived in a black cab, she'd already been drinking, he said, although she wasn't drunk. She brought with her a good bottle of red. They sat in the kitchen, drinking and talking. She was in a state. Mike had been round to clear the remainder of his things from the house, which was due to go on sale that week. While he was there, he told her that he'd met someone. Well, not exactly *met* someone, because he'd known her for some time – it was Karen, the party planner, the woman who'd organised the New Year's Eve party the night Aidan punched Mike's friend. Mike had known her for *years*. When Alex asked him how long it had been going on, he'd shrugged and said, 'It doesn't really matter now does it?'

To make matters worse, she was worried that she might be about to get sacked. After the divorce she'd accepted a (much lowlier) position at her old publishing house, but kick-starting her career was proving difficult in her current state of emotional turmoil. She had, she told Dom, taken fifteen sick days over the past two months.

'Lay-offs are imminent,' she said. 'They're going to sack at least ten per cent of the staff and frankly, if I was the one doing the sacking, I would totally sack me. I've been worse than useless lately.'

They finished the bottle of wine, opened another and ordered a pizza. They talked about me. Alex asked Dom why I was ignoring her, why I would never take her calls. Was I angry with her? Dom said he didn't know what was going on in my head any more. He told Alex about the letters, about what I said about Aidan. He asked Alex if I ever talked to her about Aidan, whether she thought I was still in love with him. Alex said she didn't know. They finished the second bottle. It was getting late. Alex said she ought to get a taxi to the station; Dom said he didn't think she should get the train home. She might fall asleep and miss her stop. He suggested she stay the night.

They opened a third bottle of wine. At some point, Alex started to cry. Dom couldn't remember exactly why, just that they were sitting on the sofa, and she was weeping, and he got up and fetched her a Kleenex and handed it to her, then he sat down next to her and held her hand, he gave her a kiss on the cheek. She put her arms around him. They held each other. How they got from holding each other to taking each other's clothes off, I'm not entirely sure, but I can imagine. I frequently do.

I came back from Edinburgh the following weekend. We'd spoken on the phone a couple of times that week, but we hadn't really talked, we'd just exchanged banalities. How's work going, are the dogs okay, what's the hotel like? He wasn't in when I got home, so I went straight upstairs and got into the shower, then came back down in my robe to make a cup of tea.

Dom had come home while I was in the shower, he was standing in the kitchen, sorting through the mail. The second he saw me, he came across to me and put his arms around me, he held me for ages without saying anything. We went upstairs and went to bed.

*　　*　　*

Afterwards, he apologised to me for reading the letters. I said it was okay, I didn't want to talk about it any more. I'd expected him to be angry about that, I expected him to throw his hands in the air, his standard gesture of annoyance, I expected him to complain about how I never wanted to talk about anything, but he didn't. He let it go. Later that evening, when we were sitting in the kitchen eating dinner, he told me that Alex had been round the previous weekend. She was upset, he said. I ought to call her. I said that I would.

It wasn't until November – late November – that he told me what had actually happened. It was a Sunday evening, I'd just come back from spending the day with my mother. We'd had a bit of an argument – and she and I almost never fight – and she'd set me straight on a thing or two.

I'd been talking to her about buying a property abroad somewhere – I had some money left over from the sale of the business and I'd always wanted to have a bolthole somewhere else. I was thinking of Morocco.

'A riad in a coastal town,' I told her, 'like Essaouira. Property prices are still pretty reasonable there.'

'What does Dom think about that? I thought he was keen on Italy?'

'He is, but I'd prefer Morocco. I'd be able to get more for my money. I'm thinking of going over there on a house-hunting trip. Do you want to come?'

'Well . . . possibly, but shouldn't you take Dom with you? It will be his house too.'

'I haven't really spoken to him about it,' I told her. 'I think it might be best presented to him as a *fait accompli*.'

When I said this it seemed to me to be a perfectly sensible idea. Mum did not agree.

'Nicole, you can't do that. You can't just go off and buy a house and not tell your husband.'

'Why not? It's my money. I can do whatever I like with it.'

'Okay,' she said, keeping her voice even, 'you can do that. You can go off and do whatever you like without telling Dom. But I think it would be a mistake, a huge mistake . . .'

'Why? Because I have to ask hubby for permission before I do anything? Jesus . . .'

'No, Nicole, but we're not talking about buying a pair of shoes, here, this is a major decision, this is one you should be taking together.'

I pouted. 'But I know he doesn't want to buy in Morocco, he's worried that it might turn out to be a poor investment.'

'Well, maybe you should listen to him.' I rolled my eyes at her, suddenly thirteen years old again. 'I'm serious, Nic, and I have to say, I'm really worried.'

'About what?'

'About you. You and Dominic, the way things are going, the way you've been treating him.'

'How have I been treating him?'

'Badly, not to put too fine a point on it. You ignore

him, you're always angry with him, you've withdrawn from him, it's as though you want to cut him out of your life . . .'

'That's bullshit.'

'Out of your real life, your emotional life. Honestly, darling, I think the time has come for you to speak to someone because I don't seem to be able to help you, and you won't let Dom help you, you barely speak to Alex any more. You're running the risk of alienating the people who really love you, and I don't want to see you do that.'

She wasn't saying anything I hadn't already heard from Dominic, but somehow coming from my mother it sounded different. It sounded true, not just like a complaint from a pissed-off husband.

'There's a counsellor who's done some work with some of Charles's patients, trauma victims, people who have lost loved ones in accidents, things like that. He's a lovely person, I think you'd really like him. I was wondering if you'd let me book you a session?'

When I got home, I told Dom that I was going to see a grief counsellor. To my horror, he actually broke down when I told him, he started to cry. I was overwhelmed, I had no idea how unhappy I'd been making him, how desperate he'd been.

'It's okay,' I kept saying, holding him in my arms, feeling him sob against my chest, 'it's okay, Dom, it's going to be okay.'

'It's not okay,' he said at last, 'it's not okay, Nic.'

We were standing in the kitchen, I'd been about to make some tea.

'It will be okay,' I said, kissing my forehead to his. 'We'll sort things out. I'm sorry I've been so hard on you lately, I didn't realise—'

'Please don't apologise to me,' he said, turning away. 'Please don't apologise.'

When he turned back to me, his face ashen, I knew something was up.

'I need to tell you something,' he said, his voice barely above a whisper. 'Let's go into the living room and sit down,' he said, but something in his expression told me I'd rather hear this news standing up.

'What is it, Dom?'

He placed his hands on the kitchen table, leaning down hard on them as though for support. His head was bowed.

'Something happened,' he said, 'when you were in Edinburgh. Something happened. With Alex.'

We didn't fight then. I was pretty calm, all things considered. I just told him that I wanted him to leave the house and he did, right away, without even packing a bag. I didn't cry or scream or wail. I took the dogs for a walk, made dinner and went to bed. I couldn't sleep, so I fetched the box set of *Six Feet Under* DVDs from the living room and watched the whole of season one, back to back.

I must have fallen asleep around four, waking

again when the sun was already high in the sky. I wondered, for a moment or two, where Dom was and why he hadn't woken me up. Then I remembered. I wanted to stay there in bed, to pull the covers over my head and go back to sleep, but I knew I wouldn't be able to. I got up and got into the shower, I sat on the tiles and let the water wash over me and cried and cried.

Dom was in the kitchen when I went downstairs, giving Marianne a cuddle. When he saw me he jumped up as though stung, as though caught in the act of doing something illicit. He looked stricken, pale, red-eyed.

'Hi,' he said.

'Hello,' I replied. I had no idea what I was going to say to him. I hadn't planned on having this confrontation just yet.

'Are you all right?' he asked me.

'I've been better. But then again, I've been worse. You?'

'I've never been worse.'

'Sorry to hear that.'

I went over to the coffee maker and tipped a couple of spoonfuls of Kenya's finest into the filter. My hands were shaking. He came up behind me, gently placing his hands on my hips. I pushed him away.

'Don't touch me, Dominic.'

'I'm sorry, Nicole, I'm so sorry. I don't know why it happened, it was just this stupid, drunken thing, we were both feeling so lonely, so cut off from you . . .'

White-knuckled, I gripped the kitchen counter. If I let go I was going to hit him.

'You felt lonely?' I asked. 'You felt lonely?'

And then the excuses came:

'I couldn't reach you . . .'

'You were always so angry with me . . .'

'I thought I was losing you . . .'

And then I started to shout.

'You thought you were losing me, so your solution was to fuck my best friend?'

I don't remember all the things I said, I just remember screaming at him to leave, never to come back. He went upstairs and packed some things; he's been staying with friends or his parents ever since.

After he left, and after I'd returned to some semblance of calm, I phoned Alex. I got her voicemail.

'I know what you did, Alex. I know what happened. Dom told me. The only reason I'm calling you now is to tell you that I don't want to hear from you, not now, not ever. This friendship is finished.'

The following day, she turned up on my doorstep, crying hysterically, begging me to talk to her, to let her explain. I slammed the door in her face and left her there, sobbing on the pathway, until eventually I couldn't stand it any more. I left the house through the back door, got into the car and drove away. When I came back, hours later, she was gone. She'd written to me, sent me a couple of letters by mail and a couple of emails since then, but I hadn't read them.

I poured myself another mug of champagne, picked up my notebook off the coffee table and looked once again at my list of resolutions. I wasn't *really* going to call the cameraman who hit on me on the *Wife Swap* shoot. I only wrote that down because for some reason I couldn't quite bring myself to write 'Call Aidan'. I'd thought about it, of course I'd thought about it. In the days after Dom moved out, when I was at my most angry and most vengeful, I thought about little else. But I never actually picked up the phone. A voice in my head told me, 'you'll only be setting yourself up for disappointment, he's bound to be seeing someone else', but that wasn't the real reason I didn't contact him. The real reason was that if I called Aidan, I'd be admitting it to myself: my marriage is over. And despite everything I'd written down in my notebook, I wasn't sure I was ready for that.

I ripped the page of resolutions out of the notebook and started on a second list.

1. Call Dominic
2. Go to see the counsellor Mum suggested
3. Try couples' counselling

4. Write to Alex
5. Lose half a stone

Then I ripped that page out of the notebook too. On the first sheet of paper I wrote 'heads', on the second I wrote 'tails'. Then I flipped a coin.

Chapter Twenty-one

30 December 2011

Karl calls me a taxi and I rush back to the hotel, as much confused as concerned.

'I don't understand,' I say to Dom when I get back to our room. 'He wasn't even due to go into hospital until Tuesday.'

'It's not the cancer, Nic,' Dom says, reaching for my hand. 'He had a heart attack.'

He's got the hotel phone tucked between his shoulder and his chin, he's on the phone to British Airways, on hold, trying to find out how soon we can get on a flight to London.

'Oh.' I don't know how to process this. 'Is it bad?' I ask, and then I start laughing. 'Sorry, that's ridiculous. It's a heart attack. Of course it's bad.'

'Well, we don't know how bad. We know that he's in . . . Oh, yes, I'm here. But it's an emergency. Yes. A family emergency. My wife's father. Yes, very serious.' He looks over at me and shakes his head as if to say,

'It isn't really serious. I'm just saying that so they'll get us on the flight.'

I open the wardrobe and start pulling out the clothes I unpacked yesterday, flinging them unceremoniously into my open suitcase. Packing to go home is always depressing. Packing to go home three days early because your father is dying, particularly so. I sit down on the bed, waiting for tears to come, but they don't.

'I need to call my mum,' I say to Dom.

'Tell her . . . tell her we'll be at Heathrow at around seven-thirty tomorrow evening . . .'

'We're on the flight?'

'Standby, but I reckon if we turn up there and cause a scene they'll find a way to get us on.' He reaches for my hand again and squeezes it. 'It'll be okay. Ring your mum. Tell her we'll drive straight from the airport, so hopefully we should be with them some time after ten.'

She picks up on the second ring.

'Oh Nic, I'm so sorry.'

'Is he gone?'

'No! No, he's all right. Well, not all right, but . . . fortunately your uncle Chris was there with him when it happened and the ambulance got there quickly. They took him to Malvern but I think he's going to be transferred to Gloucester once they've got him stabilised.'

'Where are you?' I ask.

'We're in the car, we're on our way there now. Charles is driving.'

'Have you spoken to him?'

'No, he was in surgery, so I couldn't. I spoke to Chris.'

'I'm sorry,' I say.

'What do you mean? Why are you sorry?'

'I'm sorry I'm not there, you shouldn't have to deal with this . . .'

'Don't be ridiculous. It's not a problem. I . . .' She starts to say something else, but I can't hear her.

'You're breaking up, Mum,' I say, but the phone has already gone dead.

31 December 2011

Dom puts down the phone. 'The flight's at eight, so in theory we need to be there at six, but I suppose we should get there earlier.' I look at the clock next to the bed. It's almost midnight.

'We could just go to the airport now and wait.'

He sits down on the bed next to me.

'We could, but I'm not sure it would help. Plus, JFK is not the most comfortable place in the world to hang out. Why don't we just pack, you could try and get a bit of sleep and then we'll go?'

'I don't think I can sleep.'

'All right, then. We could pack and talk. I think we need to talk.'

We finish packing. Then we sit on the bed drinking extortionately priced drinks from the mini-bar.

'I should ring Karl,' I say. 'To let him know that we won't be coming to the party.'

'We'll do it in the morning.'

'And Alex. She wanted to see me again before I left.'

'What about Aidan? Is he expecting to see you too?' I cover my face with my hands, but Dom crouches down in front of me and takes my hands in his. 'I'm not trying to start a fight,' he says. 'But I need to know. We have to – *you* have to – make a decision.'

'Not now, Dom, I can't do it now,' I say. 'I think I should call Karl. He'll be wondering what's going on.'

I ring Karl and tell him what's happened.

'Jesus, Nicole. I'm so sorry.'

'I'm sorry we're going to miss the party.'

'Forget the stupid party.'

'I wanted to be there, I really did.'

'I know.'

'And I want to come to your wedding. Promise me you won't forget to invite me to your wedding?'

'I was rather hoping you would give me away.'

I laugh. 'Are you the bride?'

'Of course not,' he tuts, 'I'm way more butch than Sean. But I don't see why only brides should be given away. It's sexist.'

'I would love to give you away.'

'Good. Ring me when you get to London. Let me know how he's doing.'

'I will.'

I call Alex who bursts into tears when I tell her that I'm flying back to London in the morning.

'I'll come with you,' she says. 'I'll get myself on a flight. I'll come to the hospital, I can help out.'

'I don't need you to, Alex.'

'But I want to.'

'I don't want you to either.' I look over at Dom, and say, 'Look, I'm not being mean, Alex, but there are things I need to sort out with Dom. I won't be able to do that with you there. It'll complicate things. Okay?'

'Okay,' she sniffs.

'I'll see you again soon. I promise.'

Dom is rooting around in the mini-bar. He holds up two tiny bottles. 'Overpriced Scotch or overpriced vodka?'

I take the Scotch, which I drink neat while Dom mixes himself a vodka tonic.

'I feel awful,' I tell him.

'I know,' he says, sitting down next to me and slipping his fingers through mine. 'It'll be okay, Nic.'

'No, I mean, I feel guilty. I don't feel upset enough. I should be hysterical, I should be heartbroken . . . but I don't think it will break my heart if my dad dies. Isn't that horrible? I'll be all right. I'll still have Mum, I'll still have you . . .'

'You'll always have me,' Dom says, putting his arm around my shoulders and pulling me closer. Now the tears come, and they're not for Dad, they're for us. Me and Dom.

We sit like this for a long time. Eventually I stop crying, dry my eyes and blow my nose.

'You know I love you, Dominic.'

'I know, Nic. You just love Aidan more.'

'I don't know, I don't know if I do . . .'

'I think you do. I think you always have. And I think I've always known.'

'Dom . . .'

'No, let me talk.' There are tears in his eyes now, and I can't bear it, I just can't bear it, I sit on the floor at his feet, resting my head on his knee as he explains to me why he thinks our marriage is ending.

'When you said you wanted to marry me, I should have said no. I should have told you, like Alex did, that we needed to wait until you were ready, until you were *really* ready. The thing is, back then I think I suspected that you never would be ready, that you would never say you wanted to marry me and really mean it, *really* want to be with me just because you loved me more than anyone else in the world and wanted to spend the rest of your life with me.'

'I did, Dom, I did want that.'

'No you didn't, Nicole. Julian was family. You felt like you had lost part of your family. You were suddenly scared, terrified of being alone, what if something happened to your mum, you'd have no one in the world . . . you needed to make a new family, just in case something terrible happened, just in case another terrible thing happened. And I knew that. I knew that you were marrying me for the wrong reasons and yet I went ahead with it anyway, because I wanted so badly to make you mine.'

I wrap my arms around his legs and hug them tightly.

'Back then, I thought that one day you would be ready, you really would be mine, your feelings for me would change, you'd forget about Aidan and you'd love me completely, like I love you.' His voice cracks a little, he strokes my hair as I start to sob.

'But you never did. And it's not your fault, there's nothing you can do about that. But I think . . . I think if we keep going the way we have been, if I keep trying to hold onto you, then we'll just end up hurting each other, even more than we already have.'

'Please don't, Dom, don't tell me it's over now. I can't do this now.'

'I know. I just want you to know that it isn't your fault.'

He's right that I married him for the wrong reasons, but I chose to stay with him for the right ones. Two years ago, I flipped a coin to decide whether I should fight for my marriage or just let it go. It came up heads: get divorced, move out, move on. And I knew right away that that wasn't what I was going to do. I ripped up that list, and I stuck with the other one. I did my best to get over it. I did my best. We both did. And it's not enough.

We climb into bed and lie there in the dark, wrapped in each other's arms, not sleeping, not talking, watching the snow fall, listening to the sound of that unsleeping city, waiting for morning, for whatever the day brings.

Chapter twenty-two

New Year's Eve, 2011
Malvern

Resolutions:
1. If I get the chance, make things right with Dad
2.
3.
4.
5.

After the first one, I can't think of anything else to write. At the moment, it doesn't seem right to write anything else.

The journey goes as smoothly as a transatlantic flight possibly can: as long as I live, I will never say anything bad about British Airways ever again. The staff are sympathetic, they get us seats in Business Class so we can try to get some sleep, and they help us rush through immigration at Heathrow, they ensure that our bags are first onto the carousel so that we can get out of the airport as quickly as possible. We're in the car a little after nine in the evening. Dom lets me drive while he rings my mum for an update.

'Okay, okay,' he says, so I know Dad's not dead yet. 'We should be there in . . . I don't know . . . a couple of hours. Maybe less. You know how Nic drives.' I smile at him, he squeezes my leg. 'We'll see you there. Are you okay, Elizabeth? Good. Good.' He hangs up.

'We're going to Malvern,' he tells me. 'They haven't been able to move him yet.'

'What did she say?'

'The operation went okay, but he's still in critical condition.' He squeezes my leg again. 'I'm sorry, Nic. Apparently it was a massive coronary, his heart has been badly damaged.'

'So, he's going to die?' I ask, my voice sounding suddenly small.

'I don't know, Nic. But you should . . .'

'Prepare myself?' That's what they say, isn't it? Prepare yourself. How do you do that, exactly? How is it that you prepare for loss? I've not done it before. Last time, I didn't get the opportunity.'

Keeping one hand on the wheel, I rub my eyes one at a time. I am beyond exhausted, I've crossed over into a weird kind of auto-pilot state. I'm pretty sure I shouldn't be driving, but what else is there to do? Dom is just as knackered. Business class or no, neither of us slept much on the plane. I just need to get there.

I open the window a little, allowing the freezing night air into the car, and press down harder on the accelerator.

Talking will help me stay awake, but I don't want to talk about the things I need to talk about. I don't want to talk about Dad and I don't want to talk about us, so instead we talk practicalities. We talk about where we should stay while Dad's in hospital, about when Dominic needs to go back to work, about whether he'll leave the car with me and take the train back to London, about whether we should leave the dogs with Matt and Liz for the time being. It's soothing, real life, but there are only so many practicalities we can discuss when everything's up in the air like this, and the conversation peters out just past Oxford.

Dom roots around in the glove compartment and under the seat in search of something to listen to. Miraculously, he finds *Let it Bleed*, and we listen to that all the way to Malvern.

We make good time: it's about ten to eleven when we get to the hospital. I leave Dom to sort out parking and run into the building, where of course I have to wait ten minutes before anyone will tell me anything. The receptionist has a lengthy discussion with someone on the phone: from her end of the conversation I gather the problem is that ordinarily they would prefer that visitors not visit critically ill patients in the middle of the night. But it appears that in this case they are prepared to make an exception. This fact alone tells me how serious things are: they are giving a man one last chance to see his daughter. Eventually, I'm directed to the appropriate waiting room, where I find Charles sitting alone, his head bowed almost to his chest, nodding gently as he falls asleep. I sit next to him and touch him gently on the arm, causing him to jerk awake with a start.

'Oh, Nic, sweetheart.' He wraps his arms around me and hugs me tight. 'Your mum's in with him now. He's awake. You go on in and say hello.'

Dad is in a private room just across the hall. The room is in darkness, but there is enough light from the hallway for me to make out Dad's figure on the bed and my mother's in a chair on the opposite side of the room. She gets up when she sees me and walks around the bed silently, she takes my hands in hers and gives me a kiss. From the bed, there is a faint coughing sound, Dad is trying to prop himself up a bit further against the pillows.

I let go of Mum's hands and go to his side. Even in this faint light I can see that his face is grey, there's a touch of blue around his lips. I bend down to kiss him.

'Hello, love,' he says in a faint croak. 'I'm sorry you cut your holiday short. You shouldn't have, you know. I'm feeling a lot better.'

'Don't be silly,' I say, sitting down next to him and

taking his hand in mine. It's like ice, and this makes me want to cry. His hands were always warm when I was a child, he was always warm. Mum said he was like a hot water bottle. I really don't want to cry now, though, it'll seem to him as though I'm admitting defeat, so I swallow hard and try to smile.

'Are you really feeling better, Dad? Are you in a lot of pain?'

'Not too bad, not too bad,' he says, but I can tell that's a lie, everything in his demeanour, the way he's holding himself, rigid, his left arm across his chest, suggests that he's suffering.

'I'll leave you two to have a chat then,' Mum says. 'I'll go and get us a cup of tea.'

After she leaves we lapse into silence. A few minutes pass, then he says: 'She's been really kind, your mum. Very kind.'

'Good, that's good.' I have no idea what to say to him now.

'Did you have a nice time in New York?' he asks.

'Yes, it was . . . very nice.'

'Good. Did you see Alex?'

'I did, yes.'

'That's good.' Dad doesn't know about the Alex and Dom incident, I've never told him.

'And Julian? How's he doing?'

'I'm sorry?'

'Julian. He's all right, is he?'

'You mean Aidan, Dad.'

'No, Julian. The Symonds boy. The homosexual.'

'Dad . . .'

'He did well for himself, didn't he? Photography. You've both done so well.'

Mum comes in and hands me a cup of tea. Dad says, 'We were just talking about Julian.'

'Oh, yes. Such a terrible thing,' Mum says.

'What's that?' he looks confused, now so does she.

'Where's Uncle Chris, Dad?' I ask, trying to steer the conversation back to safety, or at the very least to the present day. 'Is he not here with you?'

'No, he's not here.'

'He is, Jack, he just went to the twenty-four-hour shop to get himself a sandwich,' Mum says.

'Oh, yes.'

We fall back into silence and after a few minutes Dad falls asleep snoring gently. Outside in the hall I can hear people laughing and chatting, wishing each other a happy new year. I look at my watch; it's a few minutes after midnight.

'He's confused,' I whisper to Mum. 'He thinks Julian's still alive.'

'It's not all that surprising, darling. He's just had a very serious operation. He's been under general anaes-thetic, it's traumatic. Some people aren't quite all there when they wake up. You know . . . well, you know that he's not out of the woods, don't you?'

'I know.'

'The surgeon spoke to your uncle Chris, he did say

that the damage was severe. With your dad's general health not being all that good . . .'

'I know. Has he been all right with you, Mum?'

'Yes, he's been fine. Very polite, actually. He apologised for a lot of things. It was rather sad, really. I do wish he'd found someone else to spend his life with.'

'I should have spent more time with him,' I say. 'Made more of an effort.'

'Oh, Nic, you tried very hard. He was impossible, he made it impossible to be around him. You shouldn't feel bad.'

But I do, I can't help it. It's all just such a waste.

Mum picks up the chair that she was sitting on and brings it around the bed so that she is now sitting at my side.

'Did you get to do anything fun in New York?' she asks me. 'Did you see any of your friends?'

'I saw everyone,' I say, smiling at her, but the tears are running down my face now.

'Everyone?'

'Karl and Alex and Aidan.' Mum puts her arm around my shoulders and pulls me to her.

'And how was that?'

'It was good. I don't know. I felt like . . . I felt different when I was there, when I was with them again.'

'You felt like your old self again.' How does she know?

'Yeah, I did. How did you know that?'

'I'm your mother,' she says, squeezing my hand. 'I know everything. And anyway, you and I . . . we're not all that different. We've made some of the same mistakes.' She looks over at my father. She can't possibly be comparing him with Dom, surely? 'I'm not saying that Dom's anything like your dad,' she says, reading my mind. 'It's just that he wasn't the right man for me. And . . . well . . .'

'You think Dom isn't the right man for me, either?'

'I don't know, love. Sometimes I wonder. I think . . . maybe he was right for you in a certain place and time. Just not for ever.'

A nurse comes in and tells us it's probably best if we leave now, let Dad get some proper rest. Mum gets up and leaves the room, I lean over and give Dad's arm a gentle, squeeze, but as I'm leaving the room, he calls me back in a sibilant whisper.

'Nicole, please . . .'

'You need to rest, Dad. Go to sleep. I'll see you in the morning.'

'Just a few minutes,' he says.

The nurse shakes her head, but I say, 'Okay, just a few minutes,' and she doesn't stop me. I sit back down at his bedside. I take his hand again.

'I'm sorry I didn't see you married,' he says

'It doesn't matter, Dad, it really wasn't a big deal.'

'Don't say that . . .'

'No, honestly. It was just a registry office job . . .' I

am sorry that he wasn't there to see me married, but it's hardly the greatest of his offences. I would rather have had him there when I got into Oxford, or when I graduated from college, or ringing me up the day I got a BAFTA.

'I missed so much,' he says.

'I know you did, Dad.' I don't want to upset him, but there's a part of me that knows that if I don't talk to him about it now, I never will. 'I just don't know why you missed it all. I know that you couldn't bear to be around Mum, I understand that. I just don't know why you didn't want to be around me.'

'I'm not sure I know myself,' he says. 'I think I was ashamed, and when I was with you, I felt that shame most keenly. It's no excuse . . .'

It really isn't, but there's no point saying that now.

'I regret so much, Nicole. I regret so much.'

'It's okay, Dad,' I say, squeezing his hand, 'we'll just have to do better in future, won't we? We'll have to spend more time together.'

'That's right, that's right.' He lapses into silence again, and I'm about to get to my feet to leave when he looks up at me with an expression of concern on his face and says: 'He died, didn't he?'

'Sorry, Dad?'

'Your friend Julian. He died. You wrote to me, and I didn't reply.'

I bite down hard on my lip. 'He was killed a few years ago.'

'You wrote to me and I wanted to write back, I just didn't know what to say.'

'It's okay, Dad.'

'Are you all right, Nicole?'

'I should go, Dad. You need to sleep.'

A look of fear crosses his face, just for a second, and he grips my hand a little harder. 'You go back out into the world, my girl,' he says. 'Don't live a life that's less than it should be. Don't do what I did.' He coughs again, for a long time this time, he's fighting to catch his breath.

'Dad . . .' I say, but he shushes me with a wave of his hand.

'Remember,' he says with half a smile, 'it's always later than you think.' He squeezes my hand. 'You should go, love. I'll sleep now.'

I step out of the darkness into the bright corridor, fluorescent lights buzzing overhead, casting everyone – Dom, my mum and Uncle Chris, who are sitting in a row on the chairs against the wall – with a sickly yellow pallor. Charles is sitting by himself a little way off; I have a sudden flashback to New Year's Eve twenty years ago, when I saw him in the waiting room after Dad hit Mum.

'Okay, Nic?' Dom asks, and Chris comes over to give me a kiss hello, but as he does so I can hear the monitor in Dad's room change its tune, switching from regular beeps to one long flat tone.

A nurse appears from nowhere, turns on the light in the room and presses a button. It isn't like *ER*. Handsome doctors don't come sprinting into the room, no one yells for a crash cart. A doctor does arrive quickly, though, and they do shock him, once, twice, a third time. They give him shots of adrenalin, someone does CPR. I'm standing outside the room, Uncle Chris has his arm around my shoulders, Dom is holding my hand. I don't know how long we stand there, but eventually the nurse comes out and tells me to come into the room and say goodbye. It's too late, of course, because he's already dead, but Chris and I go to his bedside anyway. Chris gives Dad's hand a squeeze and I give him a kiss on the forehead, and then we return once more to the waiting room, because apparently there are forms to sign.

A little after three in the morning, we're back in the car. Uncle Chris suggested we go back to Dad's place, we could get some sleep there before heading back to London, but the thought of going to that sad, empty little house is too much for me to bear. Dom says he's okay to drive. He tells me to lie down and get some sleep in the back of the car, but I'm worried he'll fall asleep if I do, so I sit up front with him. We find ourselves making small talk again, only this time the small talk is even less cheerful: funeral arrangements, clearing out Dad's house, that sort of thing.

Dawn is breaking by the time we get home to

Wimbledon. Exhaustion has given way to a kind of delirium, we are both feeling weirdly cheerful, a pale shaft of winter sunlight seems to fall on our house and ours alone, I am beyond delighted to be home. Dom says he'll make us a cup of tea, but by the time he brings it upstairs I am already in bed and drifting off to sleep. He slips into bed beside me, spooning his body around mine.

'I love you, Nic,' he says.

'I love you too.'

When I wake up, he's no longer beside me. I roll over and check my phone, which is on the bedside table. It's just after two o'clock in the afternoon, and I have one missed call. It's from Aidan, received in the early hours of this morning. Around midnight his time. He hasn't left a message.

I get up and get straight into the shower, I stand there for ages, my eyes closed, leaning with my forehead against the sand-coloured tiles, warm water washing over me. My father is gone. I'll never see him again. I can count the number of times I have seen him over the past fifteen years on my fingers and toes, and now that number will never get any higher. I will never run out of fingers and toes.

Since Julian died, I've seen Aidan three times: on the day that I found out, at the funeral and then again yesterday. Yesterday? Was that really yesterday? It seems like a lifetime ago. Three times. Not enough for one hand, let alone a full set of fingers and toes. It isn't enough. Tears mingle with soapy water as I wash my hair. I know what I have to do, and it makes my heart ache.

I pull on a pair of tracksuit bottoms, an old fleece and a pair of thick socks and I go downstairs to talk to Dom. He's not in his study, he's not in the kitchen. I look out of the window. The car is gone. Suddenly, I feel panicky. Where is he? Has he left? I ring his mobile, it goes straight to voicemail. I'm about to run upstairs and check to see what he's packed and what he's left behind when it strikes me that he's probably just gone to the shops to get milk and a newspaper. It's possible, after all, that our local newsagent is shut on New Year's Day.

I sit at the kitchen table, feeling tearful and unhappy, drinking fennel tea. I loathe herbal tea, but at times like this you need a hot drink, and there is nothing else available. After what seems like for ever, but is actually just half an hour, the car pulls up. Dom gets out, he goes around the back of the car, opens the boot and lets the dogs out.

I run to the back door and fling it open, welcoming an overexcited Mick and Marianne into my arms.

'I thought you'd want to see them when you woke up,' Dom says as I start to cry again, 'so I drove down

403

to Matt's to fetch them.' He's also bought tea and milk and bread, as well as the most delicious cheese in the world from the farm shop down the road from Matt's place. We sit down at the kitchen table and eat cheese and pickle sandwiches accompanied by enormous mugs of builder's tea. Having run around the house and garden several times to make sure everything is as it should be, the dogs have settled, Marianne is in her favourite spot, dozing in a shaft of sunshine up against the radiator in the hallway, Mick is sleeping on my feet. The thought of leaving this makes me fearful.

Dom reads my mind.

'Once everything's sorted out,' he says, taking a swig of his tea, 'once the funeral's over and you've got everything straight with your dad's affairs, you should go. Go to Libya, go to New York, do what you need to do.'

'I don't want to leave you,' I say, my voice small and strangled.

'You do. You just think you don't right now at this moment, because you've just lost your dad and you need to be somewhere safe. It'll be like it was before. But after a while, in three months or six months or twelve, you'll start pulling away, when all this safety becomes too boring for you, and we'll have to go through this all over again. I don't want to go through this again.' His voice is small, too, small and sad. The ache in me, the ache I felt earlier when I was standing in the shower, it grows larger, it swallows up my heart. He gets up, walks around the kitchen table and pulls a chair up next to mine. We put our arms around each other.

'We'll get the dogs a passport,' he murmurs into my neck, 'if you decide that you're going to live in New York. We'll share custody. You can have them for six months and I'll have them for six months. Or something. We'll work something out. We'll be in each other's lives. We'll always be in each other's lives.'

'Promise?' I ask.

'I promise.'

At dusk, I take the dogs out to the common. The pair of them race ahead of me, bouncing up and down with the sheer joy of being back out on their favourite walk. I try to picture myself walking along a New York sidewalk with the pair of them attached to leads. I can't quite imagine it. I try to picture myself working at Zeitgeist Productions, in the building at the corner of Lexington and East 71st, sitting at a desk just metres away from Aidan's, or camping out on the sofa in Alex's tiny flat. I try to picture myself single again, unmarried.

It's exciting to me but it's frightening too, not just because it's a leap into the unknown, not just because I'm thinking of abandoning one life for another. It's frightening because I wonder if Dominic is right. He told me, back in New York, that I had to choose between him and my ghosts. Am I choosing ghosts? Maybe I am, and maybe that way sadness lies, but I have to give that life another try. I have to see if I can do it again, if I can do it better this time. I have to see if I can be me again without Julian.

I turn back as darkness falls, clenching and unclenching my hands, which are freezing even in gloves and shoved into pockets. The wind is getting up, it's time to go home, to get back to the warmth, but I don't. Instead I sit down on a bench at the side of the pathway. The dogs wander around for a bit, confused, then they settle at my feet. There is a slip of a moon in the sky, just a sliver of ivory in the black. I can't see any stars.

He seems to come out of nowhere, out of the dark like a phantom.

'You can't be here,' I say.

'I spoke to Alex,' he says, 'I got the first flight I could.'

'But, you can't be here,' I say again. 'Dominic . . .'

'He's the one who told me where to find you.'

Aidan sits down next to me on the bench and puts his arms around me. 'I'm sorry about your dad,' he says, pulling me into his chest.

'How long are you here for?' I ask him.

'Just until tomorrow. I have to get back to work.'

'Does the job offer still stand?'

'It does.'

'I want to come to New York,' I tell him, 'I want to try again. Work, Alex, everything.'

'Me?'

'Well, I don't know about you . . .' I say, laughing, and then he kisses me, and I don't feel the cold any more.

I want to stay there, on the bench, in the darkness, holding him, but I know that I can't, that it's cruel, to stay here with him when Dom's waiting for me inside, knowing I'm out here with Aidan. So I kiss him one last time and get to my feet, the dogs taking their cue and scrambling up, and I say goodbye.

'I'll see you again soon,' I tell him. 'I'll see you in New York.'

'I'll be waiting for you.'

And this time, I know he will.

All I Want for Christmas

Amy Silver

Twelve days and counting . . .

It is Bea's first Christmas with her baby son, and this year she's determined to do *everything* right. But there is still so much to do: presents need to be bought; the Christmas menu needs refining; her café, The Honey Pot, needs decorating; and she's invited the whole neighbourhood to a party on Christmas Day. She really doesn't have time to get involved in two new people's lives, let alone fall in love . . .

When Olivia gets knocked over in the street, however, Bea can't help bringing her into The Honey Pot and getting to know her. Olivia's life is even more hectic than her own, and with her fiancé's entire family over from Ireland for Christmas, she shouldn't be lingering in the cosy warmth of Bea's café. Chloe, on the other hand, has nowhere else to go. Her affair with a married man has alienated her friends, and left her lonelier than ever.

But Christmas is a magical time, and in the fragrant atmosphere of The Honey Pot, anything can happen: new friends can be made, hearts can heal, and romance can finally blossom . . .

arrow books